I, too, have suffered in the garden

Jennifer Hritz

Published by Jennifer Hritz
www.jenniferhritz.com

ISBN:978-0-578-06043-9

First Edition

Book and cover design Viewers Like You
Jacket and author photograph © Chelsea Fullerton / chelseafullerton.com

For Ken

sun, sky, birds, trees, wind

ACKNOWLEDGMENTS

So many lovely, talented people helped me bring *I, Too, Have Suffered in the Garden* to completion.

Jennifer Elsner with Viewers Like You has proven more than an ingenuous website designer; she also has a keen aesthetic and an enthusiasm for this project I didn't anticipate. Chelsea Fullerton with Mighty Bean Photography helped bring my fictional world alive with her provocative photographs, including this book's cover. David Shields labored over the typesetting with an attention every novelist deserves.

Stacey Keith has been an avid fan, meticulous reader, and all-around champion of my work. Without her faith this novel would, at the very least, be much delayed. Kristin Dorsey provided me with substantial feedback and stalwart motivation, for which I'm infinitely indebted. Olga Valenzuela served as one of my first readers and exhibited faith in this project from the beginning—way back in sixth grade. Katherine Torrini lit me up; I can't imagine taking the route I have without her compassion and guidance.

I'm thankful as well for Robert Stearn's readiness to answer every question I threw at him; my friend and neighbor, Lisa McClain, for putting me in touch with Suzanne Berkel, who provided me with the legal research I needed; Vanessa Leggett, who insisted I keep my chin up; and Linda McKenna, Jennifer Seth, and Catherine Vouvray for being early, enthusiastic readers. Peter Rock, who I met at the Tin House Summer Writers Workshop, gave me invaluable criticism and has remained a source of steady encouragement. My fellow participants at the Tin House

Summer Writers Workshop showed me just how diverse a reaction I can expect to this novel's publication. Ito Romo, a San Antonio-based artist and novelist, kindly granted me permission to use the title of one of his early paintings as the title for this novel.

I also want to thank both the Writers' League of Texas and the Houston Writers Guild for awarding this novel first place in their respective contests.

A thank you also goes to my mother, for igniting in me a passion for the written word at a wee age. And I want to thank my father, for always trying to make me laugh.

To my son, Gus, and my husband, Ken: Without your patience and support this story could not have been told. Thank you.

I, too, have suffered in the garden

1

MARCH, 1990

Bobby kneels in the dirt behind the house, his hands deep in the earth. Beside him Indy wags his tail, a brush of soil across his wet, black nose. I stand with my arms crossed over my tee shirt, trying to keep warm. It's too early, I say, but I'm ignored by Bobby as well as the dog. The branches of the maples rattle like old bones; green buds that seemed on the brink of unfurling just last week curl inward, away from the chill. Shivering, I watch as Bobby takes one of the plants from its plastic container and plucks at its roots, his fingers deft but gentle. I'm cold, I say. So go inside, Adam, he says, depositing the plant in the hole he's dug and packing it with dirt.

I don't want to go inside by myself. I want him to come with me. I want him back in bed. I've been missing him all week; I left last Monday for a business trip that lasted a day longer than I expected. When I finally got home last night he was already asleep, and he turned away from me when I slid my hand over the slope of his hip. Tomorrow, he murmured, but he took off for the nursery before I was even awake and now he's emptying the next plant into the palm of his hand.

We'll have another freeze, I inform him, examining the sky like I know what I'm talking about. There's not a trace of the sunlight that spilled golden through our bedroom windows last Sunday morning, warming our skin as we made lazy, sleepy love. Afterwards I'd pulled my grandmother's quilt over our heads and we'd lain together under a patchwork of color as rich and vibrant as stained glass. Today the clouds hang ominous and low. Looks like rain, I conclude, and Bobby sighs. Adam, he says,

3

sitting back on his heels, Are you going to help me or are you just going to stand there and complain?

I go inside. Heat rises from the floorboards and thaws my bare toes. For three hours he works, disappearing around the corner of the house at one point and coming back with the hoe. I'm reheating the soup he made last night when he opens the back door, stopping in the laundry room to peel off his muddy jeans and toss them in the washer. After he goes into the bathroom to shower I sweep Indy's paw prints from the floor.

We'll have tomatoes, he says a few minutes later, joining me at the table. Maybe, I admit as he tears off a piece of toast and gives it to the dog. Catching one of his hands, I examine his thumb, then run my tongue across the whorls on the pad, tasting soap and the singular tang of his skin. Mm, I say, but he pulls his hand from mine. I'm hungry, he says, Let's eat.

The rain starts that night as we're getting ready for bed. I told you so, I say, staring out the window. Plants like water, he tells me, his tone mild. He's lying on the bed, the dog stretched beside him, shedding long, blonde fur on my grandmother's quilt. Does he have to be up there? I ask, and Bobby rolls his eyes. But he nudges the dog to the floor, his sweat-pants pulling away from his tee shirt and giving me a glimpse of fine, white skin.

I'm allowed one kiss before he moves away. The gardening wore me out, he claims. You've already used that excuse today, I tell him. But he stops me when I try to kiss him again.

That night I dream of snow, falling from the sky like confectioner's sugar. Giddy and excited, I watch from the window, hoping it will stick. C'mon, Bobby says, taking my hand, and I follow him outside without my coat. I'm thinking of the sled Julia and I got for Christmas one year, and the hot chocolate that waited for us after our first dizzying trip down the hill behind the stable, my mother's smile as wide as her arms. But this is no snow from my childhood. The moment we step from the porch we feel the sting, and I turn to Bobby in dismay. Ice, he says, wincing. Barely audible at first, the sound crescendos until the clatter of sleet drowns out even our voices. Bobby hunches deeper into his sweatshirt, and when I reach out to him I realize I've misjudged our proximity. I try to ignore the sharp prick of fear along my spine. Holding my hands over my head for protection, I squint into the storm. Bobby? I call. I can't see him, and I spin around, losing my sense of direction in the process. Panic robs my breath, but I scream his name with what little I have.

I wake with a sob to an empty bed. Sleet rattles against the windowpane, and when I realize he's gone I bolt. Without the benefit of light I stumble toward the back door, where the dog waits, whining. Hush, I say, Hush.

Ice nettles every exposed surface of my skin as I run across the yard. Help me, he begs, throwing me a towel, but the sleet comes too thick and the weight of the towel crushes everything I'm trying to protect. Bobby, I say, giving up, but by then he's kneeling on the ground, his head in his hands. Despite the torrent of ice I can hear him crying. Jesus, Bobby, I say, dropping beside him, We'll replant. He rocks forward, moaning, scaring me. Bobby, I plead, but he presses his forehead to the ground.

Inside, once I've gotten him out of his wet clothes and wrapped him in the quilt from our bed, once I've wiped the dirt from his face, I sit in front of him. Tears still slip from the corners of his eyes. I don't understand, I say, catching one with the tip of my finger, Help me understand. I've never seen him look so wretched, and I finally take his face in the palms of my hands and kiss him, until his mouth softens under the weight of mine.

The next morning we stand in the garden without speaking. Sun warms the ice caught in the shriveled leaves of the plants we hadn't been able to cover. I bend to pull a towel from a row of tomato plants, the material stiff and hard in my hands. We'll replant, I say. I shield my eyes from the sun, listening to the steady drip of the gutters. In a few weeks, I promise, We'll replant in a few weeks.

The tomatoes come late that summer. They hang huge and round and red from the vines, and still we can't bring ourselves to pick them. A bounty, I proclaim, even as I watch their skins split and spoil. A waste, Bobby says, and I lower my eyes.

Jennifer Hritz

2

JUNE, 2005

We're supposed to have dinner together tonight, at home. Eight o'clock, Joel told me before I left for work this morning, but I know better. He's running tonight, and he has a tendency to lose track of time when he runs. I bought him a sport watch a few years back but he refuses to wear it, claiming he doesn't like the feel of it on his wrist. So you'd rather I sit around waiting for you, I say, but he just laughs. I cycle for hours at a time on the weekends, he rationalizes, and I can hardly get upset because his run takes longer than he expects. But I can, and do, and realize if I take a step back that what's really at work here is a little jealousy. I've seen him emerge from his studio, dazed and stumbling over his words, lost in whatever he has in his head; running has the same effect on him. He'll go out tonight, promising me he'll be back within the hour so we can cook something, then show up long after I've given in to the frozen pizza I've insisted we buy, or the Ding Dongs I've stashed at the top of the cupboard. Where the hell have you been? I'll ask, and in a voice drunk on his own exertion he'll tell me that he didn't realize the time. I'll watch as he pulls his sweaty tee shirt over his head, as he peels off his shorts, his legs trembling, and I'll have to bite my tongue to stop from asking how he couldn't notice that the neighborhood was shutting down around him. He'd just remind me that we're living in the middle of suburban hell anyway, and that would only start a different argument.

But he's in the kitchen peeling carrots when I get home, later than I promised since I assumed he'd be gone. Where've you been? he asks, and I set my laptop beside the table with a sigh. Drinks, I say, lowering myself onto a barstool. He looks up at me, grazing the tip of his finger

7

with the vegetable peeler. I wince at the blood but he doesn't miss a beat, automatically turning away from me and holding his finger under the faucet. Watching him, I think of the nachos and margaritas Trainor and I ordered, the beer I had at Trainor's apartment. I'd set my bottle on the flat plane of his abdomen, traced the circle of condensate that appeared when I raised the bottle again to my mouth.

Salmon, Joel says, turning back to me, though I haven't asked what he's preparing, and my stomach groans at the thought. What about your run? I ask. He shrugs, whisking the peeler across the last carrot in three swift strokes. I haven't seen much of you, he says, and I can't tell whether or not his tone carries accusation. I can't help that I had drinks, I mumble, just in case. He gives me an odd look, reaching for a glass of wine I hadn't noticed and indicating the bottle. I'm not really in the mood, I mutter.

An hour later I'm rummaging through the medicine cabinet, looking for some Pepto-Bismol, or anything else that might settle the roiling of my stomach. I'd managed to eat half my fish before confessing that drinks had turned into dinner; Joel gave me a look of barely disguised disgust. Now he appears behind me as I'm drinking straight from the bottle. You all right? he asks, and I nod, holding my fist to my mouth and doing my best to suppress a belch. He shakes his head, reaching for his toothbrush. He's a fanatic about his teeth; he's a fanatic about a lot of things now. I watch him squeezing the toothpaste, pressing the tube exactly in the center, right where it makes me crazy. So are you down for the count? he asks, starting to brush, and I say, What do you mean? He holds up a finger, and I mash my lips together and wait until he's finished. I thought we were going to hang out, he tells me, wiping his mouth with the back of his hand. What did you want to do? I ask.

It's been a few weeks, easily, more if I want to be honest with myself. I know I need to make some kind of overture, if for no other reason than to throw him off track. I've made way too many excuses lately. But guilt precludes me.

It's been a while, he tells me, and I hurry to say: Not that long. He bites his lip, a habit I used to find endearing but which I swear now raises my blood pressure. I don't feel good, I tell him, What do you want me to do?

He tilts his head to the side as if he's actually considering the possibilities. You could eat one less dinner, he suggests, and I put the Pepto back in the medicine cabinet and shut the door with a snap. So now I'm fat, I say, and he groans. No, he says, Now you're exhausting, Adam. He turns away from me. I'm going for a run, he mutters, I won't be late.

A lie if I've ever heard one. I listen for the slam of the front door, then stretch out across the bed once I know I'm alone. I could sleep if I let myself; betrayal wears me out, and I wonder, not for the first time, if Trainor's worth all this grief.

I first met Trainor in the fall of '02, at a technology expo in Vegas a couple of years after Joel and I got back together. I didn't sleep with him then, though I could have, and we kept sporadic contact, from a purely professional standpoint. I suppose I'd seen him a half a dozen times when the position at Fusion Technologies, the computer manufacturer I work for, became available last year. I called him personally, flew him down for an interview. He seemed a good fit—for the position, for the company— and I offered him the job on the spot.

Joel didn't like him from the beginning. They met a few weeks after Trainor started, when there was nothing more serious between us than a fierce flirtation. He's a player, Joel informed me after spending all of five minutes with him. Well, he can't have me, I said, which at the time I thought was less of a lie than pretending I didn't want him. When I finally slept with him this past January all I felt was relief, though I suspect that wasn't because I'd been able to let go of all that pent-up frustration I'd carried around for two and a half years. I actually think I'd been waiting to slip. Sometimes I think I even orchestrated the entire thing.

Hauling myself to my feet, I go into the bathroom. A shower might revive me, and I get undressed, taking a good, hard look at my reflection. Fat may be a stretch, but I'm definitely thicker, especially around the middle. I grab a chunk of skin between my thumb and forefinger. I need to get back on my bike, but telling Joel I'm going for a ride is the easiest way for me to see Trainor on the weekends. I can't very well come back from what he thinks is a three hour ride and tell him I need to work out. So I'm not exercising, and it probably doesn't help that I'm eating nothing but crap. That's Joel's fault; if he wasn't so obsessive about everything he put in his mouth I wouldn't feel the need to sneak junk at work. I'm lucky to find him drinking a margarita anymore: too much sugar, he says. He wants everything organic, everything whole. At first I laughed when he stopped eating meat, and gave him a hard time about the fact that he'll still eat fish. Nothing with a face, Joel, I said, Nothing with a face. I should've kept my mouth shut. Now he carries a list of sustainable fish in his wallet, and I can't eat a steak without hearing that what I'm eating will rot in my stomach. You should treat your body with more respect, he chides, and I want to kill him. Opening his veins in his bathtub a few years back falls a little short of reverence, in my opinion. Don't try to tell me that the coffee I need to get me going in the morning compares even a little with the massive amounts of cocaine he used to shove up his nose.

I step into the shower and close my eyes. Honestly, Joel hasn't said a word about the weight I've gained, though it must be fifteen pounds by now. I know his comments stem more from his concern about my stress level, from the way I'm handling my father's illness, which pretty much consists of outright denial. I know he just wants me to be healthy, so I can deal with the tension at work, so I can make another trip home. But sometimes I get so sick of listening to him. Sometimes I just want a cheeseburger.

I'm getting out of the shower when I hear him coming up the stairs. Wrapping a towel around my waist, I nod as he appears in the doorway. Hey, he says, and I can tell from the tone of that one word that he's forgotten whatever friction existed between us before he left the house. How was your run? I ask as he pulls his shirt over his head. Good, he admits. He kicks off his shoes, then hooks his thumb under the waistband of his shorts and yanks them down. I lean against the sink, watching him. His belly's flat, flatter than Trainor's, and certainly flatter than my own, and his legs quiver with muscle. He runs, and takes the occasional yoga class, and he looks better, in fact, than I've ever seen him look. Want to join me? he asks, taking note of my expression, but I shake my head. He's high enough from his run to shrug.

Once he's in the shower I go into the bedroom and rummage for a pair of shorts. I should be heading to bed soon—I have a string of meetings starting at eight o'clock tomorrow morning—but I have a feeling Joel won't let me off the hook so easily. I can't help feeling the slightest bit coerced. Though that's nothing new; sometimes I think I've felt that way from the moment we got back together.

We met over Labor Day in '97, and spent what I interpreted as a pretty fantastic weekend together before he bailed on me. I saw him again a few weeks later, and then not again for over a year. By the end of another long weekend I believed we'd crossed into a serious intimacy. But he bailed again, and when he came looking for me a few weeks after that I told him he wasn't wanted. Hours later I found him in his bathtub, his arms wide open.

We didn't speak for more than five months, and when he finally called he told me he was living in Mexico. I went down to see him, and though that trip didn't end the way I envisioned, within a couple of months he'd moved back to Austin and I broke up with the guy I was seeing so I could be with him. We lasted all of four months before he left me again.

I've never felt so alone. Not when Bobby was first diagnosed, not when he died, not when I moved here to Austin, not any of the other times Joel walked out on me. I tried to convince myself that I should feel lucky. After all, I'd loved two men in my life, and what I shared with each of them was probably more than most people ever experienced. Instead that made losing them all the more brutal.

Six months later Joel called, the same day I had Indy put to sleep. Bobby was the one who'd brought him home as a puppy, all soft paws and tail, one Saturday morning after we bought our house. Okay, I know I should've talked to you first, he said, already anticipating my argument, But Adam, look at him. He turned him toward me, cupped in the palms of his hands, as if he was sheltering something sacred. Maybe he was. Considering what he'd been through, he deserved to be loved without condition. I took one look at him, at the gentle curve of his fingers around that dog, and knew I couldn't object.

Indy lived for almost thirteen years, through Bobby's illness and death and my move to Austin at the beginning of '97. When his incontinence started a few months after Joel and I broke up for the last time I took him to the see the vet, who looked grim. Indy would not go fast, I was told, and I should give serious thought to putting him to sleep. But I couldn't do it. I just couldn't let him go, and I kept him alive much longer than I should have, much longer than was humane. He lost his hearing, and his sight, and by the last week I was carrying him up and down the stairs because he wasn't capable of getting around himself. One day I stumbled, dropping him to the floor, and when I tried to scoop him up he snapped at me. I crouched down and hauled him into my arms, where he whimpered so low and pitifully I couldn't bear it any longer. I took him to the vet that day.

Joel called the moment I got home. I'd been waiting for months for him to contact me, and now, my hands still warm from cradling Indy's head in my lap, I had Joel on the phone, telling me he needed to see me, telling me he had something to show me. I almost told him no. But he was persuasive, and I was vulnerable, and I eventually agreed to meet him at his house. The moment I stepped through his front door I burst into tears. The living room wall, the one I'd found covered with black paint the day I found him in a bathtub of blood, held what I think might just be the best work he's ever done. I'm not the only one to think so; before he sold the house he knocked down the wall and delivered it over to a local gallery, who in turn sold it for $8000. That day I stood in front of his painting, weeping, and he took me in his arms and whispered apologies until I sank to the floor beside him. I love you, he said for the first time, I love you. I just held his hand, my eyes shut tight.

Almost five years later, he's done everything he promised. Sometimes I'm still astonished when I think about how he's changed. I couldn't have asked for more, and yet there are moments when I find myself feeling just a little bit bitter about the way he made me suffer.

I get in bed and reach for the remote, clicking through the channels as I ready myself. I know what he'll want, as soon as he steps from the shower. But he surprises me. What're you doing? I ask when he comes into the bedroom and starts getting dressed. I have…, he confesses, swirling his hand beside his head to let me know that he's thinking about his work, and even though I should be thankful that he's letting me off the hook I can't help feeling hurt that I'm losing out to his studio. I thought you wanted to hang out, I say, as if he's been the one putting me off all evening, and he actually hesitates. I cringe. Go ahead, I assure him, We'll have time later. When? he asks with a wry grin, but he's already moving toward the door. We'll be fine, I mutter, and he disappears.

~ ~ ~

Hands steepled under my chin, I listen to Dave Burroughs, one of my managers, explain why his team's numbers have slipped for the fourth consecutive week. My temples throb, no doubt because I've had little to eat today beyond a couple of doughnuts and a half a dozen cups of coffee. I'd been late to the office, and now I'm running late for another meeting, and I can't seem to get rid of Dave. He's a talker, and I almost close my eyes before I catch myself.

I'm tired. Once Joel left for his studio last night I sat in front of the television before trying to fall asleep, a feat I hadn't managed to accomplish until he slunk his way across the room a couple of hours before my alarm was scheduled to go off. Hey, he whispered, seeing me awake, but I didn't answer him. I was angry, though he hadn't really done anything wrong. Maybe I just knew that when I had to drag myself out of bed in two hours I'd resent the sleeping curl of his body. He slid into bed beside me, and I caught the scent of his studio on his skin, a sort of combination of paint and sweat and turpentine. Once I found the aroma intoxicating. Now I find myself gritting my teeth whenever I catch its wind.

You hear what I'm saying, Adam? Dave asks, and I realize he's been waiting a good ten seconds for my response. Rallying, I tell him I understand his position and if he can just help me out with next week's numbers we should be fine. With a nod of gratitude he leaves, and I run my fingers through my hair. I'd be tempted to put my head right down on the desk if I wouldn't be spotted; my office, with its glass walls, shelters me from nothing. I stare out at my assistant, Darlene, who sees me watching and points to the clock. I know, I know, I mouth. I know.

Trainor's already there, along with the rest of his team, when I walk into the conference room. In theory I'm here because Trainor wants me to deliver some extra guidance with the script for our current sales promotion. Just so we can fine tune, he said when he asked me to join him. But he knows there's nothing to fine tune and that's not because of the work I've done with the script. He's just that good with his representatives. He's the only one of my managers who consistently hits his numbers, carries guys like Dave Burroughs week after week after week. A natural, my boss, Vincent, has said more than once, intimating that I have no business whatsoever taking credit for any of Trainor's success.

Vincent and I were the only two Directors to post for the position of Vice President of Domestic Sales and Marketing a little over a year ago. I was sure I'd get the job; I'd been told I was being groomed. But then I met with Miles Underwood, our Chief Marketing Officer, at the end of a grueling interview process. He wanted to discuss the plans I'd have for expansion in the second half of the decade should I be given the position, and I was honest, and told him that I felt our approach should continue in the same conservative vein. He didn't agree, and that philosophical difference tipped the scales in Vincent's favor.

From a purely financial perspective, promoting Vincent was a shrewd move. He's all about the bottom line, and he'll do anything to get there, including bulldozing his subordinates. I've spent many more late nights in my office since Vincent's promotion, been booked on many more spur-of-the-moment trips. Vincent has no qualms about dialing someone up in the middle of a Saturday afternoon, no problem scheduling a late meeting the night before a holiday. Come into work a little later than usual, or skip out early for some reason and you're guaranteed an interrogation. I want team players, he informed us early on, finding us less than satisfactory, and I swear he directed his gaze at me.

Three days after Vincent was promoted my father was diagnosed with lung cancer. I took a week: to digest the news, to go to Kentucky for my father's surgery, and when I returned to the office I found myself having to defend my absence. Vincent made a point of mentioning every meeting I'd missed, every decision that had been made without me, as if he took my father's illness, and my subsequent absence, as a personal affront. Whatever camaraderie existed between us when we'd been working at the same level disappeared. I'd just been told that my father was looking at twelve to eighteen months, and I wasn't in a mental position to cater to anyone, least of all the guy who took the job that by all rights should've been mine. For the past year Vincent has been quick to remind me of my mistake.

Now I sit to the side, listening as Trainor runs through the script with his top salesperson to show the rest of his representatives how it's done.

Writing the script last week I'd had his voice in mind, knew he'd be able to deliver. Whatever happens between us personally, I'll never regret hiring him.

When they're finished I offer a few inane comments which must leave everyone wondering why I'm even here, and then Trainor dismisses them. Long morning? he asks, sitting down beside me. Tired, I say. He moves his hand to touch me, then thinks twice and spins his pen on the table instead. He dresses well, in expensive clothing that does nothing to detract from his shaven head. Lucky for you bald is in, I told him once, realizing he'd have nothing save a semi-circle should he try to grow his hair again, but he'd been unconcerned. Hair or not, he possesses a charm all his own.

So do I get to see you this weekend? he asks, lowering his mouth to my ear. Trainor, I say, automatically angling away from him, and he chuckles. He exercises less discretion than makes me comfortable, though he has much less reason to worry. Vincent loves him. They spent time together the week I was in Kentucky, found they share a common interest in rowing; Vincent headed up his crew when he was at college and won all sorts of competitions, information he's bored me with on more than one occasion. Trainor spends almost every weekend on the water, and I've heard him talking to Vincent about some of the better places to row. You've certainly become chummy, I told him once, and he had the gall to say, Don't worry, I've got your back. I barely spoke to him for a week.

I don't know, I say in answer to his question about whether I'll have a chance to see him, but I'm lying. I'll get halfway through the day tomorrow, then won't be able to stand another second at home. Trainor knows this will happen. Somewhere in all of this I lost the upper hand, assuming I had it in the first place. I don't know, I repeat, and he nods, appeasing me. I rub my forehead, wondering why my headache hasn't gone away. Since my father's diagnosis I find myself obsessing about my body's every twinge. Heartburn? Stomach cancer. Headache? Brain tumor. Nothing can be simple.

If you want to come out to the parking lot I can take care of that headache, Trainor tells me, and I grimace. He's serious, wouldn't need convincing if I offered the same suggestion. I like to think I have higher scruples, though I know deep down my reason has more to do with a fear of getting caught than anything else. I have another meeting, I say, sighing by way of apology, and he follows me as I get to my feet, then taps his pen against my chest, one step too close. Call me, he says, and I know he's not talking about tomorrow or Sunday or even tonight. I nod, then turn my eyes to the glass. Darlene averts her gaze.

~ ~ ~

I cut out early. I don't tell Darlene, and I certainly don't tell Trainor. I don't want to be questioned, or cajoled, or followed. I just want to go home. I've been feeling guilty about the way I treated Joel last night, about telling Darlene to weed out his calls this morning, and I head south on 360, in the direction of home.

After living here for more than eight years, even taking into consideration the new construction that mars the landscape, I still can't get enough of the scenery. Driving this road back in '97 when I first interviewed with Fusion had sealed the deal, and I bought a house on the south shore of Lake Travis. Joel was impressed, too, the first time he stood at my windows and saw the hills dropping into the water, though now he'd admit nothing of the sort. He hates the neighborhood, tells me nothing's worth living so far from civilization. We're not exactly in the middle of nowhere, I've told him, and he tells me we might as well be. I resent the accusation, and remind him that he didn't have any qualms about moving in a few months after we got back together. I just wanted to be with *you*, he says, I didn't give a shit about the *house*. But he makes more use of the pool than I ever have, redesigned the formal living room without hesitation so he'd have a place to work. Remodeling cost a fortune, and I'd actually taken out a loan against the mortgage. He didn't know that, of course, and to be honest, he wanted to contribute some of the money from the sale of his house. But he had so little, and owed so much, and I just couldn't accept his offer.

When I first moved here, the area was relatively undeveloped. I thought I was getting a deal, paying what I did for a remote property overlooking the lake. But I didn't understand the way the city was already changing, couldn't have projected the multitudes that would flock here for the technology. Though that's been lucrative for Fusion, and I guess consequently for me, the sprawl has stretched far beyond the heart of the city. Now there's no debating that we live in the suburbs, and though beautiful, the houses in our neighborhood have a homogenous look that leave Joel uninspired. A wasteland, he proclaims, and even though I agree with him to some extent, even though I know how much he misses the house near campus that I convinced him to sell, I still feel myself getting angry. After all, I gave him free rein when he moved in, and though he came with few possessions other than his art supplies and a sofa he bought in college, he wasted no time making his mark. I came home from work one day a month after he moved in to find my kitchen painted a lurid shade of red. I'm not sure I can cook in here, I said. Four years later the kitchen's still crimson.

Joel's reservation about the neighborhood, though, stems more from the neighbors themselves than anything else. I've always found everyone perfectly welcoming, but Joel has been much quicker to find fault. We're a novelty here, he says, and when I'm dismissive he asks why I haven't noticed that we're treated with an equal dose of civility and wariness. That's your imagination talking, I tell him. Has anyone ever invited us over for drinks? he asks, Have you ever even set foot inside one of these houses? Enough, I finally said the last time we argued, but I'd been shocked to realize he was right. Even the dogs match, he muttered, and if I hadn't been so upset I would've laughed. The bottom line is that I hate feeling as if he's disparaging not only the neighborhood, not only our house, but the very lives we're living.

As I turn onto 2222 my cell phone rings, and when I see the number my stomach drops. Every time my sister's number, or my parents' number, or any number with an area code I recognize from Kentucky appears I feel nauseous. I've gotten way too much bad news from those numbers over the course of the last year, and I hold the phone to my ear, already preparing myself for more.

He's back in the hospital. Heart palpitations, my sister tells me, and shortness of breath, and his oncologist wants an arteriogram and another CAT scan. He just had a scan six weeks ago, I protest, and she says, in a voice that reminds me she's having a hard time holding herself together, I *know* that, Adam. Well, what are they thinking? I ask, Metastasis, a heart

17

attack, what? I don't know, Julia says, I don't think *they* know. She tells me she's going up tomorrow; I wince at the reproach in her tone. Should I come? I ask, but she says we should wait until we hear what the doctors say. How is he anyway? I ask, and my sister sighs. You know Dad, she says, He's just pissed he's looking at a weekend in the hospital.

After I hang up with Julia I call my mother's cell. My father answers himself, in a voice as thick as the smoke that curled from his cigarettes every day of my childhood. If you needed a night away from home, I tell him, I could've arranged a hotel. He chuckles. What's going on, Dad? I ask, and he gives me the same information Julia did, but in a voice so slow and thoughtful I'd swear he was talking about someone else. I still don't understand how he can be so unemotional about what's happening to him, how he can keep the resentment from getting in the way of his every thought. Instead it's my mother who carries a look of grim resignation that she manages to hide when she thinks someone's watching, a bitterness that comes from realizing my father can't possibly have the kind of time left they'd both envisioned. I know that look. I've worn it myself.

Julia says she's coming tomorrow, I tell him, and he says, She should be tending to her own family. I think she considers you a part of her family, I tell him. He grunts, then covers the mouthpiece of the phone to say something to my mother. How's Joel? he asks when he comes back. Joel's fine, I say. You boys have any plans for the weekend? he asks, and as usual I soften at the question. He always asks, always, and I'm struck again both by how easily he accepts Joel, as well as his insistence on referring to us as boys. I half-believe that he thinks we're planning a weekend that involves a campout under the stars, or riding our bikes in the rain. Not really, I say. Well, you tell him we said hello, he says. I'll call you tomorrow, I tell him, adding that someone should let me know regardless if there's any news. Julia wouldn't have it any other way, he assures me.

I hang up, not sure whether I feel better or not. My father has a way of downplaying every crisis, and I usually end up feeling confused, especially if I've just heard from Julia, who tends to blow everything out of proportion. I suppose I could've asked to talk to my mother, but she wouldn't have spoken candidly with my father in the room. I'll hear from her soon enough anyway. She knows I need the details, knows I won't rest until I've been able to mull over every sliver of information, every statistic. I was the same way with Bobby.

At home I stop in the open doorway of Joel's studio. But he's not there, and I find him a few minutes later, sacked out on a raft in the pool, his eyes closed to the sun. He's listening to his iPod, and he doesn't hear me stepping onto the deck above him. Joel, I say, testing him, but he doesn't move. I think he might be asleep, until he dips one hand into the water and then holds it, dripping, above his abdomen. Even from this distance I can see the goose bumps that rise on his flesh. Though in the winter his skin's as white as mine, in the summer he wears a tan darker than any I've had. My one indulgence, he likes to say.

Despite my affair with Trainor I haven't stopped wanting him, the irony of which isn't lost on me. From the moment I met him I've thought him beautiful. Only lately have I admitted that I'd been wooed more by the despair in his eyes that first night I met him, by his failure to break my gaze even though he tried, than anything else. Joel needed everything from me, and I let him turn me into a god. What I haven't been able to figure out is what to do now that he's saved himself.

I take a few steps closer, then pry off my socks and shoes and dip one foot into the pool. Enticed by the water, still cool this early in the summer, I roll up the legs of my pants and lower myself to the side. Ripples fan away from my calves, stirring Joel's raft just enough that he opens his eyes. Sorry, I say when he jumps, and he frowns, pulling his headphones from his ears. What're you doing home? he asks. I shrug. Just missed me, he concludes, and I allow him half a smile.

Slipping from the raft, he makes his way toward me, then stops when he reaches my parted legs and props his elbows on my khakis. You're getting me wet, I tell him, but neither one of us moves. I touch his hair, thick and warm from the sun. He used to wear it long, cuts it close enough to his head now that I can grab only half a handful. I'm sorry about last night, I say. Forget about it, he murmurs. His arms encircle my waist, saturating my shirt. You okay? he asks, and when I don't answer he pulls back to look at me. I shake my head, both refusal and warning. So he kisses me instead, and when I feel him tug I slide into the water beside him.

~ ~ ~

I talk to my mother that night, after we're out of the pool, after we've eaten a late dinner. I've told Joel the news, and he murmured the appropriate concerns and asked what he could do to help. I sent him out to pick up a pizza. Sausage, he said with a grimace when he returned, presenting it to me the way he might hand over a human head. He'd picked up a small cheese pie for himself, and a Greek salad, and I watched him dip the tines of his fork into the dressing and then spear a lettuce leaf the same way Darlene does. He'd eaten less than half his pizza; I polished off the remainder after I finished my own.

I'm just starting to feel the first twinges of heartburn when my mother calls. Phone in hand, I make my way to the kitchen where I sit at the table, rubbing my chest with my fist as she talks about blockages, and angioplasty. When? I ask. Monday morning, she tells me, and I close my eyes. Monday morning I'm slated for a strategy session with Vincent, a meeting I've been dreading and which consequently I've rescheduled twice. He's not going to be happy if I'm out of the office; I think he's already pissed that he wasn't able to get in touch with me this afternoon. I checked my voice mail while Joel was getting the pizza and found a half a dozen messages, mostly from Darlene, who'd called to tell me that Vincent was looking for me. It's a little hard to cover for you, she'd said, sounding annoyed, When I don't even know where you are.

There's really no reason for you to come all the way up here, my mother says, but she's waited just a second too long to let me off the hook, and there's no mistaking the weariness in her voice. No, I say, Of course I'll be there. I tell her I'll call her back with my travel plans and hang up, then press my hand to my chest, which is now burning with a vengeance. What's wrong? Joel asks, catching me, and I mutter something about eating too much, anticipate the look he gives me. Don't start, all right? I say, Just please ... don't start.

He's quiet, then asks about my father. Are you going up? he asks once I've told him. I lean forward, my elbows on my knees, and he squats down beside me. He'll be okay, Adam, he says, and I want to tell him not to patronize me. I know where we're headed. But I don't say a word, and he cups my face in the palm of one hand. I'll go with you, he offers, and I nod.

~ ~ ~

We land in Lexington late Saturday night and rent a car. My mother, though I've told her to get some sleep, will be up waiting for us, and I feel a pang of guilt for opting for the later flight when we could have arrived early this afternoon. But I'd wanted to see Trainor again, and I told Joel I had to go to the office for a while to troubleshoot for the beginning of next week. Truth be told, the office is exactly where I should have been. When I called Darlene to let her know my plans, she clucked her tongue and said I better leave Vincent a voice mail all on my own. I don't want to be responsible for breaking the news that you're going to have to reschedule, she told me, and I grumbled something about paying her well enough that she should do a little of the dirty work for me. I think I'm doing a pretty good job keeping your secret, she said. I'd been too taken aback to come up with a retort. Instead I emailed Vincent, then promptly turned off my phone.

When I showed up at Trainor's apartment he asked about my father, then took me in his arms in a way that felt entirely too intimate. I stayed long enough to sleep with him, made excuses when he asked me to stay. I have to pack, I said, I have to run by the bank. When you get back, he said, We need to talk. I nodded without asking why.

You want me to take over? Joel asks, motioning toward the wheel. I shake my head, taking a sip of the coffee I picked up a few miles back. Joel's drinking decaf, likens the taste to cat piss. How would you know? I ask, and he looks thoughtful. He's been more patient today than I deserve; he spent his morning doing the errands I told Trainor I needed to run, and I haven't been particularly conciliatory in response. In fact, I'd come close to suggesting that he stay home, and I might have if I hadn't realized the toll that argument would take on an already meager reservoir of energy. I glance at him, still unsure whether or not I'm glad he's here. He'll be a help, I know, to my mother, my sister. My father's feelings for him rival those he reserves for me. I just don't know that in light of my recent indiscretions I want to be reminded of his generosity.

Slouching a little further in his seat, he yawns. Should've gone for the full-strength, I tell him, indicating his coffee. And end up jittery and anxious like you? he says. He hasn't spoken with animosity; in fact, his voice sounds sleepy, but my hands tighten around the steering wheel. I'm jittery and anxious because my father's dying, I snap, and he winces. He's not the only one. I don't think I've ever said the words aloud, and the taillights of the car in front of me suddenly bleed. Why don't you pull over? he suggests, touching my arm, I'll drive the rest of the way. I shrug him off. Because I just want to get there, okay? I say, I just want to get there.

~ ~ ~

My father looks better than I expect. He's sitting up in bed Sunday morning when we get to the hospital, and he's wearing the requisite gown but complaining to the nurse about the quality of his breakfast in a way that reassures me. No one can truly be on his way out, I reason, if he's this concerned about the texture of his scrambled eggs. I lean over the bed, reaching for his hand at the same time I pull him into a hug. He tolerates this display of physical affection, giving me a couple of pats on my back before he says, Okay. I step back well before I'm ready, and Joel takes his hand. He doesn't make the mistake of lingering, and my father rewards him with a smile, which Joel returns. You don't look half-bad, Joel says. I'm not going to win any beauty contests, my father tells him, running his hand across his scalp. He's lost most of his hair because of the chemo, though he's grown some cotton-colored fuzz since my last trip home. And here last year you were runner-up, Joel says.

My father grins. They have a way between them that I still find astounding. In light of Joel's relationship with his own father, I'm always surprised by how easy he seems to feel with mine. You boys have a good trip? my father asks, and Joel looks at me before he nods. I bob my head in tandem, without speaking. I've been short with him, fell into bed last night and turned my face to the wall. Adam, he sighed, but I didn't answer. This morning he cornered me on my way into the shower and told me that he'd come to help. You need to let me do that, he said, and I told him if he wanted to help so much he should stop giving me shit about my diet. What diet? he asked, and then seeing my expression he pulled me toward him. I'm just fucking with you, Adam, he said. For a second I let myself rest against him, but then Julia rounded the corner, and though she excused herself, backing away, we'd already lost the moment.

Julia steps forward now and gives my father a kiss; Joel and I automatically give her a wide berth. She'd been sitting on the front porch with my mother last night when we arrived, but the instant we got out of the car she was on her feet. Eleven! she cried, You said you'd be here by eleven! She ran down the steps and flung herself into my arms, then hit me, a little too hard for me to think she was joking. She's been worried, she whispered. I glanced at my mother, who was just getting to her feet. She seems fine, I said, and Julia growled, soft and low. How would *you* know? she asked, You haven't *been* here. She eventually calmed down, but she hadn't apologized, and this morning she's been remarkably withdrawn, even with Joel.

How'd you sleep? my father asks her now, and she says, How did *you* sleep? My father grunts. I think he hates the fuss Julia makes over him more than anything else. He doesn't want to be treated any differently, and the mere fact that Julia leaves her family behind to drive up to see him irritates him. You have three children, I've heard him say, and she'll tell him that Ivan can handle them for a few days. I like to check in on you, she says, and though she keeps her voice light I'm not fooled. Don't get me wrong. I love Julia. She's generous, she's warm, and in a crisis, she's phenomenal. But she's been living in crisis mode for the past year, and the further my father's illness progresses, the more frenetic her energy becomes. She can't continue at this pace. Trust me, I know.

Have you eaten? my father asks us, shooing Julia away when she tries to sit down on the bed beside him. You trying to give away those eggs? I ask, and before he can answer Julia says, as if she missed my father's grumblings when we first arrived, Eggs? She peers down at his tray, frowning. Why are they giving you eggs? she asks. Because I asked for them, my father tells her. Julia gives me a look that's supposed to spur me into action. Maybe they're Egg Beaters, I suggest, and she actually picks at them with my father's fork. They're *not* Egg Beaters, she tells me. He's not eating them anyway, Julia, I say, So what difference does it make? He's having an *angioplasty* tomorrow, she informs me, and I say, So? So he shouldn't be eating eggs! she cries.

You two are going to kill him long before those eggs do, Joel mutters. My father laughs, and Julia folds her arms across her chest. You want the eggs? Joel asks my father. Hell no, my father says. You want me to see what else I can get you? Joel asks, and my father's expression turns impish. A cigarette, he says. I look away, pained by the way he's named the culprit, and baffled by its hold on him. I know he's still smoking. He won't in front of me, won't in front of any of us, from what I understand. But I can smell it on him sometimes when he comes in from outside, and I can't even look at him. A cigarette, Joel muses, settling into the chair beside my father's bed with the sigh of the formerly addicted. You have any on you? my father asks, and Joel gives his head a shake of regret, as if despite having not smoked in more than six years he'd like nothing more than to reach into his pocket and find a pack of Marlboros. They sit for a moment in quiet contemplation, and when Julia finally offers the information that my father's cardiologist doesn't want him smoking the day before surgery they both give her a dirty look. I'm going to get a coffee, I mumble. I'll join you, my sister says.

Downstairs in the cafeteria I scan the row of stale pastries, knowing I'll be sorry the second one of them makes its way into my mouth. I choose a Danish crisscrossed with icing anyway. After I pay we walk over to one of the corner tables. Bitter, Julia says, and at first I think she's making some kind of commentary about my attitude, then realize when I've taken a sip that she's talking about the coffee. Mm, I agree, biting into the Danish and offering some to her. She shakes her head, staring at the wall above my shoulder. I take the opportunity to give her a closer look, something she hasn't been still enough for me to accomplish since I arrived.

My sister's not unattractive. I've always thought her pretty, in fact, in a fresh-faced sort of way. Growing up we were both thankful for relatively clear complexions, but there the similarities between us end. I inherited my mother's features: thick blonde hair I refuse to believe I'm losing, eyes so blue Joel swears he could never reproduce the color no matter how much paint he had at his disposal. I have my mother's bone structure, too, lines almost as fine as Joel's, and long legs perfect for cycling. Julia, on the other hand, ended up with my father's almost-but-not-quite blonde hair, which I notice she hasn't been highlighting as diligently as she has in the past, his matter-of-fact brown eyes, his square jaw and blunt manner. Early summer sun has freckled her nose and forehead, and creased the corners of her eyes. She frowns, puckering her mouth, and her lipstick—her one *accoutrement* this morning—bleeds into the lines around her lips. The stress of the last year hasn't done her any favors, and the thought suddenly occurs to me that even if she took the time to make herself presentable I'd still be appalled by how she's aged. I feel like a voyeur, and avert my eyes, but not before I realize that given thirty seconds she'd probably come to the same conclusion about me.

He's not doing well, Adam, she says, and I shrug. He seems fine, I say, then amend, Well, not fine, maybe, but better than I expected. She tells me I haven't been home for three months. Thanks for the reminder, I say, but she doesn't seem to hear me. You're seeing him after thirty-six hours in the hospital, she continues, He hasn't been able to smoke, he's been forced to stay in bed, he's been on a restricted diet— Except for the eggs, I interject, unable to help myself, and when she covers her mouth with the palm of one hand I sigh. Julia, I say, on the brink of apology, and she grabs my hand with a grip so fierce the bones of my fingers grind together. Even before she opens her mouth I know what she's going to say.

~   ~   ~

Upstairs Joel sprawls in the chair beside my father's bed as if he's taken up permanent residence, and when I glance around the room I see that the breakfast tray has been cleared and the bed itself has been straightened. I wonder if the nurse has been here, or if Joel has taken the initiative to neaten things up on his own. I wouldn't put it past him. Did you two have something to eat? my father asks, and Julia nods. Coffee, I say, omitting mention of the Danish, which I had slowly and methodically torn to pieces. You didn't bring one for me? he asks, and I start. No, I say, Do you want one? Coffee sounds good, he muses. I'll get a decaf, Julia tells us, looking grateful for an excuse to leave again.

We were thinking about a movie, my father says after she's gone, indicating the television perched halfway up the wall. Yeah? I say, and he tells me there's a John Wayne special, *The Sands of Iwo Jima* and *Rio Bravo* back to back. That sounds right up your alley, I say to Joel. Soldiers, he agrees, and my father actually laughs. I smile, the effort half-hearted. I don't seem to know what to do with my hands. Listen, I finally say, gesturing toward the door when I find I can't finish. Your wife wanted us to pick her up by eleven, Joel explains. Go ahead, then, my father says, Julia will be up in a minute.

What's wrong? Joel asks as soon as we step from the room. I keep my eyes on the elevator doors at the end of the hall. If I make it to those doors before I have to say the words, I think. If I make it to those doors. What's *wrong?* Joel asks. The results of the scan, I start, and he says: No.

I want to contradict him. I want to tell him that my sister has made a mistake, that the doctors themselves have made a mistake. I want to tell him that the results of the scan show complete and total eradication of my father's cancer.

I want to hold his hand.

Where? he asks, and I swallow, as if with that motion the words will somehow come more easily, sound more palatable. The elevator doors slide open. They found lesions on his brain, I say.

He has me in his arms even before the doors have a chance to close behind us, but I worm my way out from under them. Not here, I hiss, pressing the button for the lobby. He touches me, unable to help himself, saying my name. We'll get through this, he says, He'll be okay. Blood rushes to my face, and I jab at the button, again and again. He'll be okay, Adam, he says, trying to move my hand, and I turn on him. I swear to god, Joel, I growl, I swear to god, if you tell me that one more fucking time....

The elevator doors open before I can finish, and the couple in front of us, sensing fury, hesitates. I pull my hands through my hair, then drop back a few steps to allow them entry. Offering them a wan smile, Joel joins me. Without touching, we begin our descent.

~ ~ ~

My mother's freshening up. She's in her room, where she hasn't responded to my gentle knock. Maybe I should just go in there, I say, coming back into the living room, but Joel shakes his head. He's sitting on the edge of my father's chair, his hands between his knees, and part of me wants to just kneel down in front of him and lay my head in his lap. In the car on the way to my parents' house I'd offered him an inadequate apology for unloading on him and he accepted with a graciousness that shames me, stepped to the side when we walked into the living room and my mother stood to face me. I put my arms around her, and held myself still as she cried. Whatever tears came to my own eyes I swallowed until I was nauseous, and when she finally broke away from me, excusing herself, I caught a glimpse of Joel, his head lowered. I don't know whether that was out of deference to my mother's privacy or because he was crying himself, and I kept my eyes from his, not wanting to know the answer. We waited ten minutes before I finally went in search of her, another ten before I knocked again. I don't like the fact that she's not answering, I tell him now, and he nods, as if he understands that I have a mental picture of her stroking out. Give her a few more minutes, he says. My father will wonder what happened to us, I tell him, and he says, So give him a call.

I can't. That's part of the problem. I can't call him, and I can't think about going back to the hospital either. I don't want to be there, knowing what I know, knowing that he doesn't have any idea. How could they not tell him? I asked Julia, and she told me that the oncologist thought it best to get past tomorrow's surgery before saddling my father with the news. One thing at a time, she said, probably unaware that she was using the oncologist's very words, and I gritted my teeth. I hate my father's doctor, a prick of a man as unemotional about my father's disease as my father himself. Julia doesn't understand my dislike for him, tells me I'm confusing his cool demeanor with a lack of compassion. That's not true, she's assured me, adding that I haven't spent as much time with him as she and my mother. Not wanting to get into another argument about the frequency of my trips home I've shut my mouth. But the bottom line is that I think my father should have been told, and I'm not thrilled with either my sister or my mother for allowing the doctor to convince them that it's in my father's best interest to keep him in the dark. I'm not even sure it's ethical. What am I supposed to say to him? I asked Joel in the car, and he was quiet, staring out the window. I got the impression he agreed with my sister, and I'd been just about ready to tear into him when he sighed. I don't know, Adam, he said, I honestly don't know.

I'm seriously thinking about asking him to call my father himself when I hear my mother's bedroom door open. Joel and I exchange glances as he gets to his feet. Ready? my mother asks from the doorway, and I nod, trying not to dwell on the careful set of her mouth, which trembles as Joel takes her hand. Don't, I want to tell him as he pulls her close enough to kiss her cheek, but she smiles at him. I like your haircut, she says, and Joel's free hand wanders to his hair. Yeah? he says, and she nods. I meant to tell you last night, she adds. He tells her he'll take the compliment, even if it's a day late. They're few and far between, he says, an admission which causes me to lower my eyes, though I don't think he's spoken with malice. I doubt that, she says, squeezing his hand, and I see him squeeze back.

~   ~   ~

That night we sit on the front porch, Joel and Julia and I, along with Julia's husband, Ivan. We speak in hushed tones for the benefit of my mother, who has gone to bed early in anticipation of tomorrow. But I know she's not sleeping; she can't be, given what's coming. Julia had tried to persuade her to take something, but my mother refused, and I'd defended her decision. Mom hasn't had a good night's sleep for a year, I assured my sister, And she's sure as hell not going to get one tonight, with or without a sedative.

We've had a long day. No one's looking forward to tomorrow, though my father's doctor doesn't anticipate any problems with the surgery. A simple procedure, he reiterated this afternoon, kind enough to stop by my father's room to check in on him, but we weren't paying him much attention. We were too busy thinking about what will come after tomorrow, what will happen on Tuesday or Wednesday when my father finds out what he's up against. I tried my best to keep up a front, but I've never been particularly good at smothering my feelings and I caught my father looking at me at one point toward the end of the day, his expression thoughtful. What? I asked, and then, fearful he'd ask me something I wasn't prepared to answer, I directed his attention to the television, where we were watching a western. I picked the wrong moment to point to the screen, which depicted a hapless fellow sucking on a cigarette until his cheeks were hollow. My father watched with a hungry, unhappy expression and I mumbled an apology, avoiding Julia's eye. Good work, she muttered a few minutes later when my father was elsewhere engaged, and I didn't respond. I hate what this is doing, to all of us.

Mommy? a high, thin voice calls out. I'll go, Ivan says with a sigh, disappearing through the screen door, and Julia leans her head on her hand, her elbow perched on the armrest of the swing. He's so good, she murmurs after he leaves. I nod, with little enthusiasm. I'm still nursing a wound from earlier, though Julia doesn't realize that. Joel, however, meets my eyes for one brief moment before turning his gaze toward the stable; the horses, this late at night, make soft, whinnying noises that carry on the breeze, stirring up virtually every childhood memory I own. We've not had a moment alone together, Joel and I, since we returned before lunch to pick up my mother. I'm not sure that's such a bad thing.

My brother-in-law drove up earlier with my nieces and nephew in tow, and as delighted as I always am to see them, I couldn't help but think that maybe Julia wasn't thinking things through. I'm a little concerned about Dad being able to rest, I ventured, but no one listened to me. Thirty minutes after they arrived, crowding into my father's hospital room and sucking out the air, Joel offered to take them back to my parents' house. They'll be fine, he told my sister, and when she hesitated he gestured to Lindsey, tuned into her iPod, and five-year-old Grace, who was trying to tie a ribbon around the machine that monitored my father's heart rate. Julia nodded, and five minutes later Joel left with the kids, touching my shoulder on his way. Ah, my father said in the sudden quiet, and even Julia smiled. I envied Joel, though, despite the peace. He didn't have to wade through the deceit in that hospital room. He didn't have to spend the afternoon trying to think of something to say.

By the time we got back to the house I had knots in my shoulders so rigid I could barely turn my head, and as strange as it might sound, I think the last thing I needed was to walk through the front door and realize how smoothly everything had run since Joel left the hospital. Ivan had ended up joining them a couple of hours later, and he told us when we arrived that he'd found everyone engaged in a makeshift baseball game, my nephew Rye serving as perpetual hitter and Lindsey fielding balls with a glove they must have dug out of my closet. When everyone started to lose interest, Joel persuaded them to help get something together for dinner. Chicken, he said, with orzo and sun-dried tomatoes that Grace cut herself. What are you going to eat? I couldn't help asking, and he confided that he'd made a smaller dish for himself, without the chicken, after he helped Grace with her bath. You should adopt, Julia informed us, clearly impressed. No interest, I lied, and she said, I still don't understand why you changed your mind.

I'd wanted children. A few of our friends had adopted, or had children from a hetero marriage gone awry, and I hadn't thought I was suggesting anything out of the ordinary last fall when I told Joel that I thought maybe we should follow their lead. He couldn't have been any more dismissive. I don't want kids, he said, and when I pointed out our friends who'd made the leap he simply repeated himself, as if I hadn't heard him the first time. We've never talked about adopting, he said, I don't understand where this is coming from. I tried to explain, already beginning to resent the fact that I had to defend myself. My father was sick, I was starting to question my own mortality, I wasn't entirely sure I wanted things to end with *me*. And I loved him, I loved him and I wanted to extend that love to someone else who would be a part of us. Nothing I said seemed to resonate with him. At least tell me you'll think about it, I finally pleaded, and he sighed and said all right.

So I got busy. I researched adoption agencies in Austin, talked to the few gay couples I knew who had successfully adopted, and found a connection that after a rigorous interview process would allow us to adopt from Guatemala. All the paperwork I had sent to my office, and I started envisioning a little boy with sienna skin splashing in our pool or playing in the sandbox we'd build out back. We'd convert the game room into a nursery, or maybe we'd convert the guest bedroom—a better idea, since that room faced the back of the house and afforded an incredible view of the lake. Joel could paint a mural, something sweet and quiet, and we'd scour the city for the perfect furniture. I'd even picked out a name, something I knew Joel would have to clear but that I couldn't imagine he'd refuse: Adrian, which we could pronounce with the accent, or not. The name filled my mouth, and I'd find myself at work whispering the word at my desk, or in between meetings. Adrian, Adrian, and we could hyphenate his last name as Atwater-Grayson, or Grayson-Atwater, whatever, I didn't care. Adrian. I was prepared.

And then Joel found the paperwork. Pages of painstaking information that I'd filled out during whatever free time I could find at work, or in the hours Joel spent in his studio. I'd finished everything—my educational background, my work experience, my medical history—and Joel's as well. All we needed was his signature. Still I carried the paperwork around in my briefcase, wasting time but unwilling to take the chance that he might tell me no. I was waiting for the right moment, the moment when we'd sit down with a glass of wine and he'd offer without instigation that he was ready.

But he found the paperwork a couple of weeks before Thanksgiving. I led him there without thinking, when I asked him to hand me my brief-case one night while I was working and the bag slipped from my fingers. He had the papers in his hand before I could snatch them away.

To his credit, he wasn't angry. Let's just say for the sake of argument that we go through with this, he said, Which one of us is going to take care of him during the day? I hesitated, knowing I needed to be diplo-matic. Well, I said, I suppose you would. When would I work? he asked, and seeing where we were headed I said that we could find some kind of childcare, a nanny, someone who would work around his schedule. So you want to adopt a kid and stick him with someone else, he said. I felt myself flush. We couldn't live on what you bring home, I told him, and he said, We couldn't stay here, that's for sure.

I bit my tongue, watching as he lowered himself to the floor, his back against the bookcase. So what you're telling me, he said, Is that you want to adopt a kid, and you want either me to take care of him during the day or you want to pay someone else to do it. You make it sound so callous, I protested. I'm just trying to understand how you think this will work, he said, I'm just trying to figure out where my work, and your work—not to mention friends, and cycling, and sex—are going to fit in with this vision. We had a certain lifestyle, he reminded me, and one of the advantages of being who we were was that we didn't have to worry about expectations in regard to children. The mere fact that we'd never discussed the subject un-til a couple of months ago was evidence enough. Other gay couples adopt, I pointed out, and he said, Who, Bean and Roger?

Bean and Roger were the ones who'd helped me narrow down the agen-cies that would work with us. They'd adopted a little girl from Guatemala a couple of years earlier, a sweet little thing with liquid eyes and thick, black bangs they cut themselves with a pair of kitchen shears. I'd watched them myself when I went by one night after I first started kicking around the idea. Camila stood stock-still on a towel in the middle of the kitchen floor while Bean slid the shears across her forehead, Roger offering unsolicited, unwelcome tips as he hovered over Bean's shoulder. After-wards she made a beeline for the refrigerator, where she'd been promised a homemade popsicle for being so cooperative. Apple juice and banana chunks, Roger told me, All organic. I watched Camila straddle a Dora the Explorer Big Wheel, her mouth tinged with brown, and almost couldn't believe it when I thought: yes. This is what I want.

The problem with Bean and Roger, as Joel was quick to point out, is that since they've adopted they've essentially disappeared. We've run into them a couple of times, usually at Whole Foods or Central Market, where Camila will yank Bean's hand in the direction of the fish tank while Roger shifts stray toys and sippy cups from one hand to the other. They always seem tired as they cast a wistful eye toward the cracked black olives or the bottles of wine in our cart. Don't you remember how we've laughed? Joel asked, Don't you remember how we've talked about how glad we are that we're not in the same situation? They're happy, I protested, and he said, Adam, they have no life.

That shut me up, and seeing my expression he sighed. All right, he said, Let's just say that we adopt, and we figure out who's going to watch him during the day and we set up some kind of schedule, and we over-look the fact that our lives will totally revolve around a child. He leaned forward, over his legs, which were crossed now, one on top of the other. What about what we're bringing him into? he asked. What do you mean? I said, and he gave me a look. I told him I didn't buy it, that he couldn't tell me that he believed for one second that we weren't just as capable—more capable—of raising a child than the majority of heterosexual households out there. I'm not saying I don't believe it, he said, But there are a lot of people out there who don't and they can make our lives miserable. I don't care what they say, I told him. But a kid might, he said.

I fell silent, listening as he reminded me of his own wretched child-hood. We'll make sure that doesn't happen, I insisted, We'll make sure he's protected. Joel bit his lip, watching me, then finally said he wasn't trying to antagonize me. I'm just trying to make sure I understand, he said. Well, you don't, I told him, knowing his vision would never match up to the one I carried of Adrian, You don't understand. So explain it to me, he said.

I tried. Without revealing the extent to which Adrian had become real for me, I told him that I was looking for something else, that I wanted something more meaningful in my life than the weekly sales figures for Fusion. My father's illness had forced me to re-examine some of the choices I'd made, I told him, and I wanted to make sure that even if I'd squandered some of the first thirty-nine years of my life, I wouldn't be so frivolous with the next thirty-nine. I know what's important, I said, I know what's important, and I want to share what we have with someone who belongs just to us. Childcare, money—those were immaterial. We'd figure those out. But we could bring our relationship to a whole different level by including a child, someone we could raise ourselves, someone we could teach, and love, and nurture, someone who might not have had an opportunity if not for us. By this time I was sitting on the floor beside him, and I placed the palm of my hand on his chest. Do you understand? I asked.

I thought I had him. I really thought I had him, and after a minute he curled his arms around me. I want to do this, Joel, I whispered, I really want to do this. Shh, he said, Just let me think.

The next three days I spent in a lingering high. I almost called a dozen people a dozen different times to tell them the news. But then he appeared in the doorway of our bedroom on the evening of the third day and said my name and I knew right then he was going to tell me no. He couldn't, he said, looking sick, he was too selfish, he didn't have it in him. I'm not willing to give up what I have for someone else, he told me, I'm going into this already resentful, and that's not fair. He dropped beside me on the bed, his head in his hands. Maybe I just have too much baggage, he mumbled, and I started to point out that under those circumstances he could look at adopting as an opportunity. I'm not going to use a little kid to help me deal with my shit, he said, I'm not going to do that.

I knew better than to argue. I'd only anger him, and further alienate the possibility, and deflated though I was, I thought there might be a subtler way to persuade him. Still working out the particulars, I allowed his question to bypass me without the consideration I might have accorded it under different circumstances. Is this a deal killer? he asked. I shook my head, already rehearsing what I'd say when I talked to Roger.

Here's your chance, I told Roger the next morning, but now that he'd finally been given the opportunity he sounded uncertain. Bean'll kill me, he muttered more than once. Are you kidding? I said, He's going to give you the best sex of your life. I don't know, he mumbled, and I said, Roger,

I'll book the damn thing for you myself. In the end we decided we'd try for mid-December, a one week vacation to Telluride for Bean and Roger, during which time Joel and I would be one hundred percent responsible for their daughter. When you come back you'll find her in one piece, I promised, and he said, If you don't, Bean'll have my ass. Don't kid yourself, I told him, He'll have it either way.

I was euphoric, sure that once Joel saw what having a child around the house was actually like, he'd be sold. And I couldn't have asked for a better time. Two weeks before Christmas? We wouldn't be able to fit in everything we wanted to do. I'd take a week off of work, and we'd get this settled, this adoption issue, once and for all.

I told Joel over Thanksgiving, on the flight home from Kentucky. He gave me a cautious look, as if he knew I'd planned Roger and Bean's vacation myself. You're taking the week off? he asked, and I nodded. The entire week? he said, and I nodded again. He was quiet, then finally uttered a small laugh. Never been my favorite time of year, he admitted, and I caught his hand and held it fast. He skated the pad of his thumb across my nail. We'd had a better weekend than we expected; my father was in between rounds of chemo at that point, and we'd ridden every day. All right, Joel said, and I squeezed his hand.

But when I got to the office on Monday and sent Vincent an email about which days I'd need off, he sent one right back telling me he wanted me in North Carolina. Two weeks before Christmas? I shot back without thinking, and his response was instant. Should I ask Trainor instead? he wrote. I stared at the email, confused. Trainor? I thought, and for the first time the thought occurred to me that I needed to rein Trainor in a bit. Though I toyed with the idea of sending a reply that said something along the lines of why-don't-you-go-yourself-you-insufferable-prick, I ended up having little choice. I'm happy to go, I wrote, Happy.

I decided not to tell Joel. Not until the last minute anyway, when it would have been downright cruel to make Bean and Roger cancel their trip. What do you mean, you have to go to North Carolina? Joel asked when I broke the news over the phone Friday afternoon, two days before we were supposed to get Camila. There's nothing I can do, I told him, I don't have a choice. But you had vacation scheduled, he protested. I know,

I said, I know. I'm on my own all *week?* he asked. He sounded more dazed than anything, though by the time I got home he'd crossed well into outrage. This is bullshit, he kept repeating, and I finally said, Do you think I want to go, Joel? He eyed me from the kitchen, where he was pouring a glass of wine. I got the impression it wasn't his first. You'll be fine, I said, Everything will be fine. I know nothing about taking care of a three-year-old, he told me, and I almost slipped and told him this would be good practice. You'll be fine, I said instead, You'll see.

Two days later Roger brought Camila to our house, about thirty minutes before I had to leave for the airport. He hadn't been thrilled when I told him I had to go out of town, but I'd assured him Joel was up to the task. I'm not sure Bean will okay this, Roger said, but I dismissed him. Camila will be fine, I told him, She'll be in good hands.

As my cab pulled up to the curb, though, I started to have my doubts. Camila hadn't stopped crying since Roger dropped her off. He'd been reluctant to leave, said on his way out that he'd suspected she might freak, and that he'd made Bean stay behind precisely for that reason. Bean would never leave her like this, he said, glancing over his shoulder as if he were considering that possibility himself. I clapped him on the back with false joviality. She'll be fine once you're gone, I told him, spouting something I'd heard from my sister, She'll be fine.

But she wasn't fine. Camila, I said after Roger left, Honey. I touched her shoulder and she shrieked. From a squatting position I looked up at Joel. She's upset, I told him. No shit, he said. She'll calm down, I assured him, and he said, When? I glanced at Camila, who writhed on the floor beneath me. I don't know, I admitted. Looking at my watch, I got to my feet; Joel crossed his arms over his chest. I have to go, I said, infusing the words with apology. Of course you do, he said, and feeling a rush of anger—for Vincent, who'd put me in this position, for Joel, who had to be so heavily persuaded to adopt—I snapped. Somebody has to work, I said.

He stared at me, long enough for me to realize what I'd done. Wait—I started, but he cut me off. Go, he said, pointing in the direction of the door. Joel, I said, C'mon. He waved his hands, indicating the situation in front of us. Just go, Adam, he said, I have enough to handle here without your bullshit. So I left, closing the door behind me.

35

By nightfall I'd resigned myself to the mistake I'd made, thinking he could handle Camila on his own. Nothing had improved in my absence. She'd cried for hours, Joel told me when I called, well beyond the point he would have thought possible, finally stopping when he had the idea to drive her around for a while. But he struggled so long with the car seat that by the time he'd gotten it secured she wouldn't even get in the car. She ate little dinner, fell asleep in front of the television. I have five more days of this shit, he said, and I hung up almost in tears. Adrian. Joel would never agree.

The next day followed similarly; I called during lunch, then again during a break in my meetings. Joel sounded defeated, and I felt much the same way listening to him. Camila had cried off and on all day, he said, especially when Bean and Roger called, and then Joel spent an additional ten minutes assuring them everything was fine, despite the fact that they could hear Camila wailing in the background. When she's not crying she's into something, he said; she'd single-handedly pulled all of the books off the bookshelves while he was in the shower, yanked all of the clothes out of the dresser while he was replacing the books. What's she doing now? I asked. Drinking bleach? he said.

When I called back that night, though, he sounded a little more sane. She'd gotten better, he admitted, or maybe she'd just adjusted. Late that afternoon he'd found some crayons in the stash of supplies Roger had brought, and she colored at the kitchen table while Joel threw something together for dinner. Scrambled eggs, he said, She likes them with avocado. So do you, I pointed out. She ate so much I thought she was going to be sick, he said. She's in bed now? I asked, and he said, as if he hadn't heard me, I think I'm going to let her paint tomorrow.

That was it. After that when I'd call he'd tell me what they'd been doing, as if it was a great secret they shared. He bought her art supplies—finger paints, watercolors, clay—and they worked on project after project, figuring out what she liked best. Anything messy, he said, Anything that gets her dirty. They painted on the windows with watercolors, and made gingerbread cookies, and he let her tramp through some finger paints in her bare feet. The deck's a disaster, he said, But you loved it, didn't you, Camila? I heard her chirp in the background, his name spoken in that sweet little girl voice, and I melted. She's tireless, he told me, and I almost said, I wonder where she gets that.

Heading home Friday morning, having finagled an earlier flight, I couldn't help thinking I'd closed the deal. I'd get in, I figured, well before dinner, and we'd have almost twenty-four hours before Bean and Roger were due back. With Camila under control, we'd have a chance to spend time together, the three of us. Time to imagine what it might be like, to have a family.

When the cab dropped me off at the house I stood for a moment at the front door, relishing what I had before me. Going inside, I wasn't disappointed; I found them in front of the fireplace, sound asleep. Anything I'd ever read or seen or heard about your lover lying next to your child paled in comparison to what I felt watching the two of them. Camila was sprawled on her back, her head on one of the pillows from the sofa. Curved beside her, his head propped on one arm, Joel slept with his free hand enclosed in Camila's pudgy one. I couldn't have asked for a more perfect homecoming, and I sent a quick mental thank you to Vincent for shipping me off to North Carolina. They'd done better in my absence than they would have had I been home.

I'm not sure how long I watched them, but eventually Joel stirred. You're back, he whispered, seeing me. Withdrawing his hand from Camila's he got to his feet and kissed me, then turned around and gazed down again. She hooks you, doesn't she? he asked. I murmured my assent, and we stood there, watching her, until he glanced at the clock. Hey, he said, Since you're back early, do you mind if I go for a quick run? What could I say? He'd spent six days alone with her. Of course, I said, We'll be fine. And we were fine, until Camila had the poor sense to awaken.

He wasn't gone long. I think that's what got to me the most: that he'd left the house for no more than an hour and I still couldn't pick up the slack. Awakening, Camila wasn't happy to see me, and though she wasn't to the point where she was foaming at the mouth—that came later—her little chin quivered when I knelt down a cautious distance away from her. Joel, she pouted, and I murmured something soothing which she immediately rejected. Don't cry, sweetie, I said when the tears started, and that's when she really started to wail. Trying to gather her into a hug

37

wasn't a good decision, and flailing her arms around she hit me, a good smack to the mouth that actually made me rock back on my heels. I held my hand to my lips, and checked for blood before I found myself having to duck. No! I said, probably with too much intensity, grabbing her arms at the same time, and she screwed her face up with so much fury that I winced even before I heard her scream. Scrambling away, I escaped into the kitchen until her sobs turned into hiccups. And that's when I thought of the Ding Dongs.

She ate two, one right after the other, sitting at the kitchen table with a glass of Joel's soy milk. By the time she was finished she was offering me guarded smiles, which I was thankful enough to accept. See? I said, trying to convince her as well as myself, Not so bad. I gave her a napkin and she made a clumsy attempt to wipe her mouth, allowed me to help her brush the crumbs from her lap. Maybe we should use some water, I suggested, indicating her chin, which was still smeared with chocolate, but she gave me a look of such ferocity that I let it slide. What do you want to do now? I asked her instead, and she led me to the corner of the great room, where Joel had stacked her belongings. I want to paint, she told me. Where have I heard that before? I said.

We were good for about fifteen minutes. I had her set up at the kitchen table with her watercolors and a ream of paper, and I watched for a while before she convinced me to join her. I reached for a sheet without much enthusiasm; I've never been artistically inclined, and living with Joel has done nothing to build my self-confidence in that regard. But I dipped my brush into green paint anyway, and we worked until she started to shift in her seat. Glancing up I could see that her mood had changed, and I hesitated. What's that? she asked, pointing to my painting. I eyed it with uncertainty. A tree, I finally admitted. Doesn't look like a tree, she said in a mean little voice, and I told her that maybe I didn't want my tree to look exactly like a tree. She seemed skeptical, and I found myself growing irritated. Mine's better, she told me, and looking at her picture, I saw that she was right. She hadn't painted anything specific that I could see; she'd just swirled a lot of different colors in the center of her paper. But the effect was pleasing, and I glanced back at my own sophomoric attempt and grunted. Mine's better, she repeated, circling her paint brush in the cup of water I'd given her. All right, Camila, I said, Enough.

I'm sure that's when I lost ground with her. I should have just agreed with her, and left Bean and Roger to deal with lessons about modesty. Instead I'd given her a glimpse of my vulnerability, of which she'd already had an inkling, given the way I'd fled the scene in the great room after her nap. Sensing weakness, she pounced.

I don't like you, she said, and I think I gasped. That's a terrible thing to say! I told her, which again, was stupid. I can see that now, months later. I should have asked her why, or commiserated about how frustrated she must have been, waking up to find Joel gone. But I'd spoken without deliberation, and she fixed me with those black eyes, her expression sour. You're not my friend, she said, and for some reason that pronouncement seemed a dismissal of every belief I held in my abilities as a potential father. Fine, I said, and I started cleaning up.

That's when the real tantrum started. She didn't want to clean up, she wanted to keep painting, and I shot a stubborn glance in the direction of the clock. We need to get ready for dinner, I started to say, and then realized that we actually probably did need to get ready for dinner. We were fast approaching five o'clock, and I remembered Joel saying something about eating dinner so early the past few days he was hungry again later in the evening. Should I fix something? I asked aloud, but Camila wasn't listening. She'd grabbed the paints right from my hands as I was ruminating, and now I pried her fingers from the case as she sobbed. We have to make dinner, I snapped, and she picked up her cup and launched it in my direction, with such precision I was stunned. Oily water dripped from my midsection onto the tile beneath my feet, and I stared for a moment at the mess she'd created, then yanked her off the chair. You're going to help me clean this up! I said, but she whipped away from me and threw herself on the floor, where she was still kicking and screaming when Joel came home five minutes later.

What the hell happened? he asked. She threw a cup of water at me! I told him, realizing as I said the words how childish they sounded. But he barely glanced my way, dropping to the floor and whispering in Camilla's ear. One hand stroked her back, and I watched in disbelief as she stilled, then crawled into his sweaty arms as if he were Bean himself. He kept whispering to her, sitting back on his heels, until he finally held her away from him. Better? he asked, the question striking me as a personal affront, and she rewarded him with a smile the likes of which I hadn't seen since Roger left. He hooked a strand of hair behind her ear, then touched her chin with one finger. Girl, he said, What do you have all over your face? And she ratted me out.

You gave her a Ding Dong? he asked with an incredulity that infuriated me. She was hungry, I protested at the same time Camila said, Two! She doesn't eat sugar, Adam, he said. You made gingerbread cookies! I reminded him, and he said, They were sweetened with apple juice! He stood up, lifting her with him. All right, he said, dismissing me and turning his attention back to Camilla, You need a bath. I don't want to take a bath! she wailed. Yeah, you do, he said, already turning in the direction of the stairs, Because I'm going to let you use the fish again. I want the pink one, she said, latching her arms around his neck as they rounded the corner. You promised me I could use the pink one today, he said, and I heard her giggle.

He took care of her the rest of the evening. Fixed her dinner, read her books, and when he finally came downstairs after he put her to bed he collapsed in the chair in front of the fireplace and looked at me. I was lying on the sofa, one arm flung across my forehead, saturated with defeat. Three months I'd wasted, and I was no closer to a child of my own than I'd been at the beginning of the fall. I'd lost my opportunity, and as I lay there I started to realize that I'd have to reconcile myself to the fact that I'd probably not have another. So when Joel apologized for leaving me alone with her, when he told me he should have thought about how upset Camila would be, awakening to find him missing, I snapped. Why would you treat her any differently? I asked, You've left me often enough.

The next morning he awakened with Camila, and though I stepped into the kitchen a little while later expecting rejection she seemed to have forgotten all about our argument. We had breakfast, and played for a little while, and when Bean and Roger rang the doorbell she flew into their arms as if her time at our house was already a distant memory. How was she? Roger asked, directing his question to Joel. She was great, Joel admitted, She wasn't any trouble. Well, thank you, Roger said, and then, turning to me, he added, And thanks for suggesting we go. Mm, I muttered. Seriously, he said, We'd never have gone if you hadn't insisted.

I managed to avoid Joel's eye until we shut the door behind them. So, he said then, What part *wasn't* a setup? Giving my head a hasty shake, I started in with an excuse, but he stopped me, one hand held out in front of him like a traffic cop's. You know what? he said, I don't want to fucking hear it.

He disappeared for the rest of the day. He just left, without telling me where he was going, and the one time I tried to get him on his cell it automatically rolled to his voice mail. I didn't leave a message, though after I hung up I crafted a few, none of which I had the courage to leave. And as the day wound down I was thankful I'd kept my comments to myself. Wounded as I was, I could have given him enough ammunition to leave me. Instead I kept quiet, and as the sun set I built a fire in the fireplace and sat in the dark, listening for his truck.

He kept me waiting so long I fell asleep, and the fire, when I finally awoke, glowed a quiet, scattered orange. Joel? I said aloud, though I knew by the sound of the house that he wasn't home. Overwhelmed with melancholy, I waited, and by the time he returned I was just thankful he'd come back. Here's the thing, Adam, he said.

He'd spent the day thinking, trying to understand why I'd orchestrated the previous week. You've done so much for me, he murmured, And I know you can't begin to comprehend why I won't do this one thing for you. He reached for my hand, and told me he knew what I was going through right now with my father, what I'd been dealing with at work. I want to do this for you, he said, I really want to be able to do this for you. He took my other hand, and held them together, in between his own. But I can't, Adam, he said, I can't.

When I didn't say anything he let go of my hands and sat back, shifting in a way that told me he'd rehearsed what to say, based on my reaction. I was struck by the resignation in his expression, as though he'd already heard this conversation through to the end. I love you, he said, and I noted the way he pulled back as he said the words. He was already distancing himself, and I felt a familiar panic at the thought of losing him. I love you, he repeated as I was catching my breath, But if this is something you have to do I'll give you the space to do it. I shook my head with a vehemence I haven't forgotten. Are you sure? he asked, I need you to be sure. I'm sure, I said, I'm sure.

A month later, two days after my father started his second round of chemo, I slept with Trainor. We'd been fine, Joel and I, all through the holidays; we spent Christmas with my parents, and New Year's alone, and the vast majority of the time I focused on that night we'd recommitted ourselves and not to the emptiness in my gut that seemed to spread every time I thought about what I'd given up. When Trainor and I went to Atlanta for a conference in the middle of January I was as reserved with him as usual, until he got me talking over a couple of beers one night at the hotel bar. I made the mistake of confiding what had happened, and he responded with a delivery so deadpan he caught me off-guard. I think kids are great, he said without looking at me. He was squinting at the television in the corner, one hand curved protectively over the top of his beer mug as if he expected me to slip him something when he wasn't looking. Really? I said, and he shrugged. Why not? he said. He took a swallow of beer, then looked me up and down with an admiration he made no attempt to hide. I wouldn't have told you no, he declared.

In the elevator he watched me press the button for my floor, making no move to indicate his own. Trainor, I protested, shaking my head, though I was still smiling at that point. Two steps and he had me against the wall, the doors closing behind us. Not a good idea, I managed after the first kiss, and he moaned, a soft purse of the lips that was more of a pout than anything else. He stayed right were he was, his mouth next to mine, one finger skirting the edge of my nipple in a way that did nothing for my resolve. C'mon, he murmured, You've been a good boy for three years. Four and a half, I corrected him, and he said, C'mon, then. He kissed me again, and I thought, somewhere in that haze of desire, that one time wouldn't make a difference.

Five months later I'm still sleeping with him. Sometimes I'm stunned by the way I've complicated my life, by the risk I'm taking. And yet I haven't told Trainor no, not once.

...okay? I hear, and I look up. Joel's sitting beside me; Julia's nowhere to be found. What? I say, and he holds his hand to my cheek. You're crying, he tells me. No, I say, but when I wipe my eyes I find them wet. I frown, looking to the sky as if I know how to gauge the time based on the position of the stars. He's wearing a sweatshirt he must have found in my dresser, one I'm sure he assumes mine, and he shivers, though the temperature's probably no less than sixty degrees. I'm suddenly impatient, and I get to my feet. You'll feel better after you get some sleep, he tells me, clearly oblivious to the havoc he wreaked earlier in the day trying to reassure me, and as I open the screen door I say over my shoulder, You're wearing Bobby's sweatshirt. He starts; I know his reaction shouldn't cause me such satisfaction. I-I'm sorry, he stammers. I shrug.

Jennifer Hritz

3))

My father's surgery goes as well as can be expected. Start to finish we wait about four hours for the news, what would be a relatively short time if we weren't also trying to keep my sister's children entertained. This time Julia refuses Joel's offer to take them back to my parents'; he seems relieved by her answer. Despite my gruff demeanor, it's obvious he wants to be there for me, and I vacillate between gratitude and shame at the way I've been treating him.

I don't check in with the office until my father's in recovery, until I can't wait any longer without expecting repercussions. I've made no attempt to contact Vincent since leaving him a voice mail at the office on Saturday morning, and I intentionally left my BlackBerry behind so I'd have an excuse not to check my email. Using Joel's cell, I talk first to Darlene; she asks after my father, then tells me that Vincent has been waiting for me to call. Trainor's been trying to reach you as well, she informs me, though she delivers the news as if the words are so distasteful that she might have to gargle with Listerine the moment she hangs up the phone. All right, I sigh, Transfer me to Trainor first.

How's it going, baby? he asks, and I grind my teeth together. I'm managing, I tell him. I've been trying to reach you, he says. So I've heard, I tell him, and he chuckles, as if I've said something amusing. How's your dad? he asks. Fine, I say, How's yours? You sound tense, he offers, and I tell him I can't imagine why. Was there something you needed? I add, Something work-related?

He's silent, and I close my eyes. I shouldn't provoke him this way, and not just because it's cruel. I've been stupid to let our relationship continue as long as it has, and given his friendship with Vincent I'm not in a position to extricate myself as easily as I'd like. Though to be honest, I've not thought about ending what I've started. Something's working for me, or I wouldn't have let it continue as long as it has.

I'm sorry, I say, leaning against the window. I'm in one of the hallways between buildings, and sun streams past me, warming my skin in a way that reminds me, for some reason, of Bobby's dorm room. Don't apologize, Trainor says, I know you're dealing with a lot right now. You have no idea, I mutter, seeing Lindsey approach from the far end of the corridor. She's wearing her iPod; I don't think she's removed it yet today. Your father? Trainor asks, and I say, The cancer's spread to his brain. Jesus, he says. He doesn't know, I add, His doctor wanted him to get through the surgery first. Maybe that's for the best, he murmurs, and I keep quiet, not wanting to get into *that* conversation with him. Anyway, I mutter, and he says, Well, I'm holding down the fort for you here. Nothing I need to know about? I ask. Nope, he says, Though Vincent was hoping you'd call in today.

I turn toward the window, and Lindsey walks past without seeing me. He seem pissed? I ask. You know Vincent, Trainor says, which tells me nothing. All right, I say, and sensing from my tone that I'm about to cut him loose he says, Will you call me later? I'll try, I tell him. I'm here for you, Adam, he says, and I press my forehead against the warm glass, bile rising at the back of my throat.

It takes a few minutes for the nausea to pass, and I find myself wandering toward a bank of chairs by the elevators. I'll need to sit down for this next conversation, and when I feel as if I've recovered somewhat I dial Vincent's extension. He's cordial, and poses a preliminary question or two about my father, but his voice lacks the compassion of Darlene's and Trainor's and when he immediately moves to the sales figures from the previous week I feel a sharp stab of anger. My response clipped, I tell him I'm not really in a position to talk. My father's still in recovery, I add, thinking he'll be overcome with guilt by the realization. But he could care less. Perhaps if you hadn't left the office early on Friday, he suggests, and I'm stupid enough to argue with him. To my surprise he doesn't retort, though I should know better than to think he'd be content to leave me with the last word. Will you be in the office later this week? he asks. That's my plan, I tell him, By Friday at the latest. We'll talk then, he tells me, and he hangs up before I have the chance to agree.

I snap Joel's phone shut and lean back, into the sun that shines through the windows to my right. I can't shake the feel of that dorm room, and after a minute I close my eyes. Most of the time I don't allow myself to think too much about Bobby. I can see too easily how some people lose themselves in their grief. If I let myself, I could spend my entire life reliving those six years. If I let myself, I could crawl inside and never come out.

The sun stretched its fingers across the worn linoleum in his room, softening the pillows on a single bed that didn't easily hold both our bodies. We'd curl together, or lie one on top of the other, Adam Ant or Iggy Pop or the B-52's playing on the jambox he kept above his desk, though never so loud he wouldn't hear his roommate's key in the lock. For anything more serious we'd have to go to my place, which he preferred anyway. So much more space, he'd say, though I knew that was only part of the truth. He was out enough to be seen with me, enough to allow me to catch his hand walking from a bar to my car if he'd had a few beers, but that didn't mean he wanted his roommate walking in and finding me in his bed. I don't need the harassment, Adam, he said when I pressed him, but in truth his roommate was a likable enough guy. He probably wouldn't have cared, though I'd never been able to convince Bobby of that. So the time we spent at his place was quick, thirty minutes here or there.

Physically, Bobby wasn't my type. He was slight, with skin so pale I could see his veins. He had a terrible problem with dandruff, and the one time I teased him he looked at me with wounded eyes the color of wet sand. He just wasn't the kind of guy I normally would have noticed, but when I caught him staring at me in the library one day I couldn't help being flattered. He knew who I was, and I liked the way that felt. Once I took him out, once I started spending time with him, I could've cared less that he had no ass to speak of, or that his chest, underneath the cheap clothing he wore, curved inward. He was just Bobby, and the day he took his shirt off in front of me for the first time he held me in awe.

We were at my place, in my bedroom, the windows open. We'd been to-gether for almost three months at that point, and I'd never gotten him beyond a few kisses, he'd never allowed me to do anything more than slip my hand under his tee shirt to touch the warm flush of his skin. At first I thought he was holding back because he was inexperienced, but that wasn't the case. He'd actually been with more guys than I would've thought, and a few girls, too. But I was different, he said, and though initially I would've been happy to give up that designation in order to sleep with him, I didn't push. He wouldn't even undress in front of me, and when he stayed with me he'd sleep in shorts and a tee shirt. I'd slide my fingers under the material, tracing his spine, but that was as far as he'd let me get, until that afternoon in May.

We could see the sky every time we tipped our heads back over the side of the bed, that big stretch of blue telling us that summer was practically here. Bobby had combed through my cassettes, and Pink Floyd's Meddle *was weaving its way through our conversation. I was lying at the foot of the bed, my feet stretched toward the pillows; I hadn't showered, and I was wearing a tee shirt so rumpled and comfortable I didn't care. Bobby was sitting cross-legged in the center of the bed, but with the first strum of that guitar at the beginning of "Fearless" he was on his feet. I watched him, swaying above me, his movements more liquid than I would've guessed. He usually held himself so tightly, and I think I smiled, seeing him so suddenly uninhibited. Without opening his eyes, he pulled his tee shirt over his head. By the time his fingers worked through the button on his jeans and folded them down just enough for me to see the blue stripe of his briefs I was on my knees. I had just lifted my hand when he opened his eyes. Adam, he said, Don't break my heart.*

I did a decent job for a while, for almost six years. But I let him down. In the end I let him down.

Someone touches my knee and my eyes fly open. I haven't indulged in this long of a memory since the last time I was home. There's something about my father's illness that brings everything back. Are you okay? Joel asks.

No, I'm not okay, I imagine saying. I hate my job; I hate Vincent; I hate the computers themselves. I hate the responsibility of having to bring home enough money to pay the mortgage. I hate leaving in the morning for a job I hate and coming home to find you in the pool. I hate what I'm doing with Trainor.

But for the first time I realize I'm in too deep. Yeah, I say, I'm fine.

~ ~ ~

We tell my father on Wednesday afternoon. I say "we" as if there's a group of us gathered around him, offering our support. Really, my mother has driven him to his oncologist's office herself, while the three of us—Julia, Joel, and I—bicker at my parents' house and wait for them to return. Ivan and the kids left this morning, and Joel and I leave tomorrow. While there's a part of me that feels guilty for leaving my mother and sister to deal with the fallout, there's another part that wishes I had the balls to drive to the airport right now, before my parents get home. I don't understand how I'm supposed to look him in the eye.

I pace the kitchen, watching Joel boil water for tea, though it must be near eighty degrees outside. You want some? he offers, unwrapping a tea bag that he's actually brought from home, and I shake my head. I'll take a cup, Julia tells him, and he reaches for a second mug. Why don't you sit down? he suggests, glancing at me. I give him a look which Julia catches. I wonder how much she suspects, how much any of them suspect. They must sense the tension between us, though I suppose they might point a finger toward stress arising from the circumstances of our visit more than anything else. No one has said a word, and to maintain whatever deception I've managed to create I yank one of the chairs from beneath the kitchen table. Joel takes down another mug.

We've finished our tea and I'm debating moving on to a nice, stiff bourbon when we hear my parents' Cadillac pull into the drive. Exchanging glances, we make our way into the living room, then seem to realize at the same moment that we might not want to appear as if we're just waiting. I click on the television as Julia starts picking imaginary lint from the pillow on my father's chair. Only Joel remains standing, and as the door opens I half-expect him to make his way to my father first. Daddy, my sister says, and the way the word leaves her mouth more than anything reduces her to tears. My father allows her to wrap her arms around him, and I stand, averting my eyes. All right now, he says, All right.

I move forward as Julia steps aside, my eyes on the ground. Look at him, I tell myself, but I can't. All right, he says, placing one hand on my shoulder as he walks past me. I turn, thinking I'll find Joel able to say what I can't, but he has eyes only for me. He seems saddened, as if he's

49

taken my failure and accepted it as his own. Adam, he whispers, and I can't help but take the word as a blanket admonishment. He reaches for my hand, and I leave the room.

I never learn what happened in my absence. I never ask. I hole up in the back of the house long enough to compose myself, long enough to take a shower I don't need, and when Joel finally comes looking for me I brush right past him. In the living room my father has managed to scrounge up another John Wayne movie and my mother's making a pretense of reading *Better Homes & Gardens.* Where's Julia? I ask. On the phone, my mother answers, inclining her head toward the kitchen, and in fact I can hear my sister, the low murmur of a voice that sang right alongside most of the boys in the elementary school choir. I sit down next to my mother, glancing at the television, then catch my father's eye. He doesn't speak, and I lift my hand in a gesture that means nothing. Feeling okay? I mumble, the question inane, and he nods, then looks back toward the television as if he knows that's about all I can handle.

Later we sit around the dinner table at my father's insistence. I'm not eating another meal in front of the television, he tells us, and no one dares argue. We work our way through a whole wheat pasta that Joel has concocted; I can't imagine where he got the edamame but I don't ask. He's made dinner just about every night since we've been here, seems to feel it's his duty to keep my family away from processed food. I've lost weight the past five days in spite of myself. On the one hand, I'm thankful he's stepped in—clearly, my mother doesn't feel up to the task. But I'm also annoyed, though I'm not sure I can, or want, to articulate why.

What time is your flight tomorrow? my mother asks. Early, I tell her, Six something. I guess you have to get back to work, my sister says, and I give her a sharp look. I've missed three days already, Julia, I snap. And then, realizing the way that must sound I glance in my father's direction. Of course you have to leave, he tells me, You have a life, you have responsibilities. I nod, though I'm not reassured. I have responsibilities, too, he adds, and at first I think he's talking about his illness, about the treatment his doctor has suggested, to eliminate the traces of cancer in his brain. But he starts talking about one of his horses, a recent acquisition that's been giving him trouble. I'm taking him out tomorrow, he tells us, and before my mother can say anything herself Julia's pointing her finger in protest. You need to clear that with Dr. Ungati, she says. Julia, my mother warns, and my sister throws up her hands. Well, this is ridiculous, Mom! she cries, He can't be out there in the heat training horses as if nothing's wrong with him!

My father pushes back from the table, the scrape of his chair on the wooden floor causing me to jump. Daddy, Julia says, immediately getting to her feet, but my father waves her off. Enough, he says, Enough. Holding onto the back of his chair with one hand and reaching for the wall with the other, he maneuvers his way into the living room. After a minute we hear the slam of the front door. He's not leaving, is he? Julia asks, as if she hasn't learned her lesson, and we listen for the turn of the motor. But there's nothing, and my mother sighs. I'll go, I say, stopping her before she can rise to her feet.

I find him just outside the stable, a cigarette in his hand, smoke hanging heavy and bitter around him. Seeing me, he drops the butt and grinds it beneath his boot. I follow him inside, watching as he takes a body brush and curry comb from one of the shelves. Four-ticker, he says, indicating the stall behind me. Opening the door, I whisper as I move forward. Four-ticker whinnies, the sound soft and trusting, though I've spent little time with him this trip, haven't ridden him in three months. Hey boy, I whisper, and he lowers his head, snuffling in the pockets of my jeans, and then in the palms of my hands. Edamame, I tell him, You're not missing much. He tosses his head with indignation, and I move to his left flank as my father enters the stall, carrot in hand. Four-ticker takes it from my father's fingers, throwing a dismissive glance over his shoulder. I get to work.

Thirty minutes later my father and I still haven't spoken. I can't believe he's strong enough to keep standing here, but he brushes Four-ticker with a focus and attention that leave me frank with admiration. This is how he manages his stress, how he's always dealt with anything problematic, so I shouldn't be surprised. I've found him here more times than I can count. The day I came out to him, in fact, he ended up in the stable, and when I joined him we brushed three horses in succession before we finally stopped.

51

You agree with your sister? he asks as we're finishing. He's trembling a bit, but his legs seem solid to the earth and I find myself shaking my head. He grunts, satisfied, moving to the side so I can latch Four-ticker's stall. You should've ridden him while you were here, he tells me. I know, I say, turning out the light and shutting the door behind us. We start walking back toward the house, his steps slow but sure. You go back to Austin tomorrow, he says, Take care of business. I will, I say, and he reaches for my arm, the gesture half-paternal, half-necessary on the uneven ground. Get it together, he tells me, and though I think if given the opportunity he might go on, Julia suddenly rushes toward us. You must be freezing, she cries, the look she gives me just as accusatory as the hand she throws to the night sky. Before either one of us has the chance to protest she pulls him from my grasp and ushers him across the yard and up the front steps.

Sliding my hands in my pockets, I watch them go, staring at the door through which they've disappeared for a full minute before I see Joel. He's sitting on the bottom step, just shy of the light from the living room, and for a second I swear he holds a cigarette to his lips. But he lowers his hand, and I realize I've witnessed an affectation that's come over him in the years since he quit smoking, the years that he's dedicated himself full-time to painting: his fingers, though empty, hold a brush.

Omitting a greeting, I lower myself to the step beside him. Been gone a while, he notes, and I nod, examining my feet on the walkway beneath me. The sole of one shoe has worn thin, and I catch its lip on the cement, peeling it away from the leather. Joel watches me, without comment. You finish dinner? I finally ask, and he shrugs. I'm not sure anyone loved the pasta, he admits. Does that surprise you? I ask, and when he doesn't say anything I apologize. Everyone's tired, I say, Everyone's tired, and everyone's tense. He nods, doesn't point out that we're also dealing with sixty plus years of beef consumption. Thank you for cooking, I add. Your father—he starts, but I cut him off. The man's still smoking, Joel, I tell him, If he's not going to give up his Lucky Strikes he's not going to go macrobiotic.

He's silent. Plucking a pebble from my shoe, I roll it between my fingers, and after a minute he runs his hand down my back, stopping midway to press his thumb into a knot of muscle. Why don't you come inside, he says, his voice lower, his mouth closer to my ear. I neither commit to nor refuse his offer, and his hand slides beneath my shirt. C'mon, he murmurs, I'll give you a massage. He kisses the skin below my ear, with just enough teeth to make me shiver. We'll be discreet, he whispers, slipping his free hand inside the leg of my shorts.

I want to give in. I want him to convince me to go into the house, to lead me into the bedroom, my hand secure in his. Better yet, I want him to take hold of me right here, on the steps, with my family shut inside and the quiet whinnies of the horses our background noise. I want him outside, under the night sky.

I knock his hand away. Gently at first, and when he doesn't get the message I shove him, hard enough that he has to catch himself. Please, I say, trying to soften the blow of rejection, the force with which I've pushed him, Please stop.

For the longest time he doesn't move. Then he gets to his feet, and goes inside.

~ ~ ~

Vincent's out of the office when I get back on Friday, and I breathe a small sigh of relief when I hear the news, then glance through my schedule as Darlene brings me up to date on what I've missed. How's your dad? she asks when we're finished. Holding his own, I say as Trainor raps on the open door. Darlene scoots away without saying hello. That's one woman who doesn't like me, Trainor says, dropping into the chair across from my desk. I hold my tongue, encouraging him to think that it's his personality and not the fact that I've been having an affair with him that's incurred her attitude. How are you? he asks. I concentrate on keeping my eyes on my computer, my voice absent of emotion. I'm fine, I say. I haven't heard from you in a couple of days, he tells me.

He's right. I haven't talked to him since Wednesday morning, and though I've gone more than forty-eight hours without talking to him in the past, this time feels different. Wednesday night after the incident on the front porch I'd gone into the house where I found Joel in my old bedroom, the room dark. At first I thought him asleep—I'd waited long enough to go back inside—but he spoke, his voice soft and clear. I'm trying to understand, he said, and that admittance dropped me to my knees.

I'm angry, I said. I know you are, he agreed, though of course he didn't understand all of what I meant. He pulled me up beside him, and we made love, his movements the opposite of what I anticipated, given what I'd just done. I would've imagined him sullen, perfunctory, and afterwards I realized that despite the way he's changed over the past five years I still expect him to fail me, in every way he can. Taking his hand, I silently vowed that back in Austin everything would be different.

I was busy, I say now. Trainor takes a mint from the jar on my desk and crunches it between his teeth, watching me. I was busy, I repeat. All right, he says, so easily that I frown. I remember suddenly that he told me before I left that we need to talk; I wonder what he wants to say. Schedule yourself out a little early today, he suggests, as if he knows what I'm thinking. I've been gone all week, Trainor, I remind him, and he leans across the desk. Then meet me in the men's room in five minutes, he says. I shake my head, disgusted by the unseemliness of the proposition as well as the prick of interest in my groin. You can't say you haven't missed me, he says. Sure I can, I tell him, but he dismisses that with a wave of his hand, getting to his feet. You should work, he says, ignoring the fact that he's been the one preventing me from starting. He moves toward the door, then turns back and walks around the desk. Trainor, I say through clenched teeth as he bends toward me. Four o'clock, he says in my ear, Schedule yourself out.

Vincent returns after lunch. I'd assumed him gone for the day, and when I pass by his office and see him sitting behind his desk I immediately avert my eyes, as if that might limit the possibility that I've been spotted. He's not fooled. Atwater, he calls, and I step back toward his open doorway, feigning nonchalance. We need to talk, he tells me, Close the door.

Swallowing a sigh, I lower myself into the chair across from him. Dave Burroughs, he starts, dragging his fingers through black hair he probably has to have thinned. What's up? I ask, and Vincent says, Certainly not his numbers. He slides the current sales figures across my desk and I make a pretense of looking over them. I've already seen these numbers, know they're lower even than last week's. Have you talked to him? Vincent asks, and I say, Not today, no. Are you waiting for anything in particular? he asks. I've been in meetings all day, I tell him, and hearing the defensive tone in my voice I add, But clearly I'll have to speak with him before the end of the day. Clearly, Vincent agrees.

He leans back in his chair, his hands on the armrests, examining me. I stare back with what I hope passes for quiet concern. I know you have your team's best interest in mind, he finally tells me. Of course, I say. I have your team's best interest in mind, as well, he continues, And I understand the havoc termination can wreak on morale. What are you saying? I ask, thinking for the briefest, uncertain moment that he's talking about me. I'm saying that Burroughs's time here may be up, Vincent says.

I try to give Vincent the impression that I'm digesting the suggestion when instead I'm both breathing a sigh of relief that my own job remains secure and figuring out what I can say to keep Dave on my team. His numbers have been terrible lately, sure, but he's been here longer than I have. And I know he has his hands full at home: three children, one of whom has all kinds of medical issues. Personally, I find it perfectly logical that his focus isn't on his job right now; personally, I think we should carry him for a little while.

I know Dave's numbers haven't been consistent, I start. Oh, they've been consistent, Vincent tells me, Consistently shitty. All right, I concede, Consistently shitty. Vincent nods, temporarily mollified, and I admit that I'm the one who should take responsibility for Dave's numbers. Are you sure you want to do that? Vincent asks. I look him in the eye. Do I have reason to be worried? I ask, and he smiles, without the slightest hint of humor. Are you suggesting I fire you instead? Vincent asks. I'm saying, I tell him, That you should let me talk to Dave, give him some time to get the numbers up, with my help.

Vincent ruminates, though I have the feeling he's already made a decision. He might have made up his mind even before I stepped into his office. All right, he finally says. I nod and stand to go, without asking if there's anything else he wants to discuss. Atwater, he says, stopping me just as I reach the door. I turn back. You have two months, he tells me. Fine, I say, and he says, Just make sure he understands.

~ ~ ~

That evening I lie in Trainor's bed, trying to summon the energy to get my things together and go home. We came here after drinks, which he'd convinced me to get when he saw the look on my face after Dave Burroughs left

55

my office. Making it to his apartment afterward had taken less persuasion than I'd like to admit, and I run my fingers through my hair, brooding. I'm going to need a shower, and unless I want to stop by the gym on my way home I'm going to have to take one before I leave. Sensing what I'm thinking, Trainor says, I'll join you. I shake my head, glancing at my watch. I need to get moving, I tell him, and he swings one sweaty leg over mine. Stay, he says, Spend the night. Jesus, Trainor, I mutter, sitting up and pushing his leg off of me. You spend *every* night with him, he informs me. I live with him, Trainor, I say. So what does that make me? he asks, and I say, Figure it out.

I start getting dressed, a shower at the gym suddenly sounding a lot more appealing than dealing with this bullshit. Hmm, Trainor murmurs, What does that make me? I look over at him; he's propped on one elbow, one leg bent and crossed over the other. Your mistress, he concludes. I snort. Your lover, he says. Trainor, I snap, Stop. But why? he asks. He lies back, stretching, his toes pointed in my direction. Judging from the arches in his feet, the strength in his calves, he would have made a great *danseur*. But then you'd have to get past his torso, which is thick, and full, and which he traces now without a hint of self-consciousness. I button my shirt over my own increasing girth. What am I? he muses, and I say, A pain in the ass. He smiles; I realize my mistake. I'm leaving, I inform him. Raising one limp, languid hand in my direction, he yawns. Tomorrow, he says.

~   ~   ~

I want you to try to relax a little, Joel tells me early the next evening on our way to a party at the home of a friend of ours. He's turning the air conditioning vents so they face away from him, and I automatically adjust the knob, despite the fact that I'm sweating. You've done your time today, he says, referring to the hours I told him I'd be at the office and which I'd spent, stupidly, with Trainor, You need to take some time for yourself.

I don't say anything. He already knows that I'm not looking forward to this evening; I'd actually forgotten about Kyle's invitation, and when Joel reminded me on my way out the door this morning I groaned. I don't think I'm up for the lake tonight, I said, but he told me that Kyle was expecting us. And you could use the break, he added. He made me promise to get back in enough time to leave by four, and though I'd only been a few minutes late he looked me up and down in a way that left me scrambling for excuses. He brushed them aside, told me that from that moment forward he wanted me to concentrate on having a good time.

But the lake doesn't sound like a good time to me. For one thing, I'm self-conscious about the weight I've gained, and I don't necessarily want to spend the next few hours listening to good-natured ribbing about the extra pounds. I guarantee you that few of the guys there will have any more than ten percent body fat, and most of them work out with an enthusiasm that leaves me weary just contemplating the effort. Even Kyle has lost his considerable paunch, in an attempt to make himself more presentable to Scott, a cycling buddy of mine. Scott seems not to understand the overture. They've been having an affair for almost six years now, though *affair* might not be the right word. From what I understand, Scott's boyfriend, Marcio—a Brazilian with an unbelievable body and a face that doesn't quite seem real—knows that Scott's been sleeping with Kyle but hasn't put any pressure on him to stop. My guess is that Marcio doesn't want to curb his own indiscretions, which over the years have been considerable. No one is this good looking, I'd thought the first time I met him, assuming he'd had work done. But Scott laughed when I posited the question, assured me that there's no artifice to Marcio whatsoever. Every one of us envies Marcio his allure, and I know that more than a few of us can't understand why Scott would sleep with Kyle when he has Marcio at his disposal.

Actually, I think that's the real reason Marcio hasn't protested Scott's involvement with Kyle: he's not threatened. Kyle's a lot of things, but he's not much to look at and consequently Marcio doesn't take him seriously. I'd say that was a mistake, but despite the fact that Scott has been sleeping with Kyle for six years, he's kept him at a distance. He's using him, Joel has said more than once, and lately I've begun to agree.

A few months ago Kyle sold his business, a search engine company, ostensibly because it was time to sell. In reality, at least according to Joel, Scott had been complaining about how much time and energy Kyle was pouring into his job. In other words, Joel said, Kyle wasn't available whenever Scott had a few extra minutes to see him. So Kyle found a buyer, and now that his schedule has opened up he has more time for Scott, and more time to concentrate on remaking his appearance. He's lost weight, and chiseled his upper body, and toyed with hair plugs; Scott's oblivious. I don't mean that he hasn't noticed. I mean that he doesn't understand that Kyle's making these changes because he wants Scott to leave Marcio. Whatever their arrangement initially, at some point Kyle became emotionally involved. Unable to tell Scott for fear that he'll break off the affair, he's doing everything he can in the hopes that Scott will come to him all on his own. I don't think that's going to happen. Neither does Joel, and both of us believe that Kyle probably can't go on much longer.

Just relax, Joel reminds me as I pull to the curb in front of Kyle's palatial abode, and we wind through the house and onto the three-tiered deck, where Kyle, wearing a pair of low-slung swimming trunks that show off his newly defined abs, wags his finger in our direction. You're late, he says, and Joel murmurs an apology, leaning in for a kiss. I barely recognize you, he claims. Kyle glances down at his tan, toned stomach as if he's almost forgotten, then looks up, his expression gleeful. I *do* look good, don't I? he says, and then turning to me, he holds out his hands. Instead of taking them I pass him the bottle of tequila Joel bought this afternoon. Oh, my, my, Kyle says, examining the label, You've spared no expense. I give Joel a sharp look; he ignores me, or maybe doesn't notice. But Kyle just laughs and indicates the pool with a wave of his hand. Make yourselves comfortable, he says.

An hour later I'm sitting beside the pool, sweating profusely because I haven't yet made a foray into the water. The shirt's coming off at some point, but I plan on adding at least one more margarita to the two I've already consumed before I take the plunge. We're surrounded by vegetation, but nothing large enough to provide any real shade; we're in the treetops, perched on a hill overlooking Lake Austin. Kyle has a boat docked down below, and there's talk about taking it out at some point, but so far no one has put the thought into action. Joel's in the pool, where he's involved in a competitive game of water volleyball. I'm not even sure I knew he played the game, and I watch as he sends the ball over the net, in a perfect arc.

He's good, the guy standing next to my chair says. I glance up. He's running sunscreen up and down his arms, for what must be at least the third time since I've been here, though I suppose I can't blame him. He's white, as white as Bobby was, with red hair and freckles crowding the bridge of his nose. I don't know him; I don't know most of the guys here. I like to mix and match, Kyle's fond of saying, and when he throws parties he has a tendency to change up the guest list, with the exception of what he likes to call his core. I can't imagine where he finds these guys. Though I obviously haven't been looking for a long time, I've heard more than a few of my friends say that it's impossible to meet anyone in Austin. Frat boys and cowboys, they complain, and if you're not into either one of those scenes then forget it. But Kyle has a wide array of friends; he knows everyone, and if there's one person in this city who can hook you up it's him. I met Joel through Kyle, as a matter of fact. We were at a bar at the time, though, a detail with which Joel loves to antagonize me, knowing how I disparage that scene.

You know him? the guy asks, indicating Joel with a jut of his chin. I nod without elaborating, and the guy replaces the cap on his sunscreen, then takes a baseball cap from the bag beside him and pulls the bill down over his eyes. We both watch as Joel hoists himself over the side of the pool, swimming trunks dripping, to retrieve a wayward serve. His trunks, a rich green that offsets his tan, ride even lower than Kyle's. Jewel, Joel said when he wore them the first time, and looking at them now in the sunlight I see what he meant. They shimmer like emeralds, and I'm almost sorry when he lowers himself again into the water.

Shea Shaunessey, the guy beside me says, turning away from Joel and offering me his hand. Adam Atwater, I tell him. We shake; my fingers, when I retrieve them, are moist with sunscreen. I suppress the urge to wipe them on my shirt. I can't believe this sun, Shea says, squinting beneath his cap. Hot, I agree. I'm from Washington, he explains. Kentucky, I tell him. You in for the weekend? he asks. No, I live here, I say, Why, are you just...? He nods, gesturing toward one of the few women here. My sister, he tells me. Ah, I say, and he shrugs. I'm going to get a drink, he says, You want one? I glance at my near-empty glass. Sure, I say, Why not. Watching him walk away, I lean back and cross my legs. He's young, I think, though probably not as young as Joel, and certainly not as young as some of the other guys Kyle has invited. They're children, I muttered to Joel at Kyle's last party, and he'd seen right through me. You still look good, he told me, an assessment which hadn't seemed like a compliment. Still? I thought. What do you mean, still? Look, forty is the new thirty, he kept telling me last month on my birthday. What does that make you? I asked, Twenty-three? I wouldn't go back there for anything, he assured me, and I wanted to tell him that's not what I meant.

I hate the idea of looking good for my age. I just want to look good, just *good,* without the caveat. I don't want to be thankful that my hairline hasn't drastically receded, or that I still have decent muscle tone. I don't want to get in the shower the day before my fortieth birthday—*the day before*—and find a white pubic hair.

Actually, I think my father's illness has something to do with how I've been feeling about my age. He's sixty-seven, twenty-seven years older than I am, but lately that hasn't seemed like such a big difference. I haven't asked, but I doubt if forty feels like twenty-seven years ago to him. I can't believe that I've known Joel for almost eight years, that I've lived in Austin for eight, that Bobby has been dead for almost thirteen. And in another thirteen I'll be fifty-three, and thirteen years after that I'll be looking at sixty-seven. Jesus.

You look intense, Shea says, handing me a drink. Hot, I lie, and he nods, murmuring something about getting in the pool once the game has ended. So, what do you do? he asks, pulling up a chair beside me, and I tell him about my job, realizing that I might be exaggerating my responsibilities the littlest bit. What about you? I ask, cutting myself off, and he says, I'm a nurse. I look at him, surprised. ICU, he says, Ten years now. *That* sounds intense, I tell him, trying to ballpark his age based on how many years he must have spent in school. Yeah, he shrugs, But it's pretty rewarding and the pay's good. He tells me he has quite a few stories, that he's thinking about writing a book. I'm impressed, I say.

So what do you do when you're not selling computers? he asks. I grimace. I don't actually *sell* them, I want to say, but instead I tell him that I cycle, that I've done some racing. I don't mention that it's been a good three or fours months since I've been on my bike, and when he automatically glances at my legs I breathe a sigh of relief that they still look okay. I've quit shaving, though, which Joel noticed immediately. Just for a change, I said, though in reality I didn't want to waste time shaving when I wasn't really on the bike anyway. What's a typical ride? Shea asks. Twenty-five, thirty miles, I tell him, choosing a distance I was capable of maintaining every other day last summer. I play lacrosse, he offers, and something in his voice gives me leave to examine him more closely. Yeah? I say. He makes a move as if he's swinging a stick, and my eyes fall on a swell of bicep as he bends his arm. Every chance I get, he tells me.

I glance in the direction of the pool. Joel's still in the water, though he's leaning against the side; the game's obviously over. Want to get in? Shea asks. Yeah, I say, I'm just going to run to the bathroom first. I'll wait for you, he tells me.

Without looking in Joel's direction, I skirt the edge of the pool and make my way inside, where I go into the bathroom. Now here's something to contemplate, I think, pausing in front of the mirror and trying to examine myself without the usual acrimony. I'm sweaty, though I look more as if I've been in the pool. Leaning closer to the mirror, I run the edge of my hand above my sideburns, a little long for my taste but which Joel has assured me look good. Even an hour in the sun has lightened my hair, and the few dry strands I have look golden. I'm flushed, the color of my eyes every bit as striking as the water itself. If I don't smile, I can get away without looking my age.

Outside, Shea greets me near the door. He's already stripped down to his trunks, and I pull my shirt over my head, sucking in my gut at the same time. Really, I don't look that bad; I've dropped a few pounds, probably because I've been at Joel's behest the past week. I send him a mental thank you, then turn to Shea. But he's staring across the patio with an expression I don't have to work hard to decipher. I've seen that look before, and I follow his eyes. So can you introduce me? he asks.

I try to evaluate Joel with the same dispassion I afforded myself a few short minutes ago and find the task impossible. He's talking to a friend of his who owns a dog-walking service and he's holding a bottle of water, the only liquid I've seen him consume since we arrived. His trunks still ride low on his hips, low enough with the weight of water from the pool that I catch the thinnest line of white flesh in stark contrast to the rest of his skin. Technically, Joel's not attractive in any traditional sense of the word. Though singularly he has nice features—thick, dark hair that looks good even as short as he's taken to wearing it lately; eyes he describes as gray, but which I know have just enough green to remind me of the sky moments before it rains; the most beautiful mouth I've ever seen on a man—taken together they don't add up to anything resembling perfection. He has nothing on Marcio, though I suppose if given the choice I'd go for Joel anytime. I know a lot of guys who would.

The dog-walker says something funny and Joel laughs, touching his friend's arm with just enough bend in his wrist to describe as effeminate. He's not, actually, usually holds himself so straight that I'd never guess otherwise if I didn't know him. Only occasionally do I get a hint. Only occasionally will he cross his leg in just the right way, or fall into his hip, and I'll think: no doubt. I've always found those lapses incredibly seductive, and I sigh.

Joel looks up as we make our way toward him, Shea hanging back just enough to appear shy. The affectation angers me more than it should, and I find myself quickening my steps, forcing Shea to walk faster. I'd been planning on introducing them, then casually slipping my hand into Joel's to indicate that he's taken. I didn't want to embarrass Shea, or make him feel awkward about the fact that he obviously spent the past thirty minutes talking to me only because he wanted an introduction. But as I reach Joel and turn to indicate Shea I change my mind. Shea steps forward as if he's about to receive a gift, gazing at Joel with the slightest smile, and even though I know deep down that he's not doing anything wrong I feel the blood rise to my face. Scrapping my plans, I take Joel's hand and pull him toward me, kissing him in a way I never have in public. He doesn't argue, and from the corner of my eye I catch, and relish Shea's expression. Come with me, I murmur in Joel's ear.

I half-expect him to stop me as I lead him around the pool, but when I glance over my shoulder he looks pleased. I also can't help noticing the half a dozen guys, including Shea, who watch our retreat. Yanking Joel inside, I lead him to the bathroom, where I shut the door behind us. What's gotten into you? he asks when I slide my fingers under his trunks and kiss the side of his neck hard enough to leave a mark.

As I nip his earlobe I spell it out for him. Jesus, Adam, he says, pulling away, Why don't you just piss on me next time? Before I can protest he opens the door; Kyle, spotting us, pauses with a wine spritzer halfway to his mouth. My bathroom's a sacred place, ladies, he informs us. So is my pool, I snap, naming any one of a number of places at my home where I know he's been with Scott. Kyle holds one fluttering hand to his throat, as if he can't believe my audacity. What's wrong with hubby? he asks Joel. With a huff I turn on my heel and head back outside.

But I don't have any friends out here, and I'm still hesitating a few feet from the bar, avoiding Shea's eye, when Scott appears beside me. Marcio have the day off? I ask, knowing as I ask the question that I'm going to get reamed. Marcio, Scott says, taking extra care with his words, Didn't feel like joining me. You were actually going to bring him? I ask, and Scott reminds me that with his affair, everything's out in the open. Kyle knows about Marcio, he says, Marcio knows about Kyle. He brushes one hand against the other, as if to demonstrate how neat and tidy he's managed to keep his affair, the implication, of course, being that I've made a debacle of my own.

Scott knows about Trainor. He found out early on, when I made the mistake of using him as an alibi one Saturday morning when I wanted to get out of the house. He called me on my cell when I was heading toward home to tell me that he'd run into Joel, who seemed plenty confused that Scott wasn't with me. Thirty minutes later I walked in my front door, afraid of what I was going to find; I should've remembered that Joel has a faith in me that I find stupefying. A few quick excuses and he was pacified. Later, when I realized that all it would take for Joel to find out was Scott saying something to Kyle, I asked Scott to meet me. What am I, your priest? he asked after I confessed. I just want to make sure Joel doesn't find out, I said, I'm not looking for him to get hurt. Then you should probably stop cheating on him, Scott told me.

Glowering, I eye the bar. I could use another drink; my margaritas have worn thin. Scott trails me, then picks up the bottle of tequila we've brought and pours himself a shot. Yes? he asks, poised over an extra glass. I nod, then toss it back, looking around too late for a lime. How's your dad? Scott asks.

The question catches me off-guard, and the past week spills over me like a wave, with little regard for whether or not I'm anchored. I'd almost forgotten, which is maybe one more reason that I didn't want to come here today. I don't like pretending that everything's fine when nothing has been for more than a year. Raising the back of my hand to my mouth, I look around me—at Kyle's pretty boys, at the pool spread out in front of us, a mirror of the lake below—and wish myself home. The cancer's spread, I tell him. I'm sorry, he says. I nod without speaking, squinting into the sun. Is it treatable? he asks, and I say, They're going to try. He takes a thoughtful sip of tequila; I know what he's thinking. I've wondered myself, sometimes, whether my father should continue treatment. When he's been at his worst, I've wondered how he could keep on. The desire to survive, I suppose, outweighs everything else, though that's something I should know already. By the end, there was nothing Bobby hadn't tried.

Since that day at the hospital I haven't been able to get him out of my mind. I keep picturing his dorm room, my apartment. The house we bought together after we graduated, *Bobby sprawled across the scuffed hardwoods in the middle of the living room the day we closed. I'd been staring at the chipped paint on the walls, the massive crack near the front door that indicated a serious foundation problem and the only reason we'd been able to afford the house with one month of employment under our belts. This is ours, Bobby said, and I nodded, a little terrified by the commitment we'd just made. What're you thinking? he asked. That we've just signed our lives away for a money pit, I admitted. He laughed, then reached for my hand and pulled me down next to him. His mouth, when I kissed him, tasted like beer; we'd talked about champagne, decided on a six-pack to save money. But it's ours, he murmured, tightening his arms around me, This money pit is ours.*

You all right? Scott asks, and I blink. I've blanked out again, and I touch my cheeks, afraid I'll find them wet. But they're dry, and I steady myself. I'm feeling that shot. You want another? he asks, indicating the bottle. You trying to get me drunk? I ask as he pours, and he tells me I seem to be doing a pretty good job of that on my own. The tequila slides down my throat, warming my chest; I take a lime wedge from the silver bowl on the table and suck it dry. Can we...? I ask, suddenly wanting to be someplace a bit more discreet. Come with me, Scott says.

I follow him around the pool and through a gate on the side, then down a flight of stairs to the boat. There's a breeze down here that I didn't expect, and I turn my face in the direction of the wind, letting it dry the sweat on my brow. Scott, his fingers still curled around the neck of the tequila bottle, steps from the deck to the boat, then turns back and offers his hand. I slip, just enough that both of us laugh. If I have to choose between you and the tequila, Scott warns. We sit, and I hold out my hand for the bottle. You realize this is sipping tequila, he tells me. My last, I promise, and he shrugs. You get as wasted as you want, he says, leaning back and stretching out his legs. They're heavily muscled, recently waxed; a year ago my own looked the same.

I met Scott shortly after I moved to Austin, through a mutual friend with whom neither one of us still has contact. Scott was a transplant himself, and he persuaded me to buy a bike, told me if I wanted a challenge I should try riding along 360. The traffic, the wind factor..., he said, ticking off obstacles on his fingers, There's no better rush. We started cycling together on the weekends, and whatever weekdays I could leave work early enough, and gradually I found that those rides gave structure to my weeks in a way that work never did. The exercise was great, and I found myself in better shape after six months in Austin than I'd been even in college. There was something about Scott himself that settled me, too. I wouldn't say that he became my confidant, but he was something close. He's one of a few I've told about Bobby, the only one I talked to about Joel, other than my sister. He never once passed judgment. That all changed, though, when he found out about Trainor.

Let's swim, I say, getting to my feet, and Scott eyes me with suspicion. But I've already kicked off my sandals and he watches as I clamber over the side of the boat. I've underestimated the depth, and my teeth jar together when my feet slam against the ground. The water barely reaches my chest. Tequila bottle in hand, Scott peers down at me. That's a good way to find yourself paralyzed, he calls. Feels good, I insist, and when I take a minute to sink back into the water, I find I'm not lying. I'm cool, for the first time all day, and I duck under the surface and propel myself away

65

from the boat. Coming up for air I hear Scott splash into the lake behind me. The sound throws me back almost twenty years.

I don't really like the outdoors, Bobby said when I suggested camping that first October, and taking in his white skin and nervous expression I laughed. Guess what, I said, We're going anyway.

We left early that Saturday morning and hiked a good five miles before we stopped to eat the lunch I'd packed. You're doing fine, by the way, I told him as we gathered our things together. We had a few miles left before we stopped for the night; the next day we could take an alternate route to the car, probably still make it back to Lexington before dark. It's not as bad as I expected, he admitted. Oh yeah? I asked, What'd you expect? Bugs, he confided with a shudder, Lots of bugs.

We didn't hit the river until late that afternoon. Hours had passed since we'd seen anyone, and though we'd spent the vast majority of the day talking we grew quiet when we heard the water. I was walking in front, and as the tree line broke I stopped. Sunlight, diffuse in the trees, sparkled across the river and I felt a moment of perfect calm. We'd cross, hike another mile or so and set up camp. Packing earlier that morning I'd crammed a small bottle of bourbon next to my sleeping bag, and hefting my backpack higher on my shoulders I had a quick image of us passing the bottle back and forth, curled in front of the fire. I smiled as Bobby stepped next to me, frowning. Now what? he said.

At first he just shook his head when I told him we were going to cross. Where? he kept saying, There's no bridge. We don't need a bridge, I assured him, The water's not that deep. Well, how then? he asked, and shielding my eyes from the sun I scanned the bank. There, I said, pointing, We'll cross over the rocks. What if we fall in? he asked. Then we'll get wet, I told him, starting to walk. I don't want to get wet, he said. Then don't fall in, I suggested. I kept walking, but stopped when I realized he wasn't following me. What? I asked, getting impatient, What? Adam, he said, I can't swim.

Hooking his fingers through the straps on his backpack, he flushed, color rising in his cheeks the same way it had the first day I noticed him. How did you make it through childhood without swim lessons? I asked. I assumed them a rite of passage, remembered them with a clarity that made the experience seem months in the past rather than years. Well, he said, hesitating.

He gazed off over the river, staring for so long and with such intensity at the opposite bank that I followed his eyes in spite of myself. Well, he said again, turning back to me, I had a sister who drowned.

We'd been together for eight months. I'd told him all my shit. He'd met Julia, he'd met my parents; I'd even met his, though he introduced me as a friend and the ensuing argument had almost caused us to split. I'd told him everything, and he'd kept a sister from me?

Looking suddenly uneasy, he glanced into the woods beside him and then into the water as if he found himself trapped. You had a sister, I said. He nodded. Who drowned, I said, and when he nodded again I kicked hard at the ground. He drew back, wincing as pebbles sprayed in his direction. This is so fucking typical! I shouted.

Without saying a word he cut me off, a shadow crossing his face like a shield. So that's how it's going to be, I said, watching him withdraw. Furious, I adjusted my backpack. I'm so sick of this, I informed him, and when even that didn't induce him to speak I turned and marched downstream. After a minute I could hear him following.

From a hundred yards away I'd thought the rocks larger, but unless I wanted to wade across—I bent and dipped my hand in the water to check the temperature—I didn't have a choice. Shaking my hand dry I stepped onto the first rock. My foot just fit. Beneath me the water gurgled, pleasant enough, though the current looked swifter mid-river. I took another step, then another, pausing occasionally for balance. Not once did I look behind me, though I knew Bobby was there; I could hear his tentative footing, and every so often a quick breath. The sound irritated me, and I found myself moving faster, my eyes on solid ground.

I was thinking about his parents, and the energy I'd expended trying to convince Bobby that I should meet them. They'd come up when Bobby moved out of the dorm and into his own apartment in August. I was supposed to meet them late the afternoon of their arrival; we'd decided that I should come by on the pretense of borrowing something for a class we shared. That way they won't suspect anything, Bobby said, and I grimaced. I didn't want to upset him; he was clearly nervous enough about the visit. But I hated the fact that I was something Bobby had to keep hidden. I think somewhere in the back of my mind, too, I believed he'd change his mind at the last minute and tell them the truth.

When I got to his apartment, though, they weren't there. I waited outside for a while, thinking maybe they'd just gone for a walk or something before I realized that he'd skipped out on me intentionally. He didn't want me to meet them, and as I paced back and forth in front of his door I grew angrier and angrier. I finally got in my car, determined to track them down at any one of the half a dozen restaurants they might have gone for dinner. I found them at my third stop, and watched Bobby's eyes widen as I approached their table.

I was charming. I pretended that our running into each other was entirely coincidental, made a show of begging off when they invited me to join them. I hate to intrude, I told them. Don't be silly, his mother said, We never get a chance to meet Bobby's friends. She was taken with me, and after I sat down I ordered the same beer Bobby's father was drinking, agreed with his mother when she suggested I get a plate of fried chicken. They'd already eaten, and they wouldn't hear of leaving until after I'd gotten something in my stomach. I really don't want to keep you, I said. You're not keeping us, his mother assured me.

They were provincial. His father smoked even after my food came; his mother pulled out first a lipstick, then a comb, and proceeded to fix herself up in front of a hand-held mirror as I ate my mealy baked potato. Bobby looked downright mortified, but after everything he'd told me I expected far worse. His parents were nice. They were rough around the edges, sure, but they were perfectly nice, and I couldn't believe for one second that they would disown him if they knew the truth, as Bobby claimed. They asked me questions about school and my family, and I found out about his father's work as a miner and his mother's relationship with her eight brothers and sisters, all of whom lived within a few miles of each other. Honestly, I found them fascinating, simply because of who they were: my lover's parents. I could see Bobby in each of them, and I found myself smiling as I caught his mother absently brushing her eyebrow with the back of one finger, a mannerism Bobby mirrored when he was nervous and about which I teased him. I looked into his father's eyes, and realized they were the same eyes I stared into every night before I went to bed, the color unremarkable but somehow more beautiful to me than I ever could have imagined. I was suddenly swept by a wave of emotion, and I gazed across the table in Bobby's direction.

He was utterly impassive. I couldn't have been more surprised than if he'd spit at me, and I think I actually sucked in my breath because his mother frowned. *Even then he didn't move. He just stared at me, with such dispassion that I felt sick to my stomach. When his mother asked if I had a girlfriend, all I could think was that I wanted to hurt him. Yes, I said, I do.*

I spent the next five minutes talking about Taylor, thrilled that my ex had a name that could go either way. Bobby knew about Taylor; apparently, he'd known I was involved with Taylor before we even met, and after we got together Bobby would ask about him, hoping I'd say I had no idea what Taylor was doing. To be honest, I didn't. Once I started seeing Bobby he was all I wanted, but as I talked to his parents I pretended that wasn't the case. Actually, I confided, blushing when his mother asked for a description, She has such a great body. Bobby's father looked wistful as his wife reddened, and I hastened an apology for being brutish, which she swept away. Maybe you could set Bobby up with one of her friends, she suggested, and I nodded, thinking of Taylor's friends—my friends—and how they couldn't believe I was even sleeping with Bobby. Maybe so, I said.

Shortly after that we said our goodbyes. I'm so glad I ran into you, I told his parents, and then I touched Bobby's arm, lingering just long enough for him to raise his eyebrows in alarm. See you around, I said, changing course and giving him a good-natured cuff. Bye, he said, looking right through me.

As they drove back to Bobby's apartment I followed them at a discreet distance, then waited outside in my car until they left an hour later. Bobby gave no indication that he saw me until his parents pulled away from the curb. Then he stared hard in my direction. I got out of the car, slamming the door; he automatically looked over his shoulder, as if he expected his parents to remember something they'd forgotten and return. We had a deal, I said. I changed my mind, he told me, and I said, We had a deal! It wasn't the right time, Adam, he insisted. There's never going to be a right time! I informed him, and he looked suddenly weary. Maybe you're right, he said, turning to go inside.

I yanked him back. Don't, he said, shaking me off. What're you going to do? I asked, as I followed him up the stairs to his apartment, Keep this from them for the rest of your life? What do you know? he asked. He stopped suddenly, halfway up the steps, and leaned toward me; on his breath I could smell the French fries he'd eaten, and the one beer he'd drunk. You know nothing, he said, punctuating each word, Nothing. I know that they liked me, I told him. Of course they liked you! he cried, They have no idea what we're doing! I hauled myself up another step so that even though he was one step above me I towered over him. What we're doing? I repeated, What we're doing? For just a second his eyes flicked away from mine, and I felt once again as rejected as I'd felt sitting across from him in that restaurant. What are we doing, Bobby? I asked, Tell me!

He couldn't answer, and doubly betrayed, I brought my fist down on the stair rail, so hard that the metal jangled. I hate what you're doing to me! I shouted. What I'm doing to you? he asked, What about that display back at the restaurant? You told me I could meet them! I cried, and he said, I'm talking about Taylor! He bit the inside of his cheeks, and I realized at that moment the depth of his jealousy. I'll tell you one thing, I said, tightening the screw, Taylor never made me feel like shit for sleeping with him. If you miss Taylor so much, then why don't you go to him! Bobby cried. Maybe I will, I said, Because right now I don't even want to look at you!

Crossing the river that day in October, thinking about the night we'd argued, my fists clenched. I couldn't commit myself to someone who refused me in return, and as I picked my way from rock to rock, I thought: this is it. I'm done. He just doesn't get it, and whatever excuse he might have for not wanting to introduce me to his parents, for not confiding in me about his sister, I just can't do it anymore.

Taking the last couple of steps, I hauled myself onto the bank; there was a gap between the last rock and the land and I wavered a bit over the water before I made it across. Sliding my backpack off my shoulders, I set it on the ground beneath me, then turned just in time to see Bobby slip. He was halfway across, and I knew which rock had stumbled him: the one half-buried beneath the water, slick with moss. I'd caught it myself just as I lifted my foot, stepped wide to avoid getting wet. Bobby was too late, and I watched as he wobbled, holding himself steady for just a second before he lost his balance. Though I knew the river couldn't have been more than a few feet deep, that the current wasn't strong enough to drag him away, he didn't know that, and his expression as he fell was pure panic. Smothering the impulse to go to him, I watched as he struggled to get to his feet. He was wet all right, and would need to change his clothes; that would make us late getting to our campsite, and I folded my arms across my chest, listening to him cough. That's when his eyes found mine. For just a second he paused, incredulous at my proximity, and then he pulled himself out of the water.

By the time he reached me he was furious. Bobby, I said, relenting, but he brushed right by, and when I reached out and caught his sleeve he turned on me. Don't ever do that to me again! he yelled, so close that I could feel his spit on my face. I shrank away from him and he backed off, but when I muttered something in my defense about the rocks being slick he charged me. Hitting the ground, the air left my chest with an oof. We scrambled together, but he'd taken me by surprise and within a few seconds he had me pinned. I was amazed by his strength, by the fact that though I struggled I couldn't break free, and after a minute I stopped trying. Bobby loomed above me, breathing hard. Say you're sorry! he commanded. I blinked as water from his hair dripped into my eyes, and made another half-hearted attempt to squirm away from him. Say you're sorry, Adam! he said, gritting his teeth, Or I swear to god I'll walk away from you and never fucking look back! I'm sorry! I cried, I'm sorry, I'm sorry!

Giving me one last shove for good measure, he got to his feet and walked away from me. My side hurt from where his knee had dug into my ribs, and I winced, wondering if I'd have a bruise. The sky above me, glimpsed through the dying leaves of the maples, held an ethereal quality, and I knew we wouldn't make it to the campsite before dark. I looked at Bobby. He was standing ten feet away from me, facing the opposite direction, and I watched as he took off his backpack and pulled his wet tee shirt over his head. His muscles slipped down his back, the bones of his vertebrae stretching his skin. A tremendous urge to go to him swept over me; I wanted to take each tender knob between my lips, slip my tongue between every bone. I pushed myself up on one elbow. Bobby, I said.

He didn't move, and I thought back to that night I'd met his parents, the night I'd stormed away from him and ended up sulking in my apartment. I'd lasted all of an hour before I went back to him. He opened the door without a word, and I wrapped him in my arms, my nose burrowed in the crook of his neck. He'd showered, and I inhaled the strong scent of his shampoo, some prescription he used because of his dry scalp and which had caused me to wrinkle my nose the first time I'd gotten a close whiff. I love you, I mumbled, tightening my hold on him. I love you, too, he whispered.

Bobby, I said again, and when he didn't even cock his head I planted my feet and stood up. Dirt clung to the back of my jeans and I brushed it away as I walked toward him. He finally turned, tears cutting streams through the grit on his face. I stopped, stunned. I couldn't even remember the last time I'd cried. Three years? Four? He trembled, and I gathered him in my arms and held him against my chest as he cried. I'm sorry, I kept repeating, and after a few minutes he stopped, though he continued to shake. I pulled my sweater over my head and helped him get it over his own.

While I gathered some wood and started a fire I had him sit with his back against a tree. Dusk settled as I shook out his wet sleeping bag and laid it close to the fire, then unrolled my own. We sat on the dry bag, and I unwrapped the sandwiches we'd brought, though he shook his head at the offer. Please, I said, You have to eat something. He took one bite, then a swallow of bourbon, staring into the fire. He'd said hardly a word in almost two hours when he told me about his sister.

He was young, not even three, and his sister, age six, drowned in their backyard swimming pool. Afterwards they'd covered it up, just hired a truck to pour the concrete and then lay down artificial turf. That's appalling, I said, but he just shrugged, as if he didn't know any different. I don't even remember her, he said, And no one ever talks about her. He'd seen a picture once. His aunt had shown him, a Polaroid of a little girl in a ladybug sweater holding a baby, holding him. That's the only picture you've seen? I asked, and he said, I think it might be the only one left.

He indicated the bourbon, which I was holding motionless in my hand, and after I gave it to him he took a long pull. Tilting the bottle back and forth, he watched the fire turn the liquor golden. I huddled deeper into my sweatshirt, staring into the flames. I'm sorry, I finally said. He nodded, without taking his eyes from the bottle. I love you, I added. I know, he said. No, I told him, I mean....

I didn't finish my sentence, and after a second he looked up at me. The space between us swam wide and we stared at each other, seeing everything: the past, the future, everything in between; but most of all this one moment, this one moment where we sat under a black velvet sky spilling starlight. I love you, I said again, and he smiled, his lips as perfect as the crescent moon that hung above us. Yeah, he said, I love you, too.

I'm pulled from the water, choking, Scott's arm under my chin. Half of me wishes he'd just let me slip back beneath the surface, and I struggle, whacking him across the nose. He doesn't relinquish his hold, though he curses under his breath. My eyes scan the sky; the horizon holds the last of the sunset and I realize as my lungs fill with air that I've been gone for a good long while. I croak, guttural, clogged with lake water. Seconds later my feet touch bottom. I shove Scott out of the way, but my footing isn't as firm as I thought and I get another mouthful of the lake. Scott locks his arms around my chest. Shut up, he tells me when I protest, Or we're both going to drown.

Resigned, I let myself relax in his arms. *I should have gone to him,* I think, as Scott hauls me toward the boat, *I should have gone to him.* Almost there, Scott's saying to himself. My feet stretch tentatively toward the bottom as he peels his arms from my chest, and I straighten, my legs wobbly as a newborn fawn's. He hooks one arm around my shoulders, in a gesture that helps keep me on my feet. I don't know how I'm going to get you up the ladder, he tells me, but before I can offer my own services he lifts his free hand, waving. Hey! he calls. Spotting Shea coming down the steps toward the boat, I groan. Not him, I say, but Scott ignores me. I need some help! he calls.

Shea jumps the last few steps and runs in our direction. By the time we reach the dock he's squatting above the ladder, his hands outstretched. I can manage, I tell him, placing one foot on the bottom rung. Three steps later my legs are quivering, and I give up and reach for Shea, who hasn't moved. Even with his help Scott has to hoist my ass out of the water, and when I'm finally on dry land I stagger forward with enough force that I come close to knocking Shea down. What happened? he asks.

Thankful that Scott shares my silence, I let them ease me to the ground. Do me a favor, Scott says to Shea, beckoning him aside and following his request with something I can't hear. I lean forward, staring at the muck in my toenails; I'd grabbed into the mud at the bottom of the lake with a little too much fervor. Are you sure he's okay? I hear Shea ask, Maybe I should take a look at him. He's fine, Scott says, barely glancing at me, and after a second of hesitation Shea turns and trots back toward the house. Convinced I'm going to be sick, I wrap my arms around my midsection. Scott reaches into the boat for the tequila; the mere sight of the bottle causes my forehead to break out in a sweat, and I moan. If you're going to hurl, Scott says, unscrewing the cap and holding the bottle under my nose, You might want to do it over the side.

I push him away, barely clearing the dock. When I'm finished I take the bottle of water Scott offers me and rinse my mouth. Better? he asks as I spit, and I nod. Good, he says, Now what the hell is wrong with you? I sit back on my heels, shivering as water drips down my back. If I hadn't seen you go under you'd be dead by now, he informs me, and from the corner of my eye I see Joel. I'd almost forgotten about him, and I hug my arms to my chest, watching as he sprints across the deck.

He's already reaching for me when Scott tells him about my fit of idiocy. I pull away at the touch of his hand, and that bottom lip of his works its way into his mouth. I want to rip it from between his teeth, and though I haven't said a word Joel recognizes my expression. Could you leave us? he asks Scott, stopping him mid-sentence. Scott hesitates, then shrugs. Let me know if you need anything, he says, and I watch him head across the deck and back up the flight of stairs to the party. I feel like I've lost my last friend.

How much have you had to drink? Joel asks once Scott's out of earshot. Too much, I admit. He squints into the twilight; his swimming trunks have dried, along with his hair, and I have a feeling that his skin's warm enough to thaw my own. For just a second I consider burying myself in his arms. We shouldn't have come here today, he finally says. I don't contradict him. I thought you'd be able to relax, he explains, I thought getting away from work would do you some good.

I struggle to my feet, where I teeter uncertainly. Just rest a bit, Adam, he pleads, but I shake my head. I can see Kyle at the top of the steps, looking down; I wonder what Scott has told him, what Shea has been saying. I wish you'd talk to me, Joel says, Aren't you the one who's always giving me shit about not communicating? Yeah, you don't seem to have that problem anymore, I mutter. I have my moments, he tells me, and I realize suddenly that he hasn't confided in me—about anything—for a long time. I just want to help, Adam, he says. You do help, I mumble, but he shakes his head as if he hasn't heard me. You're so angry, he says, You're just so angry all the time, Adam, and I don't know what to do to make it any better. There's nothing you can do, I say. Well, that makes me feel pretty fucking helpless, he tells me. Yeah, well, I say, Sometimes it's not all about you.

~ ~ ~

I awaken the next morning with a raging headache, and claw through the nightstand until I find a few stray Tylenol. With shaking fingers I swallow them, along with the glass of water I had the foresight in my inebriation to pour, but not to drink, before I went to bed. I can't remember the last time I was so hungover, and a wave of nausea reminds me how I got to this point: three margaritas plus the sipping tequila, not to mention a near-drowning experience. I drop back on the pillows; I'm alone, and glancing at Joel's side of the bed I realize I've probably been alone all night.

Annoyed with myself, I stare up at the ceiling, at the painting Joel finished the summer after he moved in. He'd made me sleep in the guest bedroom for a week while he worked, brought me the clothes from my closet each morning after I showered in the spare bathroom. Are you getting paint all over my beautiful furniture? I asked one night. He swore he wasn't, though he also claimed I wouldn't care once I saw what he'd done. You're pretty full of yourself, I said, but he just smiled.

A few days later he met me at the door when I got home from work. Close your eyes, he commanded, taking my hand. He led me into the bedroom, then directed me to the bed and told me to lie down. I'd thought he was going to paint the walls a different color, maybe claim one wall as his own, the way he'd done at the house he sold. When I opened my eyes I saw that instead he'd taken the ceiling. Stretching out beside me, he held my hand in one of his and pointed with the other. He'd used blues and greens and grays that blended together so perfectly I couldn't tell where one color ended and the other began, and a pink so faint he kept calling it flesh. What did you name this masterpiece? I finally asked. *Adam*, he said.

Last night after we got home from Kyle's he went upstairs and changed his clothes. I sat in front of the television, too drunk and worn out to think about maneuvering another flight of stairs. Going for a run? I asked when he came back down with his running shoes. At first he wasn't sure if he'd imagined the acidity in my tone; I could tell by the way he cocked

75

his head. Then he set his jaw, as if he was trying to remind himself not to be provoked. The gesture infuriated me, and as he got to his feet after he tied his shoes I said, Have a great run. Would you rather I just sat at home and drank? he snapped, forgetting himself and naming in the process one of the many methods of self-destruction I've seen him employ in the past. Well, I'm fresh out of box cutters, I told him, and he stepped back. This is abusive, he said. I broke his gaze, and when he finally left I dragged my ass upstairs, where I fell into a sleep I allowed myself to categorize as blameless. It's not as if he'd never taken to his arms with a box cutter.

Now I feel sick thinking about what I've said. I sit up, catching my reflection in the mirror. I look every bit my age, and maybe even older.

Downstairs, he's not in the kitchen or the great room, and I look outside to see if he's in the pool. But he's not there either, and I head down the hallway to his studio. We'd combined the formal living room and dining room in order to give him enough room to work, added windows along the north side of the house for light. When I open the door I find him standing in front of them, his back to me.

He's not as forgiving as he could be, but I can't fault him for that. I don't know what's wrong with me, I whisper, and he says, I don't either. He runs his hand through his hair; he looks like he's gotten little rest but I doubt if he's been working. Can I make you breakfast? I offer. He hesitates. I make pretty good pancakes, I tell him. Yeah, he admits, You do.

He sits at the table, watching as I scoop quarter cups of batter and drop them onto the griddle. I've let him press some kind of ointment into my temples to combat my headache; every time I turn I catch a whiff of peppermint. You need to stay hydrated today, he says. I need coffee, I tell him, and he shakes his head. He thinks I should wean myself off the caffeine, even though I've told him that I need the jump-start in the morning. Try yoga, he usually says, Or an early ride. But today he just shakes his head, absently stirring honey into the mug of tea I've brewed for him.

He eats three of my pancakes, which is more than I've seen him eat in a long time. Are you sure you're not the one who's hungover? I ask. Actually, he says, I got sick last night. What do you mean, you got sick? I ask. I ran really hard, he says. So hard you threw up? I ask, and he shrugs, taking the last of his pancake and swirling it through the syrup on his plate. Where were you? I ask. Right outside, he tells me, popping the last bite in his mouth, Why, are you worried about what the neighbors will think? No, I say. Those gays next door, he says in a hush, shaking his head and mimicking the tone of the neighbor to our right so perfectly that I have to laugh.

Joel doesn't like the woman who lives next door because she came over one evening when I was out of town to inform him that she could see our swimming pool from the window in her closet. Your closet, Joel repeated, and she gave him a pointed look, meant to indicate that she could see not just the pool but what we'd been doing in the pool. Maybe you should take your business indoors, she said. Maybe you should spend less time in the closet, he suggested. Since then she's avoided him, though she's still friendly enough to me. She's our neighbor, Joel, I said when he told me what happened. It's not as if we're shitting on her lawn, Adam, he informed me, And that's more than I can say for her dogs. He makes few apologies anymore, for anything, and though there was a time when I wished that he'd overcome his incredible self-consciousness, sometimes I find myself looking back on his insecurity with the same fondness with which a mother might remember her child before he took his first step.

You're not going to give me shit for puking in the bushes, are you? he asks, and I say, As long as you don't give me shit for puking in the lake. I carry our dishes over to the sink and run hot water over them, loosening strands of syrup that slip down the drain. My headache's nearly gone, though I'm not sure whether I should attribute that to the Tylenol or the peppermint, and my hunger seems to have gone the way of my headache. So what do you want to do today? I ask, turning, and he smiles, the first genuine smile I've seen from him in a long while.

We end up sitting outside by the pool, slide into the water at the same time and don't come out until my skin starts to burn. I'm going to take a shower, Joel murmurs, and this time I join him. He makes me sit at the bottom of the tub while he washes my hair, conjures up a lather so thick and rich it takes forever to rinse away all the shampoo. Afterward we make love the way we used to, our bodies still warm and damp from the bath. Never again, I think, his hands caught in mine. I will never touch Trainor again.

~ ~ ~

The next morning's mild, so mild that I almost can't believe my luck. I skirt through light traffic on my morning commute, and make my way into work where Vincent greets me as I'm pouring a cup of coffee. Good weekend? he asks. Pretty good, I admit cautiously, but he just nods, then disappears without another word. I close the door of my office and scroll through my schedule. Trainor's here, but because I'm locked up in meetings for most of the day I can probably get away without having to say more than two words alone to him. Maybe, I think, I can just let this whole thing fade away.

Dinner, I'm thinking later as I head back to my office to check my voice mail one last time before I head home, and maybe a movie if we have time. Knowing Joel we'll probably end up in the pool before it's all said and done. He's already accepted the invitation, and I've told him to expect me in enough time for drinks. Buoyed by the thought, still feeling pleased with myself for having successfully dodged Trainor, I almost don't notice Dave standing in my doorway. No one could ever accuse him of having a poker face, and when I see him I groan. I have a feeling I know what's coming.

Every week I get at least one call that's been passed from a Junior Representative to a Senior Representative, and then on to Dave, without resolution. No amount of coaching seems to help, and I swear I'm starting to think that threatening to take away personal time might not be a bad idea. What's the problem? I ask, and he offers me a page worth of notes. But they're all written in longhand and I make little attempt to mask my irritation. Just tell me what happened, I say, So there's at least a chance that we can get out of here before dark.

He spends ten minutes filling me in on the particulars before he lets it slip that the customer's still on hold. *Now*? I say, and he blinks myopically. I force myself not to take him in a stranglehold. Dave, I say, trying to keep my voice even, How do you feel when you're kept on hold for ten minutes? Angry, he answers without hesitation, and I stare at him. I'll just forward the call, he tells me.

I take a look at my watch while I'm waiting. If the traffic's light, the time I'm losing won't make much of a difference. We'll still be able to make the reservation I've made, even if we have to skip the preliminaries. Ms. Miller, I say, answering the phone the second it bleats, I understand we've caused you some difficulty.

The call isn't the worse one I've had. I've dealt with customers much more irate; I've been silent for five minutes at a time while I've let someone rant. I've been cursed out, too, and to those customers I simply say that I'm unable to help them until they've calmed down. I'm always smooth, and I've never, ever had to pass off a call to anyone else. Initially, this phone call isn't any different. As a matter of fact, I have her so cool within the first sixty seconds that I'm almost light-headed. Confidence and adrenaline—they're a powerful cocktail. I have to say, she confides after I've told her what we're willing to do, You've been far more helpful than your subordinates.

Everything's fine, until she changes her mind. I've spent at least thirty minutes with her, listening to her story, arranging to pick up the computer she doesn't want and placing an order for another model, when she changes her mind. It's not too late, is it? she asks. I look out the window. There's been a definite shift to the sun over the past half hour, and though Joel hasn't tried my office line I know if I pull out my BlackBerry I'll find a message. I don't want to have to go over the advantages and disadvantages of both systems again, and I really don't want to have to reenter another order. Well, I say, imbuing my tone with hesitation.

I've irritated her, and that more than indecision about her purchase causes her to change her mind. Could you hold, please? I ask. She makes a sound that I interpret as an assent, and I hit my mute button. *Goddamn,* I say. Elbows on my desk, I run my hands through my hair. There's no way we'll make our reservation, and there's honestly no explaining that to Joel. He'll say he understands, but his work experience pretty much consists of an internship at an energy company during Spring Break his freshman year in college and a five month stint waiting tables, a gig he insisted on taking when we first got back together. I'll get a sympathetic nod, but he really won't understand and he'll have a wounded look in his eyes that I'll have to rally to dispel. I don't have *time* for this *shit,* I say.

Taking a deep breath, I punch the mute button. Thank you for holding, I start, but there's no response and I frown. Ms. Miller? I say, Hello?

I glance at the phone, and there, with one finger poised over the mute button, I blanche. Oh shit, I think, please tell me she didn't hear that. Ms. Miller? I say one more time, and when there's no answer I give the mute button a ginger squeeze. Her voice comes back crisp and cool. I'd like to speak to your superior, she says.

Working late? Vincent asks, barely looking up when I stop in the doorway of his office. I have a call, I say, and he lifts his eyes. All right, he says, without asking me for the history, Patch it through.

In my office I stand facing the window. I've left my door open, though I have a feeling Vincent will close it. The sky holds a steady blue despite the hour, and I take in the view of the skyline as I have many times the past few years. It's nothing like what I can see from my bedroom, but I'd still been impressed when I moved into this office as part of my position as Director of Sales. Now I stare out at the tops of the trees, their tips tinged gold in the sun. I won't get fired, I don't think, but I've certainly given Vincent enough fuel to point me in that direction.

I wait less time than I would have expected before he calls, and as I walk down the hall toward his office I wonder what made me think he wouldn't summon me. I can't picture him sitting down across from my desk in this situation, or to be perfectly honest, in any situation. He's made it clear for the past year that I'm merely an underling, and in this instance I can't say he wasn't right to make that assumption.

He's standing in front of his window when I pause at the threshold of his office, and I'm struck by that fact, that the moment I turned from my view he stood to face his own. Vincent, I say, and he offers me a seat with the thrust of one hand. I lower myself reluctantly into the chair across from his desk; he makes no move to sit down himself. At best, he starts, This was a rookie mistake. I nod, and he leans toward me. You're not a rookie, he says. No, I agree, and he straightens to his full height and shakes his head, as if I'm a dog he's inherited and found disappointing. I'm concerned, he tells me.

I bite the inside of my cheek to keep from responding. No matter what I say, no matter how conciliatory my tone, he doesn't want to hear from me right now. Just let him talk, I think, before you start trying to defend yourself.

I'm afraid this incident might be symptomatic of a larger issue, he tells me, and startled, I forget my own advice. What do you mean? I ask. You haven't been in the game for a while now, he tells me, You've been away from the office— I was out of the office because my father had surgery, I protest, and he says, I'm not just talking about last week.

Lowering his voice, he starts speaking in a tone I'd describe as gentle if I didn't know any better. You're a solid leader, Atwater, he tells me, But lately there've been some oversights. *What* oversights? I ask, and he looks at me in a way that suggests I shouldn't be arguing with him. You're sitting in my office, he reminds me, Because you told a customer that you didn't have the time to take care of her. She wasn't supposed to hear that, I mutter, and he says, You honestly don't know when to shut up, do you?

I want to tell him that I've never had this problem with anyone but him, that there's something about his approach that compels me to antagonize him. But I'm not quite that stupid, and instead I watch as he curls his fingers over the back of his chair. I'm not happy with your performance, he says, Do you know what that means? I don't say anything. Get your shit together, Atwater, he says, Get back in the game, or you're going to be looking at some serious repercussions. My stomach turns, stunned by the sudden force of his words and the conviction behind them. Do you understand me? he asks. Yes, I say, and I'm dismissed.

Joel's in front of the television when I get home, which isn't a good sign. Other than the occasional college football game in the fall, he watches nothing. Mind candy, he tells me, as if that's a bad thing, and I sigh. I haven't been sure life is worth living since *Sex and the City* aired its final episode. Sometimes it's nice to do nothing, I tell him, and he'll agree. But does it have to be so banal? he'll ask. You're a snob, I've told him more than once, to which he nods. And in the case of television, he adds, I'll take that as a compliment.

Where've you been? he asks now, and then, before I have a chance to answer he says, Are you as sick of answering that question as I am of asking it? Something came up at work, I tell him, dropping my keys on the coffee table. Pat answer, he says, turning off the television, and I stop him before he can continue.

He listens as I tell him what happened; to my great amazement he's unconcerned. You and Vincent are always at odds, he says. I don't think you understand the magnitude of our conversation, I tell him, He hinted at firing me. Well, he had to, right? Joel asks, I mean, you told that woman you didn't have time to deal with her shit. He smiles, with the same amusement he exhibited when he first learned of my mistake with the mute button. You're not taking this seriously, I say, and he shrugs. I think you're overreacting, he tells me. Are you speaking from your wealth of employment experience? I ask, and he eyes me to gauge the animosity in my tone. They're not going to fire you, Adam, he finally tells me, They need you. Everyone's expendable, Joel, I say, Even me.

We don't go to dinner. Joel makes a salad, enough for the two of us, but I shake my head when he offers me a plate. I'm on the phone with my mother, who tells me that next week my father will start treatment for the cancerous lesions on his brain, a burst of concentrated radiation that may or may not stem the progress of the disease but will most likely leave him at least temporarily befuddled. Great, I mutter, What does Dad say? That he wasn't planning on being a brain surgeon anyway, she says. That's not funny, I tell her, and she agrees.

After I hang up I watch Joel finish his salad, decline his invitation to take a few laps in the pool. Then I'll stay inside, too, he says. No, I say, opening the pantry and staring at its contents, I'm going to bed soon anyway. There's more salad, he tells me as I take down the box of Ding Dongs. I give him a look, and he sighs.

~ ~ ~

Trainor's reaction to what happened bears no resemblance to Joel's. I tell him first thing Tuesday morning, when he walks into my office and tells me I look like shit. I've not planned on confiding in him, but I've slept little, and I'm so sick thinking about what Vincent will say to me today that when I see Trainor I figure I could use the advice. He sits in the chair across from my desk, looking grave. Joel said I was overreacting, I tell him. You're not overreacting, he says. He wants to know exactly what Vincent told me, and how I responded. You think I'm going to get canned, I say, and he shakes his head. No, he says, But you're definitely going to have to lay low for a while. He hesitates. Do you want my honest opinion?

he asks. Of course, I say. I think you should apologize, he tells me, And I think you should assure him that nothing like this will ever happen again. God, that sounds humiliating, I mutter. But it's the right thing to do, he tells me, If you want to keep your job.

I put off following through on Trainor's suggestion for most of the morning, finally make it to Vincent's office just before lunch. Sitting across from his desk in the same chair I occupied last night, I offer an apology for my behavior, and an assurance that he'll have my undivided attention going forward. He's not as encouraging as I'd like, and I leave shaking, both with anger and anxiety. How'd it go? Trainor asks in an email I pick up when I get back to my desk. I gaze through the glass to place him; he sees me watching and raises his eyebrows. I give him a cryptic shrug.

For all my promises to Vincent about getting in the game I really don't feel as if I'm even on the court. I know I should stay late tonight given the circumstances, but at five-thirty I shut down my laptop. Trainor stops me before I can leave. I've scheduled you a massage at six, he says. What? I ask. Don't tell me you don't need one, he says, handing me the directions. I glance down at the information, then back up at Trainor. Go, he says, You're going to be late.

I haven't had a massage in probably four months, though Joel swears by one every other week. As a matter of fact, the last massage I had Joel insisted I schedule; I'd taken an instant dislike to his masseuse. I'm really not comfortable with your aura, she told me before I'd even disrobed. My what? I asked. Your lover has an incredible aura, she added, and for just a second I was confused. I'd been sleeping with Trainor for about a month, and it took me a moment to realize she was talking about Joel. He does? I asked. Yes, she said, So blue. Right, I said as she gestured toward her table. Yours is sulfur, she told me, wrinkling her nose.

Raul's different. He makes me fill out a short form, then ignores what I've written and asks what areas of my body most concern me. I frown, unsure of what he's asking. Shoulders? he says, trying to help, Lower back? Both? I say, and he nods, pointing to the towel on the table. There's no music; when I had my last massage, Joel's masseuse had some meditation tape on a continuous, suicide-inducing loop. Everything off, Raul

83

says, Lie on your back, towel to your waist. I nod. I'll be back, he tells me, shutting the door behind him.

I get undressed and slide onto the table, pulling the towel to my waist just as Raul opens the door. I shoot him a quick look, trying to catch him in an indiscretion, but he's already lubing his hands. He runs his fingers in opposite directions along my brow line, then presses into my temples with a soft, gentle motion. As he works his way around to the back of my neck, I start to relax. Maybe I'll even sleep, I think as Raul kneads the pressure points at the base of my skull. I could use the sleep.

Five minutes later he asks me to turn over onto my stomach. I comply, and that's when the torture begins. Yeah, you've got some issues, he mutters, the flat of his hand deep in my shoulder. That actually hurts, I say, trying to be diplomatic, but he snorts. Gotta deal with the pain, he tells me, neglecting to add why. Hands straddling my spine, he prods the middle of my back with such vigor that I yelp. Trust me, he says, You're going to thank me later. I doubt that, and I whimper when his fingers slide lower, into the tender muscles of my lower back. Just relax, he says.

By the time he's finished I feel bruised and beaten and exhausted, but my body carries none of the tension I've been lugging around for the past year. How much do I owe you? I ask, but he waves off even an attempt at a tip. I limp out to the car, where I call Trainor from my cell. How was Raul? he asks. Thorough, I say, and he chuckles. Where are you? he asks.

I could give the question more thought. I could think about where I am not just in terms of physical space—a stoplight not far from the office, closer to Trainor's apartment than home—but in terms of psychic space as well. For just a second I can feel the wood beneath my hands as I gripped the floor of that balcony thirteen years ago, my feet dangling over the grass.

Jump, he said. Jump.

4

The Passat craters halfway to work a few weeks later in the middle of rush hour traffic. I'm mildly hungover; Joel and I spent most of the weekend arguing about whether we should spend the Fourth of July holiday by ourselves or get together with friends before we finally decided that we weren't fit company for anyone and opened up a bottle of wine on the back deck. I stared up at the night sky as the fireworks started, intercepting occasional text messages from Trainor until Joel finally said that if he'd known I was going to spend the entire evening checking my BlackBerry he would've insisted we make plans. What's the point of spending time together, he asked, making little attempt to mask his annoyance, If you're going to spend half the evening disengaged?

We've not been getting along very well, not since he reacted with such ambivalence over what happened with Vincent. The fact that Trainor stepped in hasn't helped. Instead of working harder to talk to Joel, I've allowed Trainor to become my confidant; he seems unperturbed by the role. Several times over the past few days he's dropped hints about getting away together for the weekend; I'm actually tempted. I keep thinking about that massage Trainor scheduled for me, the way he worked me over when I hobbled into his apartment afterwards.

But last night I shut off my phone, and Joel and I settled into a sullen silence. Only after the fact did I realize that I'd drunk most of that bottle of wine myself.

Absently drumming my fingers on the steering wheel, I cock my head when I hear a low, persistent whine over the sound of the radio. I turn down the volume, frowning, then widen my eyes when I realize the Passat's the culprit. Maneuvering into the right hand lane, I ease on to the shoulder and flip on my hazards. Even when I turn off the engine the sound continues, though feebly, as if in protest. Sweating in the absence of the air conditioner, I wait thirty seconds, then try again. This time the Passat belches a putrid cloud of smoke.

Trainor picks me up an hour later, as I'm signing the paperwork to have the car towed. I knew he wouldn't care about the interruption, whereas Joel—assuming he was working and not still asleep, assuming he'd even answer the phone—would sigh an aggravated sigh. I don't need to feel like an irritation today, not when I'm the one sitting by the side of the road without any air conditioning. Why don't we run by my place, Trainor asks as I wipe my forehead with a rolled-up sleeve, You can shower before we go to the office.

At his apartment he checks his email while I go into his bathroom. I've only showered here a half a dozen times; he doesn't keep his tub very clean, and to be honest I'm usually ready enough to get away that I'd rather shower at the gym. Lately I haven't been doing either, which isn't smart. Laziness could get me caught; I know this from experience.

Do you have a shirt? I ask when I'm finished. He's sitting in front of his computer, one finger curled above his lip. His pants are tight around the thighs; he's told me he has trouble finding anything that fit his legs. I do, he says, glancing over at me, But first you should come here. Why? I ask. Why do you think? he says.

I take him with me that afternoon when I buy the car. The garage has called to tell me what it's going to take to fix the Passat, and I've decided it's not worth the cost. Time to upgrade, I tell Trainor as we pull into the BMW dealership. The 500 series, Trainor suggests, and we take a test drive, in a honey of a car that climbs to 70 in less time than it takes for Trainor to count to six. Today, I say, I want to take delivery today.

I drive home as the sun's setting, in a car that shimmers in the light reflecting off its silver hood. I've just unloaded a good chunk of my savings account, and I have a car payment—a whopping one, that caused me to gulp when the sales rep wrote it down—for the first time in three years. Honestly, I probably should've spent more time deliberating. But I'm excited anyway. I need this car, I deserve this car. You're sure my job's se-cure, I joked to Trainor as we left the lot, and he assured me, in a way that made me wonder what he might have said to Vincent on my behalf. We went for drinks to celebrate, though we'd wanted back in the car halfway through the first round. Driving under that brilliant sky on the way back to Fusion so I could drop Trainor off, I felt a thrill that I haven't felt in a long time.

At home I pull into the driveway, stopping to stroke the fender before I go inside. I've never owned something so magnificent, and opening the front door I glance over my shoulder. The car glimmers, sleek and power-ful, like an animal waiting to pounce.

I find Joel in the pool, where he floats on his back, staring up at the sky. I've caught him here more often than not lately; I have no idea how much he's been working these days, or if he's been working at all. The thought makes me crazy, especially when he has the audacity to interrogate me if I come home late. After all, he doesn't know where I've been. Let me guess, Joel says, Something came up at work. No, I say, I bought a car.

As I usher him dripping through the house I tell him about the Passat breaking down when I was still fifteen minutes from the office. I just couldn't take it anymore, I confess. Opening the front door, I wave in the direction of the driveway. He looks from the car to me, and then back again. What do you think? I ask, drawn toward the car as if it's a magnet. He trails after me without speaking. Well? I say, and he lifts the edge of his towel to his ear. You bought a car, he says. Isn't it exquisite? I ask. You just went out and bought a car? he asks. The Passat was going to cost a fortune to fix, I tell him, and he says, How much? Four grand, I say, exaggerating the amount. He holds his arms out straight, the towel list-ing behind his back like wings. How much was this? he asks, nodding toward the car.

When I tell him a muscle jumps along his jaw. That's a big purchase, Adam, he says. He drops the towel around his shoulders, examining the car with dubious eyes. I thought we were going to get a hybrid, he adds, and my fists clench. You wanted a hybrid, Joel, I say, I didn't. I thought the plan was to trade in the truck, he says. The truck's running fine, I mutter.

He's talking about the shitty little used pickup he bought almost five years ago, shortly after we got back together, a purchase he insisted on making himself even though I told him we should pool our resources and get something more reliable. I've suggested a half a dozen times since then that we trade it in, and he's always found a reason not to make the time.

Don't you at least want to check it out? I ask, opening the driver's side door and inhaling the scent of all that gorgeous leather. He doesn't answer me, and I slide into the seat and caress the steering wheel. He stands with his arms folded across his chest, his jaw wired tight. What's your problem? I finally ask. My problem, he tells me, Is that we probably should've discussed ahead of time whether we should buy a $50,000 automobile. I didn't realize I needed your permission, I say. Are you serious? he asks, and I get out of the car and slam the door. Am I supposed to be clearing every purchase with you? I ask. We're talking about a *car,* he reminds me, And where in god's name did you get that ugly fucking shirt?

I glance down. Trainor, I mumble, and he says, *Trainor?* Yes, I say, walking back toward the house. Trainor bought you a shirt? he asks, following me. Trainor came to pick me up when the Passat broke down, I tell him, opening the front door, And he offered to run me to his apartment so I could shower. You took a shower at Trainor's apartment, he repeats. Stop making it sound so seedy, Joel, I say, thinking, I could be found out this easily. Did he try anything? he asks. Joel, I say, Stop. He shuts up, and I take a deep breath. Look, I can't return the car, I say, I'm sorry I made the purchase without your input, but I can't take it back so what do you want me to do? I want you to treat me like I'm your fucking partner, he says, I want you to take off that awful goddamn shirt. I pull it over my head. Well, he concedes, That's a start.

Later, as we're getting ready for bed, he tells me he wants us to see Lydia, the psychiatrist who worked with him just after his suicide attempt, and then again a year later, the last time we split. She's open to the idea, he tells me, and I say, You've already talked to her? He dips his head, as if he's self-conscious about bringing the news to light. I've seen her a few times in the past month, he admits.

So this is what I've driven him to. I'm just… trying to work a few things through, he adds. I nod, moving my mouth to say something which never materializes, and he touches my arm. I look down at his hand on my skin, faintly surprised to find it there. We've not touched, I don't think, for almost a month. Adam, he says, and I raise my eyes.

The night we met, in the darkness of that downtown bar, I'd assumed his eyes were gray. Gray, I thought, just light enough that you couldn't help but notice the contrast to his hair. Only in the bathtub later that night had I noticed the flecks of green buried in the gray of his eyes, and I'd likened the color to the sky before it rains. Promise, I told him two years later when we were in Mexico, They're the color of promise. He'd liked that; how could he not, taken as he was with the intricacies of color? Now they hold my own, and after a minute I come up for air and nod, or shake my head. He chooses to err on the side of possibility, and when he slips his arms around me I hesitate, then bend my head to his.

~ ~ ~

Three days later I find myself in Lydia's office. I've left work early, told Darlene I had a doctor's appointment I couldn't reschedule. I can't believe I'm actually here, and I settle myself on the sofa next to Joel, where he tells Lydia that I've been going through a lot. I don't know whether to break forth with a snort of laughter or address the tears that rush to my eyes. Opting for neither, I clear my throat, then realize when Joel doesn't continue that I'm supposed to say something myself. My father's sick, I finally manage, and Lydia nods. She's not what I expected, with her A-line skirt and hair so frizzy she must include an electrical outlet in her beauty regimen. But Joel swears by her, has told me more than once that with anyone else he never would've crawled his way back from the dead. I try to give her the benefit of the doubt, and clear my throat again, realizing as I do that I'm reproducing a sound that my father must make constantly. The thought makes me nauseous, and I find myself swallowing. Are you and your father close? Lydia asks. Yes, I say. This must be hard for you, she offers, and I nod, glancing out of the corner of my eye at Joel. He gives me a small, encouraging smile. Are you seeing much of him? she asks. When I can, I say, stiffening, There's only so much I can do from here.

Lydia's quiet, waiting for me to elaborate, but I've said as much about my father as I feel capable of right now. I half-expect her to hold out for more information; I know how therapists work. But she lets me off the hook. Tell me about work, she suggests.

Grateful that she's allowed the conversation to segue, I explain my function at Fusion, adding that I'd been up for a promotion about a year ago but that I was passed over. Have you considered looking for another job? Lydia asks. I'm not sure that I've really given the matter any thought, partly because at my level I'd probably have to do some considerable searching before I found anything in Austin, but primarily because I've been preoccupied. I haven't, I admit, and she nods. So you're dealing with your father's illness, she says, And you're not that excited about work right now... how would you say you're handling all of that turmoil? Well, obviously not well, I mutter, Or I wouldn't be here.

I immediately regret speaking so frankly, but Lydia doesn't seem to mind. Tell me what's going on between you and Joel, she says without missing a beat. Discomfited, I glance in his direction. But he's not looking at me, and I turn helplessly back to Lydia. There's no right answer, she assures me, taking off her glasses and allowing them to dangle from a chain around her neck. I don't say anything, and after a long moment she turns to Joel. Would you like to start? she asks.

By the time he's finished telling her about the BMW I'm shaking with resentment and he's just gathering steam. I listen as he reminds her of the comment I made about the box cutter—which he's apparently already shared with her—as well as what happened on the front steps at my parents' house. He's making me into a monster instead of the man who's supported him for the past five years, and I inadvertently fold my hands into fists. You seem angry, Adam, Lydia observes. Hey, I'm just stating facts, Joel protests before I can answer. He looks at Lydia, assuming she'll agree; I'm surprised she doesn't chide him for interrupting. He bought the BMW without my input, he continues, That's a fact. Are we really here to talk about the BMW? I snap. The BMW's symptomatic of a larger issue, he informs me, sounding exactly like Vincent.

I don't say anything. For a full minute we sit in silence, and then he glances my way, without actually meeting my eyes. I feel so distant from you, he says, You feel so far away. I squirm, and mutter something about having a lot on my mind, but he shakes his head and tells me this feels different. We don't talk, he says, We don't....

He trails off, but I know where he's going and I almost groan. Are we really going to have to address our sex life right here, right now, during our very first visit? Every time I approach you, he says, You put me off. That's an exaggeration, I tell him, reminding him that we had sex just a few nights ago, after I capitulated to his request that I come here today. That makes five times in the past four months, he tells me. You're *counting?* I ask, and he says, Not very high.

Lydia interjects before I can come up with a response. You've been concerned about this aspect of your relationship for a while, she says to Joel, and I throw him a disbelieving look. I'm in therapy, he protests. Why don't you tell Adam what you've told me? Lydia asks Joel.

This has never been a problem for us, he says, turning to me and recalling the very words I said to him one of the many times we got back together. I give my head a short nod, and he reminds me that even now when we're together everything feels right. You can't deny that, he insists, and I tell him I'm not arguing. But you still reject me, he says, Almost every time. I'm tired, Joel, I inform him. You can't always be tired, he says, and I shake my head. Five times in four months, I mutter. Yes, Adam! he says, Five times in four months! Then jerk off, Joel! I snap. What do you think I've been doing? he says.

I look hard in his direction; he folds his arms across his chest. He's not lying, and I wonder when the hell that's happening. So what? I say, I'm working all day while you're jerking off? I work too, Adam, he reminds me. Right, I say, So when does that mean you're masturbating? He won't look at me, but he glances up at Lydia through lowered lids. I think that's a fair question, Joel, she admits.

I decide that I like her immensely. I'd been worried about their history, sure she'd side with him at every turn, but she's obviously more impartial than I expected. Joel runs his hands through his hair; I watch as a muscle near his ear jumps. When he answers he speaks in a voice so muffled that Lydia and I have to strain to hear. At night, he mumbles. What, in your studio? I ask, confused. He doesn't answer me, and after a minute I realize why. In *bed?* I ask incredulously.

I have no business being angry with him. My sins are far more severe, but as I picture him lying next to me, bringing himself to orgasm, I'm overcome with fury. You could at least *try* to wake me, I say. Why? he asks, So you can tell me you're too tired?

All right, Lydia says, We're not here to take shots. Joel and I glare at each other, obviously disagreeing. Joel, she continues, Do you enjoy masturbating? I'm tempted to laugh, but Joel takes the question seriously. I don't prefer it to sex, he tells her, and Lydia turns to me. Adam? she asks. No, I say. You don't enjoy masturbating, she says. I don't…, I say. Never? she asks, and I shake my head. I can't remember the last time, and now that I'm trying to balance both Joel and Trainor—and obviously not doing a very good job—I don't have the energy. So you're not masturbating, she says, And you haven't been sleeping with Joel.

I see instantly where she's going. Panicking, I tell her that I've been consumed with thoughts of my father, with work, with money. I've gained a little weight, I say, and that's probably made me self-conscious. With everything else that I have going on in my life right now I'm feeling vulnerable, and I'm worried sex might exacerbate that feeling. I can sense Joel softening beside me as I trot out explanation after explanation, but Lydia doesn't take her eyes from mine. After a minute I have to avert my gaze.

She knows.

She waits until I look up again, until she's sure that I understand, and then she turns to Joel. Do you mind if I have a minute alone with Adam? she asks. He seems surprised by her request but he nods, touching my knee as he gets to his feet. Trapped, I watch from the corner of my eye as he closes the door behind him. For a moment Lydia says nothing, and I stare at the floor, at the swirling patterns in the rug beneath my feet. I have a profound desire to simply disappear. Joel tells me that you had a partner who died of AIDS, Lydia says.

I'm too shocked even to nod. You were young, she adds. Twenty-seven, I whisper. That must have been a tremendous blow, she tells me. I nod. You spent some time in therapy, she offers. Three years, I admit. I have clients who've been with me three times that long, she tells me. That doesn't say much for your cure rate, I manage, and she actually laughs. I like to think of therapy more as a process, she tells me, Something that ebbs and flows, depending on what you need.

I'm silent. Have you considered seeing someone again? she asks, Under your current circumstances? I shake my head. I haven't, though sitting in front of her it's easy to see why she'd ask. Tell me, she says, Why did you come here today? Joel asked me to, I say in a low voice. But why did you agree, she asks, If you're not going to be honest with him?

She waits an interminably long time for my answer. I'd probably say anything if she waited long enough, and my heart picks up at the thought. You don't know me, I finally say. No, she agrees, But Joel thinks he does.

There's the accusation I expected. I try to come up with a retort, and she watches as I scramble through my meager justifications. Staggering to my feet, I place my hand against the tightening in my chest. I suddenly can't breathe, and my heart hammers at the same moment my vision starts to fade. Adam? Lydia asks, my name spoken with more concern than I deserve. I squeeze a few short, bitter words from my mouth; they come as reluctantly as my breath. Then I pass out.

~ ~ ~

The paramedics run a quick battery of tests and conclude that I haven't had the heart attack I feared. I should probably have a more in-depth workup, they tell me, but given what happened just before I passed out they think I've had a panic attack. Have you been under a lot of stress lately? the one guy asks, before he looks around him and catches himself. I'm mortified, and only too happy to see them pack their bags. After they're gone Lydia hands me a prescription for an anti-anxiety medication. I want you to take the tests they've recommended, she says, But this should help in the meantime. I thank her, folding the prescription in half, and then in half again. I'm sitting on the sofa, where EMS placed me once they made sure I could stand. The pressure in my chest has subsided, and I take another deep breath, imagining the air's trajectory through my lungs. Joel's hand trembles in my own. I want to see you both next Friday, Lydia says. We'll be here, Joel assures her. Adam? she says, and I nod.

I sit on the sofa that night, holding one small pill in between my fingers as Joel encourages me. Trust me, he says, You're going to feel so much better. I swallow, and within minutes I feel a nice, quiet buzz. See what I mean? he asks. He clucks around me, getting an extra blanket, asking what he can fix for dinner; I watch him with increasingly little emotion. I could tell him about Trainor, I think, and probably not care too much about the implications.

I don't tell him, of course. I don't say a word. I just stare out the window, watching the last of the sun's rays stretch across the lake. Across from me, Joel follows my gaze. For once he doesn't mention the rash of construction dotting the hillside, and after a minute I let him take my hand, for the second time today. I was scared, he admits. I'm fine, I say, and in the moment I mean what I say. But he shakes his head. I was scared, he says.

~ ~ ~

I find rather quickly that every dose of Ativan further accentuates the detachment I felt that first night. I'm taking a lot, too much in fact. Five milligrams twice a day simply doesn't cut it, and by the end of the weekend I'm taking twice that much and looking for more. At this rate I won't make it to Friday, the thought of which should make me anxious enough to contemplate taking another pill, but instead makes me yawn. Who are you? Joel asks when I offer to make brunch on Sunday, but he waves me into the kitchen with a smile.

I can balance them both, I realize that afternoon. I'm at Trainor's, stretched out on his bed with little regard for the weight I've gained, which from the vantage point of the Ativan seems somewhat negligible anyway. I'm so indifferent, in fact, that though I've never smoked a day in my life I crave a cigarette. I picture myself blowing smoke rings toward the ceiling, wisps of gray getting caught in the wind from the ceiling fan. Why are you smiling? Trainor murmurs beside me. I shrug without answering him. I'd been the tiniest bit concerned that maybe the Ativan would affect my performance, but that doesn't seem to be the case. As if he knows what I'm thinking Trainor rolls over to lick my nipple, one hand already rummaging between my legs. He lacks finesse, has a blatant disregard for foreplay. We rarely kiss. I find his technique a stark contrast to Joel's, who likes to stretch a single encounter into a night's worth of entertainment. I'm not all about the orgasm, he's said when I've teased him, but now I think about what he told Lydia on Friday and wonder if I should beg to differ.

Want to go again? Trainor asks. What he's really asking is whether or not I have the time, but I don't even look at the clock. I just close my eyes, which must excite him because in less than a second he has me in his mouth. I feel somewhat smug; I'm obviously not so old that I'm not up for seconds, and my hands make their way to Trainor's bald pate. There's been a time or two lately—five times in four months, according to Joel—when I've been surprised not to find Trainor's smooth skin.

Can't stay? Trainor asks when we're finished and I'm reaching for my keys. He wraps his arms around my waist; for once I let him. I don't know what you're taking, he says, But I like you this way. Impassive? I ask without thinking. Relaxed, he tells me, tweaking my earlobe as if I'm three years old.

My mood carries into the evening, and when Joel approaches me I think about the conclusion I came to earlier, that I'm capable of dealing with them both. Instead of pretending not to understand Joel's advances, instead of making excuses, I return his kiss. His relief is palpable, and even with the Ativan I'm reminded of Bobby's reaction when I finally went to him a month after he was diagnosed. He fell against me then with such relief that he knocked me off-balance, and I did my best to banish the image I had of him in the back of our car and wound my arms around him.

The memory of Bobby does nothing for my libido, though I have to admit that my double round with Trainor this afternoon probably hasn't helped. Humiliation trickles through the façade of my medication, and after Joel has tried pretty much everything imaginable to get me to respond I mumble something about the Ativan. I hate that he's understanding. I can..., I say, gesturing in the general direction of his shorts, and that's all the encouragement he needs. He wriggles out of them, promising me he'll be fast. He's not lying, and afterwards he thanks me, with a dreamy expression. The medication barely keeps my emotions at bay.

~ ~ ~

I head to Trainor's apartment after work the next day, if for no other reason than to convince myself that my failure the previous evening with Joel has nothing to do with the Ativan itself. I find that, theoretically, I'm fine. I have no problem attaining or maintaining an erection. But my orgasm feels far from my reach, and even though Trainor coos beside me, obviously satiated, I'm in a shitty mood. What's wrong? he asks, and without caring whether or not I'm going to upset him I say, That sucked. But you came, he tells me, as if that's all that matters. I shake my head and sit up. I should be getting home anyway; a glance over my shoulder at the clock tells me that it's nearing eight o'clock. Under the circumstances

Joel will be worried, and when my BlackBerry bleats I lean over the side of the bed and check a text asking if I'm okay. Fine, I type. Home soon.

Trainor slides across the bed and braces my shoulders with his thick hands. As he kneads my muscles I close my eyes. I can feel myself slipping back into the medication, and I take a single deep breath that pleases Trainor to no end. There you go, he says in my ear. He rubs a little longer, and for some reason his hands loosen my tongue. I tell him about the panic attack last Friday, about the Ativan; he reacts with more concern than I'd like. I'm fine, I tell him when he sits back on his heels, frowning. Anti-anxiety medication can be addictive, he says, And you're taking more than your doctor prescribed.

Annoyed that I've let down my guard, I get to my feet. Did you make an appointment to get the tests done? he asks. I don't see why I need them, I tell him, If something was wrong the Ativan wouldn't be helping. He doesn't look convinced, and I remind him what he said yesterday about liking me this way. That was yesterday, he points out. I yank my shirt over my head. Well, you really don't need to worry, I tell him, Because the pills are almost gone.

The realization doesn't make me as nervous as it might have before sleeping with Trainor. The sex was just too sketchy. I'm clearly not going to have a heart attack, and while the mere memory of what happened in Lydia's office fills me with dread, I'm not altogether sure I'm destined to go through that again. I'd been caught; of course my body was going to retaliate. I'm worried about you, Trainor admits as he watches me dress. There's no need, I say, Really.

~   ~   ~

The decision of whether or not to stay on the Ativan slips from my hands Tuesday evening, when I take the last of my pills. At first I watch from the sidelines as my emotions slowly reengage, eventually leaving me right back in the middle of them, right back where I started. I haven't had another anxiety attack; instead I've developed a tight, all-encompassing rage that makes my hands quiver. Both Trainor and Joel notice the difference.

I come home from work earlier than usual on Thursday and scout around for Joel, riddled with tension. I've just talked to my father, who for the last three weeks has been treated with a heavy dose of radiation.

Does it hurt? I asked the first time. He told me no, but I have a feeling he'd disguise the truth and I've been careful not to ask again. What about his lungs? I asked my sister a little while ago, What good are we doing treating his brain and ignoring his lungs? She reminded me that we're supposed to be tackling one thing at a time. We're eventually going to run *out* of time, I told her grimly. She cried, and I apologized, and she told me that I should make another trip home as soon as I can. I can't bear the thought. If I'm having a hard time holding things together here what good could I possibly be up there?

And I can't stop thinking about Bobby. For that I blame Lydia, and I lie awake at night, memory chasing memory. The afternoon we met in the library, the first afternoon we slept together, the day I brought him home to meet my family. That Christmas, *the first one after we moved into the house. Bobby told me that he needed to go to West Virginia, that his parents would never understand if he didn't make the trip home for the holiday. What about me? I asked, and he gave me a tired look. We'd been arguing for months about the fact that Bobby still hadn't come out to them; I'd barely been able to convince him to buy the house. They're not going to understand, he told me when I suggested we pool our resources for the down payment, and I encouraged him to tell his parents that he'd stumbled upon an investment opportunity. They're not that stupid, he said. But I pressed him, and he admitted once he talked to them that it was easier than he'd expected, explaining why we'd bought a house together. Lucky for you my parents like you, he said, and remembering those words I brought them up when he told me he needed to see his parents alone over the holiday. I think you're underestimating them, I said. I know them better than you do, he assured me. So what am I supposed to do? I said, Spend Christmas by myself? You'll go to your parents' house like always, he told me. But I want to be with you, I protested. I want to be with you, too, he reminded me. Sure you do, I muttered, Just not enough to tell your parents.*

That conversation came the weekend after Thanksgiving, and in the days following I kept expecting Bobby to come to me and tell me he'd changed his mind. But he didn't, and as our vacation approached and the distance between us grew I thought to myself that this was the sort of thing that could honestly split us up. Bobby, I said the morning of the twenty-third as we packed our respective suitcases, I won't do this again. Is that a threat? he asked, and I shrugged, though the thought of losing him terrified me. I'm not going to spend every holiday alone, I said.

I left with nothing more than an ambivalent goodbye and headed for my parents' house, where my sour mood infected most of the Christmas festivities. To their credit, my parents didn't say a word. I'd told them briefly why Bobby wasn't coming, and though I hadn't elaborated, I think they understood the magnitude of what was going on between us. When Bobby called on Christmas morning I told my sister to tell him I was in the shower, and I didn't call him back.

That night my grandmother caught me on the front porch, where I leaned over the railing, sulking, ignoring the cold. I straightened at the sight of her, but she smiled, every bit as regal as the horses my father bred, and his father bred before him. We weren't that close, my grandmother and I, though that had more to do with the sprawl of years between us than anything. I had distinct memories of playing tag with her when I was a child, of catching fish with my grandfather, who'd died of a heart attack before he was sixty. Looking at her, I wondered if she ever quarreled with her husband the way Bobby and I did, if she'd made any decision she ended up regretting. I couldn't ask; I had a feeling any mention of Bobby at all would make her uncomfortable. Though she'd been polite each time she saw him, I'd caught her staring at him with a quiet intensity that embarrassed me. I didn't necessarily want to know what she thought of him, what she thought of me and my choices. What are you thinking, child? she asked.

She'd asked the question kindly, but I started at the words. What was I thinking? Yes, it made me crazy that Bobby still hadn't told his parents, but I knew that I could've fared far worse when I came out to my own. Bobby's parents were good-hearted people, but they weren't particularly enlightened. And honestly, Bobby had no one besides me. He'd never made friends easily, never participated in sports the way I had all through high school and college. If his parents didn't take the news well he'd risk alienating the only people he had in his life other than me. No wonder he was hesitant to make a move.

What am I thinking? I repeated, for my grandmother's benefit as well as my own. Then I shook my head, without answering her question. I didn't have an answer, and after a moment she reached over and patted my hand. I thought she might turn then and go back inside, but instead she gazed past me, in the direction of the stable. Did you know, she said, That when I first met your grandfather I didn't know how to ride?

I found that difficult to believe; my grandmother, from the time I'd known her, had worked tenaciously alongside my grandfather. Only recently had she stopped riding, and I looked at her now, to see her nodding. Oh yes, she said, I had not a clue. But you learned, I pointed out, and she smiled. Your grandfather was a patient man, she said.

When I got back inside I went into my parents' bedroom and picked up the phone. I'd have to apologize, I knew, first for calling so late, and then for taking so long to return his calls. But I'd tell him I was sorry, and that he should take his time, and that meanwhile I couldn't wait to get my hands on him again. We'd have our own Christmas celebration in two days. As long as we were together at some point, that was all that mattered.

Bobby's mother answered on the third ring, in a thick voice that I immediately found suspect. Mrs. Kowalski? I said, speaking with hesitation, and she burst into a litany of tears and accusations that curdled my blood. Oh my god, I thought, oh my god, he told them. Mrs. Kowalski, I said, trying to interrupt, but she wouldn't listen to me and when she passed the phone to her husband and I heard my name followed by a string of profanities I quietly placed the receiver back on the cradle. Bobby wasn't there anymore anyway. He wouldn't have been allowed to stay.

Shaking, I gathered my things. You're leaving? my sister asked, and I met my grandmother's eyes and nodded. Throwing my bag in the car, I made my way through the cold Christmas night back to Lexington. Please, I thought, turning onto our street. Please let him be home.

I found him in the living room, and though he was squatting in front of the dog when I opened the door, he straightened as I stepped across the threshold, lifting his chin in a gesture of defiance that I rarely saw from him. I stopped where I was, stymied by his body language. I'm sorry, I said. For not calling me back? he asked, For forcing me to choose? He wasn't usually so forthright, and I hung my head in abject contrition. I made a mistake, I admitted.

He didn't contradict me. Folding his arms across his chest, he shivered instead, from the chill in the room or from disappointment I wasn't sure, until he spoke again. I have no one, he said, and I immediately protested. You have me, I reminded him, and he laughed, a painful laugh rife with heartache and sorrow. I fucking better, Adam, he said, Because there's no one else.

Joel's nowhere to be found, and I pull my cell phone from my pocket with shaking fingers and dial his own, then trace the immediate ringing I hear to the kitchen counter. Well, he can't have gone far, not without his phone, not with his truck parked in the garage. I wouldn't put it past him to go for a run even in this heat. I toss my cell phone on the counter next to Joel's, then bend down to pick up the piece of paper that flutters to the floor. It's a receipt, and I glance first at the proprietor, and then the amount.

Two thousand dollars. Almost two thousand dollars he spent this morning at an art supply store, and what galls me is that he really hasn't even bought that much. Everything costs a small fortune: a tube of paint, $85; the stupid sable brushes he likes, $50 apiece; museum-quality canvas, $225. Almost two thousand dollars, and my guess is that he hasn't given the total a thought.

When Joel and I got back together, the impetus was his break with his father, who'd been supporting him. How're you going to live? I asked, but he seemed unconcerned, and made some off-hand remark about waiting tables. I didn't expect much. He'd never held a job, he'd never been on his own, and now suddenly with three hundred dollars to his name he was going to find work without missing a beat?

But he did. He put his Explorer—which has father had bought for him—up for sale, and found a job waiting tables a couple of blocks away from where he was living. I still don't understand how he convinced the manager to hire him; though not necessarily upscale, the restaurant he'd chosen was busy, and trendy, and Joel was pretty much thrown into the fray. He worked forty hours a week and sometimes more, and painted whenever he had a little free time. Basically, I never saw him. Here I'd suffered without him on and off for a couple of years, and when he finally came back to me he was so busy trying to earn the money he needed to scrape by that I rarely got to spend any time with him. Nights and weekends—that's where the money was, and Joel proved himself a satisfactory enough waiter that he was booked all the time.

I let him work like that for a couple of months before I protested. I want to see you, I said, I can't stand that I'm wishing away the weekend because at least I know I'll get to hang out with you on Monday night. What do you want me to do, Adam? he said, I need the money. I knew better than to suggest an office job, something with normal hours. He'd never go for that; it was a huge enough accomplishment that he was working at all. And the office gig wouldn't have been him anyway. But I was annoyed.

By the time we hit Thanksgiving I was trying to get him to quit his job and move in with me. Why put off what we know is bound to happen anyway? I said. We'd wasted enough time already. But he wouldn't let me dissuade him. Adam, he said, You know I have to do this. I tried to understand, and on an intellectual level I'm sure I did. If I'd been a casual observer, if I'd been asked for impartial advice, I would've told him that of course he needed to work. He needed to prove that he was capable of supporting himself, that he was capable of surviving. But I couldn't get past my own bias, and I put so much pressure on him that he finally gave in. We knew we'd work out; we'd waited long enough to get to this point. I don't want you waking up in the morning and saying you have to go home to shower, I told him, I want you to already be home. So he put the house that he loved up for sale just before the holidays, and closed before the new year.

I set it up so that he wouldn't have to pay for much. Pocket the money, I told him when he said he wanted to give me some of the proceeds from the sale of his house, but I knew that he owed his father the bulk of the cash, and that he needed to save the rest. He quit his job at my request, and spent his days painting, which is what he was meant to do anyway. He contributed some to the running of our household; I let him write an occasional check for the maid service, I let him pay the electric bill, and more and more I've let him pick up the groceries since everything he buys costs a goddamn fortune, but otherwise I've insisted that he use the time to set some money aside. Whatever you're earning from your work, I said, You need to be saving. I don't want you paying for everything, he's told me time and time again, I've done that, and I don't like the way it feels. I'm not your father, I said, And anyway, you're working.

And he did work. So much so that even with his new schedule there were nights I didn't get to see him, weekend afternoons when he'd apologize for slipping away while I had the football game on the television. Just for a little while, he'd say, returning hours later. I couldn't fault him. I knew he was doing exactly what he'd been born to do, and I knew I was making that happen. I wanted to give him that time, I wanted to outfit him with a new studio. I wanted everything for him. I liked the way that felt, the fact that I was providing him something he'd never really had before, not without strings.

But the cost. He made up for some of it, with the work he sold, though I encouraged him to save most of what he brought in. And really, the money he spent on his supplies came out of his own pocket. But sometimes I'm amazed by the number he can drop in a one hour excursion to restock. You better paint something amazing with that color, I said once when he told me that a certain blue oil had set him back more than a hundred bucks, and he told me he didn't doubt that he would.

I've wanted to do this for him. But somewhere along the line I've started to wonder. Does he appreciate everything I'm doing? Sometimes I'm just not sure when he comes back from a trip to the farmer's market with $50 worth of organic produce that can't quite fill one small shopping bag, when he picks up an expensive bottle of wine without much thought.

Almost two thousand dollars for art supplies. Jesus.

I'm still staring at the receipt in my hands when from behind me he speaks. He's been running all right; he's soaking wet, though he might have only been gone thirty minutes. That's all it would take in this heat. Hey, he says, You're home early. You spent two grand on art supplies? I ask. I guess, he says, with such flippancy that I feel like strangling him. Two *grand?* I say, and he narrows his eyes at the anger in my tone. What's your problem? he asks. My *problem,* I say, Is that you don't seem to have any qualms about dropping almost as much money in an afternoon as it takes me to earn in a week.

For your information, he says, I spent my own money. Well, you certainly don't spend it on anything else, I mutter. What's that supposed to mean? he asks, and I point out that I'm the one who pays the mortgage, the car payment— On a car you bought without me! he cries, and then he spreads his hands, as if he's trying to get a handle on what's happening. I watch as he kneads the air in front of him, then takes a deep breath and closes his eyes. He's probably trying to find his center or something, and I have this incredible urge to step a little closer and nudge him off-balance.

He opens his eyes just as I'm about to put thought into action, and though I haven't moved he shrinks back as if I have. Something inside of me crumbles. Joel, I say, changing my tone, but he shakes his head. I've crossed some kind of line, and he takes another breath, then tells me we probably need to talk, but right now he's going to shower. Let's calm down, he says, the phrase suggesting that we both need some space when in reality I'm obviously the one with the problem.

As soon as he goes upstairs I call Trainor; he's only too eager to comply. Twenty minutes later we're sitting at an open air bar and he's listening as as I rail about Joel's failure to contribute in any meaningful financial way to the household. Do you want my opinion? he asks when I finally settle down. I find that I don't. I feel suddenly empty, but I'm not sure I can decline his advice, being that I've just unloaded on him. I think he's taking advantage of you, Trainor tells me.

He couldn't be any more wrong. I'm the one changing the rules of our relationship, and Joel has every reason to be upset. I discouraged him from adding some of his own money to help pay down the mortgage. I told him to save as much as he could. I bought the car. He's done nothing untoward. But I'm just so unhappy these days that sometimes I have a hard time distinguishing the difference. Maybe it's time to get out, Trainor says. What do you mean? I ask. Maybe it's just time, he says.

Whatever center Joel has been searching for has obviously remained elusive; I see this the second I step into the great room and find him waiting for me. I came downstairs after my shower, he says, And you were gone. I concentrate on my keys, which I fondle for a minute before dropping on the table. Adam? he says. I needed some space, I tell him. Where'd you go? he asks. I roll my shoulders, trying to convey the possibility that I just drove around, then figure if he gets close enough he might be able to smell the beer on my breath. I stopped for a drink, I tell him.

Déjà vu almost sweeps me off my feet, and for a split second I remember using the same lie with Bobby. *Wine, I said as he stepped forward for a kiss, and he stopped before he got to my mouth.* Where? Joel asks, and I mumble the name of the bar, which he probably doesn't know anyway. He studies my expression; I make an effort not to look guilty. Were you alone? he asks.

He's actually never asked the question, not in all the months I've been cheating on him, and I'm so taken aback that I blink. My shock works in my favor, because even before I lie he's nodding. I believe you, he says. I let out a shaky breath, relieved and miserable at the same time. Everything's unraveling, he says, Can you see that? I lower my eyes without saying anything. Adam, he says, I'm trying to be here for you— By spending two thousand dollars on art supplies? I interrupt.

He gives me a long, steady look before changing tact. We have an appointment with Lydia tomorrow afternoon, he says, We can hash things out then. I thought you wanted to talk, I say to his departing back. I did, he tells me over his shoulder, Three hours ago.

~   ~   ~

I have to bow out of a meeting in order to make our appointment with Lydia, and I berate myself as I head to her office. Setting aside the obvious jeopardy I'm doing to my job, leaving again in the middle of the afternoon, I can't imagine anything good coming from another session. The last time I saw Lydia I almost ended up in the hospital.

Pulling into the parking lot, I scan the area for Joel's truck. It's there, sitting in the shade; he's left the windows open, which I've told him a million times not to do. Anyone can steal your car, I say. This piece of shit? he jokes, and when I tell him that even if the truck itself isn't stolen someone might take off with his iPod, he shrugs. Then they must need it more than I do, he says. I want to kill him; I'm the one who bought the damn thing.

I walk over to the truck and roll the windows up myself—they're the kind with the handle—then hit the lock. Only after I've shut the door do I see Joel's keys curled in the cup holder. Goddamn, I say, shielding my eyes from the sun and peering inside to make sure I'm right. I'm right, and ignoring the fact that I was the one who rolled up the windows and locked the car, rendering the keys inaccessible, I storm into the building. Now we'll have to pay for a locksmith on top of everything else.

Joel's reading a magazine when I step into the office. Not any old magazine, not *People* or *Us* or even *Newsweek.* No, he's got *Mother Jones* spread
out in front of him, and I smack the magazine with my sweaty hand.
What's with you? he asks. You left your keys in your truck, I say, and he
says, So? So, I say, gritting my teeth and lowering my voice in case the
receptionist is eavesdropping, When I rolled up the windows and locked
the doors, I didn't take the keys. Well, why'd you lock the truck? he asks,
letting his magazine drop on the table beside him. Why do you think,
Joel? I say, and just then Lydia steps into the waiting area. Joel smiles as
if he's witnessing the birth of the sun itself, and Lydia returns the gesture before looking in my direction. Adam, she says. I nod, trying not to
look as sullen as I feel. Why don't you two go on in, she says, I'll be there
in a minute.

I follow Joel into her office, where he settles himself on the sofa in
front of the windows as if it's a second home. We're going to have to call
a locksmith, I say, lowering myself to the cushion beside him. I guess, he
agrees, as blasé as ever. Gripping my kneecaps, I note the way my knuckles instantly whiten. That's going to cost at least fifty bucks, I tell him.
What do you want from me, Adam? he says, I wasn't the one who locked
the keys in the truck.

Problem? Lydia asks as she enters the room, but Joel shakes his head. I
can almost hear his reasoning: if we call the locksmith now, our attention
won't be on the task at hand. And I can tell from his expression that he's
ready to get down to business. All right, Lydia says, sitting down across
from us, Why don't we get started.

The first thing she wants to know is how I'm feeling. Has the Ativan
helped? she asks, and I tell her that I took the medicine for a good five
days before coming to the conclusion that I didn't like its side effects. To
which side effects are you referring? she asks. I'm actually a little embarrassed spelling it out for her. I had a problem with impotence, I admit,
And even when I did orgasm it felt.... I trail off, unsure how to explain
myself, then catch Joel's expression and realize immediately what I've
done. When did you have an orgasm? he asks.

Unconsciously, I touch my hand to my chest. I half-expect Lydia to ask
if I'm all right but she doesn't say a word, and I scrounge what little en-

ergy I have to stave off the anxiety attack hovering on the horizon. After we ... tried, I say, turning to Joel and trying to look sheepish, I wanted to make sure. I tell him I tested things out on my own, in the shower the next morning. And I was fine, you know, in that regard, I say, But the orgasm itself.... I let the sentence dangle, but he's nodding. That easily I've been able to squelch his suspicion, and I'm both thrilled and repulsed by his gullibility. I don't dare look at Lydia, who has remained silent throughout this exchange. So that's why you stopped taking the Ativan, Joel says, and I nod, omitting mention of the fact that I'd run out of pills before I could make the decision myself.

But the doctor, Joel says, You never followed through on your tests. I give my head a slight shake; we've already argued about my reluctance to schedule an appointment, and I know he's brought the topic up again specifically because he wants Lydia to know. Why haven't you seen your doctor? she asks, and I tell her that if I'd been slated for a heart attack then the Ativan wouldn't have helped. That's not necessarily true, she tells me. Well, that sounds ominous, I say, and she reminds me that a mere week ago she'd been forced to contact EMS. Look, I'll call, okay? I say, I'll call. She's silent; I think she realizes I'm putting her off. But then she changes course. I'd like to hear about your anxiety level since you stopped taking the Ativan, she says.

I don't look at Joel. Twenty-four hours later my reaction to his purchases yesterday seems ridiculous. After all, I just spent $50,000 on a car; I can't expect him to skimp on supplies. I've been a little irritable, I admit, and before I can say another word Joel jumps in and tells Lydia about our argument. Listening to him, I keep thinking about the studio I built for him, and the repeated complaints I've heard ever since about the flooring. I'd suggested wood, but he said he'd destroy them in a month. Concrete, he insisted, and a week after the floor was installed he told me his entire body was sore just from standing. Do you know, I say now, interrupting him, That I'm still paying for the remodel?

He stops talking long enough to give me a blank stare. Your studio, I say impatiently, and he says, What are you talking about? I'm still paying for your studio, I say, I took out a second mortgage so you could remodel. His mouth opens and closes a few times, like a fish out of water. You told me you had the money, he finally says. I did, I inform him, Once I took out the loan. Why would you do that? he asks. Because you needed a place to work, I tell him.

I give him a moment to let my generosity register. He looks a little stunned, and I suddenly don't feel quite so guilty; all things considered, I've been a decent partner. It's only the past few months that have tripped me up. But what he says next shocks me. I *had* a place to work, he protests.

He's talking about his house, the one near campus, and I sputter as I remind him that he could barely afford to make the payments. You were in over your head! I tell him. And you bailed me out, he says, Is that what you're trying to tell me? I point out that he'd been working fifty hours a week waiting tables, that he'd been trying to paint at the same time, that we never had a chance to see each other. So you swooped in to rescue me, he concludes, and I tell him that's not what I mean. I just wanted to spend time with you, I say.

He lets that slide without comment. Joel? Lydia finally says, and we both glance in her direction. Frankly, I think we'd forgotten she was here. How do you feel about what Adam said? she asks. Honestly, he says, I'm confused. He turns to me, and I half-expect to hear that he can't remember the last time I told him I wanted to spend time with him. If we have the kind of debt you claim, he says instead, Why did you spend $50,000 on a car?

I bought the car, I say, Because I *wanted* the car. He frowns, the furrow between his brows thickening. I *deserve* the car, I add, and when that doesn't seem to appease him either, I remind him that he has his studio, and his art supplies, and easy access to the pool and the lake. I deserve something of my own, I say, and he says, But does it have to cost $50,000? Do you know how much I owe on your studio? I ask.

He's silent, and I tell him that of course he doesn't know, I've never bothered him with the details. He just moved in, and I took care of everything. We're supposed to be partners, he tells me. Does that mean you want me to ask your advice about mutual funds? I ask, Do you even know what a mutual fund is? That's unfair, he says. I don't think so, Joel, I say, You don't know, and you don't want to know. He socks away whatever money he earns, I say, then gives little thought to spending mine. You care a hell of a lot more about whether you're eating sustainable fish than whether we can afford it, I tell him, And don't even get me started about the tequila for Kyle's party.

He wears the same stupefied look that he wore earlier, and I glower at him until he lowers his eyes. I watch as his shoulders curve inward; he's not crying yet, but that's probably coming. I am not your father, Joel, I say, sensing the accusation before it's spoken, and he looks up at me with maddeningly dry eyes. Then why are you acting like him? he asks.

His father held him psychologically captive for years. Holding money over his head like a gauntlet, his father led him to believe that he could never survive on his own. His father started burning him with cigars when he was eight.

I stumble to my feet, acutely aware as I stagger into the waiting room and down the stairs that I'm not being followed. Outside I stand with my hands on my knees, squeezing my eyes shut and concentrating on my breath. After a minute I start to worry that I'll hyperventilate and I straighten, the movement sudden enough to create a head rush. Touching one woozy hand to the glass door behind me, I wait for the stars in my line of vision to disappear, then lope tentatively to my car, spotting Joel's truck from the corner of my eye. I don't even have the luxury of fleeing the scene.

Stabbing 411 into my phone, I request the number for a locksmith, then repeat the process when no one answers the number I'm given. By this time I can feel a thin trickle of sweat running down my spine, and I wipe my forehead with the back of my arm. Forty-five minutes, I'm told when I finally reach someone, maybe an hour, and I slouch in defeat against the back of Joel's truck, then yelp when the metal burns my skin. I'm still rubbing my arm when I look up to find Joel leaving the building. He stops when he sees me, then starts walking again, his step unsure. I had to call the locksmith, I mutter before he can say anything, and he nods. I can only imagine what he and Lydia have spent the past fifteen minutes discussing, and I avoid his eyes just in case he thinks now's a good time to open up.

After a minute he sighs and leans against the side of the truck. For whatever reason the searing metal doesn't seem to bother him. How long until they get here? he asks, and I shrug. He holds his arms across his stomach; I have a feeling he's gotten sick, and when he wipes the corners of his mouth with his thumb and forefinger I know I'm right. If you're sick, I say, Then go home. He shakes his head; I honestly don't know if I can sit through another thirty minutes of this. Take the BMW, I say, and he says, That's okay. I reach in my pocket for my keys and hand them over; he declines. Just take the BMW, Joel, I say, and he screams, I don't want your fucking car!

I rip my wallet from my back pocket and throw a handful of cash in his direction. Before he can move, I'm gone.

~   ~   ~

Not a single light shines from our windows when I pull into the driveway a little after eleven that night. For just a second I wonder if maybe he hasn't come home at all, but when I hit the remote for the garage and the door opens in front of me I see his truck. So he managed to hook up with the locksmith. I slide into the garage and press the remote again, listening to the whine of the door closing behind me. But I don't move, and after a few minutes the overhead light automatically shuts off, leaving me in what would be total darkness if it weren't for the glow of my BlackBerry.

I've surprised myself. After leaving Joel at Lydia's I didn't make my way to Trainor; instead I went to the movies, where I bought a box of popcorn and a Coke that cost more than my ticket and sequestered myself in one of the back rows. When the movie ended I went into the next theater, and then the next. I'll call him, I thought, on the way home. But I procrastinated, and now he's asleep, a feat that seems unlikely in my own future.

Inside the house I move through the dark, dropping my keys on the table, and as I glance out the back window onto the deck below I see him. He's not asleep. He's sitting in one of the lounge chairs, his head bent, his hands between his knees. He imagines himself alone. Without thinking, I touch my fingers to the glass, and then I see him speak. Frowning, I scan the deck, my eyes falling back to him when I fail to see anyone else. He's on the phone. I can see his cell now, nestled between his shoulder and ear, and I try to guess who's on the other end. Kyle, maybe, though if I had to make a bet I'd go with James.

College roommates: a term that does nothing to describe the depth and scope of their relationship. There are other terms I could use—best friends, one-time lovers—but I've gotten the impression from Joel that college roommates makes James's wife the happiest. They live in Chicago, where they moved a few weeks after Joel and I got back together, and though Joel hasn't made the trek up there more than once, every so often James comes to Austin. Elizabeth's welcome, too, I told him the first time he came to stay with us, and he and Joel exchanged glances. Apparently as polite as Elizabeth has been in regard to Joel, she doesn't really want to spend time with him. Frankly, I'm surprised she lets James come down without her, and I wonder sometimes what would happen if Joel and I were to break up. I think she sees me as some kind of talisman, as if I were capable of preventing something from happening between them if they were so determined.

Their sexual relationship—James's and Joel's—didn't last long. A few weeks, from what I've been told, a mistake that almost cost them their friendship and which consequently pushed Joel over the edge. I know James believes that he's mostly responsible for Joel's suicide attempt, and though I've tried to convince him otherwise I don't think he'll ever change his mind. They went months without speaking, and an equal number of months circling tentatively around the remains of their friendship, trying to figure out if there was anything left to recover. James's move to Chicago came at the perfect time; since then they've been able to ignore each other for months at a stretch, then get together in short enough spurts that there's little time for animosity to creep back in.

I liked James at first. When he burst out of Joel's hospital room the day I met him I was struck by the intensity of his emotion, by the ferocity with which he attacked Joel's father. Knowing myself about the abuse I couldn't help but admire James's reaction. The following morning when I met him at Joel's house I found his guilt agonizing, and I joined him in a drink of solidarity. Once Joel told me the truth, though, once I found out that James had continued to sleep with him even though Joel told him he was in love with him, my empathy diminished. I was biased of course; I loved Joel, and I couldn't stomach the thought of anyone hurting him. I knew, too, what would have happened if I hadn't found him in that bathtub. But I've looked at James differently since then, and gradually, as Joel's friendship with James has restored itself, my own relationship with

James has suffered. There was a time, before he moved to Chicago, before he and Joel reconnected, that we'd meet for lunch. I don't think either one of us would suggest that now.

From my perch at the window I watch as Joel draws a flat palm across his cheek. He might be crying, and that would mean he's talking to James. I don't want to think about what he might be confiding, and I go into the kitchen, where I start to rummage in the dark for something to eat until I decide that I'm being ridiculous and turn on the light. Thirty seconds later Joel comes through the back door.

You're home, he says simply. I live here, I point out without looking in his direction, and he's quiet, digesting what I've said and probably disagreeing. I take a fresh jar of peanut butter out of the pantry and slide a paring knife through the seal around the lid. You didn't have dinner, he says. I shrug, without asking if he's hungry himself. Taking a table knife from one of the drawers in the island, I start to mix the thick layer of oil on top of the peanut butter. Adam, he says, and I glance over my shoulder. He's standing with his arms crossed, though the pose isn't remotely defensive. Instead he just looks cold, and when I get a closer look at his eyes, I feel myself caving. This is the Joel I met eight years ago, and the thought occurs to me that if I'm cruel enough I can have him back. He rubs his hands up and down his arms, in a gesture that makes me want to cup his triceps in my palms. Where were you? he asks.

I've never been so thankful for the truth. The movies, I say, and the words sound so absurd that there's no way he could ever think I'm lying. The movies? he says, wrinkling his brow. I nod. All this time? he asks, and I tell him that I sat through the first one, then snuck into the second and third when they were already in progress. And yes, I had popcorn, I confess before he can ask, But it didn't do the trick. We look at the jar of peanut butter at the same time, just as a trickle of oil slides over the side. Why can't we buy normal peanut butter? I ask, but there's nothing more than resignation in my tone and when I cut my eyes at him he's smiling. After a minute he reaches for a dishcloth, then takes the knife from my hand. Without meeting my eyes he wipes my index finger with the towel, then rubs my thumb. I watch his hands in my own. There, he says quietly, and I choose that moment to dissolve into tears.

I can't believe the gamut my emotions have run in the past week, and when I finally disentangle myself from his arms I realize he's crying, too. Come sit with me, he says, reaching for my hand, and I follow him into the living room, where we sit on the sofa, pressed together more tightly than I ever thought we'd sit again. I bite my lip, which fails to stop a fresh batch of tears. He wipes them away without a hint of bitterness. He hasn't yet let go of my hand, and I watch our fingers together, the way they twine one through the other like a safety net. After a minute he follows my eyes.

We have the most honest conversation we've had in almost a year, a conversation that lasts into the early morning hours and then continues over breakfast late the next morning. Though we start out discussing our session with Lydia, we also talk about my job and all of its disadvantages; Joel listens without judgment. I think you need to get out, he finally tells me, and though under normal circumstances I'd dismiss such an audacious comment, this time I accord his suggestion the attention it deserves. I have a feeling he's right, and we gaze thoughtfully at each other, until he nods. He makes everything seem so easy, and for the moment I allow his conviction to convince me. We have bills, I remind him. We do have bills, he says, But you also have a crippling case of anxiety.

The smile he gives me softens his diagnosis and we both laugh. The sound fills the kitchen, and even after we're quiet we don't look away from each other. Tears spring immediately to my eyes, and I lay my head on my arm. He strokes my hair as I cry, scooting his chair closer to mine. Adam, he says, lowering his lips to my hair. When I finally raise my head he cups my face in his palms. I love you, he says, and I whisper, I love you, too.

We spend the day alone, planning my escape. Nothing's concrete; we don't haul out our bank statements or try to ballpark our assets. I don't think either one of us has the energy for such an undertaking, and we content ourselves with the promise that we can deal with the logistics later, and concentrate instead on what we'll do once I give Vincent my notice. Move, Joel says, and for once I listen to what he says, though I have questions. With the equity we have in the house we could … what? There's nothing we could buy in central Austin, not unless we want to find ourselves in the exact same financial situation we're in out by the lake. Joel's unperturbed. So we'll rent, he says, And worry about someone else having to shell out the cash if the air conditioner breaks. What would I do with my free time? I ask. Sleep, he says, Exercise. He shrugs, yawning. Give yourself the time to rebuild, he adds, as if I'm a condemned building on the verge of demolition. I glance down at myself, and he must know what I'm thinking because he takes my hand. Don't be so hard on yourself, Adam, he says, You've been through a lot the past year.

That easily I'm crying again, oily tears that slip from the corners of my eyes. Joel sighs, though he doesn't seem annoyed. I honestly think he's relieved to witness me experiencing an emotion other than anger, and he holds my hand without a word.

By nightfall I'm spent. I feel raw, as if I'm wearing my skin inside out, and when Trainor calls on my cell for the fifth time I excuse myself and step outside. For the love of god, I hiss, Would you please stop calling? He's silent. I'm serious, I tell him, If I'm not calling you back there's a good reason. Like what? he says, and I tilt my head to the sky. Listen to me, I say, I have your number programmed into my phone as Scott's, and Joel's never going to believe that Scott's been calling me every hour on the hour. Then maybe you should tell him the truth, Trainor says.

In light of the past twenty-four hours, his suggestion sounds even more insane than it would otherwise. Trainor, I say, I can't talk to you now. When *can* you talk? he asks. I don't know, I admit. I'm leaving Monday afternoon, he reminds me, I want to see you before I leave. I'll see what I can do, I tell him, and I hang up before he can cajole me into promising something I don't plan on delivering.

~ ~ ~

Trainor calls the next morning when we're still in bed, and again a few hours later while we're out by the pool. Both times I let him roll to voice mail, and when he phones as Joel and I are cooking dinner that night I turn off my cell entirely. I suppose I'm taking a risk—he could call on the home number—but I honestly don't think he's that stupid. I'll see him soon enough anyway; he'll be at the office in the morning, before he heads for the airport. And then I won't have to deal with him for a week. The thought makes me light-headed.

Why are you smiling? Joel asks. He's adding currants to the couscous he's making, and I turn my attention back to the halibut, murmuring something about feeling better. He slips a currant between my lips. His fingers taste like cinnamon. Sometimes, he says, You just have to take a step back.

Over dinner we revisit the idea that's held us captive all weekend. He listens as I reinvent myself, as I tell him that I've wondered for a long time whether I should follow in my father's footsteps, as I confess that I've missed the horses more than I thought I would. I don't think I have my father's touch, I admit, but he shakes his head and lets me dream. I could start small, with just a few thoroughbreds, and then work my way up from there. We could still live central, I assure him, but maybe I could have a place just outside the city, a place that would enable me to get back in touch with whatever's been missing from my life the past year. My father would be proud of that, I think. You could wear cocoa-colored ropers, Joel tells me, And some kick-ass jeans. I should've known you'd want to dress me, I mutter, but I'm smiling, and I want to drown in the smile he returns.

After dinner he insists that I relax while he cleans the kitchen, and I wander around for a while before ending up in his studio. I don't think I've spent any time in here since last fall, and I examine the canvases he has lined up against the wall, as well as the one on his easel. He's working with water imagery; I recognize the lake in just about every painting. The colors he's chosen—blues, greens, grays, pinks—resemble those on our bedroom ceiling, but he's blended them in a way that evoke an entirely different emotion. I actually feel a faint apprehension, and I lean closer, trying to figure out why.

The calm before the storm, he says, and I turn. He gestures toward the painting in front of me, one of the largest. Here, he says, tilting the canvas toward the window when I fail to see. I stare into the paint, into the swirls of oil that comprise the water. The lake holds the reflection of the clouds, and as my eyes move from the water to an impeccable sky I gasp. With fresh eyes I scour the painting again, and though I try to draw my gaze to that pristine sky the water sucks me back.

Lowering himself to the black leather sofa that he and James bought in college, Joel tells me that he's been working on them since the beginning of the year. Has Cameron seen them? I ask, referring to the gallery owner who offered him his first show and who has been a staunch supporter ever since. A couple of weeks ago, he admits, and I say, What does he think? I'd like to know what *you* think, he tells me. They're amazing, Joel, I say.

He won't let me get away with such an elementary critique, not anymore, and he waits as I sift through the canvases again. They practically vibrate, I finally tell him. He nods, and I admit that at the same time they're unbearably foreboding. I have a feeling this one won't leave me, I say, pointing to the first one I saw, This one might follow me into my dreams. Let's hope not, he says. So what does Cameron think? I ask. Cameron's pleased, he tells me, Cameron's impatient to show them. I can see why, I say, turning to the canvas again, though night has fallen and I can no longer decipher its intricacies. I ask when he's thinking of releasing them. Spring, he says, hesitating. That seems like a long time from now, I tell him, joining him on the sofa. Well, he says, looking thoughtful, I don't think I'm finished.

We make love for the first time that weekend in his studio, surrounded by canvas. Shedding our clothes, we hold each other aloft, the way we should. The sheer weight of all that water threatens to drown us both, but instead we float, without fear of the dark. I hold his heart to mine.

~ ~ ~

The next morning on my way to the office I check my voice mail, listening to the three Trainor sent yesterday as well as the one he sent before I was even awake this morning. Apparently he was hoping I could meet him before work, but I'd still been asleep, having made a joint decision with Joel that if I'm going to make an effort to disengage then there's no reason for me to continue to get to the office early or stay late. The fact that Trainor will be out of town on business for the next week gives me the jump-start I need, and when I get to work I motion him into my office before he can follow me in there himself. I left you a voice mail, he says. You left me several, I tell him, Even though I told you to stop calling. I was worried about you, he protests, and I assure him that I'm fine. You weren't fine last week, he reminds me. Well, I'm fine now, I tell him.

He regards me for a minute, then ventures that seeing each other before he leaves for an entire week would have been nice. Is there something you need to tell me? he asks. I'm tired, I admit, deciding to be honest,

I'm sick of worrying about whether or not I'm going to get caught. So be upfront with him, he says.

That he's made the suggestion three times in the last few days shouldn't surprise me. You're not happy anyway, he adds, and I grit my teeth and assure him that there are many different reasons I'm not happy, not the least of which happens to be him. You certainly didn't seem to feel that way last weekend, he says. He's spoken stiffly, and I remind myself not to be foolish. I want to end this, but I don't necessarily want to anger him. I'm not sure how he'll react if I cut him off entirely. Would he retaliate, maybe call Joel? Would he tell Vincent?

Look, I say, I just need a little space. What am I supposed to do in the meantime? he asks, and I point out that he's going out of town for a few days anyway. Maybe this will give us both a chance to figure out what we want, I say, leaving room for him to think that I might in fact figure out that I want him. He looks me up and down, apparently trying to decide whether or not he should trust me or his instincts. I do my best not to let my gaze waver, and after a minute he sighs. We'll talk next week, he says. Absolutely, I agree.

I keep my head down for the rest of the day, barely lifting it from my desk when Trainor pops in to say a quick, professional goodbye before he leaves for the airport. I get a fair amount of work accomplished, but I manage to check in with Joel a half a dozen times, promising to come home the second I can.

The rest of the week follows similarly. I don't make any waves, nor do I make any significant contributions. I go to work and I come home, where Joel and I start tentatively talking about our assets. Every time we have one problem figured out we think of something else. Medical insurance, I say, to which he shrugs, a reaction I find juvenile. I can scrounge up some kind of part-time work, he says when our resources come up short, and I shake my head. We find that we're better off talking in generalities for now, and I set our paperwork aside, and let him tell me about the house he found for rent off 35th that might be perfect for us. I lay my head on his chest as he talks, then move lower, so that I'm resting on his belly. He runs his hand through my hair as I listen to the soft conversation beneath his skin, my eyes closed. I want to hear everything I can.

We make love every night that week, and by the time I get home from work late Friday afternoon I know he'll be waiting for me. We don't go into his studio, or out by the pool; we don't collapse on the stairs, the way we have in the past. Instead we go upstairs to our bedroom, where we lie beneath colors that meld one into the other with the same ease as our breath. What happens if we move? I ask, indicating the painting above us. I'm half-afraid he'll tell me that its fate will be the same as the wall at his old house, but I worry for nothing. *When* we move, he says, gently correcting me, We'll take it with us. I gaze up at the ceiling, then admit, haltingly, that we could use the money. Maybe, he says, But it's not for sale.

~   ~   ~

Scott gets in touch with me the next morning, which doesn't seem to surprise Joel, but stuns the hell out of me. We've not spoken since the day after the incident at the lake; he'd called to check up on me then, and I never called him back. These days I don't seem to have the time for friends, and the fact that Scott has made his feelings about my affair clear doesn't necessarily incline me toward spending time with him. I answer his call warily, but he pretends as if he's done nothing out of the ordinary and invites me to lunch. Lunch? I echo, and he says, You know, the meal between breakfast and dinner. He's spending the weekend at Kyle's, he says, so I should just come out there. Well, I say, ruminating. I glance over at Joel, who's loading twenty dollars worth of oranges into the juicer. All right, I say to Scott, I'll see you at noon.

I'm glad you're seeing him, Joel confides once I've hung up. I sit down at the kitchen table, turning my chair to the side so I can stretch my legs. I wouldn't necessarily think he'd want me to spend time with Scott, considering the way he feels about how Scott's treating Kyle. But he shrugs as if he knows what I'm thinking, then flips on the juicer and raises his voice to make himself heard. I know you talk to him a lot, he says, an observation which causes me to shift uncomfortably in my seat; after all, every time Trainor calls he appears on my Caller ID as Scott. Joel adjusts the juicer's speed, then tells me that talking to someone on the phone and actually spending time with him are two different things. You've dedicated all your time the past few months to work, he says, And you're worried about your dad....

117

He trails off. I spoke to my mother this morning, and I could tell from the tone of her voice that she thought I should make another trip home. Would next weekend work for you? she asked, and I said yes without talking to Joel, who looked pained when I told him of my plans. I have Art Reach next weekend, he said.

Art Reach comes around once a year, though it's something with which Joel's been involved for only the past three summers. Part of the city's community outreach program, Art Reach enlists local artists to teach classes to area kids, many of whom don't have access to anything more than whatever their local elementary school provides. Some artists even open up their studios for tours, though Joel has intimated that he's not interested in allowing his space to be scrutinized. To be honest, I'm consistently surprised by his involvement in the program, and when he reminded me this morning I realized again how much he has changed. I also hesitated, wanting to alter my plans in light of his schedule, but torn by the beseeching quality of my mother's voice. Go, Joel said, trying to make my decision easier, You should go, and I'll just make sure to go next time.

Now I watch as he pours the juice, then hands me a glass. Steeling myself against the pulp, I take a small sip, but he's blended the oranges until the pulp's barely discernible and I take another, larger sip. Good, huh? he says, grinning. If we move, I tell him, We're going to have to go back to Minute Maid. *When* we move, he says, We'll just drink less juice. I finish off my glass, and he pours me what's left. Go to lunch with Scott, he says, Spend some time with your friend. I nod. Go, he says.

~   ~   ~

You look like shit, Scott tells me when he opens Kyle's door. The way he's examining me I half-expect him to walk a slow circle around me, and I give him a look to stop him before he does. Ushering me inside, he tells me I might have dropped a little weight in the past month or so. But not much, he adds. Can I look forward to your critique for the full afternoon? I ask, and he says, Would you rather I wasn't honest? I *know* I look like shit, I tell him, I don't need you to remind me. He shrugs, then offers me a drink. I'll take a beer, I say, knowing full well that he's hoping I'll err on the side of something crisp and light. He shakes his head, but gestures me into the living room, then momentarily disappears, returning with a foaming glass of beer for me and a white wine for himself. Cheers, he says.

We sit on the sofa, a sleek, contemporary piece that probably cost more than all of the furniture in my great room. Hurriedly, I sip my beer, lessening my chances of spilling it on the white upholstery. Are you in a rush? Scott asks, propping his elbow on the back of the sofa and leaning his head on one fist. I shake my head, setting my beer beside me on the coffee table. Without missing a beat, Scott slides a coaster under my glass. You're awfully comfortable here, aren't you? I muse. I practically live here, Scott reminds me. Practically, I say, But not quite.

I don't know why I'm trying to antagonize him. He's invited me to lunch, after all. But the ease with which he's managed to juggle two men, without animosity on anyone's part—at least until recently—rubs me the wrong way. He's clearly not suffering as a result of his choices; if anything he looks better than he did at Kyle's party last month. Buff, brown, well-groomed... didn't I used to be all those things? I glance inadvertently at his smooth-shaven legs. So you ended it, he says. I frown. Trainor, he says, prompting me, and I say, Why would you think...? Oh, c'mon, he says, Joel talks to Kyle, Kyle talks to me.... I gulp, before he corrects me. I know you've spent a lot more time at home this past week, he says, Joel tells Kyle.... He squints, trying to remember. Joel tells Kyle, he says, That you've never been more *present*. He seems pleased that he's recalled the exact word, and he leans forward, inviting me to share his confidence. Is that why you asked me to come here? I say, So you could get the dirt?

Scott gives me a hurt look, but admits that he wanted to hear for himself whether or not I'd come to my senses. Have *you?* I ask, knowing that in his situation the question doesn't apply. He's unperturbed, and unwilling to let me off the hook. Trainor's out of town, I finally tell him. Scott lifts his head from his fist. I'm ending it, I hasten to assure him, and he says, When? Why is this any of your business? I ask. Because every other day, he says, I have to listen to Kyle yammer on about how he's worried about Joel. He gives me a minute to let that sink in, then repeats his earlier assessment that I look like shit. I get the impression, he says, That your affair isn't doing anyone any good. What do you want from me? I ask, and he says, I want to see you get yourself together.

119

I turn my eyes to the window. Kyle's view of Lake Austin far surpasses my view of Lake Travis, and I stare out at the water. There's not a hint of the turmoil I saw in Joel's paintings, and my gaze automatically shifts to the canvas Kyle has on the opposite wall, an early painting of Joel's. Will you take that shit down? Joel pleads just about every time he's here. He considers the work sophomoric, and truth be told, the painting can't compare with anything he's done in recent years. But Kyle has a soft spot for it, and when he remodeled a couple of years ago he moved the painting from his bedroom into the living room. My bedroom doesn't get the same traffic it used to, he told Joel, trying to justify its placement. Joel shook his head, grimacing when Kyle added that he liked being able to tell his guests that he has the very first Grayson ever sold. I stare into the painting, wondering how I'd feel if someone was vying for the opportunity to purchase an Atwater.

I'm trying, I mumble. How hard? Scott asks. I'm doing plenty, I tell him, and he says, ticking off a list on his fingers, Therapy, anti-anxiety medication.... He drifts off, then offers the suggestion that maybe if I just cut Trainor loose I'd fare a little better. I'm incensed, both by how much he knows, and by his presumption. You need to get control of the situation, he tells me, Because right now this situation's controlling you.

He's not saying anything I don't know. I'm clearly not the one at the helm, and I reach for what's left of my beer. I'd offer you another, Scott tells me, But I think we should eat first. *Are* we eating? I say, I thought I was here just so you could abuse me.

So how was it? Joel asks when I finally come home, and I tell him that Scott knows more details about my life right now than I'd like. He actually blushes. Kyle, Lydia, I say, James. I cross my arms over my chest. Anyone else? I ask, and he apologizes, but reminds me how much trouble we've had until recently. One week, I realize, looking at him, we've only been okay for one week. Instead of feeling reassured I see how tentative we still are. And we've got another appointment with Lydia in a few hours. Relax, Joel says, catching my expression and my hand at the same time, Everything's going to be fine.

~ ~ ~

Considering the tension that characterized our first two sessions with Lydia, our third seems almost boring. We've met on Saturday afternoon at her request because of a scheduling conflict; Joel appears grateful that she was able to squeeze us in, but I would have been perfectly happy to skip a week. I don't know that we can attribute any of the progress we've made since our last session to Lydia herself, but I'm not sure Joel agrees. He's practically glowing, and he announces to my mild embarrassment that we started talking the evening of our last session, that we've spent more time together in the past week than we've spent all year, that we've slept together every night. Lydia's careful to hold his gaze while he talks, then turns to me; she's trying to ascertain whether or not I've cut ties with Trainor. What other reason could there be for my sudden, inexplicable presence? The calm before the storm, I say, and they both look at me, eyebrows raised. But I'm only trying to change the subject, and I tell her about the paintings Joel and I examined again just last night. Sometimes I forget what a gift he has, I admit. Joel manages an expression of modesty, but I knock his leg with my own. You know you're good, I tell him. So you say, he agrees, but he's grinning and Lydia actually smiles.

I'm a little surprised when Joel tells her what we've been thinking, that maybe it's time for me to quit my job, to sell the house. I hadn't thought about sharing our plans with anyone, and spoken outside of our circle of intimacy they sound somewhat ill-conceived. We don't have the particulars worked out yet, I say, but Joel gives his head a firm shake. We will, he tells her. Lydia nods, giving me a curious look when Joel mentions my plan to breed thoroughbreds. Just an idea, I say sheepishly. We're taking everything slowly, Joel concedes, reaching for my hand, For now.

Our session proceeds without incident until the very end, when we're scheduling a time to see Lydia next week. What I'd like to do, she says, Is spend some time with each of you alone. Why? I ask, not realizing until after I've spoken how defensive the question sounds. I clear my throat. I mean, I say, If we're in couples counseling, shouldn't we be here as a couple? She gives me a patient smile, which I should consider pretty generous, being that she knows exactly why I don't want to talk to her alone. That's fine with me, Joel volunteers, frowning in my direction. Of course, I say. Good, she says, Next week then.

Are you all right? Joel asks once we're in the car. I nod, adjusting the rearview mirror. You're sure, he says, and I tell him that if he honestly wants to know the truth I feel as if I've been through therapy twice today. Scott and Lydia both in one afternoon was a little much, I confess. He's quick to offer to pick up dinner later, reminds me that we have nothing going on, not tonight, not tomorrow. We'll just relax, he says.

But I don't relax, not as much as I have the past seven days. There's too much on the horizon: Trainor's return, another therapy session with Lydia, another trip to Kentucky next weekend. I really don't think I can take much more, and Sunday night I decline Joel's invitation to curl up with a movie and opt instead for pacing back and forth in front of the windows. Relax, Joel keeps saying, Relax. Is that your new mantra? I finally snap, and he bites his lip, for the first time in nine days.

~ ~ ~

I head to work the next morning with a firm resolution to tell Trainor that I'm done. Over the past week what little contact we've had has been professional, and while I have to admit that I'm surprised by the space he's given me, I'm also grateful. Who knows? Maybe he's decided himself that we're better off without each other.

But his smile upon my arrival at the office conveys no such conclusion. I missed you, he says without mincing words once I've shut my door. Trainor, I start, and he says, When can I see you? I shake my head, my lips pressed together. Tonight? he asks. I'm busy, I say softly. Tomorrow, then, he suggests, and I lower my eyes.

He doesn't miss a beat. Instead he moves on to his sales figures from last week, and tells me that he'll send me an update about his trip to North Carolina by the end of the day. Vincent wants a copy as well, he adds. I nod, without actually hearing him. Not this easily, I'm thinking. There's no way he's going to let me off this easily. But he heads for the door when he's finished without another word about what's just happened between us. I'll email that update as soon as I can, he says over his shoulder.

I should know better than to gloat, but I can't help shooting Scott an email. Done, I write. And without a hint of bitterness. I feel oddly empowered, and the resultant energy surprises me. I take a look at my calendar, then dig in with a relish I haven't felt in a long time. I accomplish so much, in fact, that I work right through lunch, pausing long enough to touch base with Joel just briefly before burying myself again.

When I finally shut down my laptop a little after six and head for my car I can't help noticing the bounce in my step. Joel told me he's going for a run, but he's promised to be back in enough time to cook dinner, and I actually admitted that I was thinking about getting back on my bike. He seemed so pleased by my resolution that he practically congratulated me.

I've had a good day, a much better day than I expected. I'm not necessarily ready to recommit myself to this job on a long-term basis, but in the interim I have a decent gig that pays the bills, and pays them well. The fact that Trainor has kept his distance certainly helps. I'd expected him to corner me at some point, but he's afforded me the same professional courtesies he offers everyone else, and though there's a part of me that feels vaguely wounded—am I really so forgettable?—I also know that I couldn't have asked for a better parting. Even Scott admitted when he emailed back that I lucked out.

I'm not naïve enough to think that I have everything all worked out; I still have a long week ahead of me, and an even longer weekend. There's a lot of damage to undo. But today was good. Today was a start.

Jennifer Hritz

$$\overline{5)}$$

I find out the next morning that my week's about to get even easier. Trainor's leaving again to go out of town, to some conference I remember Vincent mentioning six weeks ago. I could spend more time wondering why Vincent's sending Trainor instead of me, but the easy answer is that I've spent so much time out of the office already. Of course I need to be here. And I'm exponentially grateful for the time alone.

Every day I'm away from Trainor gives me that much more confidence that I won't return, and even though I'm apprehensive about the upcoming weekend, I'm not dreading my visit with my parents as much as I expected. As a matter of fact, I can't remember the last time I was home without Joel, and my sister has informed me that she's going to take the opportunity to spend some time with her own family. I'll miss seeing you, she says, But I could use the break. I'm fine with the idea, and think that maybe I'll be able to take advantage of the time alone with my father. Maybe, years from now, I'll look back on this weekend fondly.

I have one hurdle before I can leave for the airport on Friday: Joel and I are meeting with Lydia again. I'm not thrilled with the prospect of spending time alone with her; I remember too well what happened during our first session. But I've managed to get through two weeks without Trainor, and that more than anything alleviates the dread I might otherwise feel driving to meet with her. Hey, I say to Joel when I find him in the waiting room. He grins, dropping his magazine and reaching for my hand. I know without asking how his day has been; he's changed his clothes, but paint still stains his bare arms. I brush his cheek, where a thin streak of pink has eluded him. I didn't have time to shower, he admits. And you did a half-assed job of cleaning up, I add. He laughs, and when Lydia opens the door to her office we stand with a smile.

True to her word, she reminds us as we sit down next to each other that she'd like a little bit of time alone with each of us. How was your week? she asks, and Joel glances at me before volunteering that we're actually both doing pretty well. Adam? she asks, looking at me for confirmation. I nod my head, allowing that while I'm a bit apprehensive about my trip to Kentucky, we've had a good week. Is there anything you want to address together? she asks, and when we shake our heads she turns to me. Adam, I'd like to talk to you first, she says.

I'd figured as much, and as soon as the door closes behind Joel and I'm sure he's out of earshot I tell her what I've done. I ended it, I say, hoping these three words will redeem me. She doesn't say anything, and worried that she doesn't believe me I nod. I haven't seen him for two weeks, I say, then amend, Well, I see him at work.

I've just offered her more information about Trainor than I ever have, and after a minute I can't take her eyes on me anymore. Lowering my gaze, I thread my fingers together and hook them over my knee. How long did your affair last? she asks. I wince at the word, then admit that it started after the holidays, in January. She wants to know if this was my first.

I'm hurt, though I have no right. Yes, I say, And my last. I tell her that I don't want to hurt Joel, that I never wanted to hurt Joel, that I won't tell him what I've done precisely for that reason. What do you think would happen if you told him? she asks, and I close my eyes. I don't even want to imagine that scenario, or its ramifications. I have a feeling he'd leave me, and I tell her I can't bear the thought. The last couple of weeks, I say, Have been so much better. How so? she asks, and I have to smile, a sheepish smile that she eventually returns. They've been better because I haven't seen Trainor.

So you've ended the affair, she says, And your relationship with Joel feels back on track. I nod. Cataloguing what's right in my life helps, and to the list I add the possibilities that Joel and I have been trying to work out on the side. Maybe we've come to a turning point. Maybe everything has happened for a reason.

Lydia's watching me, and I give her another smile, taking a quick look at the clock. If she's going to break up our session the way she suggested we can't have too much time together, and I actually unfold my legs, expecting her to tell me that she's ready for Joel. Instead she says, The last time we spoke alone you told me about Bobby.

I plummet from my high. In a matter of hours I'm going to be back in Lexington, driving highways we used to drive together. I look off to the side, noticing for the first time the half a dozen stuffed animals arranged on the windowsill. Are they therapeutic? I wonder. You're welcome to hold one, Lydia offers, and after a moment's hesitation I stand and walk over to the window. Does Joel ever...? I ask. A time or two, she admits. I try to imagine which one he likes, deliberating before I pick the monkey in the middle. She gives her head a slight shake, and I know I've chosen differently. I sit down anyway, plucking at the white tuft of fur on the monkey's tail. It's hard going back, I admit. To your parents' house? she asks, and I say, To Kentucky. You and Bobby lived in Kentucky, she says. I nod, then tell her that we met in college, and stayed in Lexington after we graduated. When was he diagnosed? she asks. Holding the monkey's paws between my fingers, I spread its arms wide, then fold them together. In June of 1990, I say, I had just turned twenty-five.

Lydia watches as I chuck the monkey under its chin. I know what she must be wondering, what everyone wondered when they found out Bobby was sick. Was I the one who had infected him? I would certainly have been more inclined to have multiple partners; Bobby wasn't the type. The weight of those assumptions almost buried me, and until one of our friends finally came right out and asked if I was HIV positive I walked around with the same stigma Bobby did. I realized, though, when I told our friend I was fine that he'd naturally come to the conclusion that Bobby had slept with someone else. That was almost worse.

He cheated on me, I say to Lydia. Curling the monkey's tail around its body, I laugh. How's that for irony? I ask, glancing up at her, He cheated on me, one time, without protection. I uncoil the monkey's tail. In the backseat of our car, I mutter, and she says, That was unlucky. Bobby was unlucky, I tell her. He had you, she points out, and I shift my eyes. Yes, I say. You could've left him, she says.

I knelt in front of him that day and tried to take him in my arms as he shook me away. March, he said, When you were away. I said the only word that made sense, and he corrected me, looking scared and sick and determined to tell me the truth. I don't believe you, I said, though by then I knew he wasn't lying.

He clung to me like a child, but I peeled myself away from him and walked out the door with a suitcase in my hand. When I got to Julia's I hammered on her door until my brother-in-law answered. I told her everything, drinking one bourbon after another until I finally passed out on her couch. When I came to the next morning I caught a glimpse of her and Ivan in the kitchen. From the way he was holding her I could tell she'd told him everything, and I watched as he placed one small kiss on her forehead. Then I went home.

Bobby was wearing the same clothes he'd worn to work the previous day. He was sitting on the floor beneath the window, and I walked halfway toward him, then dropped to my hands and knees and crawled. When I reached him I laid my head in his lap; he took a deep, shaky breath that seemed to come from somewhere deep inside of him. We didn't move for the rest of the day.

Adam, Lydia says, and I blink, shaking my head at the box of tissues she slides across the coffee table. Instead I tuck the monkey in the crook of my arm. He stares up at me, a red felt tongue poking through his wide lips. I touch the material with the tip of my finger. You were young, she says. That doesn't make what happened any less of a betrayal, I tell her. No, she agrees, I imagine it doesn't.

I shift the monkey to my other arm, as if it's a newborn, as if its head weighs more than a few ounces and my bicep feels the strain. I talked about all of this in therapy years ago, I finally tell her, then listen as she reminds me that I've just admitted that going back to Kentucky sends me back a dozen years, that my father's illness can't help but complicate my feelings. What would happen if you called your parents and told them you simply didn't feel up to the trip? she asks. I set the monkey on my knee; if I don't hold him in just the right way, his head flops to his chest. I just have to get through it, I say.

We decide that we'll return to this conversation next week, and she assures me that if at any point over the weekend I want to talk to her I can give her a call. I wonder if she affords all of her clients the same liberties or if she's making a special exception because of Joel. Would you like a minute? she asks, but I shake my head and place the monkey back on the windowsill. Everything okay? Joel asks when I open the door. I nod, and he touches my arm before he follows Lydia inside.

Once they've disappeared I ease myself into a chair. I could sleep right here, right now; these sessions wear me out. Every detail I recall brings another to the surface, and I close my eyes, listening to the water feature trickling in the corner and willing it to relax me. Twenty minutes, I think, closing my eyes. Maybe I can just sleep for twenty minutes.

I'm in the car with them. The air's cold; they haven't turned on the engine, and from my vantage point in the front I can see my breath. Just in case, I try to flip on the heater, but nothing ushers forth from the vents I tilt in my direction. I can hear them in the back, their short grunts and a gasp from Bobby that I know from experience can mean only one thing. I peer through the gap between the seats, one hand covering my erection. He's wearing a coat, a black overcoat that hides what he's doing, and he slaps my hand away when I try to move it aside. I can't get a good look at his face. Bobby glances at me over his shoulder; he's bracing himself against the door, his breath fogging the window. You're home early, he says. What're you doing? I cry, and he laughs, the laugh that almost killed me. The button on my jeans slides through my shaky fingers, the zipper catching my skin like tiny teeth. Sleet clatters against the windows as I take my erection in my hand. You're not immune, Bobby informs me, and I take another look at the man who holds my lover's hips. The man grins back, his teeth yellow in the glare of the headlights baring down on us. Look out, he says.

When Joel says my name I jerk upright, scrambling to my feet before I can even orient myself. Hey, he says, Hang on, hang on. I catch sight of Lydia, who stands in the doorway of her office with a concerned expression. I'm fine, I say, swallowing, I'm fine. I yank on Joel's sleeve. C'mon, I say, Let's go.

We have thirty minutes to kill before I have to be at the airport, and we stop at a coffee shop. I sit at a table while he orders tea for both of us at the front counter, ignoring my request for an Americano. Don't be ridiculous, he said when I asked, You're shaking. I didn't have the strength to argue, and now I watch as he comes to the table carrying two mugs of chamomile tea drizzled with honey. I cup my hands around the mug he offers and bend my head over the steam. Now, he says, Would you please tell me what happened back there?

Keeping my eyes on the mug, I watch as the tea bleeds into a rich amber, then run my finger along the rim to catch a bead of honey. I'm not sure what to tell him, whether I should admit that my conversations with Lydia are mostly about Bobby, whether I should confess that every trip back to Kentucky mires me in a quicksand of memories. I shake my head. Joel sits back in his chair with a sigh. Honey, he says, You're going to have to open up.

I protest, though I know what he means. Our conversations the past couple of weeks have been weightier than they've been in almost a year, but so far we've talked about nothing save for my job and the escape plan we've hatched, a plan I fear won't ever come to pass. We've barely touched on my father's illness, and I've certainly never spoken about Bobby. Holding my tea to my lips, I take a sip. He's right; the hot liquid calms my nerves, and after a minute I take a deep breath. Better? he says, and I nod.

We don't have much time to linger, but I manage to finish my tea. He watches me, doodling half-heartedly on a napkin. I'm reluctant to put you on that plane, he says when I glance at my BlackBerry, intimating that we need to leave. I'm fine, Joel, I say, and he shakes his head. I think you'd be better off here with me, he mutters. Well, I admit, getting to my feet and giving him a wry smile, I'm not going to argue with that.

~ ~ ~

I have a feeling that if Joel had driven me to the airport, if he'd put his arms around me before I could get inside the terminal, I might have decided not to go. For that reason I'm glad I drove myself, and I board my plane trying to ease myself back toward the relative calm I felt finishing my tea as I sat across from him in that coffee shop. But now that I've called Bobby to the surface he refuses to let me go. Coaxing me through time, he takes me to our bedroom, where he told me everything. I watch the tarmac disappear.

We weren't asleep, neither one of us, though we'd been in bed more than an hour. The night was dark and overcast; we were missing a moon, and even with my eyes open I couldn't see his face. But I knew he wasn't asleep. We'd come to bed too early, given how long we'd slept the night before, exhaustion catching us as we sat beneath the living room window and sending us into a sleep so deep we hadn't awakened until noon. I'd been battling a crick in my neck ever since, and I tried to rub it loose, realizing that even if he offered to knead the muscle—and he wouldn't—I didn't want him to touch me. The thought brought tears to my eyes, and I blinked them away before they could spill onto my cheeks.

I was getting tested the next day, running by the doctor's office on my way to work. We'd talked about it over dinner, a tasteless pizza and one too many beers. He wanted to come with me, and I told him no. I didn't want him involved in the testing process, didn't want him coming with me when I had the blood drawn, didn't want him accompanying me when I went back for the news. And I was pretty sure what I'd hear. We'd been having unprotected sex for more than three months.

I was angry; how could I not be angry? But mostly I was afraid, and not just because of what the rest of my life probably held in store. I knew if I turned up HIV positive Bobby would never be able to forgive himself. As much as he'd begged for me not to leave him when he saw me heading out that door a couple of days earlier, I don't think he was all that surprised to see me go. The fact that I'd returned seemed to shock him more.

Turning onto my back, I adjusted the covers around my waist. We'd parted the curtains in front of the open window, but there wasn't a breeze and I fought against the oppressive air, wanting to be cool but needing the comfort my grandmother's quilt offered me. Beside me Bobby sighed without contentment, and the thought suddenly occurred to me for the first time that I could right now be at the scene of the crime. I didn't think Bobby would ever bring someone back to our house, let alone our bed, but then again, I didn't think Bobby would ever cheat on me. Gripping the quilt in my hands I asked him.

He told me with an eagerness he couldn't belie, and I realized instantly the folly of my request. He had no one else to tell. He was barely on speaking terms with his parents, and most of our friends were really friends of mine. He wanted me to know not just because confessing would help to alleviate his guilt, but because he had no one else to tell.

I didn't want the details. I wanted reassurance that he hadn't betrayed me here, in our bedroom, beneath my grandmother's quilt, but I didn't want to hear the rest. Not that he'd been invited to a happy hour with some of his co-workers after I called to tell him that my business trip was going to last a day longer than I'd thought, and not that he'd gone along because I was forever complaining that he never socialized with anyone. I didn't want to think about the man at the bar who eyed him, causing him to flush with both embarrassment—he was afraid his co-workers would see—as well as flattery. Bobby wasn't used to being targeted. He'd turned back to his conversation, and when he looked up again the man was gone. He'd made it halfway to his car thirty minutes later when the man approached.

Though the thought pained me, I could see Bobby, standing in the balmy breeze that night and talking to the man, a stranger he doesn't describe but who must have been passably attractive for him to linger. Where can I go around here, the man asked, For a decent drink? Taking too long to answer, taken aback as Bobby was, the man smiled. Maybe, he said, I've already found what I'm looking for.

They had sex in the back of our car. They could've gone to the man's hotel— he was in town from California—but halfway there they pulled to the side of the road. What did that mean? I thought as I lay there next to him, listening to his words spill one into the other. That they couldn't wait? That Bobby was already halfway through a hand job? I squeezed my eyes shut, trying to erase the image even as Bobby created it for me. They kissed, then crawled into the back seat. Before Bobby knew what was happening the man was inside of him, and one of Bobby's knees was digging into the floorboard. That must have been uncomfortable, I said.

I spoke because I couldn't take anymore. The details were too intimate, too agonizing, the aftermath too much to contemplate without screaming. Listening to him, I thought I might. For the first time fury welled up inside of me, and I knew I'd either scream or throw up. Instead I spoke in a low voice I expected him to understand, a voice weighted down with hurt and disap- pointment and warning. That must have been uncomfortable, I said.

He laughed, and the sound assaulted my ears. I almost didn't hear him agree with me, and though I knew deep down that Bobby wasn't cruel, or cal- lous, that he was trying to make sense of what he'd done, that he was talking to me as he'd always talked to me, as his best friend, I still felt as if he'd kicked me in the gut. I turned to look at him, just as he realized his mistake. Adam, he said, and I burst into tears. Muffling my cries with my pillow, I sobbed, great wracking sobs that shook the bed.

I don't feel the flight attendant's hand until she speaks. Sir, she says, and I stare at her. His laugh echoes around me. Sir, she repeats. I look around. I'm the only one left on the plane, and I wipe my eyes and unclasp my seatbelt, mumbling an apology. A quick glance at my watch tells me that unless I move I'll be hard-pressed to make my connection. Don't forget your bag, the flight attendant says, smiling.

Staring up at the monitors after I've disembarked, I find that my next flight's delayed. I trudge to the gate anyway, turning on my BlackBerry at the same time. Joel had asked me to send him a text when I landed in Dallas and I shoot one off with trembling fingers, then hesitate in front of the bar just down from my gate. A drink might calm me, and I lean my bag against the counter and hoist myself onto a stool. Bourbon, I say when the bartender looks my way, Neat. She asks if I want to start a tab and I decline, then take a long swallow. Not as healthy as chamomile tea, maybe, but definitely stronger.

As if he can hear my thoughts, Joel chooses that minute to call. I texted you, I tell him, without saying hello. I know, he says, choosing to overlook the abrupt manner in which I've answered, But I wanted to hear your voice. I'm fine, I say. How was the flight? he asks. Miserable, I tell him. Window seat? he asks.

He's trying his hand at banter, in an attempt to loosen me up, and I smile in spite of myself. Yes, as a matter of fact, I say. A window seat in coach, he muses, Could be worse. How? I ask. But I've posed the question with too much bitterness, and he pauses. All right, he says, What's going on?

Draining my glass, I signal for the bartender. One more, I say, and she fills a glass as I pull my wallet from my back pocket. Are you drinking? Joel asks. Copiously, I say. Seriously, he says, and I tell him that I'm about to start on my second bourbon. Can you cut yourself off at two? he asks. Gee, I don't know, Joel, I say, starting to get annoyed, I kind of thought I'd stick around the airport bar for a while, see if I can't get a little drunk before my flight. I hand the bartender a ten. You don't think that's a bad idea, do you? I ask, If I show up at my parents' house wasted? Are you angry? he asks. You sound like Lydia, I mutter.

He's quiet, pretending that he's insulted though in reality he's probably flattered. I wish I was there with you, he finally says. You don't drink anymore, I point out. I know that's not what he meant, that he's not interested in hanging out at the airport bar with me so much as accompanying me to Kentucky to see my father. But he plays along with me anyway. I might have a drink, he says. Oh yeah? I say, What would you order, a Shirley Temple? Too much sugar, he admits. You're impossible, I tell him, speaking with irritated affection. That's what keeps you interested, he says.

I take a sip of my drink, glancing again at my BlackBerry. I still have a lot of time to kill, and I can already feel the alcohol. I'm not usually such a lightweight, and I wonder if the session with Lydia and the subsequent dream has anything to do with how drained I suddenly feel. For just a second I hear Bobby's laugh again, and I shake my head, turning my attention back to Joel. He's going out tonight, he says, though he wants me to call him when I land. Where're you going? I ask. Circuit party, he says.

I know he's joking, but under the circumstances I don't want to think about him dancing or partying or fucking anyone else. Honey, he says, I'm kidding. I know, I sigh. Running my hand back and forth through my hair, I catch a glimpse of my reflection in the mirror above the bar. I look exhausted. Are you listening to me? Joel asks. Yes, I say, No.

He tells me I should go. I'll be at Kyle's, he says, Did you at least hear that part? Kyle's, I repeat. Yes, he says, He invited me over to watch a movie, which is a euphemism for telling me that he wants to talk about Scott. That sounds like a beating, I admit. You've been talking to Scott a lot lately, he says, Do you have any idea what he's thinking? I don't, I say, and he sighs. Then I guess I'm on my own, he says.

I wish him good luck, and tell him that I'll touch base when I land, and it's probably the fact that he reminds me to cut myself off at two drinks that makes me order a third when I've finished the second. A more inexperienced bartender would probably point out that I could've set up a tab, but this one just slides another glass my way. I give her an extra five.

134

I'm halfway through that drink when Trainor calls. A myriad of thoughts skirts through my mind as I scrutinize my Blackberry's screen, but common sense overrides any fear I have that he's looking for something intimate. After all, he's my subordinate, and anyway, we've gone two weeks without talking outside of the office. We used to be friends once, and maybe we've gotten just enough space from each other that we can simply go back to the way things were before I made the mistake of sleeping with him. In some ways I actually miss him, and instead of realizing that maybe I should turn my attention to Scott or any of the other friends with whom I've lost touch over the past year I answer with a robust hello, made heartier by the amount of liquor I've consumed.

I'm surprised you answered, Trainor says dryly, You must be alone. Very much so, I tell him. Are you at the airport then? he asks. I'm mildly taken aback by his knowledge of my whereabouts, until I realize he probably overhead me telling Darlene where I was headed this weekend. I am, I admit, I'm at the bar.

I've volunteered this information too readily, but he doesn't seem bothered by my confession. If anything, he's amused. Not just alone, he says, But drinking alone. Well, yes, I say, and he tells me that might be a sign I have a problem. I have many problems, I inform him, Having a couple of drinks before my flight seems to be the least of them. A couple, huh? he says, and I tell him he sounds like Joel. I think he's insulted. So what's up? I ask, glancing away from the phone to check the time. I should finish my business here, and I take another, longer swallow of my drink. I miss you, he says.

Trainor—I start, but he interrupts. Let me talk, he insists. He tells me that he's given me some space for the past couple of weeks, that he's had some time to think himself since he's been away from the office. To be honest, he says, I'm surprised I miss you as much as I do. Acknowledging that our affair has complicated my life, he informs me that his own life hasn't been immune.

The word sends me right back to my dream, and I have a sudden, awful image of Trainor poised behind Bobby, his fingers digging hard into Bobby's skin. I swallow, assigning blame to the liquor in front of me. With my free hand I push the glass away. Are you listening? Trainor asks. Yes,

I say, No. Somewhere in the distance I hear my flight announced, and I mechanically remove myself from my seat. My flight's boarding, I tell him, and he says, Where does that leave me?

I could go with any of a dozen different answers, but I say the first one that comes to my lips. I don't know, I admit. I'm not happy, he tells me. No one's happy, Trainor, I inform him, and he says, Well, that's pretty fucking pessimistic. You'll get over it, I tell him. I'm not so sure, he muses, and something in his voice gives me pause. I suddenly have a feeling he's not going to let me off the hook. We're going to talk when you get back, he tells me, as if he knows what I'm thinking, and he hangs up before I can protest.

~ ~ ~

The next morning I realize that I should've known what to expect, simply because Julia's taking a break. Julia's not the type to take a break, not ever, and that she's stated a desire to have some time away should've been warning enough of what I'd find.

My father's still sleeping when I awaken Saturday morning; I've set the alarm on my cell phone, thinking I need to get up early to take advantage of the little time I have here this weekend. But I'm the first one in the kitchen, and when my mother finally appears a little after eight she seems surprised to see me. You're not usually up so early, she chides, and when I tell her why she pats my arm. Your father probably won't be up for another hour, Adam, she says, You could've used the rest.

The extra time with my mother doesn't prepare me for what I see when my father finally comes into the kitchen for his morning coffee. She's repeated what she's told me the past few weeks on the phone, that his treatments are going well, that he's not quite as confused as they'd both feared, that he needs more rest than usual but that he's coming along. So when I hear his feet shuffling through the living room I rise expectantly to meet him, already smiling a smile that freezes when I see him.

He's aged, years in a matter of weeks. His hair has disappeared again, no doubt because of the high concentrations of radiation he's been enduring, but it's his frailty that stuns me. He doesn't have to brace himself against the wall for balance, but I can see how quickly that's coming. I try to erase my expression as I move toward him. A brusque embrace confirms a substantial weight loss since the last time I was here, and I avert my eyes when we part, but not before I see him take the back of the chair in one gnarled hand. How are you, Dad? I ask, managing one question before I have to sit down. Without a trace of the bitterness that swells in my chest, he answers my question. Oh, I'm hanging in there, Son, he says.

My mother gets him coffee and prepares him a light breakfast, which he eats with shaking fingers at the kitchen table. In between bites he tries his hand at conversation, asking me about Joel, and work, and cycling, until I have to clench my hands into fists beneath the table to stop them from trembling. A bit of egg clings to his lips, and I watch, horrified and fascinated by its shimmer, until my mother gently wipes it away with a napkin. How's Joel? he asks as my mother pours him another cup of coffee. He's already asked, and I glance at my mother, who indicates that I should answer the question as if he hasn't. I do, unable to meet his eyes.

After breakfast I help my mother settle him in the living room in front of the television, where I find an old war movie that seems to spark his interest. Standing beside his chair, my arms folded across my chest, I stare at the television until he tells me I'm making him nervous. I hiccup a laugh, relieved to hear him say something predictable, and sit on the sofa. My mother cleans up in the kitchen; I listen to the faint sounds of dishes clinking and water running, and blink back the tears building behind my eyes.

After she's finished my mother runs to the store, declining my offer to make the trip in her place. Sometimes I need to get out of the house for a while, she says. I know what she means all too well, and though I assure her to take all the time she needs, I turn back to the living room once she's gone with a sinking heart. I'm on my own here, and I remember that feeling with even greater clarity. Can I get you anything? I ask my father, hoping he'll tell me to throw some laundry in the washing machine or better yet, muck the stables. That would take a good few hours. But he shakes his head, intimating that he'd rather have the company. I lower myself reluctantly to the sofa. How's Joel? he asks.

The first time Bobby got sick I woke in the middle of the night and found him missing. Bobby? I murmured, and when he didn't answer I got up to look for him. I found him in the living room, and as I sat down beside him on the sofa he moaned, as if the mere movement of the cushions was more than

137

he could bear. I held my hand to his forehead, then jerked it away when I felt the heat. Turning on the lamp, I heard him groan; he squeezed his eyes shut against the light and when I asked him to look at me and he opened them again tears ran from the corners. I tried stroking his hair, and that's when he started throwing up. I couldn't get him to stop. Bobby, I pleaded, Please, Bobby. I was covered with vomit, and I watched as it spattered on the floor beside my bare feet.

He finally finished, draped over his knees and holding his head in his hands. Shaking, I took a step away from the mess he'd made. I'm going to get some towels, I said. We'd done laundry that afternoon, and I yanked a handful from the dryer, then soaked a washcloth in the sink and ran with it dribbling from my hands back into the living room. He didn't move. Throwing one of the towels on the floor at his feet, I knelt in front of him and lifted his chin. His eyes refused to focus. Shh, I said, though he hadn't made a sound, Shh.

I cleaned him as well as I could, then wrapped him in my grandmother's quilt. I'll be right back, I promised. Ducking back into the bedroom I grabbed clothes for both of us, pausing long enough to rinse my hands, legs and feet before I dressed. From the living room I could hear Indy whine, and when I returned Bobby was slumped over the arm of the couch, one hand skimming the floor. Oh shit, oh shit, I cried. I went to him, pressing my finger to his neck and feeling for his pulse; his vein thrummed wild and erratic against my finger and I scrapped my plan to take him to the hospital myself and dialed 911.

By the time the ambulance got there I'd managed to wake him once, though he'd slipped away from me again. EMS stripped the blanket from his body; he looked so much more vulnerable, absent of even his boxers, and I wished I'd been able to get him dressed. I stood with my arms crossed over my chest, listening to Indy scratch at the back door and trying to ignore the shift in the room when I told them Bobby was HIV positive.

They wouldn't let me see him at the hospital, and I couldn't figure out if that was because they were still trying to determine what was wrong with him or because of who I was. I sat cupped in a hard plastic chair, wanting to call someone but feeling like I couldn't; Bobby and I had agreed that we'd keep his illness between us for as long as we could. They finally called my name just before dawn, when I was on the verge of reneging. He'd been *sedated, I was told, and they were running blood work to determine the origin of the fever. He was being given fluids to combat dehydration, and they wanted to keep him for a day or so to make sure that was under control. So he's okay, I said, relieved, and the doctor gave me an odd look. This is just the beginning, she said.*

I escape from the living room to take a shower, assuring myself that my father will be fine in front of the television for the fifteen minutes I'm gone. I've gotten him a snack, and ice water, and placed the phone well within reach, and I back away, keeping him in my sight halfway down the hall. By the time I reach my old bedroom my chest feels every bit as tight as it felt a few weeks ago in Lydia's office, and I sit on the bed taking shallow breaths until the pain fades away. Cocking my head, I can hear nothing except for the television; I should look in on him again, and I creep back down the hallway and peer into the living room. He's fine, propped up in front of the television with a blanket tucked around his knees.

Scurrying to the bathroom, I hurry through a shower, then throw on some clothes. My mother's still not back when I return to the living room, but my father looks up at me with a slightly less vacant expression. You showered, he says. I nod, and take the plate that held his banana. Do you want something else? I ask. Just like Julia, he grumbles, Trying to fatten me up. I'm not sure what to say, though I can imagine Joel telling him that someone should. My father seems to read my mind. I've asked you about Joel, he says, and I start to nod before recognizing the glint of humor in his eye. A time or two, I admit. He snorts, and tells me he'd bet even more. The damn treatments, he says, running his hand back and forth across his bald head, They leave me unsettled. I'm sure, I say. I lost the rest of my hair, he confides. I hadn't noticed, I tell him, but now I'm the one teasing him, and he gives me an appreciative smile. The thought occurs to me that he might just need time to reorient himself each morning, and again he seems to know what I'm thinking. Mornings, he says, Are always the worst.

We talk with a bit more ease over the next few minutes, though occasionally something on the television catches his eye. After a while I start to relax. With his wits about him he doesn't seem quite so ill, and he makes his own way to the bathroom, declining my offer to lead him there myself. I half-expect him to slap my hand away from his arm, and once he's safely ensconced behind the bathroom door I take a look at my cell to see if I have any messages, half-afraid I'll have one from Trainor. But there's nothing.

I need to call Joel; I've not spoken to him since I landed last night, and though he's obviously trying to give me time to get settled this morning he'll want to know what's going on. I've promised to check in, reminding him in the same breath that he probably won't have much time to talk. Art Reach starts at ten and runs through the evening, and he'll be lucky to catch a minute to himself. He's most likely well into the fray already, and when I call him I get his voice mail. I leave a message.

Everything okay in there? I ask, knocking on the bathroom door. I'll be out in a minute, my father calls, and I head back into the living room to wait. The television's still on, and I stare for a minute at the western unfolding in front of me. My mother should be home any minute, and for that I'm thankful. I don't know why I thought my father and I might have time this weekend to bond; as lucid as he's become over the past hour he's still not himself, and the fact of the matter is that I don't have much emotional energy left. I barely had the wherewithal to leave Joel a voice mail. Bobby sucks me dry.

I'll take care of myself, he said the day I brought him home from the hospital, as if that was going to make all the difference. But he got sick again three weeks later, and I told Julia, who wanted me to tell my parents. I have to talk to Bobby first, I said. But he said no.

We kept our secret for almost six months, until we'd both run out of sick leave and vacation, until Julia had run halfway through hers, until Bobby got so sick one night that he was shitting blood. I couldn't believe how quickly he'd deteriorated, and neither could his doctor. We'd hoped for at least a half a dozen years before the respiratory infections started, thinking that maybe in that near-decade medical advancements would've rendered the disease nothing more than a nuisance. But Bobby started getting sick eighteen months after he was diagnosed.

The night the diarrhea started I called for an ambulance; by then I knew the drill, knew half the doctors and most of the nurses at the hospital, knew where I could get a quick cup of coffee if the machine on the third floor wasn't working. I'd spent hours talking to his primary physician, though he also had a dermatologist and a gastroenterologist; a phlebotomist and a neurologist would join the team, sooner than we would've thought. I knew more about T-cell counts and antiretroviral therapy and drug resistance than I ever thought I'd know, and I found myself correcting the physicians half the time, countering one study, one piece of information, with another. Our medicine cabinet was a sea of burnt orange, and we had a significant amount of credit card debt that mounted every time one of his doctors called in another prescription.

That night I tried to call Julia and ended up reaching her husband instead. She's in Washington on business, he said, She left today. Hesitating, he asked if there was anything he could do. I knew he was sincere, but I also knew he'd just gotten comfortable with the idea that his brother-in-law was gay when Bobby first started getting sick. No, I said, I'll be fine.

I called my mother at four the next morning. She answered, fearful because of the time. Mom? I said in a perfectly normal voice, and then I started to cry, turning further into the phone booth. Adam? she said, Honey, what's wrong? Bobby's sick, I sobbed. What's wrong with him? she asked, and I waited through an awful pause until I heard the sharp intake of her breath that told me she understood. Can you come? I asked, I need you to come.

By the time she arrived we'd gotten back the results of his blood work and I'd managed to compose myself. Bobby seemed to have stabilized; he was asleep, and I walked over to the coffee pot and poured the remnants into a Styrofoam cup. I had a tendency to chew on them, breaking off little pieces between my teeth and rolling them back and forth along my tongue. Adam? my mother said behind me.

She places her hand on my arm, and I stare at her fingers without seeing them. Adam, she says again. I look up. She's standing in front of me, and my father's right behind her. They both look concerned, and I shake my head, flinging tears I meant to hide. I'm fine, I say, Where are the groceries?

My mother starts lunch as I'm hauling in the bags, and when I'm finished I fill a glass with water and watch her. She's covering thick slices of country bread with mayonnaise and weighing them down with ham; Joel would have a heart attack, and to be honest, I can see his point. I should've warned you, she says in a low voice, taking a quick look over her shoulder to assure herself that my father's still in the living room. I lean back against the counter and open a bag of potato chips, the kind my father likes, glancing automatically at the list of ingredients but keeping my mouth shut about what I find. He's always worse in the mornings, she adds. Yeah, I say, I noticed. I shouldn't have left you alone with him, she admits. You have to get out some time, Mom, I tell her, and she agrees. No one knows that more than you, she says.

They started coming up in November, every weekend they could get away. If they didn't come my sister would, and they'd sit with Bobby so I could get out of the house on the pretense of picking up groceries or running by the post office. But the truth was that I had no appetite, and I didn't have the money to pay our bills. I just needed some space, and I'd drive to the office and back, without ever stepping foot inside its doors. I'd taken to crying at odd times, parking my car by the entrance to our neighborhood park or pulling into the parking lot of the nearest convenience store and burying my head in my hands. I don't know if my tears were more for Bobby or myself, but I shed them in isolation and despair. When I got home someone would have dinner waiting, and I'd help Bobby to the table so he could eat with us. By the time the holidays came around he couldn't manage even that.

Can you ask your father if he wants to come to the table? my mother asks. I don't answer her, and she looks up from the milk she's pouring. Adam? she says. Yes, I say hoarsely, stumbling into the living room. Lunch ready? my father asks, and I nod.

~ ~ ~

Not long after lunch my mother manages to convince my father to take a nap, a legitimate nap, in the comfort of his own bed. Adam will still be here when you wake up, she assures him, a statement that ends up being false, because when she returns from the bedroom I'm holding my keys in my hand. An hour, I say, Two, tops.

But I know I'm going to be longer. I've known at least since my plane touched down last night, if not in Lydia's office yesterday afternoon, where I'd end up, and I aim the rental car in the direction of Lexington, glancing at my cell phone and letting Joel's call roll to voice mail. I drive a route I could drive in my sleep, and a little over an hour later I pull up to the house.

They've torn down the chain-link fence in favor of wood, but otherwise the house looks the same. I let the car idle at the curb, strategizing. I'll knock, and tell whoever answers that I used to live here, that I'd like to take a quick look around. They won't deny me; everyone gets sentimental about the homes they've left over the years. Resolution propels me forward, and I lift the knocker and let it fall with a thud. There's no answer.

I hold my breath but the knob turns, and with one gentle push I open the door and step back in time.

Replace the furniture and the house is ours. I know every creak in the hardwoods, every shadow on the floor. Nothing's changed, and I touch my hand to the crack in the wall, tracing it with my finger; they haven't addressed the foundation problem either, and the floor lists toward our bedroom. They have a sleigh bed, nothing like ours, but I can easily picture our headboard against this wall, my grandmother's quilt spread across the mattress. I walk across the floor, stepping wide out of habit when I reach the board I always feared would wake him. There's an air conditioning unit in the window on Bobby's side of the bed; we never had air conditioning, and we'd talk every summer about investing in a window unit, though we never did. I gaze through the glass, my heart in my throat. They've reincarnated the garden.

Retracing my steps, I stumble through the house and out the back door. The tomato plants rock gently in the summer wind; when I touch their stems and hold my fingers beneath my nose the smell brings tears to my eyes.

Every year we planted, starting the first spring after we bought the house. Bobby took over once the plants were in the ground, watering almost daily and weeding on the weekends. On the brightest days he wore a ridiculous straw hat to shade his eyes. Sunglasses would look so much cooler, I told him once, and he grinned over his shoulder, scratching his cheek and leaving a trail of dirt I rubbed off with my thumb. I envied him his patience, his commitment. Don't you like having fresh tomatoes in the summer? he'd ask. Not enough to put in all this work, I'd tell him, but I was thrilled that he felt the compulsion himself. Sometimes we'd gorge ourselves on nothing else, drizzling the tomatoes with olive oil and salt and eating until the juice ran down our chins.

I cup my hands under my elbows. Right here he fell to the ground, his forehead pressed against the earth. Ice poured from the sky as he sobbed; for three months I didn't understand why.

I let myself back inside the house, the door slamming behind me, the sound so familiar that I think Indy might come running, his nails clicking on the hardwoods. *Do you have to feed him at the table? I asked, Do you have to let him on our bed? I couldn't keep up with the dog fur, with the tumbleweeds I found in every corner. Can't you buy some kind of no-shed shampoo? I asked, and Bobby told me that he did. He was vigilant about bathing Indy, and brushing him, too, and after he got sick the job fell to me. All right, I'd say grimly, struggling to lift a recalcitrant Indy into the bathtub, I don't like this anymore than you do. But there was something meditative about lathering him with soap, about rinsing his fur, and after I blew him dry I'd brush his coat as he gazed at me with appreciative eyes. When I was finished he'd pad down the hall, and I'd hear Bobby say, Did you get a bath? I'd wait, one hand on the faucet, for the thump of Indy landing on the sofa beside him, and then I'd clean out the tub. They needed this moment, the two of them, and coming back into the living room ten minutes later I'd find them both asleep.*

I put Indy outside the day they took Bobby away. Indy knew what was going on, he wasn't stupid, and he scrabbled at the screen on the back door as they carried Bobby's body through the living room. When I shut the door behind the men Indy howled, his nose pointed to the sky. My sister burst into tears, but I watched them both with a detachment I couldn't explain. After years of therapy I'd be able to articulate what I'd been feeling: a relief that in the moment surpassed everything else. I simply couldn't bear any more, and I knew Bobby couldn't either.

The woman who opens the front door lets out a cry, swooping her child to her side in the same instant. I hold my hands out in front of me to reassure her, but find myself unable to speak. She seems equally unable to move, and we stare at each other, until her son looks up at her. Who is he? he asks. She waits for me to answer; I realize she's examining me with slightly less trepidation than concern, and when I wipe my hand across my cheek I realize why. I used to live here, I say. She nods, failing to point out that I've done nothing to explain why I've come into her house uninvited. The door was open, I add. She nods again, and I step gingerly toward her, noting the way her grip on her son automatically tightens. I'll just..., I say, gesturing toward the door, and she moves aside. As I step onto the porch I hesitate, about to turn back, but she closes the door behind me.

~   ~   ~

If my mother couldn't tell from the tone of my voice when I talked to her on the phone on my way back from Lexington that I've had a difficult afternoon, my expression convinces her. I've been gone almost four hours, a foolish amount of time given the length of my visit this weekend. When I come through the front door she and my father don't just look disappointed; they're downright worried. I'm fine, I say, the words sounding every bit as unconvincing to my own ears as they obviously do to theirs.

In an effort to make amends I offer to buy dinner, then instantly regret the suggestion. My father's not in a position to venture out, and he can only feel frustrated by my invitation. But my mother tells me I could pick up a pizza, and she sets the table while I drive into town. Joel calls on my way; I've already talked to him once, after I spoke with my mother on my way back from Lexington. How are you? he asks, and I know he's not asking the question lightly. He's already told me he should have skipped Art Reach, that I shouldn't be up here alone. He actually called my parents' house this afternoon when he couldn't get in touch with me on my cell, fueling their fear that something was wrong. I'm picking up a pizza, I tell him. That sounds good, he says, and I'm wondering whether he's having a hard time refraining from asking what kind, whether or not we'll be eating something loaded with fat and sodium, with a healthy dose of growth hormones to boot when he adds, But that doesn't really answer my question. I'm tired, I admit. Ready yet to tell me where you spent the afternoon? he asks.

I wouldn't tell him when we spoke earlier, after I picked up the series of voice mails from both him and my mother. No, I say, and he sighs. All right, he says, Though my bet's Lexington. Startled, I keep quiet; he takes my silence for agreement. You went to your old house, didn't you? he asks, and when I babble something that sounds like protest, he says, Honey, please. Did you talk to Lydia? I ask, suddenly furious that she's repeated what I told her in confidence. But he sounds confused, and I remember our first session with Lydia, when she asked to see me alone. She'd mentioned Bobby immediately. Maybe he understands what's going on more than I've given him credit for. You're back in Kentucky, he says now, confirming my thoughts, You're helping to care for someone who's terminally ill....

His analysis, however accurate, exhausts me and I pull into the parking lot of the pizza shop and lay my head against the steering wheel. Adam, he says, Give yourself a break. He tells me that I have every right to mourn what's happening to my father, what happened to Bobby. But he doesn't know where I'm going tomorrow, and after a minute I lift my head. I need to get the pizza, I say. He allows that he should get back to his own festivities, and I remember to ask him how his day's going; I don't listen to his answer. Go, he finally says, Pick up your pizza, and get some rest. What about you? I ask. C'mon, Adam, he says, I'll be here when you get back.

~ ~ ~

The sweatshirt Joel wore the last time he was here, the one that belonged to Bobby, has been neatly folded and tucked into the top dresser drawer. I wonder if my mother realizes to whom it belongs. With some apprehension I lift the material to my nose, but the smell evokes nothing more than the detergent she uses, nothing more than the springtime scent of an everyday fabric softener. Pulling the sweatshirt over my head, I sift listlessly through the rest of the clothing, knowing I'll find nothing else that still carries his smell.

For that I have to go into the attic.

She gave us the quilt just before Christmas; we'd come to visit my parents early, planning on spending the holiday alone, for the first time. The previous holiday still held us ransom, and I'd occasionally catch Bobby's expression when he thought I wasn't looking, and be overcome again with shame by the sacrifice I'd made him offer. He always knew what I was thinking, and he'd touch my hand or give me a quick smile, which I appreciated. We have each other, his touch reminded me, but I knew that without me he was alone and I went out of my way that year to accommodate him, any way I could. He didn't want to get together with friends to go ice skating? No problem. Not interested in a rousing trip through the neighborhood singing Christmas carols?

We'd stay in. I was happy to give him whatever he needed, but by the time we got to my parents' house the weekend before the holiday I think we were both eager to be done with everything. We were cordial enough; we played games and toasted each other with mugs of eggnog and hot cider, but we were anxious to be on our way and my grandmother had to beckon me back as we made our way to the front door, ready to escape. I was impatient with her, and I took the package she pressed into our hands, wishing her a happy holiday over my shoulder.

When we got home, I shoved the gift under the Christmas tree Bobby and I had decorated with cheap ornaments and silver tinsel. A sweater, I assumed, something thoughtful but unimpressive. I certainly wasn't in a hurry to see what she'd wrapped, so when we finally opened the gift on Christmas Eve I knew I'd have to beg her forgiveness.

She'd taken pieces from the clothes we'd left at my parents' over the last few years, tee shirts and baseball caps that we'd forgotten in our haste to get away. These she'd stitched together with material the color of jewels, sapphires and emeralds and rubies and amethysts, the colors so vivid I half-expected them to stain my fingers. Taking one end and offering Bobby the other, we spread the quilt across the floor right there in front of the Christmas tree, where we poured over the individual patches, recognizing some and coaxing each other into remembering others. She made this for us, Bobby finally said, sitting back on his heels. I nodded, watching as he reached out to stroke a piece of denim that we'd both claimed as our own. I think we were overwhelmed by the generosity of the gift, but Bobby in particular seemed awe-struck. When he looked over at me his eyes were shiny and bright. She made this, he repeated, and I realized suddenly how much he'd needed this validation, this year more than any other. Yes, I said, She did.

We kept the quilt on our bed, though we weren't above taking it into the living room and curling up with it in front of the television. We wrapped it around our shoulders when we were cold, and tucked it under our chins when we were sick. Secure in its embrace, we made love beneath the Christmas tree, on the living room sofa, in the confines of our bedroom. Bury me in this, Bobby said once when he came home from one of his many stints in the hospital, but I knew I wouldn't. I took the quilt from beneath his cold hands the day he died and packed it away.

When my parents go to sleep I search their attic with single-minded purpose. I moved the box here myself before I left for Austin; I was making a fresh start, and didn't want anything other than a few pictures to remind me of what I'd lost. But now I can't remember where I stashed it, and when all of the boxes my parents have accumulated over the years start looking the same I decide to rip into every one.

By the time I find the quilt, strips of packing tape and pieces of cardboard litter the attic floor, along with the contents of a half a dozen boxes. My breath comes in short, rapid bursts, and when I realize what I've found I let out a moan I have to cover my mouth to mute. Burying my nose in the material, I search for his smell, coming up with nothing at first other than sickness, and death. But I burrow deeper, until I find him, buried in the clothes we once wore, in the colors we held over our heads the Sunday before he left me. Clutching the quilt I sink to the floor, where I inhale him with one shuddering breath after another. A half-moon trickles watery light through the narrow window above me as I curl into our quilt, where I cry myself into an exhausted sleep.

This is how my father finds me early the next morning, so early that only the very beginning of a gray dawn seeps through the attic window. I sense his hand on my shoulder and let out a sharp cry, scuttling away from him and dragging the quilt along with me. I barely feel the splinter that embeds itself in the palm of my hand. Adam, my father says softly, and that quickly I come to my senses. Struggling to disentangle myself from the quilt, I look around the attic with dismay. I'd lit into the boxes with the fury of a small cyclone, and I meet my father's eyes with a humiliation I don't try to disguise. He might as well have stumbled upon me jerking off up here by the light of the moon. Son, he says, his expression a patchwork of sadness and concern, but I get to my feet, folding the quilt at the same time. He moves more slowly; I should offer him my hand but the quilt snags on the splinter in my palm before I have a chance. Wincing, I pull the splinter from beneath my skin, along with a pearl of blood, then drop the quilt into the box beside me. Before he can say another word I turn and go downstairs.

~ ~ ~

My father tries to talk to me several times before I leave for the airport that afternoon, but I assure him, not very convincingly, that I'm fine.

I don't want to shoulder him with any more burden than he's already carrying. I wouldn't know where to begin anyway; I can't explain even to myself what's happened this weekend, and I go through the motions, aware of my father's impatience but unwilling to appease him.

My father's not the only one looking for answers. Joel calls mid-morning, after I've showered and eaten a breakfast I couldn't stomach at the time and now don't seem to want to hold down. I didn't hear from you last night, he says, and I don't know what to tell him. Simply conceding that the weekend has been more difficult than I expected seems ridiculous.

I leave my parents' house an hour early so I can finish what I've started. Once I'm in Lexington I maneuver my way past our old neighborhood and on into downtown, where I easily anticipate I'll lose my way. After all, it's been almost thirteen years. But my hands seem to know how to direct the steering wheel despite the passage of time and I turn on to his street, my heart hammering every bit as hard as the first time I made this drive. I won't go inside, I promise myself, not unless I'm invited. This time I'm better prepared.

But I'm still not ready for what I find.

I stare at the empty lot in front of me, then at the remnants of the former residences that stand to either side. They're both vacant, plastered with signs advising against trespassing. They'll be bulldozed, too, to make way for a parking garage, or the trendy loft apartments that characterize the rest of this revitalized neighborhood. As a matter of fact, a refuse trailer sits in one of the meager front yards; I don't know how I could have missed it.

Against my better judgment, I get out of the car and step onto the sidewalk. The chain link fence has disappeared, but my hand lifts anyway, as if it remembers that I'm supposed to open the gate. I walk toward what was once the front door, half-expecting him to appear in front of me; a hot wind ruffles my hair, but I only have to close my eyes to feel the crisp, autumn air.

The breeze that came through the window in his kitchen was cool, and scented with cloves. I sat at his table, one leg crossed over the other, a glass of wine at my fingertips. I wasn't wearing shoes. From over his shoulder he gave me a smile, insouciant, inviting, the kind I'd been missing for months. I held my own; he knew what I was doing, and didn't protest. Instead he brought me

149

pad Thai, spicy noodles soaked in sesame, which he set on the table between us. We ate from the same plate without utensils, an act so intimate that I shivered thinking about it later. Afterward, I licked the oil from his fingers; he never took his eyes from mine. Miles Davis cried in the background, albums that I'd eventually start bringing him myself, plundering our meager resources in order to afford. I refused to look at my watch.

When I told him I had to leave he never asked me to stay. Instead he walked me to the door, where he waited to see what else I was willing to offer him. At first I couldn't meet his eyes and he'd let me slink into the night without a word. After a few weeks I managed a nod. The day I fell asleep in his bed I turned back. Our kiss pressed us up against the door, where I stayed for half a beat after he pulled away. I didn't want to leave.

Those last moments were the ones I'd scrub from my lips on the way home, as if Bobby wouldn't be able to tell what I'd been doing from the wine on my breath, or the chili-oil that stained my fingers. I was worried, he said one night when I stumbled in too late to claim a happy hour. He'd been up half the previous night, sick to his stomach, and he'd finally curled into a sad, little heap on the bathroom floor, where I lifted him myself and carried him to bed. I'd checked in with him from work a half a dozen times the next day, relieved for more than one reason to hear that he was okay. I feel a lot better, he told me that night. I know you do, I said, trembling, I know you do, or I wouldn't have been gone so long.

I come to with a raging headache, and shield my eyes from the sun's glare. The breeze has all but disappeared, and I wipe my hand across my sweaty forehead, catching a glimpse of my watch in the process. My plane's probably boarding at this very moment. Stumbling back through the lot, I collapse into the front seat of my car, where I let the air conditioner work its magic for a few minutes, then reach for my cell. I can get a later flight, but I'll be looking at a three hour layover in Dallas and an arrival time after midnight. Ruminating, I rub the base of my skull. I'm tempted to stay here—not in the empty lot, necessarily, but at a nearby hotel. But that would mean missing at least a half a day of work tomorrow, and I shouldn't test Vincent any more than I already have. I'm leaving today, and I give the empty lot beside me one more glance.

The last time I left I didn't know I wouldn't be coming back.

~   ~   ~

Trainor's waiting for me beside my car after work the next day; I opt for a no-bullshit stance, which fails. I thought you left already, I say, unlocking the doors and hoping he'll realize I don't have the time to linger. I've had a long day, which started after about five hours of sleep, and I want nothing more than to go home and crawl into bed. I wish I lived in a city of perpetual rain, somewhere I could cozy up to a fire and fall asleep. Here the sun shines with a vengeance, and I know that even with the BMW's tinted windows and stellar air conditioning, even though I have the luxury of parking underground, I'll be sweating as I start my way home.

I thought we could go for a drive, Trainor says, oblivious to my thoughts. I don't have time, I tell him, opening the door and depositing my laptop in the backseat. I make a move to get inside myself, but he stops me. I'm talking about a conversation, Adam, he says. I don't have time tonight, I mumble. What does that mean? he asks, That you don't have the time tonight but you'll make time tomorrow?

He's left me alone most of the day, pursed his lips when I declined his invitation to join him for lunch, but didn't persuade me to change my mind. Now, one look at the way he's leaning against the BMW's rear bumper tells me he's not going to let me leave for the day without a fight, and after a minute I gesture him toward the passenger seat with a resignation that frightens me. Where am I going? I ask, starting the engine and checking my rearview mirror. I don't know, he muses, taking the liberty of adjusting his seat, Why don't you just drive? I back out of the parking space, suppressing the urge to ask him to duck when we pass a handful of his representatives. I wonder, sometimes, what people know. Just because we're leaving together doesn't mean we're doing anything suspect, but that also doesn't mean we aren't the subject of scrutiny, of gossip. I glance in my rearview mirror after we've passed, trying to glean something from their body language, then end up braking hard to avoid smacking into the car in front of me. Trainor braces himself against the dashboard, glancing at me out of the corner of his eye. Trying to get rid of me? he asks. That's not a bad idea, I tell him.

Once I'm out of the garage I turn in the opposite direction of home, and find myself in bumper to bumper traffic. I went to North Carolina the week before last, Trainor says. I know, I tell him. He'd extended his business trip through the weekend, informs me now that he went to see his ex. Huh, I say. He's quiet; from the corner of my eye I can see him examining me. So how'd that go? I finally ask, and he looks out the window without answering. I get the impression I've hurt his feelings. Sighing, I ease off the brake, just enough to edge forward another three feet. What do you want from me, Trainor? I finally mumble, and he says, I want you to care.

Stunned, I turn to look at him. I want you to be jealous, he says, I want you to wonder what I might have done without you. I don't say anything, and he shakes his head. I slept with him, he tells me.

I try to picture Trainor with this ex-boyfriend of his, someone I've never met, someone who may or may not be better looking than I am. I try to envision Trainor touching him the way he touches me, or kissing him. Other than a prick of something ancient and territorial I honestly couldn't care less. Trainor, I say, Every night I go home to someone else. I know, he says, And that bothers me more than it used to.

I close my eyes. I wanted the upper hand; now it's mine. I'm not sure I can handle the complication. For all I know he's about to confess his undying devotion, and I swear to god that if he does I'll take this car right off the road. Adam, he says, using a tender tone I've never heard from him, and instantly I hear his voice, rich and thick and golden. *Adam, he said, and I felt the color rise to my cheeks, a blush that made him smile and take another step in my direction. David, I said, trying his name in my mouth, and he said again, Adam.*

I open my eyes in just enough time to realize I'm mere inches from the car in front of me. Disoriented, I grope drunkenly for the brake and find the accelerator instead. With a *vroom* I plough ahead.

~ ~ ~

Heartbreaking though I find the damage to the BMW, I'm grateful no one was hurt. The woman in the car in front of me had two toddlers in the back seat, twins from what I could tell, who sobbed for five minutes straight until their mother found their pacifiers. We called EMS to be on the safe side, but the twins ended up being fine. I was shaken, though, and almost relieved by the citation the police officer handed me once he listened to a description of the accident. Here, at least, was punishment for my sins.

Because the bmw has a busted headlight I have to wait for a tow. But none ever shows, and Trainor and I eventually get back in the car, though I sense reluctance on his part, as if he doesn't think I'm capable of getting us back to the office without incident. What happened back there? he asks as I pull away from the shoulder. I don't answer him, and he shakes his head. You should've seen your expression, he says, You weren't even there.

I make the half-mile back to the office in record time now that the traffic has subsided. Trainor's quiet as I pull into the empty garage and ease into the parking space beside his car, and then he puts his hand on my leg. I'm suddenly miles away, and I watch from what feels like a great distance as he starts kneading my thigh. Stop, I say, but the word lacks conviction. He moves closer. Trainor, I whisper, but he ignores me, reaching for my belt and whipping open my zipper in less time than I can make sense of what he's doing. You're not immune, I hear Bobby saying, and I close my eyes.

~   ~   ~

I slink into the house a little after nine, half-hoping that Joel's forgotten about me, that he's decided to go for a run, that he's caught up in his studio. That way I can go upstairs and take a shower. I can wipe away what I've done, and make false promises to myself that I'm strong enough not to let it happen again. But he's waiting for me. I called, he says, Several times. I know, I say, I'm sorry. I tell him I had work to finish, a business plan that Vincent wants first thing tomorrow, a deadline he sprung on me but which I wasn't in a position to refuse. Warming to the task, I rail on Fusion, admitting that Joel's right, I have to get out, we have to make a plan. The more I talk the stronger the quaver in my voice becomes.

Meetings, I claimed, A happy hour I couldn't skip. He looked at me without speaking, and for a quick second I feared that he'd tried to call the office and been told the truth. You should've called, he finally said, I was worried. Forcing myself to maintain eye contact, I apologized, and when he sighed and offered of his own accord that he was feeling better I nodded. I knew you were, I said, I knew you were or I wouldn't have stayed out so late.

I knew you were okay, I say, but when I lift my eyes I find a different man than the one I'm expecting. He's frowning. I had an accident, I confess.

153

What? he says, and I lead him out to the garage, where he stares at the BMW's smashed front fender and then me. Shit, he finally says, Are you okay? I nod, though I'm obviously not. The past and the present bleed too easily together, and half the time I don't know whose hand I'm feeling on my shoulder, whose gaze I'll find staring into my own.

Ushering me out of the garage, he settles me on the sofa in the great room. Beside me, oblivious to the countless betrayals I've wracked up not just in the past six months but since the moment I dropped from that balcony thirteen years ago, he runs his fingers up and down the ridge of my spine. I want to reject the comfort he's offering me, but instead I close my eyes as he traces the muscles that line my vertebrae. After a minute he pulls my shirt from my pants and slides his hand beneath the material. With his hand on my skin, he whispers that I'm okay, we're okay, he knows I'm having a terrible time right now but we'll make it through. His conviction crushes me. Carefully, he pries my hands away from my face, then looks into my broken eyes. When he kisses me I kiss him back, desperation seeping from my every pore, its stench so powerful that I can't believe he doesn't reel away from me.

I lock my arms around him, but I'm afraid my hold isn't tight enough.

~ ~ ~

I wake the next morning with a fury equal to the one I felt in the days after going off the Ativan. I can't believe what I've done, the jeopardy in which I continue to put my relationship with Joel, and I ease the BMW out of the driveway, thankful at the very least that I'd managed to move quietly enough while I was getting ready that I hadn't awakened him. I don't want to have to meet his eyes this morning, and I certainly don't want his arms around me as he tries to coax me back to bed. His loyalty overwhelms me, and I scrub hard at my mouth, thinking about the way I'd kissed him, my mouth still tasting of someone else.

As I head to the office I make a vow not to think about Bobby. He's at the crux of the problem, and I cringe when I think about the way I behaved over the weekend, leaving my parents' house and fleeing to Lexington, then returning and crashing in the attic with that goddamn quilt pulled over my head. And yesterday, the way I'd fumbled for the brake, lost in David's voice. No more.

Swinging into my parking space at the office, I screech to a stop and eject my key, then stride to the elevator with some measure of resolve before I spot Trainor holding the door for me. Loathing rises in me like bile, and Trainor raises his eyebrows. You look like you're going to puke, he says. I step past him into the elevator, watching as he punches the button for our floor. You know, he continues, but he pauses as a woman from Accounting slips between the doors just before they close. I lean back against the wall, out of his reach, and he moves beside me, too close for me to surreptitiously wriggle away. How are you? he asks in a low voice, I was worried last night when I didn't hear from you. I don't look at him and he nudges my shoulder, automatically reaching for me when one floor later we're left alone. I shove him away and he stumbles, then grins, a slow curl of his mouth that tightens my hands into fists. I want to hit him, to smash into the jowl of his left cheek and watch him spit blood and teeth into the palm of his hand. I actually take a step in his direction, and he seems to know what I'm thinking because he offers me his chin. Go ahead, he says.

The elevator doors open, and Vincent pauses, looking from one of us to the other. Gentlemen? he finally says. Morning, Vincent, Trainor says, stepping easily across the threshold. I watch him make his way to his desk, stopping to chat along the way with some of his representatives. My arm still twitches. Atwater? Vincent says, Are you coming or going? Sorry, I mutter, ducking past him. I don't turn around, but I can feel his eyes on me as I head to my office. I can only imagine what he's thinking.

~ ~ ~

I'm locked up in meetings for most of the morning, but I have a working lunch that includes Trainor and I brace myself as I head into the conference room, where I doggedly ignore his attempt to catch my eye and busy myself preparing a sandwich from the lunch tray. Beside me Dave Burroughs layers thick slices of turkey on one slice of bread. Hungry? I ask, and he gives me a lopsided grin. Busy morning, he says. I nod; I know what he means, and I also know that he's serious. He's been making more of an effort lately, and though his sales figures haven't moved all that much I appreciate the fact that he's trying. I've made sure to send Vincent weekly progress reports; he rarely responds, and I'm hoping that's more an indication that he's busy than that he's already made up his mind.

Trainor appears beside me as I'm piercing a black olive, and I sidestep Dave and take my place at the head of the table. I'm not sure why I bothered to make myself a sandwich; I'm running this meeting, and I won't be able to take more than two bites before we'll have to get started. I'll make up for it, though, with the chocolate chip cookies I've already spotted next to the coffee. Nodding in answer to a question from one of my other managers, I watch from the corner of my eye as Trainor seats himself at the opposite end of the table. All right, I say, Let's get going.

For the next hour we run through the latest script, which Trainor and I wrote together before his trip to North Carolina. Vincent had suggested the collaboration, and Trainor and I knocked it out fairly quickly one afternoon, Trainor having a little too much fun in the process. Now, after giving him credit for co-writing the script, we do a few practice runs, getting feedback on what needs to be changed, what might be problematic. We don't have much time to implement advice; college starts in the next few weeks, and we already have a higher call volume than normal, though for some reason the sales figures haven't reflected the extra time on the phone, at least for my team. I don't know how to explain that yet, but I'll have to come up with something. Vincent will want to know.

Throughout the meeting Trainor maintains his distance, keeping an air of professionalism despite our altercation in the elevator. No one here could ascertain the tension between us, not until I've dismissed everyone and Trainor hangs back, asking a second too soon if I have a minute. Goddamn it, Trainor, I hiss, and I catch Eleanor raise her eyebrows. Well, that's perfect, I think. Now everyone will know something's going on. How do you know I don't need to talk to you about something work-related? he asks. I'm not that stupid, I tell him, and he says, I beg to differ.

Vincent's grooming him to take over as Director of Sales-West Coast when Liberty, who currently holds the position, starts maternity leave at the end of the year. She'll only be gone six weeks, I remind him, and he assures me that Vincent has heard from a reliable source that Liberty's not planning on coming back. So how do you know Vincent's grooming *you*? I ask. He gives me a look and I shrug; I shouldn't have to ask. Trainor's put in his time here. The fact that Vincent has sent him to North Carolina in my place, that he's made it a point to have Trainor and I collaborate on scripts to give him more experience, serves as further evidence. I've known for a while now that he has what it takes; Vincent would claim he knew from the moment I hired him. Good for you, I say grudgingly, and he manages a self-deprecating expression before he tells me that of course no one's supposed to know. I grumble, a little put-out that all of this reorganization has been going on behind the scenes, without my knowledge. Vincent assumes, Trainor continues, That you won't have any objection mentoring me.

I give him a suspicious look. Mentoring? He could handle the job today, without anyone's help; he doesn't need to be mentored. For the first time, I wonder if Trainor has confided in Vincent, if Vincent knew well before spotting us in the elevator this morning that we're involved and that he's somehow managed to allow Trainor to convince him of a way that we can spend more time together. I'm not sure I want to know the answer. Whatever, I say instead, and Trainor nods, his expression suggesting that we've come to a much more complicated agreement than the one on the table. We'll start tonight, he suggests. No, I say, I can't. He shrugs, unconcerned. Tomorrow, then, he says, smiling, We have plenty of time.

~ ~ ~

Joel's outside when I get home; I'd made a point to call mid-afternoon to apologize for missing him this morning and to tell him when I'd be back. Now I pull the car into the garage, then join him in the front yard, where he's holding a paper bag in one hand and a garden trowel in the other. What're you doing? I ask, watching him scan the grass in the twilight. Picking up dog shit, he says flatly, inclining his head in the direction of our neighbor's house. I'm surprised you're bothering, I admit. Yeah, well, he says, I went to check the mail and I stepped in it. I automatically glance at his feet; he's wearing sandals, but he shakes his head. I was barefoot, he says grimly. Are you sure it was her dog? I ask, and he rolls his eyes, then bends down to flip another chunk into his bag. I'm tempted to squat on her lawn myself, he mutters.

I follow him into the garage, where he opens the garbage can and drops the mess inside. In the kitchen I pull out one of the chairs and lower myself with a sigh. Have you eaten? he asks, lathering his hands with soap. I shrug, implying a myriad of answers: yes, no, yes but I could eat again. Are you hungry? he asks, trying a different tact. I could eat, I admit. I'll make sandwiches, he offers, drying his hands on a dish towel and then flipping it over his shoulder. Opening the refrigerator, he starts rummaging through its contents and lining up ingredients on the island behind him.

So I can do a veggie sandwich, he says after a minute, examining what he's found, Or I can make some kind of breakfast taco. Dinner taco, I correct him, and he says, Whatever. I shrug, disappointed as usual with the contents of our refrigerator. Would you rather I just hand you the phone so you can order a pizza? he asks, exasperated. Veggie, I say, and he whisks the eggs off the counter, pleased with my response, then starts lining slices of whole wheat bread with shredded carrot. Can I at least have cheese? I ask, but he's nonplussed, now that I've given in to the vegetables. I have goat cheese or mozzarella, he tells me. Mozzarella, I mumble, and he opens the refrigerator again.

I watch in silence for a few minutes as he slices mushrooms, speaking up only when he reaches for the sprouts. He sniffs but acquiesces, and I yawn, stretching my arms above my head. Tired? he asks. He hasn't looked in my direction; he's busy cutting the sandwiches. A little, I admit as he hands mine over. I lift the top slice of bread. I've got carrots, mushrooms, green peppers, and mozzarella. Can't you drizzle this with ranch or something? I ask. Be my guest, he says, sitting down across from me with a sandwich of his own.

So, he says, munching contentedly, like a rabbit, I talked to your parents. I lift my head, wiping the side of my mouth. Your dad's fine, he quickly assures me, He's fine. Why did they call? I ask. I called them, he confesses. Oh, I say, taken aback despite the relationship I know he shares with them. Joel touches my arm. They're worried about you, Adam, he says, We're all worried.

I have a brief, unpleasant memory of collapsing into him last night, and I wince. When did I become the one who constantly needed comforting? There was a time at the beginning of our relationship—for almost three years, really, before we got together for the last time—when he was the one who fell apart at the drop of a hat. Now I'm the one struggling to maintain composure. There's no reason for you to be worried, I say, and he frowns. You sobbed in my arms last night, he reminds me, adding insult to injury, Or don't you remember? Stroking my arm with the tips of his fingers, he tells me that I need to let him take care of me, that I need to let my parents help, too. They realize how difficult your trips to Kentucky have been, he says, How traumatic this past weekend was for you.

I stop chewing. Tell me, I say, my mouth still full, That you didn't talk to my father about my trip to Lexington. Honey—he starts as I swallow, and I jump to my feet in protest. What the hell is wrong with you? I cry. He's your father, Adam, Joel says. I groan, humiliated all over again by the memory of my father catching me in his attic. The idea that Joel has been divulging the particulars of my breakdown seems even more of a betrayal, and the anger that's been coiled in the pit of my stomach since I awoke this morning, the anger that left me trembling in front of Trainor with a clenched fist, rouses itself. The last thing my father needs right now, *the last thing*, is to expend what's left of his energy worrying about me. I picture him, sitting in his chair with my mother by his side, trying to make sense of what Joel's told him, no easy task under the best of circumstances but nearly impossible in his current state of mind. You had no right! I shout.

Adam, Joel says, getting to his feet. He's going to try to placate me; I can tell by the patronizing way he steps toward me, and my fury unfurls, every bit as lethal as when I faced Trainor in the elevator. Folded into a fist, my hand has a mind of its own. I pull my arm back like I'm cocking a trigger, then catch Joel's expression at the last possible second. Turning, I bury my hand in the wall.

~ ~ ~

We sit in the emergency room, where Joel has insisted on driving me, despite the fact that nothing's broken. Sprained, probably, but not broken. I would've expected more pain; I hadn't made contact with a stud, but I'd ploughed right through the sheetrock, my fist at the wrong angle. I gaze down at my swollen wrist, lifting the ice pack Joel made as I sat at the kitchen table. Beside me he's filling out paperwork; I'm glad something's keeping him busy.

I've given myself over to a vague numbness that most likely has something to do with why I'm not experiencing much pain, why I've allowed myself to be driven to the hospital. I feel almost drunk, and I notice, when Joel asks for my insurance card, that the fingers of my left hand move thickly, clumsily. I wonder if my words would be slurred, should I choose to speak?

In fact, I've not said a word. After I pulled my fist from the wall we stood in stupefied silence, staring at each other, the roar I'd let loose still lingering in the air. Then I winced, glancing down at my hand. My wrist was already tender to the touch, and I watched the skin swell as Joel got an ice pack together without speaking. By the time he finished I'd sat myself down in one of the kitchen chairs, where I examined the wall with something bordering on dispassion. He took one look at my wrist, and another at my face, and told me we were going to the emergency room.

After he hands my paperwork to the admissions clerk he sits down again beside me, emanating a nervous energy I barely recognize, it's been so long since it's come from his direction. I don't think we'll have to wait long, he says, though how he came to this conclusion I haven't an idea. Crossing my legs, I stare at my shoes, a pair of weather-beaten sandals Joel gave me for my thirty-ninth birthday, before I was passed over for promotion, before my father was diagnosed, before I slept with Trainor. My detachment would surprise me, if I weren't already so detached.

True to Joel's word, we're summoned quickly; he insists on accompanying me through the double doors, and once we're inside I find out why. He wants to tell the doctor not only about this episode, but about my anxiety attack weeks ago. He wants someone to know that I should have undergone tests. As he's speaking he keeps glancing in my direction, expecting me to protest, but I don't say a word. I'll submit to anything he asks. Mr. Atwater, the doctor says, and I raise my eyes. The movement seems to take a long time. How did you hurt yourself? he asks. I punched the wall, I say. Uh-huh, the doctor says, Well, you've sprained your wrist. He's holding my hand lightly in his own, prodding the bones. Does this hurt? he asks. Yes, I say, and he nods, letting go of my hand and jotting something on his clipboard. Your friend here tells me you've been having a hard time lately, he says, Are you talking to anyone about that? We're in counseling, Joel tells him, and the doctor looks to me for confirmation. I nod, or shrug, some movement that appeases him. All right, he says, Well, I'd like to run some blood work, get that EKG, make sure we're not dealing with something else here. He makes a few more notes, then gets to his feet. We'll have a tech come in to get some blood in just a minute, he tells us.

After he leaves Joel wonders aloud if he should call Lydia. I glance over at him. He seems relieved to be here—that I've agreed to come, that we're going to get the tests done that I've been avoiding—but he also looks apprehensive about what we're going to discover. I want to tell him not to worry, that there's nothing physically wrong with me, other than a sprained wrist that any minute someone will come to wrap. It's funny. For months I've been concerned about every ache and pain, and god knows I thought I was dying that day in Lydia's office. But there's nothing wrong. Nothing. My body's not the problem.

We're seeing her Friday, he continues, I guess we can wait. No, I say. I should call her now? he asks, and I shake my head. No, I say, I'm not going to see her on Friday. All right, he says, appeasing me, We'll reschedule. But I shake my head again, and though part of me wants to erase the panic in his expression I don't have the energy. I feel remarkably calm, almost as if I've taken several rounds of Ativan, and I wonder if maybe I've found my answer. Sprained wrist notwithstanding, I may have figured out the best way to deal with my anger. No, I say. No what? he says, No, you don't want to reschedule?

I run my fingers back and forth across my lips. I'm suddenly thirsty; maybe I'll ask the tech to get me a cup of ice water, since I have a feeling Joel won't be up for the task. I don't want to reschedule, I finally admit, and he says, What does that mean?

Leaning back, I close my eyes. I could sleep here, maybe sleep right through having my blood drawn. More than water my body needs rest, and without answering him I let my head sink into the pillow. Adam? Joel asks. I'm not going back, I tell him without opening my eyes, and I can hear the fear in his voice when he asks why, why, when I'm obviously making headway. Is that what this is? I say. Adam—he starts, but I shake my head. No, I say, You're going to have to figure this out on your own.

~   ~   ~

I have about twenty-four hours to enjoy the remnants of my buzz, twenty-four hours of respite from work, ignoring Joel's pleading that I listen to reason and avoiding Trainor's text messages. But by Wednesday night I'm painfully sober, and I set about the grim task of repairing the wall. I've gone to Home Depot, and I cut the mesh screen I've bought, then spackle over that with a putty knife. The whole process would probably take no more than an hour, but because of my injury it takes almost two, during which time Joel wanders back and forth between the great room and the kitchen, giving me nervous, sidelong glances. Do you need any help? he asks at one point, pausing behind me, but I don't answer and after a minute he resumes his pacing.

I take a shower when I'm finished, and when I open the bathroom door Joel's sitting on the bed, waiting for me. How's your wrist? he asks. Sore, I say. So far I haven't touched the pain medication I've been prescribed; until a couple of hours ago I still felt anesthetized. But now that the numbness has worn off, now that I've tackled a spackling job, I have a feeling I'm going to need those pills.

As I go back downstairs Joel trails me, hovering in the kitchen as I ransack the pantry, trying to find something appetizing. I can make you something, he offers. What would that be, Joel? I ask, A sprout and carrot sandwich? He lowers his eyes, but allows that he'd be happy to call for a pizza. Don't bother, I say, holding up an unopened jar of peanut butter, There's plenty to eat here.

Closing the pantry, I opt instead for a bourbon and water, which I certainly don't need, given the way I've just swallowed a double dose of pain medication. Joel hesitates as I pour, and I count the seconds before he finally ventures that I probably shouldn't mix the two. Probably not, I agree, screwing the cap back on the bottle and feeling just a little bit frightened by how quickly and with how much intensity my anger has returned. Unconsciously, I glance at the wall, where the spackle gleams white. I'll have to wait until tomorrow to paint, and for now the patch of white looks like bare skin, or bone.

Sipping my drink, I make my way into the great room where I set the glass with a clunk on the coffee table and reach for the remote. Joel perches on the edge of the sofa, eyeing me with uncertainty, as if he thinks at any moment I might jump to my feet and attack the television with the same sense of vengeance I afforded the kitchen wall. Will you please stop? I ask, and he starts apologizing before I can explain what I mean. Just give me some space, I say, Would you please just give me some space? I want to help, he says, I'm afraid we're going to end up right back where we started. I tell him if he truly wants to help he should listen to what I'm saying and give me some distance. Go paint or something, I say, Okay? Still he hesitates, as if he doesn't know anymore if he should take what I say at face value. *Go*, I say, and after a minute he does.

Jennifer Hritz

Over the course of the next couple of weeks, to use Joel's words, we're right back where we started. I leave for the office in the morning before he's awake; he's still asleep because he stays up late working, skulks into the bedroom at three or four in the morning when he could have just as easily crashed on the sofa in his studio for a couple of hours, thus eliminating the risk of awakening me. Within minutes he's asleep, and I stare at the ceiling until I accomplish the same feat, usually about a half hour before my alarm's scheduled to go off.

We don't talk during the day. I come home late, eight o'clock or nine, and find him already in his studio. He'll break when he hears me, but our attempts at conversation end in petty arguments and I break off contact when he mentions Lydia. He's still seeing her; I know because he tells me. Please come with me, he pleads, but I shake my head.

I've never gotten around to painting the wall, and as I reheat leftover pizza I mix myself what has quickly become my nightcap, glancing occasionally at that patch of white. Sometimes from his studio I can hear music; sometimes he talks in a low voice, which I know means he's on the phone, most likely with James. One night I stop by his studio to tell him I'm going to bed early, and find the door cracked. Hesitating, I listen to his end of the conversation, wincing when I hear him say that he doesn't know, he just doesn't know. I go to bed without saying good night.

At work I exhibit none of the energy that characterized my first seven years at Fusion, or even the attention to detail I displayed just a few weeks ago, when Trainor was out of town. I've had some explaining to do about my wrist, and I concoct a story about bracing myself too hard against the dock as I was getting off a friend's boat, a story that everyone except Trainor seems to believe. To him I told the truth, that I got into an argument with Joel and shoved my hand through the sheetrock in my kitchen. You throw punches like a girl, he said, examining my wrist. I don't know what pleased him more: that I had an argument with Joel, or that I was angry enough to take something out.

We haven't been together since the day I crashed the BMW; he's not as upset by that as I would've expected. Without my elaborating, he seems to know that I'm not sleeping with Joel either, and I get the impression that he's biding his time, waiting for the moment when my defenses have sunk even lower. For now he convinces me to meet him for drinks, and sometimes dinner, always on the pretense of helping him to prepare for his next step at Fusion. Work, I say to Joel when I come home after nine, as late as ten, Drinks. You're supposed to be distancing yourself from the office right now, he reminds me. That sounds great, I tell him, But in the meantime somebody has to pay the mortgage.

~ ~ ~

Are you listening to me? Joel asks a few nights later, Did you hear me say that James is coming? Tomorrow? I groan, and he points to the calendar on the refrigerator, the one I insisted he start using so I wouldn't be caught off-guard. Sure enough, he's written James's name in red ink on every block for the next three days. I mentioned it last week, too, Joel tells me. I don't remember, I say, and he says, Well, I did. He sounds petulant, and glancing over at him I find his arms folded across his chest in the defensive gesture I came to know very well during the first couple of years we were together, and haven't seen often since. I must not have heard you, I tell him. You don't hear much these days, he agrees. All right, I say, I don't want to argue with you. I don't want to argue either, he tells me. I lean against the counter, rubbing my eye with the heel of my hand. I'm tired, I finally say, I'm tired, and I was really looking forward to spending the weekend alone with you.

He has every right to look skeptical, but his expression still angers me. I wouldn't mind a weekend alone with you, either, he admits. Stepping closer, he tells me he misses me. We need some time together,

Adam, he says, and I tell him that after this weekend, after James's visit, maybe something can be arranged. Yeah? he says, Like maybe a bed and breakfast or something? I nod. Okay, he says, looking relieved, All right.

He's in a good mood for the rest of the night. Lying on the sofa, I watch as he readies everything for James's arrival, as he throws a load of clothes into the washing machine so his favorite shorts are clean, as he makes homemade granola. You're coming with us tomorrow night, right? he asks, sitting down across from me with a mug of hot tea. How can you drink that in the middle of August? I ask, ignoring his question, and he holds his hands over the steam. I find it comforting, he informs me. I roll my eyes; he takes a sip. James wants Mexican food, he tells me. Well, then we'd better go for Mexican food, I say, and he tries to kick me, his foot just missing my leg. You'll come? he asks. I wouldn't miss it for the world, I say.

~   ~   ~

Atwater, Vincent calls as I pass his office the next morning, even before I've made it into my own. Let me grab some coffee, I tell him over my shoulder. Adam, he says, and I stop. He's never used my first name, not even when we held the same job title, and I take a couple of steps back and look into his office. He's sitting behind his desk, his expression far more serious than the last time I saw him, and I know instantly what he wants to discuss. His numbers are up, I tell him, closing the door behind me. Not by much, he says, and before I have the chance to argue he adds, Not by enough. We've had a tough month, I admit, and he shakes his head. We can't keep making excuses, he tells me.

Once again I try to explain Dave's personal issues. I think we've been patient, Vincent tells me. He places his hands on his desk, palms down, and I realize that he's made up his mind, that he didn't call me into his office to talk things over. Nothing I say will make a difference. I think about my last conversation with Dave, the way he crumbled when I laid out the ultimatum, and can't bear the thought of going through that again. Vincent, I say quietly, His daughter's sick. Vincent's face reddens, and he leans over his desk, one small blue vein ticking in his temple. Are you going to do your job, Atwater? he asks, Or am I going to have to do it for you?

Leaving his office I make a detour into the restroom. I'm shaking, and I stand in front of the sink examining my reflection, my complexion every bit as flushed as Vincent's was a few moments ago. Hey, Trainor says, opening the door. He glances around to make sure we're alone, then sidles over, frowning as he gets a look at my expression. I have to fire Dave Burroughs, I tell him.

He doesn't look surprised, which infuriates me. His numbers haven't really gone up, have they? he asks, leaning against the sink. They've gone up, I say, grinding my teeth, And everyone else's have flatlined. Trainor ignores the shot I've just taken at him, shrugging. He's dead weight, Adam, he tells me. His daughter's sick! I cry, and he looks at me without speaking. She's sick, I repeat, and he reaches out to stroke my arm. I whack his hand away from me. Look, he says, You have to make this decision unemotionally. I haven't made *any* decision, I tell him, That's the point.

I turn around and lean back against the sink. I hate my job, I mutter. No, you don't, he says. I'm seriously thinking about quitting, I tell him. No, you're not, he says. Trainor—I start, and he says, Dave Burroughs is going to be better off somewhere else. I don't say anything. You know I'm right, he tells me, He's done good work here, but for whatever reason he can't handle the pressure anymore. He shrugs. He'll be fine, he says, He'll do something else, and he'll be fine. You want to tell him that? I mutter. Are you kidding? he says. I award him half a grin, and he smiles. You'll do a much better job than I ever would anyway, he assures me, brushing my arm with his knuckles. I snort. I'm serious, he says, his voice dropping as he takes a step closer, You'll know just what to say.

The door opens and we snap apart. Abel, Trainor says, nodding at one of his sales reps. Morning, Abel mumbles. I'll talk to you later, I say, not wanting to stay long enough to find out what Abel may have seen, and Trainor turns to the sink to wash his hands. Let me know how that meeting goes, he says over his shoulder. Right, I say, Will do.

Dave's already sitting in his cube, and he looks up when I pause beside his desk. You need to see me? he asks. Yeah, I say, I do.

~ ~ ~

Joel calls midway through my lunch, half of a Hershey bar that I found in my desk and the cup of coffee I had to forego until after I'd told Dave he was being let go. He'd been more composed than I expected, ended up apologizing for letting me down. Horrified, I told him that wasn't the case. I assured him I'd be happy to keep an eye out for him, that he could count on me as a solid reference, but saying the words did nothing to make me feel any better, and when he finally thanked me and shut the door behind him I was overwhelmed with hunger, inexplicable because I got up early this morning so I could try some of Joel's granola. I'd had to put off eating anything, though, because through my front window I could see Dave packing his things. His reps hovered in the background, looking shell-shocked; once Dave left I had to call them all into the conference room and assign them temporarily to the other managers. One of the women cried. Demoralized, I fled to my office once again, to find a voice mail from Vincent telling me that he'd made a tee time for us at his country club, for one o'clock. I hate golf. I've never learned to play well, and I can think of nothing worse than capping off my day with eighteen holes in hundred degree weather with Vincent. My wrist should give me an out, but Vincent waves off any concern that I might re-injure myself. You seem fine to me, he says, and I realize I have no choice.

Needless to say, when Joel calls my patience has thinned. I listen, swallowing a mouthful of burnt coffee, as he tells me that James's flight is running late, but that he should land by around two. Is this information I need? I ask, and he falls silent. I gesture to Darlene, who seems to have taken Dave's termination personally. She comes to the door with a sour expression, nodding when I ask if she knows how to get to Vincent's club. Are you going to keep the directions to yourself? I ask as she lingers. She leaves the office, eyes narrowed and lips pursed. Not my fault, I call to her departing back, then turn my attention to Joel. I thought you might want to come home before dinner, he's saying. I thought that was the plan all along, I tell him.

Darlene opens the door to my office again and hands me the directions I need. I calculate drive time, gritting my teeth. I have a feeling that once we've finished the round I'll be looking at a forty-five minute drive home. Maybe you should go ahead without me, I tell Joel, I have a tee time with Vincent at one. You're playing golf today? Joel asks. He sounds incredulous, and I don't want to know whether that's because of the short notice or because only a moron would play in this heat. Don't start, I tell him as Trainor raps on the door of my office. Without waiting for my response he comes in and plunks down in the chair across from me. I have to go, I mutter. Well, what should we do? Joel asks. You're a big boy, I say, You make the call.

Want to ride together? Trainor asks after I've hung up. I didn't know you were playing with us, I tell him. He nods. Underwood, too, he says, and I frown. I don't know that I've spoken more than a half a dozen words to Miles Underwood since my interview, and I stare across my desk at Trainor, trying to figure out why Vincent would be including him. Maybe you're up for a promotion, Trainor says. I don't think so, I say, and judging from the way Trainor avoids my eye it's clear he doesn't think so either.

The afternoon doesn't go well, from any perspective. For one thing, I can't handle the heat. If I were in better shape, if I hadn't put on fifteen pounds since last summer, then maybe I'd be okay. Instead I sweat profusely, and I find when I catch my reflection in the restroom mirror at the turn that brushing my hair back from my forehead doesn't produce the same sleek effect for me as it does for Vincent. I look pink and rumpled and hot, and I watch with a sort of grim admiration as Trainor swipes his towel across his bald head, removing any trace of sweat. A liberal application of sunscreen and he's fine. Even Miles had the sense to bring along a baseball cap, and he eyes me as I comb my fingers through my hair and wipe the sweat on the damp material of my khakis.

I play a terrible game. The harder I try the worse I play, and I end up hacking at the ball from every sand pit on the course. On the back nine I hit the ball with an awkward whack, and shield my eyes from the sun, following the ball's trajectory far to the right. No one says a word, and I climb in the cart beside Trainor, thankful at least for the sixty seconds we'll spend under the shade of the golf cart's roof. You're having a rough day, he says, pressing his sweaty leg to mine. Trainor, I say, Shut up.

We discuss no business, which doesn't escape my notice. There's a reason why we've met today, and there's little doubt in my mind as we finish up the last couple of holes that I've just been through some kind of test. I can't imagine I've done well, and the thought angers me, especially given what I've been through today with Dave. Plans tonight? Vincent asks, seeing me glance at my watch, and without thinking I nod. Vincent looks at Miles and Trainor, who shrug. Let's get a drink, he says to them, offering me a wave. Struck dumb, I watch them walk away.

When I get home Joel and James are outside by the pool, sitting with their feet in the water, entirely too close for my liking. Smoke from the joint they're passing back and forth hangs haze-like above them, and they look up as I make my way down the steps. James jumps to his feet, offering me his hand and then changing his mind and pulling me into a hug before I can stop him. Good to see you, man, he murmurs, and I nod something similar, looking over his shoulder. Joel leans back, with a beatific smile. You're home, he says.

They're starving, but I tell them I have to shower first. They're so high, and so easily distracted that they don't protest. I watch as James lowers himself beside Joel again, as Joel offers him what's left of the joint. You want? James asks me, and I shake my head. Shrugging, James takes a toke, holding the smoke in his lungs so long that Joel nudges his shoulder to get him to release. Laughing, they lean toward each other. I don't wait around to find out what's going to happen next.

Driving the two of them to dinner is like chauffeuring a couple of teen-agers. They've brought along their beers, which they drink without self-consciousness, even when we pull up to a stoplight. Hey, James says at one point, pulling himself forward and grasping the back of my headrest, Did you know that Joel had a BMW in college? The year after college, Joel corrects him, and James says, I totaled it. I glance at him in the rearview mirror, trying to refrain from asking him to please buckle his seatbelt. Yeah, you did, Joel says, smiling at him. I grip the steering wheel as he and James clink bottles, as if they've got reason to celebrate.

At the restaurant they order margaritas; I can't remember the last time I saw Joel drink one. He draws the line at the beef fajitas, though James cajoles him. I can't eat that shit anymore, Joel says, and when James shakes his head Joel grabs him and buries his hand in his hair, which is brown and wavy and thicker than mine will ever be again. Do you ever fucking comb this shit? Joel says, and James grins. I want to kill them both.

After dinner they manage to convince me to take them to some bar they used to frequent when they were in college. There's a guy at the door checking IDs, and once we're inside I find that while Joel and James could definitely be considered some of the older patrons, I'm a dinosaur. Why are we here? I hiss at Joel as we're winding our way through the crowd, but he acts as if he doesn't hear me. I should leave them, I think, ditch them both and tell them to take a cab home, but instead I follow them onto the back patio. We find a long bench in the back, and since they collapse on that together without leaving me enough room to join them I go in search of an extra chair. They're deep in conversation when I return, and I prop myself glumly in front of them.

This wasn't something Bobby and I ever did. We went out, and we did the bar thing occasionally, but we certainly never went to straight bars. I look around me; I'd deem every one of these guys straight, but I know Joel would correct me. The guys in Austin, especially the younger ones, are at the very least bi-curious. Or so he says.

What're you thinking? Joel asks, breaking my reverie. He's drinking a beer that I didn't see him order, and the sight of the bottle in his hand I find both repugnant—it's so uncharacteristic these days—and provocative. Nothing, I say, then shrug and tell him. Bi-curious, James muses from a half-prone position. He turns to Joel. Is that what I am? he asks. He'd have to be drunk to ask the question, and I know Joel's drunk when he laughs, because he usually clenches up at any reference, however nominal, to what happened between them. I don't think you're curious anymore, honey, he says.

It's the term of endearment that gets to me. For the first time I feel what Elizabeth must feel every time James heads to Austin, and I wonder what would happen if I wasn't right here in front of them, if I wasn't in the picture at all, if Joel was drunk enough, or James persuasive enough. For the first time I really picture the two of them together, not just now, but at the moment when they first connected, when they were ten years younger. The thought makes me ferocious with jealousy.

I tell them I have to use the bathroom. They barely nod when I tell them I'll be back.

It takes me a few minutes to find it, a hovel near the bar with a door so low I have to duck to enter. I shut it behind me, squinting in the dim light at the graffiti covering the wall above the urinal as I unzip my jeans.

"AUSTIN SUCKS" in block letters, "you suck" scrawled beneath. A handful of phone numbers that would amount to naught if I took the time to punch them into my cell. Drivel unbecoming the bard for whom this establishment was named.

I tuck myself back in and flush, then wash my hands in tepid water; catching my reflection in the mirror above the sink, I'm momentarily taken aback. I could've guessed that the lighting would do nothing for my complexion, but I look positively ghoulish. I stare into the mirror, half-horrified, half-fascinated. My eyes appear sunken, and I look a little closer, noticing lines I didn't know I had. I'm getting older. There's no denying that fact any longer, and I wonder with a start what Bobby would think if he could see me now. Would he be as captivated as he was the day I felt his eyes on me in the library? Or would he be as appalled as I am by the way I've changed?

But he would've changed, too, if he'd lived. He'd be my age, and I close my eyes, trying to conjure an image of him as a forty-year-old man. I'm unable.

The knocking I've heard off and on for the past few minutes becomes more insistent, and I shake myself. A minute, I say, but the words barely reach my ears as I stare into the cracks and crevices of my face. Would his look the same, if our roles had been reversed? Did his look the same, the night he betrayed me?

The first time, a few weeks after he told me, a week after my results came in negative, he almost wept in my arms. I think somewhere in the back of his mind he believed that I'd never touch him again, and when I did he fell into me with a relief I hadn't expected. I made the determination to dismiss any thought of what had led us here, and I took him the way I would have taken a long drink if I was dying of thirst. Afterwards I examined his expression for any trace of what I'd managed myself to banish, and realized when he didn't return my gaze that it would never be just the two of us again.

After that he didn't want me to touch him. He claimed he was too afraid that the condom wouldn't offer the right protection, that we'd turn on the news and find out nothing served as a barrier to the virus after all. Nothing I said alleviated that worry, and though every once in a while I'd manage to convince him I was usually sorry I had. He held himself so far away from me, and that was worse than imagining him with a stranger.

For a while we pretended that the veritable absence of sex from our lives wasn't so strange. But he knew what I was missing, and at one point, after he'd gotten sick a few times, he offered an alternative. You could always..., he said, trailing off. What? I asked, and he shook his head, his eyes darting to the side. He couldn't be suggesting what I thought, and still aching from another botched attempt at love-making I screwed my hands into fists. As long as you're discreet, he said, half to himself, As long as it isn't anyone we know. He was wearing one of my long-sleeved tee shirts, and he pushed the sleeves, which hung below his wrists, up to the middle of his arms. I'd managed to coax his jeans around his ankles, but he'd already pulled them back up and secured them around his waist. They have services..., he said, and I jumped to my feet. You're right here, Bobby! I yelled, but the look on his face told me otherwise. Furious, I kicked the side of the bed with my bare foot, then howled at the pain. He watched me without intervention until I finally sat back on the bed, my injured toe cupped in my palm. Adam—he started. Never, I hissed, cutting him off, and when he was silent I turned to look at him. I will never sleep with someone else, I insisted. Sure you will, he said, Once I'm dead.

Blows rain on the door behind me, and I grab for the knob.

He's young; if I had to make a bet I'd say he used a fake ID just to get in here tonight. Theoretically, he could be my son. The thought doesn't make me feel anything paternal. What the fuck is your problem? I snarl, and he holds his hands out in front of him, in a gesture that's both melodramatic and patronizing. Sorry, Grandpa, he says, trying to sidestep me.

Even before my hands clench he senses what's about to happen. He ducks when I take the first swing. But he's not fast enough.

I have the initial advantage, but he manages to get in one quick jab that fills my vision with the light of a thousand stars. Momentarily befuddled, I shake my head, and he knocks me to the ground. We roll together as the crowd gathers; I'm only dimly aware of them. He pins me for just a second before I heave him off of me. As he scrambles away I grab his leg; when I pull he comes down hard, with a sharp cry of pain. The sound should stop me in my tracks, but instead I'm incited and I crawl on top of him. I hit him once, twice, with delicious precision, his eyes squeezed shut against the onslaught. I've just brought my fist back for a third try when I'm lifted away from him. Fighting back, I realize too late who holds me.

They have me in cuffs before I know what's happening. I'm read my rights and shoved through the crowd; on the street I'm crammed into the backseat of a patrol car. Shut the fuck up, one of the officers says when I open my mouth. I search the people who throng the sidewalks, but Joel's nowhere to be found, and after a minute I avert my eyes from the gaping crowd.

They take me to the lock-up downtown, where I'm finger-printed, photographed, and shoved into a cell that holds a dozen other men. I avoid eye contact, rubbing my wrist, which I'm fairly convinced I've re-injured. With my back against the wall, I ease myself down until I'm sitting on the floor. Cold concrete seeps through my jeans. I can barely see through my right eye.

I'm still there an hour later when someone calls my name. By that time I've almost gotten used to the smell, a sort of medley of alcohol and sweat and fear, and I get to my feet. Phone call, the guard says. For just a second I'm confused. Someone's called me *here?* But as I follow her down the hall I realize what she means. This is my one call, and I pick up the phone, my finger automatically reaching out to stab the first number of Joel's cell.

But then I hesitate. Who's to say he'll answer? Who's to say he and James haven't disappeared? They certainly weren't in the crowd outside the bar when I was in the back of that police cruiser. For all I know, they're not even aware I've been arrested. I picture the two of them together on that bench, and that settles the decision.

You're *where?* Trainor asks. Cupping my hand around the receiver I lower my voice. The guard's not looking at me, but how am I supposed to know if what I say will somehow incriminate me? Are you going to help me or not? I hiss. Of course, he says, Just give me some time.

~ ~ ~

I'm released late the next morning and I step outside, blinking in the sudden, harsh light. Trainor stands beside me, waiting as my eyes adjust. He'd pressed his lips together at the sight of me; I can only imagine what I must look like, in my rumpled jeans and blood-stained shirt, after a sleepless night. Every so often I probe my swollen eye. That kid hit me hard enough to crack the bone.

Wait here, Trainor says, I'm going to get the car. I'm too tired to argue, and I lean against the side of the building, trying to ignore the offside glances I get from passerby. Trainor had to front me the cash so I could post bond; I'll have my work cut out for me on Monday, rearranging accounts in order to pay him back. The thought sickens me, almost as much as what I did to land myself in jail. In the light of day the rage that consumed me last night seems pathetic, and I close my eyes. I'm just lucky the kid's okay; I have a feeling the judge would've set bond even higher if he'd ended up in the hospital.

I shift my weight, opening my eyes just briefly to make sure that Trainor hasn't appeared in front of me, then closing them again when I see that he hasn't. I don't know what I'm going to tell Joel. I might be able to convince him that Trainor was in a better position to come up with fast cash, but he won't forgive me for keeping him in the dark until this morning. I suppose I could slough that off on Trainor, make that his fault. But how to explain why I ended up arrested in the first place? I'm humiliated to admit that one condescending word had the power to push me over the edge, and I can't even begin to figure out how to tell him what held me captive in that bathroom. What can I possibly say?

I sense Trainor's car pulling up to the curb and I open my eyes, then make my way forward. Falling into the front seat beside him, the air conditioner blissfully cool against my fevered skin, I thank him. He nods grimly, and I pull the visor down to check my reflection. Want me to swing by my apartment? he asks, So you can make yourself presentable? I start to say yes, then wonder if maybe my state of disarray might play on Joel's vulnerability. He'll be considerably more pissed off if I show up freshly showered, especially if he learns that I've just come from Trainor's apartment. Drop me off at my car, I say.

Trainor doesn't argue, and we're silent for a couple of blocks. At a stoplight I stare out the window, watching as people stroll along the sidewalk, slide in and out of restaurants, enjoy their Saturday. Joel and I did the same thing, once; Bobby and I did the same thing. Now I'm sitting in a car with a black eye and a felony charge.

Listen, Trainor says, You might want to work on trying to get that swelling down. I automatically raise my hand to my face as he shakes his head. You do not want to come into the office on Monday looking like you've been in a dogfight, he tells me. What're you saying? I ask, suddenly remembering the way Trainor, Vincent, and Miles banded together yesterday at the golf course. You have some pretty serious charges against you, Trainor reminds me, And until they're resolved I don't think you want to appear as anything less than the professional you are.

He's smooth, I have to hand him that. A warning and flattery, all at the same time. I could call him on it, tell him I see right through him, but he's probably right and instead I nod. What are you going to tell Joel? he asks, pulling into the lot where I've left my car. I shrug. I'll get you the cash on Monday, I tell him, and he waves me off. I know you will, he says.

In my car I check my voice mail. I have eight messages, each and every one of them from Joel, beginning about an hour after I was arrested. He's querulous in the first, worried by the third, downright panicked by the last. I squirrel away my guilt by reminding myself that he spent a good, solid hour with James before he even realized I was gone. Maybe he deserves to be a little concerned.

The moment I pull into the driveway he bursts through the front door, though he stops short when he sees me. I watch whatever words he held on his lips disappear.

I got in a fight, I admit, noticing James hanging on the periphery. A fight? Joel repeats. James takes a few steps closer, gawking at my eye and my blood-stained shirt. I hope you look better than the other guy, he says. I shrug, grimacing. I don't understand, Joel says. Yeah, well, I say, You were a little preoccupied last night.

I haven't been able to keep the jealousy from my voice, and James manages an expression of contrition; Joel simply looks impatient. I still can't think of a single explanation that might appease him. The sun beats down with relentless force on my thinning scalp, and I brush away the gnats that have taken an interest in my swollen eye. I feel ripe, and as I inhale I catch a strong whiff of body odor that I know isn't wafting from Joel, with his coconut-verbena scented shampoo. I shift from one foot to the other, then glance over my shoulder in the direction of my car. I have to quell the urge to make a run for it.

In the end I figure I have no choice but to speak the truth. He's going to find out anyway, if I end up embroiled in a lawsuit. I tell them I'd had words with some guy after I came out of the bathroom, that the situation went downhill from there. He just clocked you? James asks. Something like that, I mumble.

They're less than satisfied with my answer. Joel folds his arms across his chest; I squint at him with my one good eye. Sweat has begun to trickle down my spine, into the seat of my jeans. I squirm, both from discomfort as well as his scrutiny. I hit him, I finally confess. You hit him? Joel says, Without provocation? There was provocation, I tell him. Well, what did he say? James asks.

I glare at him. He shouldn't even be a part of this conversation, this confession. What did he say? Joel echoes, and now I'm trapped. The BMW waits behind me, sleek, ready to flee. In her throne I feel strong, potent, invincible. I have to force myself to stand still. He called me Grandpa, I mutter.

James guffaws. I scowl at him; Joel joins me, and I'm grateful for his mercy, until he turns back to me with narrowed eyes. He called you Grandpa, he says, And you attacked him? I wouldn't say I *attacked* him, I say, annoyed by the unnecessary repetition of the word "Grandpa." And then what? Joel asks. What do you mean? I ask. Don't blow me off, Adam! he says, I want to know what happened! I got arrested! I shout.

With their widened eyes and opened mouths they're almost comical. I couldn't have taken them any more aback, and there's a part of me that wants to tell them there's more, there's so much more, they couldn't even begin to understand how much I'm carrying right now. Secrets scurry back and forth beneath the surface and I clamp my mouth to prevent their escape. The tightening of my jaw rouses them both, and I watch as Joel scans the neighborhood to be sure we haven't been overheard. So now you care what they think, I mutter, but he just grabs my arm and pulls me in the direction of the house. James trails us, and when the front door shuts I almost weep with relief; we're finally out of the sun.

In the great room I collapse into the chair in front of the fireplace; my interrogators take up position in front of me. Why were you arrested? James asks, You weren't even drunk. I tell them how I'd come up swinging, how I'd inadvertently caught one of the officers on the chin. Even James seems speechless, and I have to reiterate that I hadn't done anything *intentionally,* that I was caught up in the moment, that I didn't even know the police were there. The admission doesn't seem to make them feel any better; Joel actually looks like he might throw up. So this is serious, James finally says. I grunt. For an intellectual James can be remarkably inane.

A full minute passes. I think we're all digesting James's words, when he speaks up again. How did you get out this morning? he asks, Did you post bond? Why are you *here*? I ask, pissed that we might have been able to skip over this part of the story without his interference. He sniffs, offended, and I glance at Joel, who has his eyebrows raised. I called Trainor, I admit.

Joel doesn't move. But I can see him weighing the news, turning it over in his mind to examine it from every angle, testing it for weakness. Before he can find fault I remind him that he was with James. And you'd been drinking, I say, thrilled that I've remembered this key piece of information, And smoking pot. The last thing I needed, I tell him, was to have him bail me out, reeking of marijuana. I rub my hands together, almost gleefully; I'm amazed by how easily I've been able to put the onus on him. Why didn't you just post bond yourself? he asks. I don't have easy access to that kind of money right now, I tell him. What kind of money? he asks.

I'm beset with a host of emotions, not the least of which is an instant self-loathing. I'll consider myself lucky simply losing the money Trainor had to put up to post bond; if I have to come up with the cash for an attorney as well I don't know what I'll do. I'm also frustrated by my own wording. "That kind of money" implies a sum worthy of the catch I feel in my throat every time I think of what I'm going to have to give Trainor this week. Approached differently, I might've accorded the matter a little less heft, might've been able to convince Joel that the amount of money we were talking about wasn't all that worrisome. The way he's looking at me now, though, I don't have that luxury. I tell him.

For the first time James looks like he wishes he could leave the room. I try a shrug, but even I'm not fooled. We're talking about a lot of cash, especially considering the purchase I made last month. I'll figure it out, I say, I'll move some things around. Joel doesn't say anything; I know what he's thinking. There's no way we'll be able to follow through on our plan, and after a minute I can't take his expression. When I get to my feet and mumble something about taking a shower he doesn't try to stop me.

~ ~ ~

I wake from a fitful sleep early that evening, remember everything that's transpired in the past twenty-four hours, and groan. When I realize that not only Joel but James as well wait for me downstairs I have half a mind to burrow under the covers for the rest of the night, the rest of the weekend. I'm almost surprised that they haven't already come to get me. I listen hard, first from my current vantage point, and then at the door, but I can't hear a thing. Maybe they've gone out; I should be so lucky. More likely they're in the pool. At the window I crane my neck, but I can only make out part of the deck, already in shadow.

I take a moment to examine my eye. The swelling's worse, and I wonder if I'll end up having to call in sick on Monday morning. That won't go over any better than showing up wounded; I've missed way too much work this year, and Vincent doesn't need any more ammunition against me. I don't know what Trainor's thinking. I'll have to concoct some fiction.

I open the bedroom door, then make my way downstairs. They're in the kitchen; I can hear James's voice, and from his inflection I gather that he's asked a question. Joel answers, low and agitated. I've thought about it, he admits as I round the corner, and I have just a moment to register what I see. They're sitting at the kitchen table, across from each other, but they're both leaning forward. Joel's forehead rests on one hand; with his other he fingers a half-empty bottle of beer. James watches him with a focus I haven't been able to conjure for months, a lock of hair in his eyes. Their intimacy feels thick and impenetrable, and I pause on the threshold, acutely aware that I'm interrupting.

Joel meets my eyes first. Without speaking, he sits back in his chair. After a reluctant moment I croak out a hello, darting a glance at James to include him in my greeting. He stares back with a hostility I hadn't expected, and I suspect that in the hours I've been asleep he's been told something that Joel previously kept from him. What, I wonder. Has Joel confessed that I bought the car without his approval? Has he divulged the secrets of our session with Lydia? Could he possibly be aware of what I've been doing with Trainor? I try to hold his gaze and find the task impossible. Lowering my eyes, I turn to Joel. Can I talk to you? I mumble.

He follows me outside onto the deck, then down the stairs to the pool, where he folds his arms across his chest. Please, I say, reaching out and touching his wrist, but he says, I have every right to feel defensive. I drop my hand. How do you expect me to react? he says, I mean, really, Adam. I wait for him to tick off his list of grievances, but he doesn't. He's actually waiting for an answer, and I finally mutter something about making a mistake. Everyone makes mistakes, I add lamely. There've been a host of them lately, Adam, he says, and I snap, You've made your share, you know.

He's quiet. He'll probably spend the rest of the evening taking inventory; I should offer to help, in case he's forgotten anything, and I watch as he ruminates, sucking on his bottom lip. Lately, he finally says, his voice trailing, and then he shakes his head without finishing. I turn away, my eyes snagging on the sun as it slides through the sky. Time's running out, I think, and he speaks again, this time with more conviction. Lately, he says, I get the feeling that you're trying to see something through to the end.

I feel a chill that starts smack in the middle of my chest and spreads outward, to the very tips of my fingers. His perception unnerves me. He's articulated something I haven't fully admitted to myself, and I struggle with the truth of his words, shivering all the while.

All that summer I wanted to escape. But there was nowhere for me to go, other than to work and then home again, to make sure Bobby was all right. And for the most part he was fine, so fine that I found myself getting irritated when he sloughed off my invitations to go to dinner, to the movies, to the parties that our friends threw every other weekend. I can't drink, he said, making excuses, I shouldn't sit in the hot tub. But the truth of the matter was that he didn't want everyone staring at him. You look fine, I said, which wasn't really the truth. Your friends don't care what you look like anyway, I added, and he told me that I might be right but he wasn't going to be that guy. What guy? I asked, exasperated. But I knew what he meant and he knew he didn't have to elaborate. What about me? I wanted to ask, but I never did. Instead I humored him, and by the end of the summer I was rigid with resentment.

One afternoon as I was picking up a few things at the grocery store I ran into a friend of ours, and I eyed the contents of his cart and compared them with my own. Beer, a dozen bottles of wine, a collection of lemons and limes that could mean only one thing. I glanced at my own meager collection of cot-

ton balls and Band-Aids—necessities because of the blood thinner Bobby had to take—and the whole wheat bread Bobby wanted because he was paranoid about eating the white stuff. Hey, you guys are welcome to come over tonight, Paul said after I told him that Bobby was actually hanging in, he was actually doing all right. Yeah, I said, knowing I'd never be able to convince Bobby, Sounds good.

I broached the subject anyway after I got home, and true to form Bobby refused the invitation. But you should go, he suggested. Without you? I said, and he told me that I could use a little time away from the house. You're not the one who's sick, he reminded me. Neither are you, I pointed out, and he gave me a look. He hated when I played semantics with him. In his mind, he was always sick, regardless of whether or not he was capable of making it out of bed in the morning. I'm not going without you, I said.

But he didn't change his mind, and sitting in front of the television with him that night my bitterness swelled. They were cracking open the first bottles of wine, I knew, and they'd probably make daiquiris or margaritas while they cranked up the stereo. They'd all be there, all of our friends, and we could be right there with them. Even though Bobby might have to suck it up and take a pass on the alcohol that didn't mean we couldn't enjoy a little conversation. I was so sick of just sitting there, so sick of waiting. If he couldn't let go when he was feeling well, what was the point? I was debating throwing my argument in the ring one last time when he said, Adam, just go.

I went. I went without him, after I made sure he had everything he needed, after I promised him that I wouldn't stay long, that I'd go for one drink, maybe two. You're sure you're okay? I asked one last time, and for just a second I thought I might have pressed my luck. But he erased his expression, and I let myself believe he never looked unhappy in the first place. Go, he said, Have fun.

To be out on a Saturday night when I'd spent the entire summer watching movies and doling out medicine felt like an incredible indulgence, and I let the windows down as I slid through the night. I felt sleek and primal, and stopping at the liquor store on my way to the party I threw a smile to the cashier that made her blush. Slipping my beer into the paper bag, I took a healthy swig as I swung back behind the driver's seat. Yes, I thought, heading into the night. This is what I need.

But the moment I stepped through Paul's front door I realized my mistake. He hadn't been lying when he said there'd be a crowd, and I glanced around me with a sinking heart. I don't know what I expected, but the sea of drunken men surrounding me, after what I'd been through the past few months, seemed the epitome of hedonism. Watching a half a dozen men make their naked way through the sliding glass door onto the deck where the hot tub beckoned, I caught Paul's eye. He waved me forward, and I closed the front door with a reluctant snap. Bourbon, I said, offering him the bottle, and he linked one hand around my neck and pulled me close. Where's Bobby? he asked before he let me go. Didn't feel up to a party, I said, realizing how smart he'd been to stay home, and Paul gestured around the living room. Well, you've got plenty to distract you, he told me, and though I knew he probably meant that I needed the diversion of simply being out of the house, I felt myself flush. Bobby's not dead yet, I wanted to tell him, but I kept my mouth shut and allowed him to introduce me to a few of his friends. One drink, I thought. Just one drink, and then I'm out of here.

But I found it impossible to leave. You just got here! Paul protested when I tried to beg off, and his boyfriend attempted to persuade me to get in the hot tub with them. He was half-dressed, and half-hard, and I shook my head. I should really check on Bobby, I told them, but I realized in the miserable moment that I stepped away from them that I didn't want to go home either. I didn't know what I needed, and instead of fighting my way through the crowd to the front door I fought the tears in my eyes as I ducked up the back staircase. A few guys wandered the halls, but I avoided eye contact and slipped into the last room on the left. Double doors led onto the balcony, and I pushed one open and gulped in the night air. I was alone, and after a minute I draped myself over the railing, looking down. I could hear snatches of laughter from the hot tub downstairs, but because I faced the side yard I couldn't see a thing.

When the door opened behind me I winced. Sorry, he said, seeing me in the shadows. I shrugged and he hesitated, one hand on the door. I gave him a second glance, and recognized him. Bobby and I had seen him a couple of times at random parties, though we'd never been introduced. Way out of my league, Bobby said the first time we spotted him, Though not out of yours. I didn't deny the observation; I learned early on that Bobby hated when I tried to pretend that he was better looking than he was. Should I talk to him? I remember asking, teasing him, and Bobby grabbed my ass. Don't you dare, he said.

Thinking back, I was reminded of why Bobby felt threatened. From a purely physical standpoint he paled in comparison to the man standing in front of me, who seemed to shimmer in the moonlight as if he'd been touched by the hand of god. You're not usually alone, he said in a voice as thick as honey, and before I could let myself wonder if the words tasted sweet on his tongue I blurted out the reason why.

He watched as I got myself together, then stepped onto the balcony beside me. I'm David, he said, extending his hand. Adam, I said, embarrassed, and he leaned against the railing next to me and repeated my name in a way that made me blush. He could have come tonight, I confessed, But he said he didn't feel like being around a bunch of pretty boys. They are obnoxious, David allowed, and I managed a smile, then looked down at my hands.

I couldn't speak; I couldn't disguise the treachery in my voice, and he saved me by asking how I knew Paul. We played softball together, I said, A few years ago. I told him that we'd run into each other this afternoon, remembering the way I'd felt staring into Paul's basket while I shifted Bobby's pharmaceuticals from one hand to the other. He must have been making the rounds, David said, I saw him this afternoon, too. They hadn't been in touch for months, but Paul told him to come by anyway. And I didn't really have anything better to do tonight, he added. I took a closer look at him. He couldn't possibly be sincere, but he didn't even blink as I examined him. Anyway, he said, inviting me to share his smile, I've found that you meet people at the most unlikely times.

He was flirting with me. He was flirting with me, and I didn't know how to respond. Words came to my lips, and I held them back, wrestling with what was right. Before I could come up with something we heard braying laughter, and glancing over the railing we watched a couple of guys round the corner below us. One of them, spotting the full moon, dropped to his knees and howled. Should we duck? David whispered, and I snickered, loud enough for them to hear. Who's up there? one of the guys called, scanning the back of the house. David rolled his eyes in my direction, then acknowledged the question with a wave of his hand. Who's that? the guy asked, walking through the grass and squinting up at us. His friend, having lost an audience, got to his *feet and brushed off his jeans. This is Adam, David said, inclining his head in my direction, And I'm David. He leaned forward, his hands dangling over the edge of the railing; I watched the change in the man's expression as he got his first good look at him. Well, hi, the man said. He peered into the shadows, trying to place me, and I took an unwilling step into the moonlight. Hi, he said.*

Introducing himself, he added a nod in the direction of his friend, who gaped at us with little discretion. Nice to meet you, David said. I mumbled something noncommittal, and the initiator cocked his head. He had a scruff of beard I found wholly unappealing, and I grimaced as he stroked a smarmy tuft of chest hair protruding from the v of his shirt. We're thinking about going dancing, he told us, dropping the name of a club I knew by reputation only. What do you think, Adam? David asked, You feel like dancing? I shook my head, though my spine suddenly shivered at the thought of having him that close. Sorry, boys, David said, turning back to the men, his shrug failing to convey the apology his words suggested. Well, what about if we come up there? the initiator blurted, and David looked at me, his eyebrows raised. God no, I whispered, and he laughed, the sound as perfect and warm and miraculous as a summer rain. My own laughter spun helpless and out of control.

Minutes later I hung suspended over the side of the balcony. The men who had lingered below us were now inside, making their way up the stairs and through the dark bedroom; David waited for me in the soft grass. Jump, he called, his voice steady, low, and still I hesitated, trying to remember who first decided that there was no other escape. My fingers, gripping the edge of the wood, turned white before my eyes. There's still time, I thought, there's time. Jump, David insisted beneath me, and I let go.

With a whump I hit the ground, but I scrambled to my feet as I heard the door open. Grabbing David's outstretched hand, I ran with him around the corner of the house, where we leaned into each other, breathless, straining to hear. I don't know, a bewildered voice said as we collapsed into muffled laughter, and the same voice called David's name, then mine, with a petulance we found exhilarating. Maybe they jumped down, the other one suggested, and David and I looked at each other in alarm. Come with me, he said, reaching again for my hand when we heard the door close, and I followed him through the night, in between one house and the next, the grass slick beneath our shoes. He finally dropped at the edge of a grove of trees, in a spread of grass

185

that shone silver beneath the moonlight. I fell beside him, and he held his finger to my lips. Wet grass bled into the back of my shirt.

His kiss was terrible and wonderful and I had just one opportunity to change my mind, when he pulled away to see my reaction. I almost wept in his absence. Pulling him toward me again, I closed my eyes, then opened them as I felt his tongue on my neck, along the edge of my collarbone, below my navel. The moon held steady above me, rock hard and full. I couldn't tear my eyes away, though they watered in its brilliance.

Afterward, I pulled my jeans to my waist and buttoned them with fingers still shaking. David handed me a tissue, and I wound it around the condom we'd used and slid it into my pocket. Without speaking, we walked back toward Paul's house; I slowed to a stop when we reached my car. Adam, he started, and I wondered, before we were distracted by the couple opening Paul's front door, what he would say. Then I recognized the men as friends of mine, friends of Bobby's, and I averted my eyes. In a low voice, as David moved away from me without ceremony, he told me where he worked.

I left. Halfway home I remembered the condom, and I lifted my hips off the seat to take it from my pocket. The tissue had leaked, and I unrolled my window and threw the mess into the wind, then wiped my fingers on my jeans. The next morning I'd find the stains along with grass and mud from where I'd knelt behind him, and I'd scrub them with a brush before I threw them in the washing machine along with the rest of our laundry.

When I got home I let myself in without a sound. Bobby was asleep; at least that's what I let myself believe. I undressed and slunk down the hall to our only bathroom, where I closed and locked the door and sat on the toilet with my head in my hands. I couldn't get the taste of him out of my mouth, and I don't know that I wanted to. Ten minutes passed before I admitted to myself that I was pressing my luck. I washed the best I could without risking a shower, until I couldn't smell him anymore. When I got into bed Bobby turned away from me, as if even in sleep he knew what I'd done. I rolled onto my side and stared out the window. The moon held me in its gaze.

Adam? Joel asks. I give my head a vehement shake, and when my vision returns I realize I'm clutching his arm. I fling my hand away as if I've been scalded and back away from him, out of the reach of his beseeching hands. Bed, I manage, and then I turn and scramble up the stairs.

In our bedroom, shielding my eyes from *Adam,* I curl on my side under the covers. I don't answer when Joel says my name.

~ ~ ~

The rumble of the garage door awakens me, and I can almost hear Joel's truck turning over once, then twice, before finally catching. He's taking James to the airport, which means he'll be gone at least an hour and maybe more; I should use the time to figure out how I'm going to explain myself. Instead I stare listlessly out the window. I never closed the blinds last night, and I guess Joel didn't either. Judging from the tight pull of the blankets on his side of the bed, he didn't sleep here at all.

With a tentative finger I touch my swollen eyelid. There's still some discomfort, and I absently trace the bone. Above me the ceiling fan sits inert; apparently I didn't take the time to turn the fan on either, and my skin feels moist, despite the air conditioner. I'm tired of the heat. By the middle of August every year I'm ready for fall, but I know I've got another solid month of hundred degree weather before I'll have a chance to cool off. For years now the pool has been my only saving grace.

I sit up at the thought. Maybe if I spend some time in the water I'll reappear invigorated and armed with an excuse for my appalling behavior.

At ten o'clock in the morning I can already tell that we're on track for another scorcher. Squinting in the bright light, I approach the pool, then drag my toe in the water and find to my dismay that it feels more like a bath. I lower myself in anyway, swimming the length of the pool before I come up for air.

I'm tired. I'm tired and out of shape, and I lean against the side, wondering how I've managed to let so much go, in such a short time. Shouldn't exercise be something you can store, like knowledge? What good is it to cycle more than one hundred miles a week one summer if the next I can barely make it from one end of the pool to the other?

Again I think of Bobby, of how he might have aged, had he been given the opportunity. And David. I close my eyes, the water lapping against my skin. What would he be like now? Do I want to know? Because I could probably find him, if I was so inclined. I could do a search online, or I could try to track down some of my friends from Kentucky, guys with whom I haven't had much correspondence since Bobby died, since I moved to Austin. I could ask around. I could email him, or call. I could ask him what he thought that day, when I never showed, when I never contacted him again.

But that would be even worse. To talk to him again, to hear his voice: that would be an even greater betrayal. Bobby's was the last voice I heard, and to override his with David's seems like unfaithfulness of the cruelest kind. Still I wonder. Would he be involved, would he have children? Would he be happy to hear from me? Because he would remember me. I know he would remember.

Shivering, I open my eyes. I've stayed in the pool a little too long, and I hoist myself onto the side before I realize I've forgotten a towel. Hugging my arms to my chest, I run up the stairs to the back door. The breeze prickles my skin, and goose bumps rise along my shoulders. With a wet hand I turn the knob.

Joel's waiting for me in the kitchen. I don't know how long he's been standing there by the window, watching me, and I cast a hasty glance at the clock. I don't have the time to make any kind of calculation before he says, You're dripping water all over the floor, Adam. I automatically head in the direction of the stairs but he holds me back. Hang on, he says, I'll get you a towel. Teeth chattering, I wait while he goes into the laundry room. I can hear him rummaging through the dryer, and then he's back, offering me one of the bath sheets from upstairs. I drape it around my shoulders like a cape. You look like a wounded super-hero, he says ruefully, and relieved that he's trying to lighten the mood, I offer him a wan smile. He shakes his head, as if he's warning me that he's not going to let me off the hook, not that easily. Go take a shower, he says, And then we'll talk.

I go upstairs, thankful that he hasn't forced a conversation as I stood there in my wet trunks, and agitated at the same time by the no-nonsense tone of his voice. I've obviously had a bad weekend. I'm not sure I want a lecture, too, but I have a feeling that's what I'm going to get, and I turn on the shower, pulling off my swimming trunks and leaving them in an untidy puddle on the bathroom floor. Steam slowly coats the mirror.

When he was at his worst, when he was close to the end, I had to give him sponge baths. He wouldn't let anyone else touch him, and I'd fill a bowl with warm water and set it beside his bed. Ringing out a thick washcloth, I'd start with his face, wiping his forehead, his cheeks, his chin. I had to move slowly, gently; his skin was so sensitive. From the medication, I'd say, and with what little energy he had he'd roll his eyes. Because I'm dying, he would've said if he had the strength. His lips were cracked and sore, and I'd rub them with Vaseline because that was the only thing that helped. After I finished washing his face I'd lift his shirt, biting the inside of my cheeks at the sight of every new lesion, every inexplicable rash. When I was finished with his chest and stomach, after I'd helped him into a sitting position so I could reach his back, I covered the top half of him with our quilt, then worked his briefs down his legs. We'd already given up on pajama bottoms by that time; the drawstrings knotted too easily, the elastic dug into his tender skin.

Washing the rest of him took a fortitude I didn't always have. I kept my expression impassive, but I almost couldn't bear the sight of him. His legs, which had always been slender, had become so thin and frail that I was half-afraid the bones would break apart in my hands. His feet I rubbed with lotion, something hypo-allergenic but which I still feared would somehow cause him pain. I kept his nails clipped, but they were stained an unhealthy yellow, and the toes themselves were brittle and gnarled. Changing the water, I'd soak the washcloth, then carefully touch his penis. If I looked up at him I'd find his eyes closed, and a couple of times I had hope that maybe, somehow, he'd grow hard in my hands. But we were long past that point, and after I cleaned him I eased his legs apart and simply wiped between them.

The sponge baths were bad, but they weren't the turning point for Bobby. What he couldn't handle was the chair I insisted he use in the shower when he first started slipping. Suddenly light-headed, he'd grab for the shower curtain as he fell, taking the whole thing down with him. After the second time I told him he was going to have to sit down to bathe. He wouldn't hear of it. I'm not that far gone, he insisted, but the very next day he passed out. I found him in an inch of water, and when he finally came to I told him I wasn't going to take no for an answer. I bought a hard plastic chair at a medical supply store that I was beginning to patronize with a frequency that alarmed me, and placed its rubber stoppers firmly in the bottom of the tub. Bobby watched from the doorway, angry and frightened. Well? I asked after he took his first shower sitting down. But he wouldn't admit that the chair made bathing easier, and he held a grudge for a long time.

I've been in the shower long enough to use all the hot water, and I reach behind me for the faucet. Stepping from the tub, I wrap a towel around my waist, then lean forward to wipe the mirror. My face, disembodied and distorted by the steam, stares back.

~ ~ ~

Joel and I spend the better part of the afternoon dissecting our finances, trying to figure out the best way to get Trainor his money and make sure we have enough for the criminal attorney that I'll inevitably have to hire. I'll have calls to make tomorrow; Trainor has already given me a few names, and Joel suggests Kyle as another resource, rubbing his temples. He's been complaining of a headache, and I watch him, his eyes closed, his brow furrowed. I've been told in no uncertain terms that I'm going back to see Lydia, and I've agreed, fearing that if I refused he'd tell me he was leaving, for good.

Now he passes one hand across his forehead like a true Victorian lady. He hasn't accused me explicitly, but I know I'm the one to blame for his headache. Take some Advil, Joel, I mumble. But he won't take anything unless he's dying, and I gather up the last of our paperwork. I'm going upstairs, I tell him. He nods without opening his eyes, and for just a second I wonder what would happen if I covered his face with a pillow and put us both out of our misery.

When I finally awaken night has fallen. I'm surprised Joel hasn't come after me, and I make my way downstairs and find him in the great room, in the dark. He winces at the warm glow of the lamp, shielding his eyes as if I've just turned a spotlight in his direction. Still have a headache? I ask, and the lines between his eyebrows deepen. Nut up and take something, Joel, I say, A few Advil can't compare with all that shit you smoked this weekend. Mumbling something I can't hear, he holds his hand to his head. What? I ask. I already took some Advil, he repeats. Frowning, I take a closer look at him, then place the palm of my hand on his forehead. Oh honey, I say, You have a fever.

I try to convince him to go upstairs, but he doesn't want to move. You'll be so much more comfortable, Joel, I say, and he tells me that he doesn't want to be alone. The admission crushes me, and I squat down in front of him and tell him that he won't be alone, I promise, I'll be right there with him. He gives me a look as if he doesn't quite believe me. What am I doing? I think. What have I done? But I help him to his feet and guide him up the stairs and into bed. I'm cold, he protests when I try to lift his tee shirt over his head, and I let him slide under the covers fully clothed. Tucking the blankets around him, I start to stroke his hair but he shakes his head and I end up folding my hands in my lap. Get some rest, I say.

He's sick for three days. His fever spikes late every afternoon and disappears each morning; he's just starting to think he's feeling better when his headache returns. I make good on my promise, and refuse to leave him alone. Three days in a row I call in sick to work despite his protests, and I set up camp beside him while he dozes on the couch. You're pushing your luck with Vincent, he warns me, and even though he's probably right I tell him he's wrong. I have only a handful of sick days left, and I know that means I'll be taking time without pay at some point, as my father worsens. But I refuse to capitulate, and each morning I bring him tea and toast and sit beside him. I don't want to be anywhere else.

I avoid Trainor's calls, evade his text messages. Whatever correspondence I've had with him I've forced through email, and I've kept those as short and impersonal as possible. I'll have my work cut out for me, trying to explain myself, and I lie awake the night before I start work again, listening to the soft sound of Joel breathing beside me. Whatever's coming won't be good.

~ ~ ~

I'm in the middle of a phone call early the next morning when Trainor comes into my office without knocking. I saw him arrive, saw him shoot a glance my way as he spoke with Vincent, who for whatever reason hasn't commented on my absence. I shake my head when Trainor shuts my door, mouthing that now isn't a good time, but he folds his arms across his chest in a way that tells me he's not going to let me put him off. Let me give you a call back, I say into my headset.

I can see Darlene through the window; talk about avoidance. She's barely spoken to me in the past month, and she looks up at us now with an irritated expression. Please remember that everyone can see you, I warn Trainor. I really don't give a shit, he says. He leans over, his fists on the desk. You can't expect me to post bond for you on Saturday and then just disappear, he says. I didn't disappear, I mutter. You were out for three days and I barely heard a word from you, Adam, he says. Joel was sick, I explain, and he says, I don't care if he was on his fucking deathbed!

I've never told him about Bobby, but I'm still put off by the insensitivity in his tone. This is not the place, I tell him, getting to my feet. You're right, he agrees, But I can't seem to get your attention outside of the office. He reminds me that he's the one I called Friday night, he's the one who posted bond. I deserve some acknowledgement, he says, and I fumble with the tie I've chosen, thinking an impressive wardrobe might counteract the fact that I've been missing in action for the past three days. I have an unwelcome image of my finger poised over that phone, ready to dial Joel's cell and choosing Trainor's instead. He didn't miss a beat, had me out of there in less than twelve hours.

At the very least, he adds before I can say anything, We have business to discuss. I sent you an email, I mumble, I'll have the money for you later today. I'm not concerned about the money! he says, Jesus, Adam. Falling into the chair across from me, he rubs his hand across his bald head, then peers across the desk in my direction. Sit down for Christ's sake, he says, and I slowly lower myself to my chair. He watches me for a minute, the palm of one hand muzzling his mouth, as if he's about to say something he'd rather not. He finally sighs, muttering something about his better judgment. He knows a few people, he says, and he's made some calls. I've gotten your charges dropped, he tells me.

I stare at him in frank disbelief. How? I ask, and he shrugs, looking pleased with himself. I know a few people, he repeats, and I say, You're having an affair with the D.A., too? He chuckles, though he doesn't deny anything. The fact that the kid was under twenty-one helped, he admits.

So he was underage; I'd figured as much. And he's okay? I ask. Looks worse than you, Trainor assures me. You saw him? I ask, and Trainor nods. I wanted to get his story before I started asking for favors, he says. He tells me the kid's missed a few of his classes this week, that he has a broken nose and a couple of black eyes, but that he's far more concerned about his parents finding out he was at a bar. So that's it? I ask, I'm free? You're free, he says, and he gives me a look so coy it straightens my spine.

~ ~ ~

I tell Joel that Trainor's managed to get my charges dropped; he's thrilled, but quick to guess that Trainor's motives aren't altruistic. He just wants to get laid, he assures me. I don't think so, I mumble, but Joel shakes his head. He's setting a trap, he says. I don't have the heart to tell him I'm already caught.

Joel wants to go away for the weekend; so does Trainor. At this point I'd rather go to Kentucky, and I call my mother, half-hoping for a request that I won't be able to deny. Instead she tells me that my father has wrapped up the last of his treatments, that he has a good solid month of recuperation before they'll do another scan to see how everything looks. Maybe I should come up, I say, but she tells me that in all honesty they could use a little time to themselves. And you know how difficult these trips are for you, she adds.

She's right, though I'm embarrassed to hear the words. I don't need to go to Kentucky right now; that's probably the last thing I need, and over the next few days I let Joel talk me into a weekend getaway right here in Austin. I know what he's doing. He wants to plant us in some turn-of-the-century house near downtown in an attempt to evoke last month's conversation, and I want nothing more than to be convinced that's possible. But Trainor's right there at every turn, texting me, calling me. I string him along, mired in guilt.

When Joel catches me at work he tells me about the bed and breakfast he's found; he's surprised he was able to get a reservation over Labor Day weekend with such short notice. Must be fate, he says, referring to the fact that this weekend will mark eight years since we first met. I've already told Trainor that I'll be unavailable starting Friday afternoon; one look at his expression had me scrambling to appease him, and I've somehow led him to believe that the weekend is a preliminary step in leaving Joel. You're ending it, he said, and I lied and told him soon, soon. Maybe, I think, Joel and I will go away for the weekend and never come back.

~ ~ ~

I leave work early on Friday, under the scrutinizing eye of Vincent. I'm half-afraid he'll stop me, and I pick up my pace on my way to the elevator, catching Trainor's eye. I spent time at his apartment last night, where he'd forced me to reiterate my plans for the weekend. I'm laying groundwork, I lied, I don't want to take Joel by surprise. Now he nods a quick goodbye, rising to his feet and intercepting Vincent; I manage to duck into the elevator.

Outside Joel's waiting for me, the BMW humming at the curb. The moment he sees me he slides from his seat, as if he can't stand another second behind the wheel. Hey, he says, giving my arm a quick squeeze. Hi yourself, I say, and he walks around the back of the car. I get in, my nose automatically wrinkling. When I lift my eyes to the rearview mirror I see them.

Tomatoes, ripe and sweet, spill from their bags, fill the backseat, topple onto the floorboards, permeating the air with a thick, unrelenting aroma that knocks me backward, across a decade and a half. Gagging, I stumble from the car.

We couldn't stay outside, couldn't stand the smell, couldn't stand the sight of all those tomatoes rotting on the vine. They grew anyway, a bumper crop. Even Indy tired of them, and when we let him out the back door he started avoiding the garden altogether. We should pick them, I said one afternoon, Even if we don't eat them we should pick them. I'd been looking out the window, but I turned to place Bobby; he was tapping medication into the palm of his hand, and he shook his head. No, he said, and the flatness of his tone angered me. Everything angered me: the medication, the sound of him swallowing his pills, the chill that had seeped into our bed the weekend of that cold front last spring and that we couldn't seem to banish, even in the middle of August. I didn't want to pick the tomatoes any more than he did. What I wanted was to pick a fight, and when he recapped the medicine and glanced up at me I said, Someone might want them, Bobby.

His jaw tightened, but he didn't say anything; still I goaded him. Why are we wasting them? I asked, When we could give them away, or eat them ourselves? Is that what you want? he snapped, You want to eat them? The thought made me nauseous, but I nodded anyway. We could make spaghetti sauce, I said, though by now my voice was weak. Fine, he said, flinging the prescription bottle on the counter. Barefoot, he brushed past me and opened the back door. Without a word I watched him go.

But once he'd brought the wheelbarrow from the side of the house I changed my mind. Opening the back door, I let it bang shut behind me as he started picking, without stopping to examine the fruit in his hands. Every tomato made it into the wheelbarrow, ripe, rotten, or otherwise. Bobby, I said, trying to stop him, but he shook me away, stripping every tomato from the vines until the wheelbarrow overflowed, until tomatoes tumbled onto the ground, splitting in front of us and oozing their insides onto the green grass. Bobby, I pleaded, but he shut me up, blocking my hand with his arm. I trailed him across the yard, where he hoisted the wheelbarrow up the steps, grunting and grimacing. Wrenching the screen door open, he forced the wheelbarrow through the doorway, scraping the paint on the doorjamb. Jesus, Bobby! I said, and he turned on me with a roar. You wanted the fucking tomatoes, Adam! he shouted, dumping the wheelbarrow, Well, here they are!

They rolled under the kitchen table, splattered underfoot. The smell of their squished insides filled the kitchen; even Indy balked in the doorway. Bobby, I whispered, and he reached for the tomato nearest him and drilled it, right at the window. With a sickening thud it split, coating the glass with its juice. He threw another, and another, with sharper precision then I'd ever seen him throw anything, and when I cried for him to stop he lobbed one in my direction. I ducked, but it caught me on the shoulder; the moment it made contact he burst into tears. I want to take it back, he sobbed, I want to take it back!

Joel's shaking me, and my head snaps backward, hard enough to hurt. Moaning, I hold my hand to my neck. His mouth moves, but I can't hear anything but Bobby's voice. *I want to take it back! he cried, and I wanted to shut him up because I knew what he was going to say next and I couldn't bear to hear the words. I couldn't bear them. Bobby, I begged, but he said them anyway, dropping his hands and looking up at me, his eyes raw and red and dripping with tears. I can't, he whispered, I can't.*

I feel Joel's hand on my back and sense myself being eased to the pavement. I'm dimly aware that a crowd has gathered. Gradually, the world shifts, and I realize that I'm lying on the sidewalk next to the BMW; I can hear the soft purr of its motor, and after a minute I can see an iridescent cloud emanating from its right flank. My eyes move toward the sound of Joel's voice. He's kneeling beside me; over his shoulder a half a dozen people peer down at us. I clear my throat and try to sit up, which causes everyone to murmur. Don't move, Joel says, but I shake my head and maneuver myself until I'm perched against the curb. I think he's okay, someone says, and slowly, one by one, they make their retreat.

I glance at Joel. He's ashen beneath his tan. What the fuck? he says. The tomatoes, I say, So many. I got them from Kyle, he says, and I force myself to my feet as Joel protests. Lurching toward the car, I jerk open the back door.

There in front of me sits one small sack of tomatoes. One. I stare at the brown paper bag. I thought…, I say, I thought…. What? Joel asks, and when I don't answer he says, Get in the car, Adam. Get rid of them, I say hoarsely. The tomatoes? he asks, surprised. Get rid of them, Joel! I cry, and he does.

~ ~ ~

He's insisted on driving and I've acquiesced, partly because I don't think I'm capable and partly because I don't know where we're going. He's already scouted out the bed and breakfast, and I've told him to take me there now, instead of to the emergency room or Lydia's office, where he's suggested we go. I just need to rest, I assure him, leaning back in the passenger seat and closing my eyes.

Beside me he shimmies with nervous energy. I can feel the vibration surrounding him, and I wonder what his masseuse would say now, what color she'd assign his aura. The thought makes me chuckle, and I sense Joel turn his head my way. What's so funny? he asks, and I shelve the truth and open my eyes. Nothing, I say, Everything. He takes a quick glance at the highway in front of him, then looks again in my direction. I'm going to ask you something, he says, And I want you to be honest with me. Would you just concentrate on the road? I mumble. How much of this has to do with Bobby? he asks.

Bobby. The first syllable escapes my mouth with an exhalation, an ahhhh of satisfaction and remorse; with the second I try to recapture what I've lost. Bobby, I said when I introduced myself, shaking his hand across the table in that library, thrilled he already knew who I was. I breathed his name, moaned it into his mouth that Christmas, my grandmother's quilt wrapped around us. The night I woke to find him missing, the night the garden took him away from me, I crooned the word, tried to bring him back. And when I realized we'd never be the same I sobbed his name into my pillow, as he touched me with a tentative hand.

Joel, I say, my voice sounding far away, Let's just get to the hotel. He bites his lip; I've given him the answer he expected, and I turn away from him, hunkering down against the window. The glass feels cool against my forehead, and I stare out at the landscape, until I can't tell if it's the speed of the car or the tears in my eyes that blur the horizon.

~ ~ ~

I have to hand it to Joel; we have exceptional accommodations. After we register we're led up a discreet staircase to our room, where we find an antique four poster bed covered with a soft, creamy quilt that beckons us. Tasteful paintings adorn the walls, and we have an adjoining bathroom with a claw-footed tub, though it's also outfitted with a shower head. A chair sits at the foot of the bed, a wing-back upholstered in dusty pink. I'm tired, I confess. I can't imagine why, he says.

At his urging I slide beneath the bedcovers. We can sleep, he says, but his hands suggest otherwise. A month has slipped by, an entire month since we've been together, but I still have nothing for him. He's not discouraged; in fact, I think he'd go on all night if I let him, and I finally stop him, when I know I'm not going to be able to will anything to happen. He murmurs reassurance, telling me that we'll nap and try again later. Yes, I say, All right.

Later I'll wish that I'd paid attention that night, the last night we spend together. The press of his leg against my own, his hand clasped in mine, the soft sound of his breath beside me; I'll wish I'd noticed more. But I'm so tired, and I fall into a sleep so deep that I don't wake until ten o'clock the following morning. In the hazy realm between dreaming and waking I see a figure perched on the window bench as the air conditioner stirs the long, gauzy curtains. For just a second I think I've found Bobby. I watch as he takes a bite of a tomato, then smiles, juice dripping from his bared teeth like blood.

At first I'm not aware that I've slept through the night. I start talking dinner; Joel points to the clock, and smoothes the wrinkles from my forehead with his fingers. You needed the rest, he tells me when I apologize, and I can't argue. Even now I feel weary, stripped bare by my dreams. What have you been doing all this time? I ask, and he shrugs, easing back into bed beside me. Nothing, he says. Nothing? I ask. Thinking, he says,

197

Sleeping. Trailing one hand across my chest, he tells me he's happy I've slept, that our intention this weekend should be recovery, reconnection. We don't have any responsibilities right now, he says, Other than to ourselves and to each other. Lowering his voice, he tells me that he loves me, he misses me, he'll do whatever it takes to get us back on track. To punctuate this last point he kisses my shoulder, then lingers.

I know instantly that nothing's going to happen. Joel doesn't seem to mind taking his time, but I can't erase the image of Bobby I had when I woke and I tell Joel when I've finally persuaded him to stop that maybe my body's out of whack. Maybe I just need to eat something, I add, and he nods, frustrated and fairly unconvinced. You're not taking that medication again, are you? he asks. You know what, Joel? I say, That doesn't help.

We've missed breakfast in the parlor, and Joel suggests brunch instead, or lunch if I'd rather. He's willing to be flexible, he says, but apparently not so much that he'll grab burgers and a couple of beers. What am I supposed to eat there? he asks when I bring up the name of a place not far from us that he frequented in college. We're about a block from our bed and breakfast when he asks; he wanted to walk and I'd agreed, though now I wish I hadn't. The heat's unbearable. Anyway, he says without looking at me, I don't know if a hamburger is the best thing for you.

Whether he's talking about my weight or what happened this morning is beside the point. What would you like me to eat, Joel? I ask, A salad? What's wrong with that? he asks. I haven't eaten in twenty-four hours, I tell him, I want something more substantial than a salad. He shrugs, reminding me that he hasn't eaten in twenty-four hours either. I snort. I can picture him depriving himself of food for an entire week and labeling his behavior a cleansing ritual. Look, he says, I don't want to argue. Pointing at the deli across the street, he tells me that we should just get something, fast. You're irritable, he says.

We order mediocre sandwiches and salads, but we eat everything on our plate, quickly, without saying a word. Better? he asks after I've gnawed my pickle spear to a nub. I nod and his mouth slides to the side. Now that you've been fed..., he says.

But we don't make it back to the room. There's a turret that overlooks the garden at our bed and breakfast and Joel wants to check it out. We talk to the proprietor, who hands us a slim, black key and gives us directions to the top of a second flight of stairs we didn't know existed.

The room's small and round and sparsely furnished. It's also unbelievably warm. God, the light, Joel says, turning slow circles in the middle of the floor. From an artist's perspective I see what he means. But those ancient windows do nothing to insulate us from the heat, and I wipe my forehead with the back of my arm. I could sketch you, he says, turning back to me. No thanks, I say, stepping forward to peer down into the garden. He's silent, and I glance in his direction. I'll die of heat stroke, I protest. Fine, he says, shrugging, but I know I've hurt his feelings and I turn back to the garden, swallowing a sigh. All right, I say, Get your things.

He leaves before I can change my mind and I stare out the window. Below me the garden grows thick and lush, ivy twining up the trunks of pecans, branches heavy with a coming crop. Crepe myrtles bloom fuchsia and lavender, drip petals onto the verdant earth. My own yard looks dry and brittle; they must be pumping an obscene amount of water into this garden to keep it flourishing so late in the season, and I think about pointing that out to Joel when he comes back, though he'll probably just shrug. He picks and chooses his causes, insisted on converting our pool to a salt water system because of the chemicals, but indulges in the longest, hottest showers of anyone I've ever met.

Something scurries along the perimeter and I watch as two squirrels dart up the trunk of one of the pecans, chased by a small, yapping dog who must belong to the owner. From the crook in the tree the squirrels chatter. Joel had a pecan tree at his old house; he reminds me every year, before he points out the lack of vegetation on our own property. I usually just gesture out the window in the direction of the lake.

We had a pear tree in our backyard, Bobby and I. The pears ripened in late October, *branches bending beneath the weight of its fruit. I'd eat them right from the tree, without washing them first. You should at least check for bugs, Bobby would say, and I'd roll my eyes, my mouth filled with the sweet, aromatic juice. But Bobby liked them, too, and we'd pick as many as we could, knowing they'd keep forever. He'd bake them with cinnamon and nutmeg, and in those days before Halloween we'd breathe in that rich smell as we watched*

the skies, waiting for the cold. Every year he made them, including the Octo-
ber before he died. I didn't eat them that year. The day he baked them I was
with David.

Joel's footsteps echo behind me and I turn, running the back of my
hand across my sweaty brow. He tosses me a bottle of water, which misses
my outstretched hands. You okay? he asks as I bend to retrieve it, You
look kind of pale. Where do you want me? I ask. He glances around the
room, then points to the sofa. Why don't you start there, he says.

I've probably sat for Joel a hundred times in the past five years. At first I
found the work fascinating, even provocative. His fervor held me captive, and though I knew his focus carried over to any subject I loved being
the recipient. He liked sketching with a pencil, and the sound of the lead
scratching across the paper would soon become the only thing we could
hear. He rarely spoke, and when he did it was with an authority that
didn't usually infuse his voice. Look at me, he'd command, or, God, that's
good, don't move. I never spoke myself; I can't imagine that he would've
heard me if I had.

Gradually, though, over the past year, our sessions have become
tedious. I don't want to be examined with such intensity; I don't want to
be picked apart. The last few times he's asked me I've declined his invitation and he sketched me anyway, surreptitiously, on a post-it note or on
the back of an envelope. A few months ago I was clearing out the junk
drawer in the kitchen and found a dozen drawings that must have been
from the beginning of the year. I could tell, because in every one I was
wearing a sweater he'd bought me for Christmas. He'd used paper from a
small, spiral notebook, and he'd obviously caught me at a private moment. Thin blue lines cut through my distracted expression, and I stared
at the pictures in my hand, wondering what I'd been thinking and feeling
utterly, positively invaded. You really need to ask me first, I told him that
night, showing him the drawings, and he apologized and said, Of course,
of course. But he does it anyway, and he probably always will.

Now I sit on the edge of the sofa as he flips open his sketch pad. What do
you want me to do? I ask, and he glances up at me from where he's lowered
himself to the floor. Lie down, he says. I do, with a sense of relief. This I
can handle, at least until the heat gets to be too much. Turn toward me, he

says, and I shift until I'm lying on my right shoulder. The sky surrounds us; we're too high to see even the tops of the trees. I look at Joel. His pencil's already moving across the paper, though his eyes haven't left mine.

Sometimes I marvel at the two men who have informed my adult life. Bobby was nothing like Joel. He wouldn't have been able to sketch me to save his life, and he probably would've flushed with self-consciousness if I'd asked him if he could. He liked computers, and knowing how things worked; he relished structure, and precision, and was fastidious to a fault. Rarely excitable, I could've easily accused him of dispassion, though that wasn't the case. He adored that dog, for one thing, and there were moments, many of them, when I knew he couldn't be any more alive.

He'd been sick off and on for almost five months, since just after Thanksgiving, and finally, finally, he was feeling better. All day Saturday he spent in the garden as I chided him, worried that he'd work himself to exhaustion. I'm fine, he said, taking off his sweatshirt and tying it around his waist, I feel great. Smiling at me over his shoulder, he brushed off my concerns, even though by then we both knew that one little cold could render him incapacitated for an entire week. Should I help? I finally asked, squatting beside him, and he laughed. Sure, he said, handing me a spade, Why not?

That night I woke to find him missing, and I stumbled from the bedroom, calling his name. But he wasn't in the bathroom, or the living room either, and just when I was starting to panic I saw him through the window. Bobby, I said, banging open the back door, and he turned to me wearing an expression of such ecstasy that I stopped in my tracks. Adam! he said, I feel so alive! Holding his hands out in front of him, he laughed. I'm tingling, he told me, I'm actually tingling. I looked at his hands; I could see them shaking, even in the moonlight, and I realized he'd wandered outside in nothing more than a pair of pajama bottoms and a tee shirt. But he ignored my suggestion to return to the house, tilting his head back to look at the stars instead. Everything's so beautiful, he murmured, Don't you see? Shivering, I crossed my arms over my chest. Beside me he smiled, stretching his arms toward the sky. I'm not scared, he said, For the first time I'm not afraid.

Six days later he was cooking dinner, and as he reached into the refrigerator and his shirt slid above his waist I saw the lesion. Against his pale skin it looked positively gruesome, and I had to steel myself before I spoke. I'm fine,

he protested, I'm feeling fine. He told me we'd wait a few days to see if it disap-
peared. Bobby, I said, and he brushed my hand away. I'm fine, he said.

But the following day he spent mostly in bed, claiming he wanted to catch
up on his reading. Instead I caught him disappearing into the bathroom
every twenty minutes. Sometime after lunch I demanded an explanation; he
lifted a trembling hand to his mouth, the skin beneath his eyes a faint, pale
blue. I think, he said, I think I'm sick.

Judging from the tone of Joel's voice he's said my name more than
once. I snap upright, but he's still sitting on the floor, his pencil poised
over his sketchpad, furrowing his brow. Maybe we should stop, he says. I
look around me. The floor's littered with failed attempts. Okay, I say, but
he stops me before I can get to my feet. Why don't you rest a minute? he
says, You look peaked. With one hand he smoothes the hair back from my
sweaty forehead. I focus on the feel of his palm against my skin, and after
a minute he leans in to kiss me.

I want this time to be different, but my skin lacks sensation and I watch
with detachment as he pulls my tee shirt over my head and slides his
tongue around my nipple. Closing my eyes, I think of Trainor, trying to
recall that moment in the elevator of that hotel in January, when I let him
convince me to take him back to my room. But he does nothing for me,
and as Joel moves lower I search for something else, my hands moving to
the back of his head out of nothing more than habit. Bobby, I think, but I
can't. I can't.

Sensing Joel's impatience, I squeeze my eyes shut in concentration.
Joel, Trainor, Bobby. Gary, the boyfriend I had while Joel was in Mexico;
Chad, the guy I started seeing after Joel left me at the end of '99. Travis,
my first, the older brother of a friend from high school. Every man I've
ever had or wanted, every man who at some point crossed my path and
about whom I thought: maybe. I comb through them all, and then suddenly he's there, *sweat cementing our bodies as we moved together in his*
bedroom, the evening sun staining the walls with its bloody light. We kept our
eyes open, right to the end, because I wanted to see him, because the feel of
him beneath me wasn't enough.

I've instantly stiffened, and I hear Joel's appreciative murmur at the
same moment Bobby appears before me, wearing an expression of dis-

gusted reproach. My eyes spring open, and I pull back, away from Joel's mouth. What? he moans, but even he can see how quickly I've deflated. As I wrestle with Bobby's image he falls back against his heels, then stretches out on the floor, one arm covering his eyes.

Look, I finally say, I'm sorry. He shrugs, without bothering to lift his arm. I button my shorts, wiping my hands on my tee shirt. It's fucking hot up here, I mutter. It's an old house, he says, sighing.

After a minute he gets to his feet; I wait as he gathers his drawings, bending after a minute to pluck one from the floor myself. His lines are crisp and cool in places, smudged in others; I know if I examined his thumb and forefinger I'd find traces of lead. On the page he's barely touched my body, but my eyes loom large, too large for my face, wrinkles I know I don't have spiraling out from the corners. I hold out my hand for the rest of the drawings; he relinquishes them without protest, and I shuffle through them, my heart pounding, trying to find one, just one, that might give me hope. I look haunted in every one. Hey, he says, trying to catch my hand, but I pull away from him. I'm going downstairs, I say, and he lets me go.

~ ~ ~

Later, after we've showered and gone to dinner, after we've agreed to end the day early with the idea that tomorrow might be different, we lie together in bed. Lamplight colors the room the same pink as the chair across from us. Joel hasn't reached for me, but I know he will and my eyes roll in their sockets like those of a spooked horse. We'll take it easy tomorrow, he murmurs beside me, We'll sleep, go for a swim. Propping his head on his fist, he runs his hand across my skin. We can do anything, he says, he'll go along with anything I suggest. Even hamburgers, he tells me, and when I fail to smile he bites his lip, hard enough to draw blood. With a shaking finger I wipe it away. Tomorrow will be different, he promises, and I nod, closing my eyes. I have a feeling he's right.

I made it twenty-three days without contacting him. I slipped back into my life, convinced that refusing to think about what had happened with David was tantamount to erasing it. I'd slipped one time, just once; Bobby had practically encouraged me to do so. And I'd used protection, which was more than Bobby had done. There didn't have to be ramifications.

But the problem was that I couldn't stop thinking about him. Midway through a conference call at work, walking to my car with my dry cleaning, the sweet smell of that grass would come out of nowhere. Are you okay? Bobby asked one night as I set the table for dinner, and when I nodded, hot and dizzy, he placed one hand on my forehead. I jerked away before I realized what I was doing. I didn't want him to break the spell.

I called him on a Monday, just over three weeks from the day we met. I looked up the name of the company he'd told me and dialed their main number. There was no mistaking the voice that answered, and I dropped the phone on its cradle. For a full minute I didn't move, and then I picked up the phone and dialed the number again.

I met him that night after work. He told me how to get to his place, a wood frame house just east of downtown, and I eased to a stop alongside the curb. There was a chain-link fence around his front yard, and I let myself in the gate and let it creak shut behind me. He opened the door when I knocked; he was wearing jeans and a thin white shirt, but no shoes. He'll kiss me, I thought, as soon as the door closes behind us. But he didn't, and I realized as he offered me a drink, keeping his distance, that he wasn't going to make the first move again.

I wish I could say that I changed my mind, that I shared a glass of wine with him and then said goodbye. But the truth of the matter is that I reached for him before he could even open the bottle. Judging from the way he'd been holding himself back I half-expected him to stop me, but he opened his body the same way he had that night in the grass. I could've dropped him right to the kitchen floor, but instead I let him point the way to his bedroom. He pulled a curtain over the window as I unbuttoned his shirt; I held his waist in the palms of my hands.

I wish I could say that I hurried to finish, that in five minutes I was dressed and ready to leave. But the truth of the matter is that I lingered over his body. He was long, and tightly muscled, and his skin was smooth and golden beneath my fingers. When I slid my tongue over his hip he shuddered; my teeth, at the nape of his neck, made him squirm. I savored his moan, the skip of his breath, the low plea in his voice when he said my name. I wanted it all, needed it all, and sitting back on my heels and looking at him stretched out before me I had not an ounce of regret.

I wish I could say that I never went back, that I went home to Bobby and never saw David again. But the truth of the matter is that I called him three days later, and then two days after that. The afternoon I left work early and fell asleep in his bed I stopped trying to convince myself that I wasn't going to see him again.

I didn't know what I was doing. I wasn't thinking. I was just reacting, and though somewhere in the back of my mind I must have known that it couldn't go on I didn't want to stop. Maybe a part of me thought that if I was taking care of Bobby—if I was getting him to the doctor, staying on top of him about taking his medicine, making sure he was eating and drinking and shitting the way he was supposed to—then a couple of hours here and there with David didn't matter. They didn't matter.

But the more time I spent with David the less I wanted to be at home. I went through the motions, waiting for the moment I could leave. I didn't think Bobby noticed. I honestly didn't think he noticed, and then one Saturday on my way out the door he stopped me. I'd hurried through the morning, counting the hours until I was free; David had been out of town for four days, and though we rarely saw each other on the weekend I'd made plans to spend the afternoon with him. I barreled through my chores, setting Bobby up with lunch, my energy frenetic, and as I headed for the door he said, Who is he, Adam?

I turned and he was standing with his arms over his chest like he was afraid that if he moved his insides would spill onto the floor. But there was a tilt to his chin, a matter-of-factness in his tone. I can't even be angry, can I? he asked. He looked down at the floor; when he looked back up his eyes glittered. Indy's almost out of food, he said, Can you pick some up while you're out?

At the pet store I bought Indy a sixty pound bag of dog food and a couple of chew toys. I tried to pay with a check but my hand was shaking too hard to hold the pen and I ended up using one of my credit cards. I remember being afraid that it would be declined. At home I balanced the bag of food on my shoulder; Bobby barely glanced in my direction when I opened the front door. Without a word I carried the bag into the kitchen, where I slit the top and emptied the contents into a bin. Indy poked his snout around the corner, his toenails clicking on the hardwoods. I offered him one of the chew toys and he took it between his teeth, then trotted toward Bobby and dropped the toy at his feet. All bone, Bobby squatted down in front of him; I winced at the sharp jut of his elbows as he cupped Indy's head between his hands. Good boy, he crooned, Good dog.

The bathroom door opens. Joel, I say, I'm having an affair.

For a long moment he doesn't move. He's still in bed with me, still relieved, still satiated. It's been seven months, I say, I'm sorry. He shakes his head, and I watch as he fumbles for the question that will be the beginning of the end. Who? he asks. My eyes skirt past him. He makes a sound like a small, wounded animal. Not Trainor, he says, Please don't say Trainor.

I'm silent, and a low, anguished moan fills our room. Are you in love with him? he asks. *I was captivated. I was infatuated. I was alive.* No, I say. Then why? he cries, *Why?*

~ ~ ~

In a silence as stifling as the humidity we make our way to the BMW. I've told him nothing; he disappeared at one point to throw up, and when he came back he started packing. After a minute I helped him. Now I search in my pocket for the keys, and as my fingers close around them he stops. When? he asks. What? I say. *When*, Adam? he asks, When did you...? January, I say, and he holds his hands to his head. Oh my god, he says, This is because of the adoption.

I can't argue with the timing. I asked you if that was a deal killer, he protests, and when I don't say anything he yells, I asked you if that was a deal killer! Joel, I mumble, trying to urge him in the direction of the car before someone hears us. At the sight of the BMW his eyes narrow. Was he with you when you bought the car? he asks. I look away from him, at the inn's proprietor, who's hurrying down the sidewalk toward us. Was he with you when you bought the fucking car, Adam? Joel screams. Yes, I say. Gentlemen, the woman interrupts, Is there a problem?

Joel doesn't look at her. I'm not altogether certain he even sees her, and he searches my expression as if he's never seen me, as if we haven't spent the past five years staring into each other's eyes. Who are you? he finally asks. I don't answer him; he stumbles away from me. Sir? the proprietor says. I'm sorry for the noise, I tell her. Unlocking my door, I slide behind the wheel; she hesitates as I start the engine, but she finally turns and goes back inside.

I drive slowly as I make the block, but Joel's nowhere to be found.

~ ~ ~

Darkness engulfs me as I climb the stairs at home, feeling my way along the wall until I reach our bedroom. Little light falls through the open blinds; there's no moon tonight, and I stand at the windows, contemplating the faint gleam of water in the distance. I keep expecting Bobby to appear before me, but he doesn't. I can't even picture his face.

By the end of the weekend everyone was gone, leaving me with a refrigerator full of food I didn't want. I had a dull headache that for five days I'd been blaming on my fall—I'd fainted when I came out of our room to tell everyone he was gone—but which I suspected had something to do with the fact that I still hadn't cried. I'd sat with dry eyes across from the funeral director as Julia blubbered into a handful of tissues, stood in front of Bobby's open grave without shedding a tear. He'd drawn a decent crowd; I had a lot of friends. But his parents weren't there, and David wasn't either. I wondered if he knew.

I was going back to work the next day and I went to bed early, slipping beneath the new blanket I'd bought at a department store late that afternoon. The material felt rough and cold beneath my fingers. Upstairs in the attic, my grandmother's quilt was neatly folded, tucked into a box. Beneath the earth, Bobby started to rot. There wasn't much of a moon.

~ ~ ~

Joel comes home late the following afternoon. I watch from the window in the study as Scott's car pulls to the curb, mentally combing through the sequence of events that would lead Scott to bring Joel home. I wait to see if he's going to linger, but when he pulls away with a quick honk of his horn I head downstairs, where I meet Joel at the door. He hasn't slept, or he hasn't slept well; I can tell by the bruise-colored circles beneath his eyes, the gray pallor of his complexion. Scott knew, he says as soon as he sees me. I nod. Who else? he asks. No one, I say, No one knows. No one at work? he asks, and I hesitate. You weren't working late, were you? he says, Any of those times. No, I say.

Last month, he says, Was a lie. No, I say, I meant everything I said. But I can see from his expression that he doesn't believe me, and I tell him that Trainor had been out of town, that I'd told him before he left that it was over. I didn't go near him for three weeks, I say, Not until after I came

207

back from Kentucky, not until the day I wrecked the car. You were with him when you wrecked the car? he asks, and I know he's remembering the way I fell into his arms that night. We always used a condom, I say, Always. Well, thanks, Adam, he says, starting to cry, Thank you for not endangering my life on top of everything else.

He buries his head in his hands. When my cell phone rings I pull it from my pocket without thinking; Joel snatches it from my hand at the exact second I recognize the number. A quick scan of the Caller ID and he has the phone to his ear. Scott? he says.

He turns his eyes in my direction. I lower mine to the floor.

~ ~ ~

For sixty hours we hardly speak. He disappears into his studio after Trainor's phone call on Sunday and doesn't come out until Monday afternoon. Even overlooking the hammering I hear—which means he's stretching his own canvas—I can tell by his expression when he finally emerges that he's been working. Joel, I start, but he shuts me up with a look that tells me I should know better than to interrupt his rhythm. I watch as he takes a yogurt from the refrigerator, withholding comment about the paint stains on the handle. Later I stand outside his door, listening for a sign that he's finished. I finally give up and go to bed, then try again in the morning. I can't tell if he woke up early or if he never went to bed at all.

At work I head straight for Trainor, without bothering to acknowledge the half a dozen representatives who offer me tentative greetings. Come with me, I say, and he gets to his feet, looking sheepish. He knew he wasn't supposed to contact me over the weekend, and he follows me into my office, where I close the door behind us. Sitting in the chair across from my desk, he runs his hand back and forth across his skull, looking mildly apologetic. It's over, I say.

He breaks into a smile I didn't expect and I realize, horrified, that he's misinterpreted my words. No, I say, trying to interrupt him as he tells me I'll be so much happier, so much more relaxed. When he stands and takes a step in my direction I reel away from him. No, Trainor! I say, *We're* over!

If I had anything left I'd feel for the man in front of me. Instead I stare at him with a dispassion that rivals any I've known. No, I say, I'm done.

~ ~ ~

When I get home I hesitate on the threshold of Joel's studio, then press my ear to the door. I can't hear a thing, and when I knock there's no answer. I step inside, calling his name just to be sure. My voice trails off as I catch sight of the canvas in front of me.

His core colors haven't changed, but the inclusion of another makes me sway on my feet. He's chosen a green so dark I could mistake it for black, a green devoid of possibility. The color swirls around the others, confusing them, consuming them. At first I think I'm looking into a funnel, or maybe a water spout, but I should know better than to think he'd do something so amateur, so sophomoric. Despite the chaos I find lines almost mathematical in their precision, and I look more closely, to see if I can find pencil beneath the paint. I can't see a thing, and I back away, then shut the door behind me.

He's upstairs, asleep. He's changed his clothes, but he hasn't showered; I can tell, by the paint that stains his bare feet, the faint brush of pink on his cheek. That color, the color of decay, caught in the webbing of his fingers. Even in repose the skin between his eyebrows creases. Joel, I whisper, but he doesn't stir.

An hour later I hear the shower running, and when he comes downstairs he looks better than I would've expected and as if he's on his way out. Where're you going? I ask, and he gives me a look of such incredulity that I flush. I start teaching tonight, he reminds me, and I feel doubly slapped, for questioning his whereabouts when I haven't been upfront about my own, and for not remembering. I'm sorry, I murmur, but he acts like he hasn't heard me. I watch him slide a handful of papers into a satchel I've never seen. What time will you be home? I ask, wincing as I ask a question for which I know I don't deserve an answer. Why? he asks.

I don't say anything, and he looks at me with a defiant expression I haven't seen in almost thirteen years. Did you want to talk? he asks, Were you ready to tell me why you've been lying for the past seven months? Joel—I protest, but he's already heading for the door. Joel! I cry, and he turns. This at least he should know. I ended it, I tell him, and he gives me a wan smile. Yeah, he says, You did.

~ ~ ~

Trainor hasn't once tried to contact me; I think he realized that I wasn't leaving room for negotiation, and when we encounter each other at the office he assumes an air of professionalism that surprises me given the circumstances.

So you ended it, Darlene says, loitering in the doorway of my office on Friday afternoon, and I look up from my laptop. Yes, I say. What about Joel? she asks. That's over, too, I admit, and she shakes her head. Seems a shame, she tells me. What's that? I ask. That you didn't realize what you had, she says.

When I get home that night Joel's truck isn't in the garage. Inside nothing has changed, but he wouldn't have taken the furniture from the great room, he wouldn't have taken anything from the kitchen, and I walk down the hall to his studio.

The room's empty, like a cadaver laid bare.

I feel remarkably little satisfaction. I expected something: a wellspring of relief, a sudden absence of weight. Instead I'm cagey, and I prowl upstairs to our bedroom, where I wrench open the dresser drawers and peer into the closet. He's left nothing, nothing except for his key, which I find on the nightstand when I lower myself to the bed.

And the ceiling. His painting stretches above me, and I stare into those colors for all of five seconds before I get to my feet.

I won't be able to sleep in here again.

7

Vincent sends Trainor out of town three weeks in a row, first to the same technology expo where we met, and then to North Carolina. I'm glad to see him go, even though his representatives languish in his absence. I feel little compulsion to motivate them. I'm having a hard enough time just getting here in the morning.

Outside of work I don't leave the house. The weekends come and I pass them in front of the television, picking at food I can't really taste. I've started to lose the pounds I've gained in the past year, and my swimming trunks, when I lower myself into the hot tub to ease my aching back, fall loosely around my hips. No one's here to notice.

I don't talk to anyone except for my parents, from whom I temporarily keep my news. I don't want to worry them; they have enough going on as my father starts a third round of chemotherapy. The tumors in his lungs have grown, and when I call to check in I brace myself for the inevitable: the nausea, the headaches. Without my help, my mother and sister have to cope with everything. But I don't suggest a visit. I can't.

Julia finds out what happened soon enough anyway. She calls me one day at the end of the month, bawling, and I experience five seconds of sheer terror before I figure out why she's crying. I don't know why the thought never occurred to me that she might contact Joel herself; despite their rocky beginning they've developed a decent relationship over the past five years, and as I listen to Julia sob I realize for the first time the way my split with Joel will impact my family. Why? she says, Why would he leave now, when Daddy's dying? He didn't tell you? I ask, and she wails, He told me I should ask *you!*

211

So he's left it up to me to be the bearer of bad news. Well, why not? I'm the asshole in this scenario. I had an affair, I tell her, and she moans, as if she's the one I betrayed. Why? she asks, Who? You don't know him, Julia, I say. How long did it last? she asks. Seven months, I say, And I'm not answering another question. But Adam, she says, *Why?*

I call my parents as soon as I hang up. I have no choice; as soon as Julia gets off the phone with her husband my parents will be next in line. Never mind the fact that I told her to give me time to tell them myself. She won't be able to keep her mouth shut. Mom, I say when my mother answers, I have some bad news.

She's devastated, and that's before I explain why he left. Once I drop that bombshell she's irate as well. I feel like a chastened five-year-old. She finally passes off the phone to my father, telling me I'm going to have to give him the news myself. I don't want any part of this affair, she sniffs.

My father takes the news better than my mother. He's quiet at first, then asks in a somber tone if I'm all right. I silently note that my mother failed to ask. I'm fine, I tell him, and his voice tightens as he tells me that he's not so ill that he's stopped caring about his children. I wonder at the use of the plural tense. Does he mean me and Julia? Or me and Joel? I'm fine, I repeat, When I'm not I'll let you know.

~ ~ ~

Scott contacts me midway through October. I take his call even though I ignored the half a dozen voice mails he left me in September. He'd finally sent an email saying he wasn't going to hound me. I knew where to find him if I wanted to talk. I'd almost laughed. I'm not an idiot; I know where his allegiance lies. After all, he was the one who brought Joel home.

But a combination of curiosity and loneliness gets the better of me and I agree to meet him one day for lunch. You've lost weight, he says, raising his eyebrows. Some, I admit. It's not as if I'm trying. I just don't have an appetite these days, and when the server approaches I order a salad. Have you been cycling? he asks. No, I say. You should, he tells me, watching as I douse my iced tea with artificial sweetener. Yeah, I sigh, I probably should.

Scott's still seeing Kyle, still living with Marcio. How's that working for you? I mumble. Actually, he admits, Kyle's been a handful.

Every November for the past five years Kyle has hosted a citywide AIDS benefit at his home the weekend before Thanksgiving, and though he complains about the workload everyone knows that playing host to the entire gay community is right up his alley. Truth be told, I don't think anyone could pull off the affair with quite as much aplomb. Joel and I have been in attendance every year, and for the past three I've volunteered a considerable amount of time and energy. Though Kyle does a lot of the work himself, he also collaborates with area restaurants who donate food and man-power; for three years running I've been the liaison. Preliminary schmoozing starts mid-summer, so Kyle must have decided to go with someone else this year. I probably have Joel to thank for that. Despite my personal problems Kyle would've cracked his whip, unless Joel asked him to keep it to himself.

Now that Kyle has sold his company he has more time than usual to devote to this project. That, Scott tells me, is part of the problem. Kyle's obsessing about the details, falling to pieces when something goes wrong, then rallying with an enthusiasm Scott finds unnerving. I can't stand the drama, he says.

On top of everything else, Marcio plans on going this year. For five years he's let Kyle appropriate his partner for the night, but over the past year a couple of his friends in Brazil have died and now he wants to be a part of the show. Oh, he'll be a part of the show if he goes, I assure Scott. That's what I'm afraid of, he says. What does Kyle think? I ask, and he tells me he hasn't yet broken the news. Kyle can be unreasonable, he explains. You're going to make the situation worse if you're not upfront with him, I caution, and he gives me a look, which I sheepishly return as our server arrives with our salads. So, he says, How are you anyway?

I let my shoulders roll in a noncommittal shrug. Don't give me that shit, he says, How are you? What do you want me to say, Scott? I say, I'm fine. Don't you at least wonder how he's doing? he asks. How's he doing? I ask mechanically. How do you think he's doing? Scott asks. I don't know, I mumble, and he shakes his head. Well, since you're obviously indifferent, he says, Maybe you can hook up with someone at Kyle's benefit. I'm horrified. I'm not looking, I assure him, And anyway, what makes you think I'm going? Because you always go, he says, And because you're probably already feeling guilty that so far you haven't lifted a finger to help. That's where you're wrong, I inform him, but he shakes his head. I'll see you there, he says, The question is whether or not you'll bring a date. If I don't, I tell him grimly, impaling a tomato with my fork and setting it aside, I can always borrow one of yours.

~ ~ ~

The trick-or-treaters catch me unaware this year, and I'm forced to rummage through the pantry before I come up with a forgotten box of Ding Dongs. Handing them over I feel a faint nostalgia, and when I've closed the door I unwrap the foil from the last one and take a bite, standing there in the entryway. Even the sweet, creamy filling does nothing for my taste buds. I turn off the porch light to discourage the next round of children, then hesitate in front of the window. Clomping down the sidewalk, spurs jingling, a four-year-old holds hands with his father. I suddenly have to press my lips together to keep from crying.

My father has decided to stop chemotherapy. He told me himself this afternoon, claiming he'd rather have a few months of relative normalcy than a year of suffering. I couldn't argue, couldn't be sure that I wouldn't make the same choice if I were him. But I know my mother will struggle with his decision, and Julia, too, and I promised him the only thing I could. I'll make a trip home. You come when you're ready, he said, letting me off the hook the way he has every day since July.

I'm leaving the day before Thanksgiving, returning the following Sunday. I'll have to take two days without pay; I've run out of personal time, and I don't know what that will mean for Christmas. I can't imagine not going home. This holiday season will be my father's last.

A shout from the front lawn turns my head and I watch as a small troupe of pre-pubescent boys weaves through the smaller children, their loot swinging carelessly by their sides, their voices deep and new. I feel suddenly ancient, and I move away from the window and make my way back down the hall, pausing in front of Joel's studio, the door of which I haven't opened even once since the day he left. At night I sleep in the guest room; in the morning I go into my bedroom just long enough to get dressed. I've considered moving my clothes altogether.

Other than my parents and Scott I haven't spoken about him with anyone. It's as if he died, or never existed at all. Are you happy now? I whisper, but Bobby doesn't answer.

~   ~   ~

Theoretically, there's no reason for me to skip out on Kyle's benefit. Nothing's required of me other than to make an appearance, and it's not as if I have other plans. I'll see people I haven't seen in a while—some of whom might actually still be speaking to me—and I'll have the satisfaction of knowing I'm supporting a worthy cause. I'll also get to see how Scott's going to manage Kyle, who still doesn't know that Marcio's planning on attending. For that reason alone I should go.

But Joel will be there, and that I'm not sure I can handle.

The afternoon of the benefit I still haven't decided, though I'm leaning towards staying home. I'm tired; I've got a long week ahead of me; I think I'm getting sick. I don't have anything to wear. So go shopping, Scott says when he catches me on the phone. He has little patience for my excuses, given his own issues with tonight's event. Considering the support I've given you the past year—he starts. *What* support? I interrupt, You made it clear from the beginning how you felt about what I was doing. And yet I never told a soul, he reminds me.

He has a point, but I grit my teeth. You know what? I say, If I go tonight it's going to be for one reason only. What's that? he asks, and I say, To watch you fall flat on your ass. He's quiet for a long moment. I don't know what happened to you over the last year, Adam, he finally says, But you've turned into a real prick.

I go that night to spite him, though as I pull up to the valet in front of Kyle's house I question what I'm doing. The fever I've managed to stave off all day catches me as I hesitate behind the BMW's wheel, and as I step from the car I sway on my feet. I have a feeling I'd be better off at home. But I steel myself, and follow a handful of Austin's best-dressed through Kyle's opulent front doors.

I spot Kyle immediately. He's wearing a blue silk kimono, and he's in his element, flitting from one small group to another, gushing compliments. He doesn't see me at first, and when he finally does he raises his eyebrows. Scott obviously didn't tell him I'd be coming. I watch his eyes in case he's trying to warn Joel, but they hold my own, and he floats toward me, offering his cheek for me to kiss. You look divine, he says, which couldn't be further from the truth. Still, I have to admire his poise. I know he must hate me. You do, too, I admit, and for just a moment I think he's going to turn a full circle in front of me. He remembers himself just in time, and calls forth a discreet blush. Where's Scott? I ask.

I've been cruel, but he doesn't find my question out of the ordinary. Oh, he's around somewhere, Kyle says, flinging his hand, and then he nods as someone catches his eye. Enjoy yourself! he calls back to me over his shoulder. Apparently that's all the attention he's going to muster for me and I grunt, turning to assess the room. I don't see Joel, I don't see Scott. I certainly don't see Marcio. I don't see more than a dozen people I know, and I find as I make my way around the room, lifting a glass of champagne from a tray, that while everyone's perfectly polite, no one seems overjoyed to see me. I end up making small talk with people I don't even know, and the combination of stilted conversation and fever and alcohol leaves me with a piercing headache. I squint past the sharp pain buried in my right eyebrow. I could be home, I think, in front of the television or curled up in bed. I give my watch a surreptitious glance. I've been here less than thirty minutes and I'm already contemplating my escape.

And why not? Joel's not here, not that I can see. Not that I would've approached him. What could I possibly say? I don't want to see him, not in this environment. I'm not sure I want to see him under any circumstances. And as far as Scott and Marcio are concerned, obviously Scott came to his senses and forced Marcio to stay home. There's no way Kyle would be holding himself together otherwise.

I'm just getting ready to excuse myself when I hear someone tapping a glass. Heads turn toward the west side of the room, where Kyle's holding court on the two short steps that lead to the master bedroom. Scott stands below him, but there's no mistaking the fact that they're together. Ladies, Kyle calls, clapping his hands together to quiet the chatter. The sleeves of his kimono billow out beside him like the wings of a dove. If he's not careful, I think, they're going to catch the flame from one of the hundreds of lit candles in here. Can I please have your attention? Kyle says.

A graduated silence settles across the room. There's no way I'm going to be able to get out of here until Kyle finishes whatever speech he has planned, and though I've never had a problem with tight places I edge toward the back door, pulling my collar away from my neck as Kyle begins a long list of people he wants to thank for helping to coordinate this year's benefit. Those he singles out wave from their respective spots around the room, bowing under the weight of the crowd's adulation. I'm almost to the back door when I hear Joel's name, and I throw a glance toward Kyle, expecting him to add something about Joel's absence. Instead I hear applause.

I don't see how I could have missed him. He's standing just a few feet away from Kyle himself, leaning against the wall, and he raises one brief hand at the mention of his name. The bastard's gone ahead and grown his hair out, and he tucks a stray strand behind his ear before he lowers his arm. He's lost every trace of his tan, and his pale skin shimmers in the candlelight. For the first time in months my heart skips a beat.

A murmur rises from the crowd, and heat creeps up my neck to my already flushed face. I think they're talking about us, about Joel and me. Uh-oh, someone behind me giggles. I turn to look at him, but his eyes travel past me.

Marcio looks amazing. Dressed in a sharp, black suit with a creamy scarf around his neck, he lingers in the open doorway until he's sure every eye has found him. Then he steps coolly into the room. I glance at Kyle. He seems frozen, and he watches along with the rest of us as Marcio makes his way toward Scott, whose own eyes have fallen to Kyle's marble floor. As Marcio slips his arm through Scott's the crowd sighs. Kyle rocks unsteadily on his feet. Next to Marcio he looks positively ridiculous, like an aging, exotic bird. I cut a quick look at Joel. He's every bit as devastated as Kyle, and anger begins to build slowly in my chest.

Avoiding Marcio and Scott, who stand mere inches from him, Kyle goes back to his list, though in his haste he probably leaves out a few names. He's supposed to say something else, too; last year he convinced everyone to share a full sixty seconds of silence for those who've died. But tonight he skips the reminiscences and goes right to the toast. To everyone we've lost, he says, holding his glass with a hand shaking so hard even I can see it from my vantage point, And to everyone who helped.

We drink in spite of his blunder. As soon as Kyle lowers his glass and steps down into the living room Joel moves to his side. I distinctly see his mouth form the word "no," and then he whisks Kyle away, toward the back of the house. Marcio watches them go, releasing Scott's arm the moment they disappear.

I don't move. Rage renders me immobile, and I listen to the wisps of conversation that surround me, that dissect the drama unfolding in front of us with little regard for its participants. A group of men half my age— half, I think in wonderment—label Kyle a priggish queen, and claim that they've never understood what Scott sees in him anyway. Money, one of them says, and they all nod. I glower at them but they don't seem to care. They're too young, and too disrespectful. They have no idea what I've gone through, what any of us who came of age in the eighties had to endure, and despite their presence here I'm not altogether sure that they care. They're too busy reaping the benefits of the groundwork we were responsible for laying. You're not being fair, Joel told me once when I offered these same thoughts after one of Kyle's parties, They have their own set of issues. Like what? I said. He just shook his head. He knew what I'd been through, and he knew he wasn't going to change my mind.

I just can't stand the sense of entitlement I see, the defiance that I find undeserved. In the locker room at the gym last fall some kid—he couldn't have been more than eighteen or nineteen—told me he was HIV positive. I didn't even know him; we'd shared a couple of sets of bench press together and found ourselves in the locker room at the same time, but I didn't even know him. His announcement came with little regard for who might overhear, or what my reaction might be. He wore his diagnosis like a badge of honor, and that I just couldn't understand. Now I turn to the idiots in front of me. Show some fucking respect, I snarl, The man's your host.

I don't think I've made much of an impression but I don't wait around to find out. Ducking outside, I loosen my tie and gulp in the still, cold air. But I'm not alone. Kyle has installed heaters and a dozen tables with chairs, and half of his guests have chosen to mingle out here, where they admire the thousands of dollars worth of flowers that float in his pool. Joel would've fought him on that; think of the fossil fuel that goes into delivering them, he probably said. But he'd have to admit that they look beautiful in the light from all these candles. Beeswax, he'd say, Because lighting up the others is as good as smoking a cigarette.

Everything all right? Scott asks beside me, and I turn. What's wrong with you? I hiss. Scott darts a quick glance at Marcio, who shrugs. Don't you see what you're doing? I ask, starting to tremble, Can't you see what you're doing? Marcio says something to Scott, lowering his voice and speaking in Portuguese. I didn't even know Scott understood the language. But Scott nods, and as they turn away from me I spot Joel standing in the doorway. I could cross the distance between us in less than five seconds. My heart rocks in my chest. Don't you see that you're killing him? I cry.

Scott pauses. Marcio tries to pull him forward; from the corner of my eye I see Joel take a concerned step in my direction. My eyes swim with hot, fevered tears. Kyle's in love with you, Scott! I cry, He's been in love with you for years!

Everyone's mouth falls. Scott's, Joel's. Kyle's. I see him now, standing behind Joel and looking as if I've just socked him in the stomach. Regret fills my mouth like bile. Only Marcio doesn't look surprised. Bending his mouth to Scott's ear, he whispers something I can't hear; Scott shakes him away. Kyle? he says. But Kyle doesn't answer. Instead he flees, his kimono swirling around him.

In his absence Scott turns to me. I can't meet his bewildered eyes. Skirting past him, avoiding Marcio, I move toward the doorway. When I reach Joel I pause. I'm close enough to touch him, close enough to breathe in his smell. I take the liberty, though I don't have the right. His face swarms with emotion.

I leave before he can say my name.

~ ~ ~

I land in Lexington late Wednesday night, wracked with fever and hours behind schedule. I've missed two additional days of work because I've been so sick, and under any other circumstances I would've called my parents to tell them I wasn't coming. Instead I took a handful of Tylenol and dressed in layers, which I shed on the plane as if I were molting. Now I trudge to my rental car, my sweaty skin forming what feels like a thin layer of ice under my long-sleeved tee. With chattering teeth, I try to

219

shrug into one of my sweaters without losing hold of my BlackBerry. I've already called my mother to tell her that my flight would be delayed, but I'll need to call her again to let her know I've arrived. She'll wait up for me, even though I wish she wouldn't. I don't want to talk.

Shivering, I shove my suitcase in the trunk of the car and get behind the wheel. Even with the heater running full-blast I can't seem to warm up, and I shut my eyes, trying to recall that moment on the plane when I thought I might melt right in front of everyone if I couldn't get any air. Beneath my chest my heart thrums at twice its normal speed.

After a few minutes my skin starts to thaw. I breathe into my hands as my pulse slows, then ready them on the steering wheel. I have at least an hour of driving ahead of me, and possibly an inquisition once I've arrived. I need my strength.

Julia's already at my parents' house, along with the rest of her family. I've barely spoken to her over the past couple of months, and to be honest, I'm a little apprehensive about how I'm going to be received. Between my mother, whose disposition toward me has cooled since I told her about my affair, and Julia, who can hold a grudge for a length of time that staggers me, I'm not sure I stand a chance. Only my father's demeanor hasn't changed, and while I'm thankful that he at least will welcome me I have my own reasons for not wanting to see him. Despite my mother's assurance that he's doing much better now that he's terminated chemotherapy, I know he's dying. Sometimes, my sister said in a hopeful voice the last time we spoke, The cancer just goes away. That's bullshit, Julia, I told her tiredly, And you know it. She hung up on me, and we haven't spoken since.

The highway spreads before me like a rumpled blanket. I take the hills slowly, putting off the moment when I'll have to call my mother. I haven't found a tolerable radio station but I've brought along a CD, one that Joel burned for us when we knew we were going to be heading this way last Thanksgiving. I keep the volume low, so the sound doesn't hurt my tender ears; by the time I reach my parents' house I'll be due for another dose of Tylenol. In the meantime I sip from the bottle of water I bought at the airport, feeling the cool fluid slip down my throat. You need to stay hydrated, I hear Joel saying, and I look to my right, expecting to find him in the passenger seat where he belongs. Instead I'm alone, and I pinpoint the last moment I heard those words, the morning after Kyle's lake party as I made pancakes in our kitchen. Even then, at the beginning of the summer, I knew we didn't stand a chance.

I haven't spoken to him. I haven't spoken to anyone, haven't apologized for my behavior Saturday night. I have no idea how Kyle's coping, whether he and Scott have split. No one has contacted me, and that more than anything reminds me of how utterly alone I've rendered myself. I should be glad I'm going to my parents' house. In their absence I'd have nowhere else to spend the holiday.

I'm closer now, and I pick up the phone. I won't be long, I say when my mother answers. She asks how I'm feeling; I'm careful to rein in the tears that spring to my eyes. I just need some sleep, I tell her, doing my best to keep my voice even. We hang up, and I clear my throat. Even alone I don't want to cry.

~ ~ ~

Thanksgiving's a boisterous affair with Julia's children, and I stand to the side with a bourbon in hand as my mother and sister labor over the meal and snap at Grace and Rye, who peel through the kitchen, skirting the edge of the open oven door. Julia finally chases them away, yelling for my brother-in-law to keep them occupied. He nods, catching Grace as she flies past. He looks every bit as exhausted as I feel, and I realize for the first time the toll my father's illness must be taking on his family. I watch him whisper something in Grace's ear; she nods solemnly, then trots off again after her brother. Thirty seconds later we hear shouting from the back bedroom. Want a drink? I ask Ivan, holding up my own as an example, but he already has a glass. Give me five minutes, he says, And you can make me another.

I turn back to the kitchen, where Lindsey has hoisted herself onto a free space on the counter. She's tuned into her iPod, her legs dangling above the floor. Without missing a beat, Julia shoos her off the counter, reaching at the same time into the cabinet above her daughter's head. If you're not going to help, Julia tells her, pulling out one of Lindsey's earphones, Then please leave the kitchen. Uncle Adam's not helping, Lindsey points out. I'm supervising, I inform her, and she rolls her eyes, throwing out her hip in a way that must madden half the boys at her junior high. You're *drinking*, she says. Thanks for drawing attention to that, I mutter, and she smiles in a way that would probably make her father crazy if he caught her. Can I have a sip? she whispers, sidling up to me. Are you kidding? I ask, lowering my voice, Your mother would kill me. But I throw a look over my shoulder and hand her my glass. She takes a generous gulp, startling me when she doesn't sputter. Not your first time? I ask, and she shrugs, as only a twelve-year-old girl can. Are we going riding later? she asks, taking another swallow. Not if I can help it, I tell her, reaching for my glass before she polishes off the rest, Now listen to your mother and get out of the kitchen.

She leaves, repositioning her earphones, and I reach for the bottle of bourbon with a sigh. Don't think I didn't see that, Julia says, hacking at a potato with a vegetable peeler. What? I ask, and she rolls her eyes, looking every bit like her daughter. What kind of example are you setting? she asks. Probably not a very good one, I admit, recapping the bottle of bourbon. I look toward the living room, where my father's nestled on the sofa, the pillow from his bedroom cupping his bald head. I'll be in the living room, I say, Holler if you need anything.

My father looks up as I enter the room, then struggles to sit up. I move to help him but he waves me back. I was just resting my eyes, he says as he achieves an upright position. He's been resting since he awakened this morning, saving up his energy for Thanksgiving dinner itself, though he probably won't have much interest in the meal. The chemo stole his taste for just about everything long ago, including his morning coffee. What about cigarettes? I asked my mother when my father was out of earshot, and she set her mouth in a way that told me everything I needed to know.

Overall, he doesn't look that bad. I'd prepared myself this time, but there really wasn't any need. He's a little thinner, but according to Julia he's actually gained some weight in the past month. Once he stopped the chemo, she said, He bounced back. I eye my father now, marveling at her choice of words. I'd hardly use them to describe the man in front of me, who holds a handkerchief up to his mouth as he coughs a slow and obviously painful cough. But I'd expected worse, and I'm thankful that he's at least able to carry on a conversation.

As if he knows what I'm thinking he asks how I'm doing. I'm fine, I
say, turning my eyes to the television, which someone has tuned to the
Weather Channel. I indicate the remote. Do you want me to try to find
something else? I ask, but he shakes his head. How's that fever? he wants
to know. Low-grade, I say. You need to rest up, he says, So you can take
Four-ticker out tomorrow. I nod. How's that dinner coming anyway? he
asks, jerking his head toward the kitchen as something crashes to the
floor. Slowly, I inform him, and he grins.

~ ~ ~

We make it through dinner with minimal commotion. My sister ushers
my father to the head of the table, where she spreads a napkin across his
lap before he gently slaps her hand away. She wants each of us to share
something for which we're thankful; my father nips that in the bud. The
food's going to get cold, he says, and Julia has to make do with a blessing. Even then she manages to tweak everyone's emotions, and when
she finishes we all sit in silence, too tearful to move. I finally reach for
a bottle of wine. Can I have a glass? Lindsey asks. No, Julia says. Why
not? Lindsey whines. Because you're barely twelve years old! Julia snaps.
I lean over and put my mouth to my niece's ear. You can have some of
mine, I whisper. For god's sake, Julia says, and my father interrupts. No
one's mounting one of my horses if they've been drinking, he announces. Well, that eliminates both of us, I mutter to Lindsey. She accepts
my glass, giggling. Adam, my father sighs, turning his attention to the
turkey, Behave yourself.

Lindsey and I don't ride after dinner. Ivan takes Grace and Rye to the
stables while Julia and my mother start to clear the table; I offer to help,
but they soundly decline. Take care of your drunken niece, Julia tells
me. My father shakes his head and retires to the living room, and I follow Lindsey onto the front porch. She's not really drunk, but she's definitely tipsy. I lower myself to the swing, watching as she leans over the
railing. She dresses like all the other girls these days, in jeans entirely
too low and shirts that leave little to the imagination. I could get you a
sweater or something, I tell her, If you're cold. She smiles; I'm surprised
she realized I was going for irony. The alcohol warmed me up, she says.
Great, I mutter, lifting my own glass to my lips. I really haven't had that

much; two drinks before dinner and maybe one full glass of wine. Any more and I'd have to rest my eyes like my father, especially since I can still feel my fever behind them.

So, I say, examining her, Do you have a boyfriend or what? She shrugs. I'm actually into girls, she tells me. I gape at her, and she bursts into merry laughter. You should see your face! she crows. Very funny, I say, reaching out to give her a light smack. She grins, collapsing onto the swing beside me. After a minute her smile dwindles. Actually, she says, There's a guy.

She hasn't met my eyes; I return the favor, gazing toward the stable and then into my wine glass. Someone from school? I ask, and from the corner of my eye I see her shake her head. He's older, she says. Yeah? I say. Fifteen, she admits. I keep a straight face, though on the inside I'm wincing. He's really hot, she says, speaking eagerly now, And he's pretty smart. I nod, knowing if I'm quiet that she'll tell me the problem without my asking. Margaret likes him, too, she finally says.

I wrack my brain, trying to remember Margaret. My best friend, Lindsey says helpfully. Right, I say, pretending I already know. She doesn't call me on my lie. Instead she brings her feet up to the swing and wraps her arms around her knees. I can see a glimpse of the little girl in her when she's in this position, and my heart aches over the wine I've shared with her. I suddenly wish she was small enough that I could pull her into my lap.

They've been going out for three weeks, she says. Margaret and this guy? I ask. Tom, she says, and I say, Margaret and Tom? She nods, resting her chin on her knees. I wait, spinning my wine glass slowly between my fingers. In the distance, Ivan emerges from the stable, Rye and Grace trailing behind him. None of them are riding Four-ticker. Beside me, Lindsey shudders from the weight of her secret. I squint up at the sky. I have a feeling she's not going to say any more, and after a minute she drops one foot to the floor of the porch and starts idly pushing the swing back and forth. Uncle Adam, she says, Why did you and Uncle Joel break up?

I have a feeling she knows, and at first I'm angry at her for asking, for teasing me with the truth. But when I turn to look at her I find her eyes glistening with tears that she holds back as carefully as I've held my own. The impulse to pat her leg and patronizingly tell her that the situation's complicated disappears. I had an affair, I admit. Why, though? she asks, I mean, he's not really my type, but Uncle Joel's pretty cute. I bite back my smile, at the idea that a gay man twenty years her senior isn't really her type. Yeah, I say, He's pretty cute. So why then? she asks, Did you just like, get tired of sleeping with him?

I cut my eyes at her, but she's asked the question in earnest, and I understand why my sister didn't want me siphoning her daughter any wine. Lindsey's growing up so fast. No, I say. She frowns, contemplating; I have a feeling I know her secret. Was the other guy better looking? she asks. I shake my head. But you liked him better, she concludes. No, I say, I didn't.

She's thoroughly confused at this point, and I'm beginning to find our conversation wildly inappropriate. Look, Lindsey—I start, but she interrupts. Mom says that Joel told her that you're having the mother of all midlife crises, she informs me. I look at her, startled. Well, that's…, I say, That's….

What? I think. Insulting? Preposterous? The truth? Your mom talked to him? I ask, and she shrugs with a nonchalance that unnerves me. I guess, she says, but she's looking at me carefully from beneath lowered lids. I suddenly remember her asking Joel about the scars on his arms the first time she met him, when she was only five. You miss him, she says, Don't you?

For five days now I've breathed in the scent of his shampoo. For five days I've stood across from him, inhaling with my eyes half-closed, as if he were a drug and I the addict. Tremendously, I whisper. Do you think he misses you? she asks, and I nod. She lets out an exasperated sigh. Then Uncle Adam! she says, You should just apologize so you can be together! It's not that simple, I tell her. Why not? she asks, Because you slept with someone else? Because I lied, I say, Because he doesn't trust me anymore. So promise him you won't do it again, she tells me.

I'm not about to admit to my twelve-year-old niece that I have a track record. I'm not about to tell her that I have a penance to pay. Maybe, I say, to put her off, but when I lift my eyes I see that I haven't fooled her. I glance toward the stable. In the distance I can see Ivan with the kids; an occasional *whoop* punctuates the silence. Beside me, Lindsey leans her head back against the swing and sighs. Uncle Adam, she says after a minute. I turn to look at her. One shiny tear escapes from her eye. I miss him, too, she says.

~ ~ ~

My sister doesn't seem thrilled with the time I've dedicated to her daughter. I have a feeling she's eavesdropped on at least part of our conversation, and when she asks what's wrong with me I have a hard time not telling her that Lindsey's most likely fooling around with her best friend's boyfriend. She's entirely too young to be listening to your problems, Julia snaps, and my father, who has been watching us argue, chooses that moment to break into a fit of coughing. At first I think he's trying to distract Julia, but his cough lingers until even my mother looks concerned. He waves us off, claiming that the day has simply taken its toll. My sister gives me a pointed look. What? I say. As if you don't know, she hisses, and I bring the palms of my hands together, my fingertips pointed toward the ceiling. Dear Lord, I intone, mimicking the blessing we had to endure, Thank you for bringing all of us together today on this most precious of occasions....

She bursts into tears, and my mother gives me the same look my sister turned in my direction ten seconds ago. Honestly, Adam, she says from where she sits with her arm around my exhausted father. I mumble an apology, including Lindsey in the sweep of my eyes. I don't know what's wrong with me, I admit. I do! Julia sobs, You're an asshole! Julia, my mother warns. No wonder he left you! Julia cries, ignoring her, No wonder he left! That's enough! my father says, raising his voice, and with her hand clasped over her mouth my sister flees. I meet Lindsey's widened eyes. Adam, my mother says, but I shake my head. No, I say softly, She's actually right.

I meet Ivan and the kids halfway to the stable; he takes one look at my expression and asks if everything's okay. I nod without elaborating, and he extricates Grace's hand from mine. Uncle Adam needs a little time to himself right now, he tells her.

A thick animal heat envelopes me as I enter the stable. I breathe in the smell of trampled straw and manure, then rummage in the bin in front of Four-ticker's stall. He whinnies, and I hand him a carrot, caressing the soft skin on his nose as he chews. When he's finished he nuzzles the pockets of my jeans, looking for more. I hold his great, strong head between my palms and press my face to his. Let's get brushed, I whisper, You want to get brushed?

I start with a curry comb, then move on to a stiff-bristled body brush, working my way from his boney shoulder to his hip with swift, sweeping strokes. He stands obediently in front of me, flicking his tail as I labor; I'm warm, and probably still fevered, and sweat drips onto the straw beneath my feet. You need to ride, don't you? I murmur. My father has been paying someone to look after the horses, but I'm not sure they're getting the same level of exercise they were getting six months ago. Maybe tomorrow, I say, reaching for a finishing brush, Maybe tomorrow we'll ride. Four-ticker stamps his foot as if he understands what I'm saying. Tomorrow, I promise.

But I don't ride him the next day, or the day after that either. I'm too sick, and I hole up in my old bedroom, where Julia accuses me from the doorway of sabotaging her children's health as well as my father's. I feel too awful to do more than moan. Somewhere along the way I've developed a sinus infection, and my head aches with fever and congestion. My mother brings me medicine and asks if I want something to eat; I know she has her hands full and shake my head. Julia, who lingers in the doorway, informs me that I should've stayed home. My mother doesn't argue, and when Lindsey tries to slip past them to say hello they tell her I'm not to be bothered.

I sleep off and on for a good forty-eight hours, my dreams so vivid that I'm never really sure if I'm asleep or awake. Several times I reach for the man next to me without knowing who I expect to find. They all haunt me, the living and the dead mingling with the missing, until my fever breaks Saturday evening and I open my eyes, sure of my whereabouts for the first time in two days.

I honestly think I was better off asleep.

I make my way into the living room, where my father's stretched out on the sofa in front of the television. I almost don't remember what he looks like when he's not prone. His fragile skull shines dully in the light from the living room lamp. I can barely look at him, and I wonder what Joel would say if he was here. I don't think he'd have any problem taking my father's hand in his own. I don't think he'd have any problem touching my father's back as he's wracked by another fit of coughing. Who are you? Joel asked as we stood in front of my car in the broken night, and the answer brings tears to my eyes. I'm the kind of man who made love to someone else as his lover lay dying. I'm the kind of man who doesn't learn his lesson and repeats the same mistakes. I'm the kind of man who can't look his father in the eye.

I leave the room without announcing my presence and sneak into the kitchen. Going without food the past couple of days has sharpened my hunger, but nothing appeals to me as I quietly search the pantry. I can make you something, my mother offers behind me. I turn, watching as she fills a teapot with water and places it on the stove. That's okay, I finally say. It's no trouble, she adds, taking a ceramic mug from one of the cabinets. I lean against the counter and slide my hands in the pockets of my jeans, the ones I bought last year and haven't been able to wear since. You've lost weight, my mothers notices. I shrug. You should eat something, she chides, Keep up your strength. What did you have for dinner? I ask. My mother takes a teabag from the box on the counter and drops it in her mug. Ivan picked up a couple of pizzas, she says, They wanted to eat dinner before they left.

I've already opened the refrigerator to hunt for leftovers, and I straighten at the news. Left? I say, They went home? My mother nods, reaching past me for the milk. There isn't any more, if that's what you're doing in there, she says. But they didn't say goodbye, I protest, letting the door snap shut, and my mother gives me an exasperated look. Under the circumstances..., she says. I fold my arms across my chest, unsure whether I'm more annoyed that my sister whisked her family homeward without a word or that they didn't buy enough pizza. I'm not sure what you expected, Adam, my mother continues, Given your behavior. Please, I say, You really don't have to spell it out for me.

Leaving my mother to her tea, I wander back into the living room. Fever break? my father asks. I drop into the chair across from him and nod. I don't ask how he's feeling; I haven't asked once since I've been home. Now I eye the television, which drones on in the background like a persistent mosquito. For once I can see why Joel tried to convince me to get rid of ours. If I had a brick I'd smash the screen without an ounce of regret.

As if he can read my thoughts my father reaches for the remote and turns off the power. Almost instantly I wish he'd turn it back on. The silence that builds between us feels far more threatening, and the muscles in my quadriceps tighten as I stare at my lap, until I honestly think I'm going to explode. I lift a cautious eye. My father's watching me, and I offer up a meager smile, hoping to buy myself some time. Quiet in here, I croak, and he takes a breath, as deep a one as I've seen him take in a while. Son, he starts.

Springing to my feet, I start jabbering about my flight tomorrow afternoon and all the packing I still have to do. I practically trip over the rug in my haste as I back away from him, and I have to steady myself with a trembling hand. My eyes light everywhere except on him. Good night, I say, Good night.

In my room I turn out the light and get right back into bed, where I tremble as if my fever has returned. Still damp with perspiration, my sheets cling to my chest and legs, and after a few minutes I fling them off of me. Quietly, I steal into the hallway and take a fresh set from the linen closet. With one ear cocked I listen for my name, for a sign that my parents might at this very moment be discussing my behavior. But I can't hear a sound, not even from the television, and once again I close my bedroom door behind me.

After I've stripped the bed and replaced the sheets I crawl back under the covers. Exhaustion holds me in its tenacious grip, and I close my eyes, willing sleep to release me. Instead, images from the past skirt beneath my lids like shadows, Bobby and David and Joel and my father blending together until I'm on the verge of weeping, right here in my childhood bed. Even pressing the heels of my hands against my eyes doesn't banish what I'm seeing, and I finally open them and sit up, a quick glance at the clock telling me that at the very least my parents are probably in bed. I can go into the living room and park myself in front of the television until sleep has no choice but to overtake me.

But the sight of my father's chair, the scrunch of the worn cushion, changes my mind and I wheel around and head for the back door, which I fling open with a bang. My father, leaning against the railing of the back porch, turns to look at me. Couldn't sleep, he grunts, and I nod, already backing away from him, unsure if he was asking me a question or delivering a pronouncement of his own. Stay, he says, ushering me forward, and I hesitate, then step onto the porch in my bare feet. He makes no move to extinguish his cigarette; at this point I wouldn't dream of making the request. Instead I watch as he lingers over the butt in his hand, occasionally examining the hot, glowing tip. Every time he inhales he chokes a little, then coughs wetly into the handkerchief he's pulled from his back pocket. After a minute I can't watch anymore.

I wonder how many cigarettes he has left to smoke in his life. I wonder how many nights. I wonder if he's scared or angry or just so used to holding everything inside like every other man of his generation that he doesn't know himself. I wonder what I'd do if he suddenly decided to open up.

Tough weekend, he says, startling me. Yes, I say, and he nods, grinding out the last of his cigarette. I wait, thinking that he's going to say something else, but he's quiet and we both look up at the moon, which hangs half-lit from a night sky patchy with clouds. The thought eventually occurs to me that maybe he's waiting for an apology. He certainly deserves one, and I utter the words in a low voice, keeping my eyes to myself. He sighs through his nose. Son, he says, You don't have to apologize. Tell that to Julia, I mutter, Tell that....

My father places a warm, calloused hand on my shoulder, and without warning I start to cry. Quietly at first, and then before I can stop myself I'm sobbing, as hard as I ever have in my life. My father pulls me roughly toward him and I bury my face in his coat, my nose filling with the scent of hard-worn leather and tobacco. All right, now, he says, in the same voice he reserves for one of his new acquisitions, All right. Still I cling to him, gripping his coat, kneading it with my fingers. As if I was a small child he cups the back of my head with the palm of his hand. Shh, he whispers, until I finally break away from him, wiping my nose. Silently, he fishes a clean handkerchief from his back pocket, one of the last true gentlemen. I take it, mumbling a thank you and dabbing at my eyes, which continue to stream. Dad, I say, my voice breaking, I cheated on him. I know, he says quietly, and I shake my head. I don't mean Joel, I say. Son, he says, I know.

My eyes swivel in his direction, and the gaze he returns holds a compassion greater than any I've ever known. We spent time with you, Adam, he says, It wasn't hard to see.

Covering my face with my hand, I sob as my father watches over me. Does Mom know? I finally ask, and he shakes his head. I don't think so, he says. But Bobby..., I say. You were young, Adam, he tells me. That doesn't matter, I whisper, and he takes me by the arms, holding me with a grip so fierce that for just a second I struggle away from him. You were twenty-seven years old, he says, And you watched your partner die the most terrible death I've ever seen. He squeezes my arms, then slowly releases them; I take a step back, until I'm leaning against the railing, tears running down my neck and into the collar of my tee shirt. How long are you going to punish yourself? my father asks, Because I'm here to tell you, Adam, that you don't have as much time as you think. What am I supposed to do? I say. Tell him! my father says, sounding an awful lot like his granddaughter. How? I say, and he takes my hand and holds it to his chest, beneath his coat, where his heart beats hard against my fingers. Here, he says, You speak from here.

~   ~   ~

There's one thing I have to do first, and I leave for the airport late the following afternoon, with just enough time to make one stop along the way. I'm still a little light-headed from that fever, and as I step from the car and make my way through the cemetery I have to stop often to steady myself. Fast-moving clouds sail across the sky, the sun a bit too warm for the date. But I know a front will come soon enough, and I shift my bundle from one arm to the other, my arms sweating beneath the thick material. When I see his headstone I stop.

I've not come here since I moved to Austin almost nine years ago, and I'm embarrassed by how neglected the earth surrounding the stone appears. No flowers adorn this spot, no plant.

But I've been thinking of him, nevertheless.

The sun dips behind a thick bank of clouds and I take the opportunity the sudden shade affords me. Shaking the quilt, I let it settle around my shoulders. With closed eyes I take a deep breath.

Three months after Bobby died a friend of ours stopped by on the pretense

231

of checking up on me. I say pretense, though it's possible he came with no ulterior motive. I'd never considered him before, and when he came into the living room and fell onto the couch beside me in front of the television I thought nothing of his proximity. But halfway through the first period of the game we were watching I gave him a sidelong glance, which he returned. We wrestled into position, and when he told me he had a condom I didn't blink. Getting dressed afterwards we didn't look at each other; eye contact, I think we both knew, would evoke Bobby's memory more than what we'd just done. I walked him to the door and waved a noncommittal goodbye as he climbed into his truck. Then I picked up my beer as if he'd never come by.

But I soon lost interest in the game, and I found myself an hour later staring out the kitchen window, my beer warm in my hand. I took a swig anyway, looking out toward the garden. We'd planted nothing that spring; Bobby died before he had the chance. But some of the vegetation from the previous year had grown, inexplicably, despite my refusal to cultivate the soil, despite the frost, and I cocked my head to the side, examining the few leafy tomato plants, the thick bend of their stalks. I could leave them alone, I thought, and within a month or two I could slice tomatoes thin as paper and sprinkle them with sugar, the way Bobby liked them. I could chop them and mix them with peppers to throw on a sandwich, or I could blanche them and peel them and freeze them for the cold winter months. I had options.

In the end I went into the garden and systematically pulled up every plant by the root. Each and every one. When I came back inside I waited for the tears to come. But they didn't, not for months, not until that moment I touched my sister's swollen belly and felt my niece kick back and realized for the first time that he was never, ever going to come home.

Slowly I unwrap the quilt from my shoulders, breathing in his scent for the last time. I should've given this to you, I say, I'm sorry. I cover the headstone, draping the material until his name disappears. Against the gray the quilt shimmers, and for just a second I finger a patch of denim, the piece we both insisted was our own. Then I turn and walk away.

~ ~ ~

I haven't said his name aloud in weeks and I test the word on my tongue late Sunday evening, to see how it tastes. I linger over the last letter, and then I open the door to his studio and step inside. Even after almost three months there's an energy in here that I find unmistakable, an odor that makes my eyes water. Sinking to the floor in the dark, I spread my hands, fingering the drips of paint he left behind. Joel, I say.

His name echoes in the empty room, boomerangs back into my heart.

~ ~ ~

He's renting a house east of 35, a white clapboard with purple trim. I know because I talked to Scott, who came by the house unexpectedly. Bad time? he asked, taking in my towel and the slow drip of my swimming trunks on the tile beneath my feet. No, I said, and he followed me into the great room but shook his head when I offered him a seat. I gave my legs a cursory wipe and squeezed the edge of my trunks with the towel as he fingered the candle on top of the mantle. I left him, he finally said. Marcio? I asked, and he nodded. He didn't take it well, he added. But Kyle—I started, and he said: Kyle's pissed. That wasn't my place, I admitted. No shit, he said.

I mumbled an apology but he was already shaking his head. I wasn't seeing, he said, I wasn't seeing what was right in front of me. He gazed past me, in the direction of the windows, and I turned to follow his eyes. But the sky was long past black, and there was nothing to see save our reflections. I suppose I owe you a thank you, he said. You do? I asked, and he shrugged. We're going to try to work it out, he told me. You and Kyle, I said. He nodded, offering me the most grudging of smiles. I love him, he confessed, and the words themselves must have liberated him because the smile he'd been holding suddenly broke free. I blinked in its radiance, my arms crossed over my miserable heart. What about you? he asked, and I burst into tears.

Now I pull to the curb in front of Joel's house, examining the peaked roof and the ramshackle screen door. His truck's parked under a dilapidated car port; I half-expect to see the roof collapse right in front of me. He has no idea I'm coming, but as I search for the strength to get out of the car some sixth sense must speak to him. He opens the front door.

Even from this distance I can tell that the sight of my car parked in front of his house has thrown him. He stands halfway down the front steps, and I lift my hand in a foolish attempt at a wave. He's wearing jeans, and a long-sleeved tee shirt, and his bare feet rock back and forth on the cold cement. He's been working; I can tell from the trickle of paint on his cheek, a faint crimson rivulet. Like blood, or a tear. I could take him in my arms right now, I think, stepping toward him. I could take him in my arms right now, and there's a chance he wouldn't stop me. Could I talk to you? I ask instead.

From outside, I was able to convince myself that everything about our situation was transitory. But once I step across the threshold I realize how much time I've lost. His couch, I thought beforehand, and his art supplies, and maybe a second-hand chair or coffee table. But it's not even the new furniture that stuns me. It's the pictures on the walls, the half-melted candles above the fireplace, the soft dent in one of the pillows on the chair that crush me. He's settled here, and everything I've rehearsed fades from my memory. Oh my god, I say, Oh my god, I've been so *stupid*.

Burying my face in my hands, I start to cry. Tears slip through my fingers as I apologize, and when I finally get myself under control and lift my head the sight of the tears in his own eyes shames me. I want to hold him, to try to tuck behind his ear the lock of hair that swings toward his mouth. I want his arms around me, the sweet lock of his hands behind my back. He says my name, for the first time in three months, and at the sound of his voice I dissolve. Joel! I cry, I miss you, please come home!

I might have had him, without that final plea. But as I reach for him he backs away, flicking his tears with a matter-of-factness that stuns me. I don't know that I have the strength in my legs to carry me, and I sway on my feet before sinking, uninvited, to the sofa. He doesn't protest, and encouraged by that small concession I start to babble. Everything happened so fast, I say, I don't know what happened, but he meant nothing to me, Joel, nothing!

Don't you realize, he says, How much worse that makes me feel? I nod, bobbing my head as he leans toward me. If you'd come to me and told me that you felt more compatible with him, he says, If you'd told me you didn't know what you were feeling, that would've made a difference. I know, I say, I know. No, you don't! he cries, You don't know! He leans closer still, close enough that I catch a whiff of his studio. Do you know how many lies you had to tell in order to keep him a secret? he asks.

I couldn't tally them if I tried, and I try to remember the number of times Joel has lied to me. I can think of none since we got back together for good, and those that came before were lies of omission more than anything else.

I was good to you, he says, and I realize he's right. He was good to me, better than I deserved, better than I ever was to Bobby. You were, I whisper. Then why? he says, Because honestly, Adam, I've been trying for the past three months to figure this out and I can't.

I stare down at my hands. The windows to the soul, I've heard my father say, and for the longest time I didn't know what he meant. I thought, at first, that he just didn't know the saying, but I don't think that's the case. I think of everything he's chosen to do with his hands, the gentle caress of his horses, the quick offer of a shake when he greets someone, the feel of his palm on my shoulder just two nights ago. I think about Joel, about what he's created with his hands, about the slide of his fingers through mine.

I cheated on Bobby, I say, When he was sick.

For a long moment he stares at me, and then he turns his eyes to the ceiling, as if whoever's up there can commiserate. You've got to be fucking kidding me, he says. Holding up one hand, he starts to tick off my excuses on his fingers. Your father was sick, he says, You didn't get the promotion, I wouldn't go through with the adoption, and now you're going to blame what happened on someone who died thirteen years ago?

I'm sorry, I whisper. Fuck that! he says, his voice trembling, Apology not accepted! Hugging his arms to his chest, he starts to cry. Don't touch me, he says when I rise to console him, and with my hands hanging helpless by my side I watch as he breaks down in front of me. Please, he finally whispers, Just leave. Joel, I say, but he shakes his head. Please, he says, Leave.

~ ~ ~

I'm being let go. I find out Thursday morning, when Vincent calls me into his office. As of December 31st, Fusion will no longer have need of my services. If I weren't so wretched I might be able to concentrate on what Vincent has termed his justification, which I receive verbally but which he's been kind enough to type up in case I forget. He offers me a three month severance, provided that I go quietly, provided that my office has

235

been emptied by the end of the year. I sit across from him, catching a glimpse of Trainor through the glass. Who's taking over my position? I ask. That hasn't been decided, Vincent says, but my gut tells me that Liberty's planning on coming back after her maternity leave. My gut tells me that Trainor knew all along.

I go back into my office, where I shuffle through the work on my desk. I'll have to put feelers out there, I'll have to update my resume. My eyes close when I think of the emotional investment that will entail, and when the phone rings I almost let the call roll to voice mail. At the last second I glance down at the Caller ID.

I can't sleep, Joel says, I can't work. He sighs, and I hear the weariness in his voice; his brow will be furrowed, and I want to smooth the wrinkles with the pad of my thumb. I curl my body inward, as if I'm holding more than the phone. I wish to god you hadn't contacted me, he says. I know, I say, I'm sorry.

We're both silent, and I wonder if I've already said the wrong thing. I shouldn't have apologized again. Is he giving me another chance? Joel, I start, and he says: I need to see you. I release breath I didn't know I was holding. When? I ask.

He wants to get together tonight, and I agree to meet him at his house. Or we could go to dinner, I offer. This isn't a date, Adam, he tells me. I know, I say, chastened, and he says he'll see me at seven. He hangs up without saying goodbye.

~ ~ ~

I'm hoping he'll offer me a drink, open up a bottle of wine, but he collapses into a chair after he's let me inside. For a brief moment his hands cover his face, and when he takes them away he says, Have you seen Trainor?

I've just lowered myself to the sofa, and I start at the question. No, I say, and then I decide to amend my answer in keeping with the truth. I see him at work, I admit. He nods, then asks a question which baffles me. Why aren't you seeing him? he asks. Because, I say, surprised, I don't want him. What do you want? he asks.

He's asked the question even though I've already told him. I was clear when I saw him the other night, when I apologized for the way I'd treated him, when I told him I wanted him to come home. But he's looking for a different answer, and I search his eyes as if they hold a clue to what he might be thinking. Windows to the soul, I think, and then automatically glance at his hands. He laces his fingers together, and I wonder if I'll ever be able to separate them. I want to try, Joel, I finally whisper, I just want to try.

He promises me nothing, but I have to think I stand a chance. He's spent no more than five minutes with me, but he hasn't asked me to leave and I have to think I stand a chance. Tell me about Bobby, he says, and I swallow. This I'd expected, though now that he's asked I'm not sure where to start. I want to know what you left out, Adam, he says, And I want to know why.

Lies, I think, have a way of turning on you, of turning you in, and I decide not to mince words. I tell him everything, more than I've ever admitted even to myself, and the words conjure the curl of David's hair around his ears, the damp, musky scent of his skin, the desperation I felt in his arms. When I finally stop talking and glance in Joel's direction I find his eyes as wet as my own.

How's your dad? he asks, changing the subject, and I automatically cover my mouth with the palm of my hand. Alarmed, he sits forward. No, I assure him, He's fine. I wipe my eyes, and tell him that I spent Thanksgiving there, and he nods and says he knows. Julia, he says, and I think, of course. She'd be keeping him abreast. I take a deep breath. We're hoping he can make it through spring, I say.

We're both quiet, contemplating, the room soft with candle color. Maybe, I finally venture, We could go to dinner tomorrow.

He doesn't say anything for a moment, but he finally nods.

~   ~   ~

I dress for our date as if it's our first, carefully choose and discard first one and then another pair of trousers, peel a pale blue sweater over my head and exchange it for a gray one. I brush my teeth with vigor, gargle with a capful of mouthwash, cram a stick of gum in my mouth in case that's not enough. Running my hands through my new haircut, I examine my reflection in the mirror. I'm thin again, and I adjust my collar, taking a second to meet my own eyes. My hands, my mouth: everything trembles with anxiety.

We're meeting downtown at Joel's suggestion, and when I find that I'm the first to arrive I settle myself at the bar where I gulp a half a glass of bourbon trying to calm my nerves. My eyes dart back and forth, snagging each time the front door opens, until he finally appears. The air electrifies, and I sit up straighter, pushing my drink away from me as he meets my eye and starts in my direction. Halfway there he throws an acquaintance a smile, and my heart lodges in my throat. I don't want anyone else to be the recipient of his affections. Don't be fooled, he says when he reaches me, as if he knows what I'm thinking, I cried myself to sleep every night for a month.

I stare down at my hands as he orders a glass of wine. Beside me he fidgets on his barstool, and when his drink has been delivered he takes a good-sized swallow, one that suggests either that he's as nervous as I am or that he wants to get this evening over with as quickly as possible. I come to the conclusion that it's the latter. He doesn't want to be here. I can tell by the way he averts his eyes when I ask him a question, by his monosyllabic answers. Panic rises in my chest, and as he sucks the last of his drink, breaking what must be some kind of record for speed, I put my hand on his leg. He jerks as if I've hit him with a closed fist. Please, I say in a low voice, Don't end this yet.

Leaning both elbows on the bar in front of him, he drags his hands through his hair, his eyes closed. I touch his back, my fingers spread like a starfish. For just a second he lets me. Then he straightens, and asks me why. I mean, seriously, Adam, he says, Why are we dragging this out? Please, I say, Just come with me.

He follows me to my car, where we climb inside and sit without moving. After a minute I turn on the engine and adjust the heat. We can't go back, he finally says. No, I admit, But we can move forward. He shakes his head, his eyes on something I can't see. C'mon, I say, buckling my seatbelt. Where're we going? he asks, and I pull away from the curb. Anywhere but here, I say.

As I drive I tell him about work. My speech comes haltingly, reluctantly, as if he's asking me questions I don't want to answer. Maybe I'm just afraid he'll place the blame on my affair. But the farther I drive the more I warm to the task and before long I've told him that I don't know what I'm going to do at the end of the month, what I want to do next. I could try to find something along the same lines somewhere else, I say, Or I could stay right here. I don't dare look in his direction as I posit my possibilities; it's enough that he's listening to me.

I'm driving back roads I've never seen, the BMW clipping smoothly along the highway under a thin skein of stars. The dashboard glows orange in front of us, a CD burned in another time softening the silence. Beside me Joel stretches his legs as far as they'll go in the confines of the car, leaning his head on his hand. His hair falls over his ears in thick strands that I ache to touch, to thread through my fingers. But I settle for keeping him in my line of vision, glimpsed from the corner of my eye as I take another turn, easing the steering wheel beneath my hands. What about you? I ask, but he doesn't turn his gaze away from the road. What about me? he murmurs.

I suppose I'm asking in a roundabout way if he's okay, if he's making it without any financial support. However much I might be screwed if I can't find something soon, he can't be in a much better position. For the first time I realize how much more difficult our breakup must be for him, from a strictly logistical perspective. I have half a mind to offer an apology, and even more. But before I can speak he tells me he got a grant. A pretty decent one, he allows, and now I look over at him. You're kidding, I say, and he grimaces, as if I've called his talent into question. I hurry to explain myself, mumbling something about grants being so competitive, that he'd never mentioned applying. Well, he says, and I realize that he may have had an idea long before I did that this is where we'd end up. He may have understood a long time ago that he needed to protect himself. Congratulations, I manage, and he nods.

For a long while we're quiet. The miles drop away from us; every so often I take a deep breath, memorizing the smell of his shampoo, the scent of his skin, which I know lingers just beneath the fold of his shirt. I'm amazed that I ever took him for granted. Joel—I start, but he interrupts me. I keep seeing you with him, he says, With David. Why? I ask, and he sighs. You led me to believe that I was the one with the secrets, he says, That I was the one with the past. We all have a past, I tell him, and he says, Then why couldn't you tell me about yours?

For a moment I don't answer him. I'm thinking about the many confessions he made during the first couple of years we were together, the times I watched him sob as he told me about his father, his mother's suicide, his relationship with James. I'm thinking that there wasn't space for my burdens as well, that even though I'd told him about Bobby—early on, before we got back together for good—our roles had already been set. He was the one who needed to be saved, and I was the one who could offer him salvation.

Sometimes, he says quietly, as if he knows what I'm thinking, I have the feeling that you liked me better when I was fucked up. I protest, even though on some level I know he's right. After Bobby I wanted a chance to redeem myself. Do you realize how awful that makes me feel? he asks, How guilty I feel every time I accomplish something, how worthless I feel every time you refuse to let me help you? I'm sorry, I say, I'm so sorry. He holds his hands to his eyes. I still love you so much, I whisper. After a minute he lowers his hands; I catch the closest one in my own. Please, I say, holding his fingers to my heart, Please.

To my surprise he doesn't let go.

~ ~ ~

He hasn't made any promises. In fact, he's been careful to tell me that he wants some space, that he needs some time to work through what he's feeling. I'm not ready to make a commitment, he says, and I tell him I understand, that we can take things as slowly as he wants, that I won't put any pressure on him to make a decision. I'm just thankful for what he's willing to offer.

There's little left for me at work, and I slowly begin to hand the reins over to Trainor. I've softened toward him since Joel called; I can't continue to fault him for what's happened. But seeing him reminds me of what I've done, and though we have contact I continue to make it a point not to be caught alone with him. I'm not sure how receptive he'd be anyway, if I were to invite him to lunch, if I were to ask him to grab a coffee. I haven't treated him well, either.

I've made no decisions about what I'll do at the end of the month. I'm waiting to see, I guess, what Joel wants. In the interim I dream of what we might be able to accomplish together, circling through our conversations

from the summer. I think about moving someplace altogether new and
starting from scratch, selling the house and the BMW and trying something fresh. I think about parking ourselves right in the middle of Austin,
the way Joel has always wanted, about moving out to the countryside
just west of town, where I might be able to raise horses the way my father
has. Closing my eyes, I picture us one year from now, five, ten. I picture
us growing old together, helping each other, partnering each other. I
picture lying next to him in forty years, his hand held fast in mine.

By the time I arrive at his house for our next date I've wedded myself
to this fantasy, and when he opens the door I almost pull him into my
arms. I'm thinking he'll invite me inside, but he steps onto the porch,
pulling the door shut behind him. I've got someplace in mind, he says
once I've asked if he's hungry, and I bite the inside of my cheek. I'd made
reservations.

We end up with fish tacos and a beer apiece from a stand down the
street. We eat quickly, sitting astride an outdoor picnic table in weather
we've heard will change within the hour. Beside him he has a coat, and
I imagine the gloves he keeps in his pocket, a pair he picked up when
he was in Tahoe almost nine years ago. I've a coat of my own, and a
cashmere scarf he gave me last Christmas, a creamy one, flecked with
a Caribbean blue that brings out the color of my eyes. I don't ask if he
has any plans to stay warm over the upcoming weekend; I'm hoping
that information will come organically, as the night progresses, even
though within twenty minutes he's wiping his mouth and crumpling
his napkin. Here's the reason I made reservations for tonight: for all
practical purposes, our dinner date appears to be over. But instead of
checking the time he holds his bottle of beer to his lips and squints.
How was your week? he asks.

Taking a chance that he's not simply indulging in small talk, I tell
him. Not about the way my job's being phased out before my eyes, not
about my father, but about anything whimsical I can call to mind: the ice
cream cake I took the time to order yesterday for Darlene's birthday; the
woodpecker I found drilling a hole in the side of our neighbor's house;
the ridiculous display of Christmas decorations going up at the house
on the corner. Before long his contribution to the conversation echoes

my own, and he tells me about the neighborhood cat who awakens him almost nightly with its yowling, and the massive quantity of pecans he picked from his own backyard. I guess you're set for Christmas baking, I tell him, and he laughs. Have you ever tried to shell those things? he asks, They'll be sitting under my car port until summer.

Briefly relieved of any guilt or blame we smile at each other, until he shifts his eyes from mine, pulling his bottom lip between his teeth. I marvel at the gesture. C'mon, he finally says, and I follow him as he gets to his feet. We wander through the still night air, our coats draped over our arm, skirting the edges of poorly kept lawns whenever a car passes our way; there are no sidewalks in Joel's neighborhood. Streetlights seem strung fewer and farther between than out by the lake, and after a minute I ask if he runs at night, and if so, whether or not he wears an iPod. I have an image of a car bearing down on him as he runs without awareness. I'm careful, he assures me, but I shiver anyway. For just a second his sleeve touches mine.

Down the street from his house we pause at the entrance to a dilapidated neighborhood park, outfitted with creaky swings and rusty monkey bars. Any minute now the weather will turn, but before I have a chance to say something about seeking shelter, he pushes open the gate. Our feet crunch through the dead leaves. Think these will hold our weight? I ask as we lower ourselves to the worn rubber strips of swing. He doesn't answer, and I watch as he spins in a slow circle, knotting the chain of his swing at chest level, and then higher. Beside him I rock back on my heels, then forward onto the tips of my toes, scuffing the leather of my shoes. At the last possible second, with a chain tangled to the top of the swing set, Joel pushes against the ground with his boot. His swing spins a tight circle, his hands gripping the rusty chain as it quickly unwinds, then starts to knot in the opposite direction. Watching him I'm almost dizzy, and when the swing finally slackens I say, Doesn't that make you nauseous? Sort of, he admits. Then why are you doing it? I ask, watching as he starts to knot his chain again. He shrugs, but he doesn't stop.

For ten minutes we don't speak. Over and over he entangles and disentangles himself, until we feel the sudden drop in temperature. Woozy? I ask as he stands, lifting his arms to check his balance. Something, he says, and I take a chance and hold him steady, my fingers curved around his triceps. He doesn't move. The wind winds itself around us. I kiss him, and he braces his body against mine.

Then we move quickly, silently, fists shoved into the pockets of our coat, shoulders hunched against the cold. When he opens his front door a burst of warm air spills over us and we shrug out of our coats; before I can close the door he's sliding cold fingers beneath my sweater. I rake mine through his hair. Tripping over each other, we fall onto the couch, sealing the space between us. With trembling lips I kiss the taut vein on the side of his neck; he twists to the side and I bury my tongue beneath his ear.

I expect him to stop me. After all, he reminded me just yesterday that he's not sure what he wants, that he doesn't want to rush into anything. But he lets me take him right there on the couch, in the soft glow of a tableside lamp that bleeds amber shadows on his skin. Every regret I've harbored the past eleven months releases as he lifts to meet me. We both moan with relief.

When we're finished I don't want to slip away from him. Joel, I whisper, but then I get a look at his face. He looks shell shocked, as if he's just realizing that he slept with the enemy, and for a second I hesitate at his expression. Then I yank my briefs hastily over my hips. Don't move, I say, I'll be right back.

In his bathroom I hurriedly urinate, then wash my hands in the stained porcelain sink. Opening the door I cock my head; I can hear him moving in the living room, and I picture him stepping into his jeans, pulling his tee shirt over his head. I need to talk to him, before he changes his mind, before he tells me to leave. But across from me another door, left slightly ajar, beckons. Without thinking I push it aside.

The room doesn't hold a candle to the space I created for him at home. He's dealing with a second bedroom in here, and though windows line three of the walls my guess is that he doesn't get the light he needs. There's no sink, no room to stretch his own canvas. But the work itself drops my jaw.

They're character sketches, all of them, and I move from one sheet of drawing paper to the next. I'm in every one and so is he, our features blurred together and pulled apart in an agony too awful too contemplate.

With these drawings in front of me there's little doubt about how he feels, about how terribly I've hurt him, and when I hear him step behind me I can't even turn my head. Joel, I say, my voice fracturing, These sketches.... I trail off before I can finish, before I can tell him that they break my heart. But I'm also proud of him, I realize, proud of what he's done, of who he's become, proud that over the past three months he's been able to channel his grief into something so powerful and inspiring when I've not done a thing. I know I've hurt him. But I also know that I gave him the space he needed over the last five years to work, and that what I'm seeing in front of me might not be if not for that sacrifice. That's got to count for something, and I cast a glance over my shoulder.

One look at his expression and I'm stepping backward. His eyes narrow even further. Get the fuck out of here, he snarls, and I almost gasp, at the same time I realize my folly.

I have no right to be looking through his work. He allows so few people a glimpse of his process, and though I've always been one of the privileged I'm not any longer. Hastening an apology, I step around him. He follows me into the living room, shaking with an anger he makes no attempt to belie. Please, I beg as he throws my clothes in my direction, and that quickly he's screaming, tears choking his accusations. With closed fists he pummels my chest; I let him, until he finally collapses against me, then jerks away when I try to wrap my arms around him. I'm sorry, I say, over and over, I'm sorry.

Already I'm priming myself for his assurance that my apology isn't accepted, that he hasn't forgiven me and won't, not ever. But as I quiver in front of him his fury disappears. I know you are, he finally says, I know.

~ ~ ~

I talk to my father Sunday afternoon. The news I have to report feels fragile, fleeting, but I close my eyes and infuse the words with an optimism I've struggled to maintain since I left Joel's house late the other night. I don't know where we go from here, he admitted, and I ventured that maybe we didn't need to know. Maybe we could just see what happens. He nodded, but so wearily that my heart trembled. Since then I've tried to focus on what happened before I stepped into his studio, on the way he abandoned what was obviously his better judgment in favor of what he felt in the moment. I don't think about the look on his face when I lifted my body away from him.

I've agreed to give him time and space to think, and as a result we haven't seen each other this weekend, not once. I've managed to slip in a couple of phone calls, though, conversations which I imagined would be long and languid and which instead lasted less than a few minutes apiece. You promised, he said in a low voice at the end of the last one, and I hung up berating myself for calling in the first place. I'm doomed to fuck this up, and I admit as much to my father, who tells me I'm going to have to trust myself. My track record—I start, and he interrupts, sounding impatient. Let me tell you something, Son, he says, If you can't let go of the past you will never move even one step forward.

I mull over these words as I shower Sunday night. There's so little I can change, I realize. I will forever be the man who cheated on Bobby; I will forever be the man who cheated on Joel. Closing my eyes, I tilt back, letting the water rush over my forehead. I'm also the man who nursed Bobby until he died. I'm the man who saved Joel's life; without me he would've perished in that bathtub, and so many lives would've never been the same.

I'm not necessarily the man I wanted to be; I'm not necessarily the man I've led others to believe. I've made mistakes, tremendous ones that have cost me almost everything. But I'm ready to move forward, and as I step from the shower that thought alone fills me with hope.

I'm just reaching for my keys, promises be damned, when the phone rings. I want to tell my father what I've decided. I want to hear a last few words of encouragement before I make this leap. I want to thank him for telling me to trust myself. Hey, I say, and my mother starts to cry.

~ ~ ~

Through a blanket of fog we drive to my parents' house. Poor weather has delayed our arrival and I squint into the gathering dusk, adjusting my wipers. Beside me Joel offers to take the wheel, in the same quiet voice he used last night when he asked if I wanted him to accompany me to Kentucky. This time I shake my head no.

Neither one of us has slept. After I hung up with my mother I went to him; he pulled me into his arms without a word, murmuring something about the end—a stroke—being quick and merciful. We knew the way it

245

could've looked: lungs so polluted no air could penetrate, a death remarkably like drowning. I had just talked to him, I whispered, and he took my hands in both his own. For that, he said, You can be thankful.

We'll have a viewing tomorrow, the funeral the day after that. Travel has rendered me impotent today as far as helping to make arrangements are concerned, but Joel has reminded me that this is the sort of work my sister needs right now. I wipe my eyes and Joel silently hands me a tissue. At the very least he's here, and he reaches for my hand and slides his fingers through mine.

We arrive to a full house. Everyone crowds around us, and I realize as Lindsey breaks from my grasp and tumbles into Joel's arms that I should've known what a homecoming this would be. Hey there, he whispers, brushing his lips across the crown of her head. My chest swells, and when Lindsey finally steps back and he folds my mother into his arms I have to bow my head.

By the end of the day I swear I've begun to think that my father orchestrated his death in order to get Joel and me back together. Joel belongs here, every bit as much as I do, and as I watch him interact with my family I remember with a sharp pang of regret how much I resented his support last summer. Now I see that I couldn't ask for anything more. We need to get you to bed, he tells me, and I nod, the thought of sleeping beside him a luxury I can't quite believe I'm allowed.

We curl together beneath a mound of blankets. His arms encircle me, and I press against him, as tightly as I can. Thank you, I whisper, and his hair slides gently across my cheek. Sleep, he says, Just sleep.

~ ~ ~

My father wanted an open casket, and as I stand at the back of the funeral home, steeling myself, I thank god that with Bobby at least I was spared this moment. Joel waits behind me; I've agreed to take my mother first, and when she indicates her readiness I guide her slowly up the aisle. She's held herself together remarkably well over the past twenty-four hours, but when we reach the casket her knees falter. Without my support she'd probably keel right over, and I tighten my arm around her.

My mother touches my father's hand. She may be waiting for me to make the same gesture, but I'm having a difficult enough time holding myself steady and I simply nod when she finally says that they did a good job. For a second longer she manages to hold her tears, and then she turns to me, leaning her head against my shoulder as she cries.

Julia's next. She walks to the front with Ivan, her children following dutifully behind as I slide my finger beneath the collar of my shirt at the back of the room, suddenly short on air. You do not have to go back up there, Joel tells me, and I nod, because I don't think I can. Instead I watch as he makes his way himself after Julia and her family return. With lowered head he stands in front of my father, his hair slipping over his ears. When he comes back to me we step into an embrace that lingers, until Lindsey says beside me, Uncle Adam, they're here.

For the next two hours I accept condolences, standing with my mother on one side of me and Julia on the other. Lindsey and Rye stick together, watching their little sister, who I frankly can't believe Julia has allowed to attend. She's well-behaved enough, thanks to quick intervention on the part of both Ivan and Joel; I see their intercessions from the corner of my eye, and when my sister intimates during a break in the flow of mourners that someone could always run Grace home I tell her that's fine, as long as she's not thinking that Joel's going to be her minion. Even if he's not right beside me I need the quick glances he gives me. I need the thirty second pause when we meet in the quiet hallway leading to the restroom and he touches his forehead to mine.

Though fraught with emotion, the evening's not as difficult as it could've been, and for that I know I have Joel to thank. I drive my mother home in my father's car; she sits beside me in the passenger seat, but Joel's right behind me, meeting my eyes every time I look in the rearview mirror. I'm impatient to be alone with him, and once we're home and my mother has bid everyone good night, once Julia and Ivan have ushered the children into bed and exchanged glances as if they might appreciate a moment together themselves, I lead him into my old bedroom. For the briefest second I think he's going to reject my kiss; he pulls back just slightly, and my heart quivers in my chest. But then he sighs, and his lips, when I touch them with my own, part as easily as they did the first time I kissed him, all those years ago.

~ ~ ~

Though I'm reluctant to slip away from his sleeping body, I wake early the next morning and go for a ride. A tribute to my father, I think as I saddle Four-ticker, and the two of us make our way through the cold toward the west field. Great puffs of air stream from Four-ticker's ample nostrils as I lean over his neck, my knees braced against his heaving sides, my boots secure in the stirrups. He runs with abandon, and a wave of exhilaration sweeps over me as we sail over a fence, airborne longer than I would've thought possible. By the time we return we're both soaked in sweat, and I wipe Four-ticker down, my own legs shaking.

I had a feeling you were riding, Joel says when I appear in the kitchen in my stocking feet. Rye and Grace swarm around him as he holds a steaming cup of coffee just out of their reach. Someone needs a shower, he adds, handing me the cup and wrinkling his nose, and I have to bite back the grossly inappropriate invitation, under the circumstances, to join me.

I'm oddly jubilant considering the solemnity of the day, but I have a feeling my father would understand. I think more than anything he wanted to see us back together, and when I said as much to Joel last night he agreed, though when I added that my father might have timed his death to suit that very purpose he murmured something soft that indicated nothing. I spent half the night talking, knowing I should sleep but needing to tell him what was on my mind. I'm at the cusp of something, I told him, a new beginning. I'm ready to sell the house, ready to start fresh. With my father's passing—even though I'll miss him, even though I know I'll have to be there for my mother—I can put this portion of my life behind me. Everything we talked about over the summer can happen now, if he'll only give me a chance. We can stay in Kentucky for a few days; the tickets we purchased are open-ended, and though I'll have to go back to Fusion at some point because I really can't afford to forfeit my severance, I can probably get away with staying here for at least another week. I can help my mother with my father's affairs, and then we can get away, take a weekend trip, or maybe something longer. Let's hole up in a cabin somewhere, I said, And never come out.

He let me talk, and eventually I grew sleepy, dreaming about our life together. Together, I murmured just before I drifted off to sleep, one arm slung around his waist, We'll do this together.

Now I watch as my nieces and nephew vie for his attention. My god, I think. I've never loved him more.

~ ~ ~

Joel has a more difficult time at the funeral than I do, which touches me in a way I can't describe. Blinking back my own tears, I hold tightly to his hand as he cries; on my other side my mother holds herself together, her hand pressed into Julia's. Several of my father's friends speak on his behalf, men with whom I've made scant conversation in my life, and I remind myself to track down each of them after the service and thank them for their contribution. A couple of them have agreed to be pallbearers, and as we file into the aisle of the church and surround the casket at the end of the service I take a quick glance at Joel. I've asked him to help as well, and though pale, he meets my eyes with a resolve that I feel on a cellular level. With his support, even this seems manageable.

Dozens of friends and family members return to the house after the trip to the cemetery; I keep Joel close to my side as I make idle chit-chat with people I barely know, or haven't seen in years. He holds up his end of the conversation admirably, and every so often I give his shoulder a squeeze. I know how much he hates small talk. I can't imagine how I'll ever be able to thank him.

As evening falls our guests begin to gather their coats. I walk someone to the door, realizing Joel's absence as I head back through the living room. I'm tempted to go looking for him, but one person after another steps in front of me, offering one last handshake, one last murmur of sympathy. I thank them all, and when there's no one left I make a quick apology to my mother for leaving her and go in search of him.

The mild weather of the past two days has begun to turn, and I make my way toward the stable, wishing I'd brought my coat. I find Joel just inside the door, his collar turned up against the wind; he looks over his shoulder as he hears me approach. You disappeared, I say. I wanted to give you some space, he tells me, and I nod, knowing that his intentions were pure, though I would've preferred that he never left my sight. Everyone's gone, I add, sliding my hands in my pockets. How are you holding up? he asks. I'm okay, I admit. I toe the straw beneath my feet, glancing in the direction of Four-Ticker's stall. I couldn't have gotten through this without you, I say. He's quiet for a moment, and then he speaks, his voice quiet and sad. I love you, Adam, he says, I think I always will.

His words should thrill me, should put to rest every fear I own. Instead they send a chill down my spine. You're going home, I say, Aren't you.

~ ~ ~

He leaves the next morning, the day breaking along with my heart. I stand with him on the porch, wind stinging my eyes; through my tears I watch as the last of the leaves tear from the maple trees. His cab idles in front of us, its tailpipe exuding a long, white plume; I've offered to drive him to the airport, but he gently refused. I'll be fine, he said, and I'd known all too well that he was right. He'll be fine.

I have no such hope for myself. Last night I turned on my heel and went back to the house, where he followed me thirty minutes later, his eyes bearing no trace of the redness I know my own revealed. Though I was polite to him I managed to let the rest of the evening escape without having to see him alone. But he came to me long after everyone else had fallen asleep, finding me in the kitchen where I was standing in front of the pantry, trying to pinpoint when I'd last eaten. I turned at the pad of his feet, and we stood at opposite sides of the room for what seemed like a lifetime before we met in the middle. What am I supposed to do without you? I asked, and he touched my cheek; I covered his hand with my own. Move on, he said, You're supposed to move on.

Will you call me when you get in? I ask now, and after the briefest hesitation he nods. He'll call me, I realize, to let me know his plane has landed, to check in. But there will be days, and weeks, and months in my future when I won't hear from him at all. The thought brings a sob to my throat and I choke it away before he can catch it; he knows me too well, and touches my hand. I fear I don't deserve even this gesture, but I cherish it all the same.

Well, he says, but I'm not ready. I hold fast to his fingers, and for just a second longer he lets me. Then with one quick squeeze he lets go.

8

OCTOBER, 2006

I sit at my computer, in the second bedroom of the townhouse I've been calling home for the past nine months. The rain outside my window comes in fits and starts; I've turned down the music, hoping to hear its patter on the roof, but for all the gloomy weather I've witnessed since I moved here I've yet to see anything like a good old-fashioned Texas thunderstorm. I can barely hear a thing, and when I part the blinds and squint into the dark I see little more than a mist skirting beneath the streetlight. Resigned, I sip from the mug of tea I've brewed. Nights like these are the times when my solitude feels most acute.

I've made few friends here in Seattle. I'm pleasant enough at the office, and I've been known to succumb a time or two to happy hour requests. But most of the time I'm content to work, and go to the gym, and come home to a hot shower and a quiet, solitary dinner. I have occasional plans on the weekend; I'm invited to one house or another, but I imagine that my presence must be as peripheral to my host as it feels to me. I'm simply not invested, and I usually beg off early, my excuses as tired as my smile.

I've been on three dates, each more discouraging than the last. *Move on,* I keep hearing Joel say, and so in June, spurred by the early summer weather, I allowed myself to be introduced to a friend of a friend. We met at a wine bar, and over a flight of California whites I asked what he did for a living. I run a preschool, he admitted. Intrigued, I asked him a few questions, until he finally heaved a great sigh. Anything else you want to know? he said, Because I sort of feel like I'm being grilled here. Taken aback, I apologized, but we never recovered. Twenty minutes later he left, and I finished my wine alone.

Having made it past that first hurdle, though, I was determined to try again, and a few weeks later I returned the gaze of the barista who made the Americano I bought on my way to work in the morning. A couple of flirtatious conversations later I asked him out, and that weekend we met for dinner, where he informed me that he'd lied about his age, his living arrangements, and his educational background. Anything else I should know? I asked, and he smirked in a way that left me ill at ease.

I'd sworn off meeting anyone else, and then one Saturday morning a few weeks ago I struck up a conversation with the guy next to me at the fish market who was buying five pounds of salmon. That's a hell of a lot of fish, I offered, and he grinned. I like to smoke it, he said, With hickory and honey. He reached forward to take the package, then turned to look at me, the silver earring in his ear catching the sunlight. Want to try it? he asked. I took in the long sweep of his hair, the black gloves with the fingers cut away. Why not? I said.

I arrived at his houseboat later that evening, and hesitated on the dilapidated threshold. She won't sink, he laughed, beckoning me forward. Moonlight made its reluctant way through the windows, casting milky shadows on the floor as I gave my surroundings a quick glance. Beer? he asked. I'm good, I started to say, but he'd already ducked into the small kitchen. I listened to the creak of the refrigerator as I took a closer look around me. Thanks, I said when he returned, and he clinked his bottle to mine.

The sex wasn't unpleasant. But it left me feeling melancholy, and even though I stayed for a little while afterward I think he could tell that he wouldn't be seeing me again. We went through the routine of exchanging phone numbers, but I have a feeling that my card ended up in his trash, the same way his ended up in mine.

Since then I've had little inclination to meet anyone. Instead I spend a lot of time at the office, which isn't necessarily a bad thing. I feel as if I have something to prove. I have a good job, one I probably don't deserve. I have a competitive salary, a challenging workload; I'm lucky. Because I knew the moment I got back to Austin after my father's funeral that I couldn't stay.

I told Joel in person. We'd spoken twice since he left Kentucky, once when he called to tell me he'd arrived safely in Austin, and again a few days later. But that last phone call was even more perfunctory than the first, and I held the memory of that conversation in my mind when I made the decision to move. Once I knew for sure I was leaving, once I'd gotten rid of the car and sold most of the furniture, I gave him a call. I had some news, I said, and I'd prefer he heard it from me.

We met that night at a coffee shop. His hair was a little longer, and he kept sweeping it behind his ears, where it held for a few seconds before falling toward his cheekbones again. I held my hands still in my lap. How's your mom? he asked, and I told him she was holding her own. He blew through the hole on the lid of his cup, then took a sip. What about you? he asked. I'm moving to Seattle, I said.

For just a moment he froze, before he started nodding. Microsoft? he asked. Yes, I said, and he ran his fingers back and forth across his mouth as I tried to get a better read on his reaction. When? he asked. Friday, I said. Not wasting any time, are you? he asked, and I told him I didn't have the luxury. He looked away from me then, and when he turned back his eyes were as impenetrable as diamonds. Well, he said.

I've not spoken to him since. I hear about him, mostly from Scott, who now lives with Kyle and spends time with Joel as a result. I know Joel's work is going well, that he has a show opening in DC in the spring. I know he's still living in that purple and white house east of 35, that he's scouting around for a larger place to work. I know he's seeing someone new.

Move on, I hear him say, and I'll try. He's left me little choice. But I'll still ask after him, I'll still wonder how he's doing. I'll still sit here most nights, checking my email and hoping. I'll remember him, the same way I remember Bobby.

These men I once held like jewels in the palm of my hand.

COLOPHON

This book was designed by Viewers Like You in Austin, Texas. It is type-set in Comenia Serif, designed by František Štorm in 2006. Incidental typography is set in Omnes, designed by Joshua Darden in 2006 . Chapter numbers are set in Colonna released by Monotype in 1927.

Jennifer Hritz

Jennifer Hritz lives in Austin, Texas, with her husband and young son. Readers may visit her website at www.jenniferhritz.com.

DISCUSSION QUESTIONS

1   *I, Too, Have Suffered in the Garden* begins with a brief glimpse into Adam's life with Bobby, then quickly segues into his life with Joel fifteen years later. How would you characterize Adam's relationship with Bobby, based on the few pages of text the author provides at the beginning of the novel? How does Adam's relationship with Joel appear in contrast?

2   Adam wants to adopt a child, though Joel does not. What do you think of Adam's plan to convince Joel otherwise? Why does it backfire? Despite the fact that the two men never adopt, Adam and Joel both seem to have a bond with their nieces and nephew. How does Adam's conversation with Lindsey on Thanksgiving Day impact him?

3   Adam earns a fair wage as Director of Sales for Fusion Technologies, but few of the luxuries that his job provides—a suburban home with a view of Lake Travis, a BMW— fulfill him. In fact, these *accoutrements* become a point of contention for Adam and Joel. How does Adam feel about the fact that he's supporting Joel financially? Do you think Adam enjoys his work? How do you think the two men might have fared if Adam had quit his job and they'd moved to the countryside, as they discuss at one point? Why do you think Adam takes a job with Microsoft at the end of the novel?

4   The reader learns about Adam's relationship with Bobby mostly through flashbacks. What do you think of these scenes? How do they fit into the larger picture of the novel?

5   Over the course of the novel Adam must come to terms with his father's illness. In what ways does caring for his father bring Bobby's struggle with AIDS to the surface? How does his father's death bring Adam closer to Joel?

6   Guilt precludes Adam from sleeping with Joel, though he's clear about the fact that he hasn't lost the desire for him. As a matter of fact, he agrees with Joel when Joel points out that sex "has never been a problem" for them. Joel also tries to support Adam emotionally. Why, then, does Adam have an affair with Trainor? Once Joel learns about the affair, why does Adam cut ties with Trainor?

7   When Adam comes home with a BMW Joel insists they begin couples counseling. Why do you think Adam acquiesces? Do you think Lydia helps or hinders the men's relationship?

8   Joel tells Julia that Adam is suffering from the "mother of all midlife crises." How fair do you find this assessment? How do aging and body image come into play in Adam's life right now? Why do you think Adam behaves so erratically the night he's arrested?

9   Adam appears to be intensely jealous of Joel's relationship with James. Do you think he has reason to be suspicious? Do you think his jealousy is justified, especially in light of his own affair with Trainor? What do you think James provides Joel that Joel isn't getting from Adam?

10 Infidelity plays a prominent role in Adam's experience: Bobby's betrayal of Adam with another man, Adam's betrayal of Bobby with David, and Adam's betrayal of Joel with Trainor. In light of such morally questionable behavior, do you feel sympathy for Adam? Repugnance? Can his behavior be justified or at least understood in either instance?

11 Scott's affair with Kyle creates an interesting contrast to Adam's own. How does this sub-plot compare? What do you think of Adam's outburst at Kyle's party? How does Scott's decision to break up with Marcio ultimately affect Adam's decision to reinitiate contact with Joel?

12 Adam seems to waffle in regard to how he feels about Joel's painting, claiming that the scent of Joel's studio, once an aphrodisiac, now makes him grit his teeth. What do you think of Adam's involvement—or lack thereof—in his partner's work? Why do you think Joel reacts with such ire when Adam enters his studio uninvited at the end of the novel?

13 The garden serves as an important thematic device in this novel. How does their backyard garden change for Adam and Bobby over the course of Bobby's illness? What significance do the tomatoes hold? What purpose does the garden at the bed and breakfast serve?

14 The last chapter finds Adam alone in a condo in Seattle. He and Joel no longer speak, though Adam hears about him through mutual friends. What do you think Adam has learned over the past year and a half? Do you feel any faintness of hope that Adam and Joel could reunite? Would you want to see them back together? Or do you think Adam deserves to be without a partner?